■

'You don't have to like James Rainer Willing to like *Noise*, the exuberant lampoon of which he is the over-elegant centrepiece. And a good thing too – dour, self-absorbed, the most pretentious restaurant critic ever to hit the pages of a trendy tabloid, Willing is a throwback to the hilariously unsatisfactory heroes and heroines of Kingsley Amis and Evelyn Waugh. Smith, whose 1994 novel *How Insensitive*, mined similar territory – the lives of Toronto's helplessly hip – offers here a more polished portrait of a distracted magazine writer for whom *la vie bohème* is rapidly becoming *la vie* ho-hum. Smith picks on the effete and the dowdy with a bracing even-handedness: he's just as good at nailing what makes motel dining rooms so creepy as he is at skewering performance poets.' Frank Moher, *Saturday Night*

D1422256

RUSSELL
SMITH
NOISE

The Porcupine's Quill

CANADIAN CATALOGUING IN PUBLICATION DATA

Smith, Russell, 1963–
Noise

ISBN 0-88984-197-7

I. Title.

PS8587.M58397N65 1998   C813'.54   C98-930504-X
PR9199.3.S64N65 1998

Published by The Porcupine's Quill,
68 Main Street, Erin, Ontario NOB 1TO.
Readied for the press by John Metcalf; copy edited by Doris Cowan.
Typeset in Trump, printed on Zephyr Antique Laid,
and bound at The Porcupine's Quill Inc.

The cover is after a photograph by Russell Smith.
Author photo is courtesy of Ceri Marsh.

Represented in Canada by the Literary Press Group. Trade orders are
available from General Distribution Services.

We acknowledge the support of the Ontario Arts Council,
and the Canada Council for the Arts for our publishing program.
The financial support of the Government of Canada
through the Book Publishing Industry Development Program
is also gratefully acknowledged.

1 2 3 4 • 01 00 99 98

For my parents,

Ann and Rowland Smith

His phone rang, again, a jangle like shock torture in a wet cell, and James Rainer Willing swore, again, but this time not cursorily, not a mere acknowledging grunt; this time he swore loud and long. He put his sweaty arms over his head as he had seen Arab mothers do on the news and wailed. *Keening*, he thought, is what we're looking for, and although he wasn't entirely sure about the proper pitch and length of a true keen, he made an educated guess, adding non-Western ululations for authenticity.

But his wail was engulfed, as he had known it would be, in the noise of his little room: absorbed and subsumed into the whir of fan and hulking, obsolete computer cooling system and shrieking telephone and by the undifferentiated roar seeping through the window and walls: the pounding of two stereo systems (one next door, teenage girls; the other, much worse, from a fridge-sized car stereo parked in the alley, teenage boys), plus the whine of two differently tuned archaic radios (ancient gardeners pottering out in the sun with squash trellises), their tinny speakers frantic with Portuguese ads for discount carpet warehouses.

James put his head down on his arms, knowing that dripping sweat might damage his keyboard, and waited, tensing, for the machine to take the call.

Two articles due: a review of the new Thai-Greek place in Brampton for *Edge* and a supposedly humorous piece on rising fee structures for *Dental Week* now two days late. And the fucking goddam *fucking* Loon Lake reading tonight, *SHIT*, at the Culture Corner, which he had promised he would cover for *Reams and Reams* because the goddam Prairie poet novelist playwright and *dramaturge*, whatever that was, would be there. Flown in all the way from Medicine Hat.

'Medicine Hat,' shouted James with all the disgust he could muster. Above the noise came his own voice saying he wasn't home.

'James,' said a male voice which sounded equally edgy, 'James, pick up the phone. James. It's Franco Giardini.'

James sat back, relieved. Only his landlord; non-editor calls had low priority.

'James, I hope you're not out of town. I've been trying to get you for two weeks now. Please call me, James. It's very important.'

'Sorry, Franco,' said James to his screen. 'Not important enough.'

'Okay,' said the voice, 'I guess you're really not there. I have to tell you that –'

James lunged for the volume control, and Franco's voice vanished. James had a strict policy against listening to possibly troubling messages in the middle of the day.

He read the paragraph which was the sum total of the afternoon's work.

and Kazimoto Stockwell, a design team best known for their faintly proletarian industrial-gothic fancies, notably the dazzlingly brutal Control (Ritchie LeBlanc's first brief but memorable indulgence). The new Chimera combines a fin-de-siècle eclecticism with a frankly nostalgic discomfort: a Victorian rethinking of a grunge-youth's playroom or large sports arena restroom. And of course the visual references to stock-car racing do add humour.

He closed his eyes and tried to remember what he had eaten. There was a good soup, rather plain. But his readers preferred the artistic stuff, the pickled tempura bok choy, the Cajun durian. And the gossip.

'GONNA STROKE YOU UP,' boomed the car stereo.

James felt his chair vibrating. Above the bass, the boys outside were shouting at each other.

'She's a cow, man. She's a fucking *pig*.'

'You fucking know shit, Armando. Fuck you, man. Stop pulling the hair out of my ass.'

'Suck my hairy –'

To his momentary relief, someone cranked up the booming even louder, and the voices were lost. He watched his water glass

8

slowly edge across his desk. He wondered what a seismograph would read in his neighbourhood on any midafternoon.

He typed,

But Chimera's greatest draw is of course the young chef's name: Damian Buhr, a wunderkind trained by a wunderkind, the first sleek little porker to emerge from the now-famous sty of LeBlanc (whose soon-to-be-opened restaurant, by the way, I have on good authority, will be named Mirage). The lucky few familiar with Buhr's previous success will know to make reservations immediately at Chimera: it has now been open for three weeks, which is about his lifetime endurance record – two weeks longer than the spectacular Pursuit, one of those flares in the night that burns short and bright.

He pushed his chair back, exhausted, to wipe his head. The room was dim, the blind drawn to keep out the toxic sun. He wore nothing but a pair of damp shorts. He could feel his nose ring burning in his nostril like an iron. Thirty-six on the thermometer, forty-three on this alleged humidex. James wondered if humidex meant anything at all. It was just like the wind-chill factor in winter: the rule seemed to be you just added ten degrees either way.

There had been an 'air quality advisory' on the radio that morning, which meant, as far as James could understand, don't breathe if you can avoid it.

Next door, the teenage girls responded to the boys with their romantic tune, the little stereo stretched to breaking, fizzing with white noise. 'And I. Will always. Love you.' Cigarette smoke in his room. The girls were home all day these days; school out, parents at work. If he put his head out the window he would be able to see them on the sundeck below, in their shorts and T-shirts, smoking, fighting, frequently sobbing. He thought of their long hair, the lipstick and braces, newly Neeted legs glistening in the sun, and tried not to.

He typed,

A young ginger pancake, satisfyingly crisp and refreshingly free of the tart marinades becoming so tiresomely common, soothes the early-meal tongue (rendered prickly by the delicate fire of wasabi on the quail egg *amuse-gueule*), but I suspect that this city's rather suddenly torrid affair with young ginger may be drawing to a close. When the Holiday Inn's brunch menu includes this ingredient, you can be sure that LeBlanc's and Buhr's downtown coterie will be eagerly seeking new terrains for exploration.

He stared at his scrawled notes. What else had he eaten?

One of the girls was swearing violently – at one of the boys? At another girl?

There was one blonde who wore tight spandex T-shirts; she would smile aggressively at him whenever he locked his bike to the front steps. The tops were short, exposed a little brown tummy.

The night before, James had watched a science-fiction film downtown so as to spend two hours in an air-conditioned room. There were laser beams and metal armour and the imagined insides of computers, all crashing and killing. He came out onto the street and into the wall of heat, a street full of motorcycles and long hair and tightly outlined breasts and nipples, and he instantly felt quite weak with lust. It was a dizziness, a hysteria that clutched at his throat, made him want to whimper.

That night he had dreamed he was an eighteen-wheeler thundering down the twelve-lane 401 in darkness and stripes of orange light, the lanes of traffic shifting left and right, hurtling forward. Silver factories and office blocks flashing by like cursors. He was a juggernaut and a sort of weapon, travelling inside brightly lit wires to seek out noise to destroy it and replace it like a mortar shell smashing into the neighbours' ugly yard. And there was music, the music he had been listening to all day, a sort of throbbing song of fax machines and touch-tone phones, a sad electrical music that was violent and lamenting and a part of the spinning images of highways, breasts with swollen nipples, wires.

He rose and went to his own stereo. He took a disc from the pile of freebies sent him to review – something hardcore from Holland, its cover all psychedelic fractals, the song titles all synapses and wandering neurons – unwrapped the plastic and put it on. He chose a track called 'Soap Orbit Funk (Reptile Didjit Mix)' by someone called Hostilator X.

A tapestry of bleeps blanketed the other thumps.

In the thumping, unvaried and simple as silence, he sat down and tried not to think about nipples again. He typed,

But one wishes Buhr's flirtation with citrus – the echo of starfruit on the Thai-Mexican sirloin, the edge of grapefruit a mere aromatic cloud in the champagne ice – would grow

And paused again. He changed 'grow' to 'swell'. Swell was a good word. He sat still for a moment and thought about swelling until he was dizzy again, and then abruptly stood up.

He hesitated for a moment, then, stealthily, as if the girls could hear him, he tiptoed through the dirty clothes towards the window, then climbed onto the bed to reach the blind.

He stopped himself before he lifted it. They were teenagers; they had braces. He shook his head. He returned to the computer and typed rapidly,

swell from prim courtship into ardent embrace: why not a hint of fig, for example, in the lamb's otherwise instructive tandoori crust? Or, say, a daringly wholehearted embrace of satsura with the amusingly named but demurely raspberried Nintendo Duck? Positively *carnal* would be the interbreeding of durian and

He was just getting excited when the phone rang. He slammed the keyboard. He waited for the message, trying some deep breathing exercises. IN-two-three Hi, this is James, I'm not available to take your OUT-two-three, please leave a message IN-two-three-and-BEEP.

'Hi James,' came the languid voice of his editor at *Edge*. 'It's Julian, listen, I was just wondering about, ah ...' James could hear him pausing to pull on his cigarette. 'About a couple of things. Wondering how Dining is coming, you know, and I also have something else for you, don't know if you're interested, it's a movie review, kind of easy money if you ask me, but I thought of you, and –'

'Fuck,' said James, and lunged for the phone. 'Julian?'

'Hello James. How are you?'

'Oh, fine, fine, a little stressed. A little warm.'

'Warm out there?' James could see him in his air conditioned office: a linen shirt, leather brogues.

'Don't think about it, Julian. Listen, Dining's coming along fine, it should be in tomorrow, no problem, but listen, I'm way overloaded right now, I couldn't take on –'

'Oh, James, I know, you always say that. But just listen. You heard of Judd Hardbird?'

'Movie star.'

'Yes.'

'No.'

Julian waited patiently.

'I mean, I've heard his name, but I don't think I've seen him in anything. But I'm not really interested in any profiles right now, Julian, I –'

'No, not a profile. He *is* in town, and I would love to give it to you because I know you'd tear him apart, which would be delightful, but we can't afford to alienate the publicist right now. Just a review of the new film. There's a press screening tomorrow night. No interviews, nothing. Just write what you think. A day's work.'

James puffed out his cheeks. 'What's the film?'

'You've seen the posters. It's this blockbuster romance about scientists in Alaska, although they filmed it in B.C., so it's got a Canadian angle.'

James snorted. 'What's it called?'

'*Breaking the Ice*. It's got Alicia Montgomery, too, and –'

'Babe,' said James. 'I like her. Why can't I interview her?'

'She's not in town. And we don't want her. We just want something northern in this issue. It's been a huge hit in early screenings, and everyone's talking Oscars.'

'What's it about?'

'Oh.' Julian took another puff. James could hear phones bleating at the other end. 'These scientists – the tough guy and the babe – who fight and have different views on ecosystems or whatnot, go

up to the Arctic Circle and bond with the quaint native people and
have a love affair and then they have to defend them against the
evil chemical company who wants to develop the area or build a
factory or something and destroy the native way of life, and these
guys ... you know, it's one of those "we're all people too" things.
It's *Dances with Seals*. It's a great idea. It's based on that book, you
know, that book that was on the bestseller list for years and years.'

'I wouldn't know.'

'Oh, I know you wouldn't, James, and that's why you'd be perfect for it. You'd *hate* it.'

'It sounds *vile*, Julian, you *know* I just offend people when I
review that mainstream stuff –'

'Yes, but that's okay, James, you're very entertaining when
you're snarky. If you can give me snarky on this one, I'll be happy.'

James heard the jaw-clenching beep that signalled another call.
'One minute.' He punched the button. 'Hello?'

'Well, I'm surprised to get you.'

'Hi Mom. Listen, I'll have to call you back, I'm on the –'

'Oh, I know, lovey, you always are when I call.'

'Oh, Mom, please –'

'No, listen, I understand you're busy, so I won't chat your ear
off. I just wanted to remind you *again*, because I'm sure you've forgotten, that it's Kurt's graduation next week and he'll be *very*
upset if you don't come up.'

James made his clubbed-seal face. 'Mom, I'll do my best, but
you know, I'm not sure if he will be so upset if I don't –'

'We *all* will be. You can stay a few days and take a rest. You'll
have to, anyway, because the party is two days after the graduation. It was the only way we could plan it.'

He sighed. 'Okay. I'll do my best. I have to –'

'We'll pick you up at the bus, and you can have your old room,
it's all repainted now. It's a guest room.'

'Okay, Mom, I have to go now.'

She disappeared, businesslike, and he punched Julian again.
'Sorry.' But Julian's line was dead; he was taking another call.

'*And I ... will always love you-oo-oo –*'

The girls were singing along now, in high and emotional voices, under his window. James's stereo was chanting, 'Technology. Philosophy. Technology. Philosophy.'

'James?'

'Yes. Okay. Listen, I really don't think I can do this review. I've just got way too much, and I've got to go away next week.'

'Three hundred words. One hundred and fifty bucks.'

James considered, sweating. There was no way he could fit it in, but he was going to miss a week of work in goddam Munich.

'GONNA STROKE YOU UP.'

He closed his eyes. 'That's a day's work for me. A hundred and fifty isn't worth it. Besides, it'll just make me angry. Sorry. Get Mary-Lou Snelling on it. She loves that stuff.'

Julian was chuckling. 'Ah, James. I can always rely on you to be the hippest. I can just hear that awful noise you're listening to and know that there's not the faintest trace of bourgeois pleasure in it anywhere. What *is* that noise?'

'Just some new Amsterdam stuff,' said James stiffly. 'Ambient industrial stuff. Helps me concentrate.'

Julian laughed, delighted. 'You're *such* a *hipster*, James. Don't ever change.'

'I have to finish Dining now.'

'Can't wait to see it. I hope it's snarky.'

James hung up and typed,

A wine-list of compassion, generosity and near-Proustian comprehensiveness – but a toothache-sweet intra-course sherbet shrivels the more ethereal choices. A gregarious duck in blood orange sauce consorts freely with wild rice, raisins, almonds and vinegary cabbage – a precarious success, arranged with the zest of fauvist painting. Marrakech Tuna steak on soya-sake butter of chocolatey richness (both salt and rice only distant notes, perfectly balanced), plus amusingly proletarian tempura onions.

He pushed his chair back, his chest running with sweat, his stomach churning. 'Amusingly proletarian' was good. He realized he was hungry. Perhaps a pizza slice from next door.

'Technology. Philosophy. Technology. Philosophy.'

He rose and lay down on his dirty sheets, limp with effort. 'Hipster,' he said aloud. 'I'm such a hipster.'

He sat up and turned off the blanket of industrial rattle. He lay back down and began to doze in the blur of sounds.

There was a noise like a fire alarm inside a jet fighter cockpit and James jumped an inch off the bed before realizing that it was the phone again.

'Hello James?' came the uncertain and vaguely English voice of Raymond Cottager of Canada's Largest Publishing Journal. 'It's, ah.'

While Cottager paused, James listened to the boys outside getting in and out of their car. 'Armando, you're getting in the fucking back, you *fuck!*'

'Hey, suck me dry, jerk-off, I saw your little sister –'

'Raymond,' said Cottager decisively. 'It's Raymond, from *Reams and Reams*, as, ah …' He paused again, chuckling. 'As you no doubt surmised.' He let out a huge sigh. 'Um. What was I …'

'*You're always in the fucking front, you little fuck!*'

'Oh!' said Cottager. 'I know! This thing about Boben, this reading tonight. I don't suppose you've heard, I mean we've all just heard it ourselves, that he's just won an award, a *prize* if you can believe it, for his last novel, which is or will be what he will be reading from tonight, or whatever.' Cottager stopped again, dizzied by his wandering verbs. James pictured him putting his fingertips to his brow. 'Anyway, he's won this prize from some Western literary magazine called *Prairie Afternoon* and it's rather a big deal, it's worth five hundred dollars, can you believe it? It's a prize called, what is it, here it is, no, that's not. Wait a – here it is. *Prairie Afternoon*. It's called the Responsible Fiction Award. Anyway, if –'

'Jesus,' said James, and reluctantly hauled himself up. He interrupted Cottager in mid-pause. 'Hello Raymond! What's all this about?'

'Ludwig Boben has won the *Prairie Afternoon* Responsible Fiction Award.'

'GONNA STROKE YOU UP.'

'Yes, I heard that, but I mean so where do I come in?'

'Oh,' said Cottager, 'well, it's just that … you are still planning to go to the reading tonight, aren't you? Because we do *need* an interview now and he's notoriously hard to get a hold of. He's something of a recluse. Lives in a log cabin with husky dogs or something like that.'

'Good Christ,' said James. 'You do know that this isn't exactly up my alley, right, Raymond? I mean you do know I'll just hate it, don't you?'

'Oh, I don't know. I thought you were remarkably kind to that whale book from Vancouver. I could never have got through it myself.'

'Thank you,' said James. 'Thank you so much for giving it to me then. Raymond, why *do* we have to review these things?'

'Oh, come on, James. Boben is one of the West's senior writers, he's published six novels and eleven books of poetry with Pussy Hollow before they went under, now he's with Outbuilding ...'

'I know, I'm sure, each one just as god-awful as the last, which doesn't answer my question.' He listened for a moment to an interesting Portuguese folk song outside, which blurred into a news broadcast that was yelled like everything else, the announcers always sounding furious or frantic or both.

'Well,' said Cottager. 'I know. The thing is, I know what you mean. But the thing is we have to do the West or they won't stock it in the newsstands out there and we get outraged letters and ... and besides Caroline is very big on this.'

James stiffened. Caroline was the editor-in-chief.

'The thing is,' said Cottager, 'we've got our grant situation in review here, and all the deadlines are coming up. And Caroline has some inside knowledge on the Council juries this round, and she says the gay-coming-out-in-an-immigrant-community stuff is all over, even child abuse is wearing thin, believe it or not, and she doesn't know what the next big thing is, but the West and First Nations are always safe, so we have to go with that. So we're going to show them what we have coming up in the next issue and ... you get the picture.'

'Jesus Christ,' said James. The broadcast outside had turned to an apoplectic commentary on an apparently unbelievably exciting soccer game at a critical moment. 'What's the title of the book?'

'*Fields of Glass,*' said Cottager. 'Referring to snow, I believe. But it's mostly about explorers sleeping with natives. In the best way, I mean, of course.'

James grunted, aware of some connection or memory that he couldn't pinpoint.

'And you see, James, I was going to get Mary-Lou Snelling to do this thing tonight –'

'She'd love it,' said James. 'She'd totally love it. She loved the whales thing.'

'I know, I know, but she can't, she has to go to a wedding or something.'

'GOOOOOOOOOOOOAL!' screamed the commentator.

After receiving assurances from Cottager that all he would have to do was review the reading and get a few quotes from Boben and that under no circumstances would he have to read the book, James promised again that he would attend the Loon Lake Reading Series in the back room at the Culture Corner, and he hung up.

He reread his review. He typed,

Adult desserts are inspirations to the rest of this tiramisu-besotted city: barely sweet grapefruit ice and champagne fill a flute with a cold pink glow, chaperoned by Riesling-tart berries and inky cocoa shavings; ultra-soft crème brulée quivers under cracking crust.

That would just about do it. He tidied it up and printed it.

Once the printer stopped its unpredictable jerking and grunting and humming and ratcheting and had reset itself internally, laboriously, as if it had painful digestive problems, James was stacking up the pages when he realized that he was in silence. One of those sudden silences that came from several pieces of music ending, by coincidence, at once: a simultaneous changing of channel and pause between songs. The boys were slamming car doors and revving engines as if in preparation for departure. The girls' stereo hissed, demanding a new CD.

James was always thrown by these silences, the moments when the overlap failed; he counted their frequency (sometimes once a week, sometimes three times in a day; sometimes thirty seconds, sometimes a frightening ten-minute stretch, as if a bomb had dropped), and they disoriented him. It was like dead air on the TV; it signalled a lack of planning, a failure somewhere.

You had to take advantage of these moments. He put his article into a file folder, and then, with willed containment, scrambled for the hidden discs, under the bed.

They still had their plastic wrap.

There was a Shostakovich String Quartet, a new recording, and a new weird Richard Catherell orchestral suite, which would require a good hour of quiet, late at night. The Shostakovich had a clean Malevich painting on the cover, all angles and precision, so impossibly, romantically clever and urbane it made James want to just fly away, rocket up through the roof of the Victorian house and into the stratosphere of steel-spectacled Russian intellectuals he knew he would never find, or just give up, just lie down and cry. He ripped open the plastic.

He had the score, had bought it the same day, and hidden it in a cardboard file-box of scores on a shelf. You would never know to look at it that it was full of scores; it was labelled MILAN −BARS. James lowered the blind before he slid it out. It was just superstition, but you couldn't be too careful. The strings played and he opened the score.

The beginning was breathless and agitated, *moderato*, and repetitious, like all the Shostakovich chamber music. James tried to follow all four staves at once but it went too fast. He caught a little echo of Beethoven and then it went into what could have been a crude twelve-tone thing, though it resolved on D flat major, which was perfectly tonal, and then went into straight conventional expressive polyphony, which was troubling and possibly humorous, an acknowledgement and rejection of twelve-tone, and if so just *ridiculously* clever, James thought.

He thought once again about trying to write something about it and again couldn't think of anyone who would be interested and felt like crying again. He decided he should get out of the apartment more.

He put aside the score to listen to the playing. That bastard Yakamori again, with the Niedviecki. A long high note, just soaring and steady. Lots of rubato. Yakamori was emotional, intensely emotional, but never soppy. Not too much vibrato, not romantic, the way the Borodin Quartet did it. James hated to admit it, but he actually preferred this to the Borodin guys. It was subtler, more refined than all that mad Russian emotionalism.

He hated to admit it because Yakamori had been at Martin Luther at the same time as James, and they were about the same age. Of course he was probably playing a Guarnieri or some such now. Easy to sound like that if you have a hundred-thousand-dollar instrument.

He stopped the music and sat in silence for a second. He picked up the cover and looked at the Malevich painting again and simultaneously loathed Yakamori and wanted to talk to him. He wondered why he had turned the music off and realized it was because it was too good and caused him pain.

Then he did what he did about once every two weeks: he bent and pulled a long, curved case out from under the bed. He blew the dust off it and opened the brass catches. He took the violin out.

He tapped it on the back, out of habit. It said, as usual, *bownk*, but there was a very feeble echo of *doo*: the strings' vibration hanging in the air.

Dumbrowsky used to say – perhaps half joking or perhaps not, James could never tell – that James should have been a drummer.

He ran his fingers over the tuning pegs, nervously, followed the scrolls with a fingertip. He straightened the bridge which didn't need straightening. He touched the matte black of the fretboard which he hated. He didn't hate this fretboard because it was a bad one; indeed, it was extremely smooth and without blemish and as a result extremely fast, because it was extremely expensive; he hated all matte black fretboards because of their sternness, their blankness. The fretboard was impassive because unmarked. It was impenetrable; it gave you no guidance. You only knew you were on the wrong place on it when you made a horrible sound. It was unforgiving. And indifferent to him.

James took out the bow and tightened it. He felt the fine roughness of the fibres, imagined a million tiny barbs. He took out the little cake of rosin and smelled its strangely dirty smell, a smell that always reminded him of cheese. Slowly and carefully, he pulled the cake of rosin up and down the bowstrings.

He took out the metal pitch pipe and blew B flat, and began to tune. After the first note, the open G, thin and whiny as creaking machinery, he fumbled around in the case again and found the mute. He clamped it over the fretboard and tried again.

G (not too bad).

D (way out).

A.

E (nice).

Circle of fifths. He thought once again of writing an essay about how the whole system of Western music is embodied in the four notes of the violin, each representing a key a fifth higher than the last, and indeed almost put the violin down to make notes, but forced himself to concentrate on the task at hand.

(Who would print it, anyway?)

He tuned with the tuning pegs and then once again with the fine-tuning knobs at the bottom end of the strings.

There was still, unbelievably, silence in the room. He took a deep breath and tightened the bow again. He shook out his hand and brought the instrument to his shoulder, nuzzled the permanently greasy chin-rest. He brought the bow perpendicular, relaxed his shoulder and his wrist, and played a scale. He missed C completely and it squawked.

Deep breath. Wrist loose, little finger just resting on the end of the bow. Upstroke and downstroke just like breathing in. And breathing out. He got the next scale okay.

He played the first few bars of an easy partita and his hand began to tighten. He heard, as he knew he would always hear, for the rest of his life, Dumbrowsky's voice, again: the *fore arm* does the work. He always separated the two words, pedantically, with great trilling r's. The *forre arrum*. Not the wrist, the wrist is loose, it is as if it were broken, it is *broken*, yes?

'Yes,' said James, playing. He got a better attack on the downstroke and started to get some nice full notes, long and hollow. The orangy wood glowed. Its vibrations under his chin were like purring. 'There you are,' he said to the violin, in Dumbrowsky's voice. 'We do not speak long time, yes?' He could feel that the instrument was grateful, pathetically grateful, for being touched.

He tried some vibrato, which wasn't really appropriate for the Bach. He couldn't get much anyway.

Dumbrowsky's voice again: not the finger, the whole arm. The whole arm moves.

His hand was aching, somewhere in the palm. Some booming started up from the stereo next door, and he tried to ignore it. Sweat dripped onto the varnish.

The song from next door interfered with his concentration and suddenly the whole thing was gone. By the end of the partita his hand had clamped up completely.

Which was what always happened.

He shook his hand out and stood up. He had to find a public fax machine. And then maybe a burger. He put the violin away.

'Daybreak slipstream, your
reptile lizard door, I open with
freezeframe, under your naked.'
An interminable pause. A full three seconds of silence.
'Whiplash.'
Another pause.
'Eye.'
All around James, the audience tensed, staring expectantly at
the bearded man in the spotlight, unsure if the poem was over.

James tried to breathe deeply. He felt the sweat sliding from
under his arms down his sides. There was an odour of feet. The
man stared at his sheaf of pages, the spotlight shining on his forehead. A few discreet coughs.

Loudly, the poet announced, *'Lightbulb.'*
'Bluelight.'
'I open.' He shuffled his sheets of paper, and the audience
exhaled as one.

James sat back in his chair, rubbing his temples. Perhaps this,
finally, was the end of the set. His watch said ten-thirty and there
were still *three* more poets before the star attraction. He glanced
with yearning over his shoulder at the bar at the back of the room.
It was crowded with the lucky young people who were under no
obligation, as he was, to listen.

And immediately he had taken in the two new women, black
clothing and bare legs, a possible tattoo on one now-crossed ankle
– not because their clothing was unusual in a room with such a
high proportion of students, but because they were the only spec-
tators whom he had not seen at that week's two other interminable readings at two other unventilated bars. He knew every face
here; indeed, these were even the same poets and the same poems
as at the last.

James wrenched his neck even farther as the fat oaf from

Squirrel Brook Books – Mac? Jack? Zack? – chattering to no one and waving chapbooks, as usual, obscured the two young women; now he could only make out one pair of legs, heavy clogs, short skirt; definitely a tattoo.

There was a sputter of applause as the bearded man clambered off the stage, and James turned back, wiping his neck and trying not to think about the tattooed ankle, the slender leg shining slightly with heat. Dick, shiny-nose Dick of the Loon Lake Reading Series, still unbelievably and impressively wearing his grey cardigan, was on the stage, shading his eyes and giggling, as he usually did to prelude his introduction of the next reader.

'Thank you, Bob,' said Dick, and giggled. He rubbed his head and clasped his hands together, then unclasped them. 'Now,' he said in an almost inaudible voice. 'You and, uh...' He cleared his throat and looked around as if suddenly distracted. He frowned, then brightened. 'I, you and I both, all know that there's really very little I can say to introduce this next ... this next ...' He began to look around him again, and James couldn't help turning his head back towards the bar. The girls had vanished.

Perhaps they were sitting, perhaps even sitting close to him. Crossing their long legs in the heat.

James took a deep breath, tried to concentrate.

'Augusta has published seven books of poetry and three collections of stories, most of them with the, ah, sadly now, ah ...' Dick's voice was diminishing further, and he was frowning harder, rubbing his knees together on the stage. '... *sadly* now defunct Weeping Sister Press ...'

The dishwashing machine at the bar came to life with a mighty buzz, and Dick's voice was drowned. Simultaneously, someone in the front bar put money in the Dukes Of Hazzard pinball machine, and it awoke with a synthesized William Tell overture and a fanfare of bells.

Conceding defeat, staring dolefully at the floor in an attitude of total penitence, as if to imply that further resistance was not only futile but dangerous and that they should all, all of them, give themselves up peacefully to avoid any trouble, Dick continued his introduction inaudibly. James was distracted by a shuffling of

chairs and murmured apologies to his right, as someone looked for
a seat in the darkness, banging knees and stepping on bags. The
entire audience turned to watch, as a young woman – not one of
the sets of bare legs at the bar, a new one, an entirely different one,
in a black leather jacket – sat down, carefully hanging her tiny silver knapsack on the back of her chair.

James tensed, opening his eyes wide. Radioactive red hair in
matted tendrils, the early stages of dreadlocks, the tops of brown
thighs flashing between tights and miniskirt. She turned away
from him before he could see her features, but he was sure she was
the one. He sat up straight and inched to the edge of his chair,
squinting at her form, trying to read every detail he could from the
back of her neck. Black leather jacket, wild red hair. What colour?
Scarlet, vermilion – what colour was vermilion, exactly? It was
pinker than vermilion, less natural. What was the red of the
three-colour video projector – yellow, cyan, magenta. Magenta.
That was it. Not on the spectrum; something electronic. Magenta.

He realized he was holding his breath. It must be the girl from
the Pursuit opening, who had smiled at him. He tried to breathe
deeper, tried to release his grip on the sides of his chair. If only she
would turn around and he could be sure.

She folded her hands on her lap and crossed her legs. The hair
on James's arms stood up. He clenched his jaw, closed his eyes,
and began trying to focus every ounce or amp, or watt, or whatever
psychic energy was measured in, to willing her to turn her head
towards him. He visualized the force beams emanating from his
forehead, turning her head like a giant magnet. He ground his
teeth together to strengthen it.

'Thank you, Dick,' came the faint voice of the next poet. She
sounded close to tears. 'I want to read a few poems tonight, about
a very painful experience in my life, and in the lives of many many
women, many of whom are still forced to remain silent.'

'Hee haw!' screamed the pinball machine.

James opened his eyes, unclenching his jaw. The seated woman
had taken off her leather jacket, revealing a cropped white T-shirt
that glowed faintly in the darkness. Ghostly pale arms, an exposed
midriff. From where he sat, he could see the bumps of vertebrae at

the base of her spine. He knew it was her. Someone had said she was a photographer.

She had hung her heavy jacket on the back of the chair, too, which meant she had turned around when James had had his eyes closed.

'I don't have to leave,' bellowed a drunk at the bar. 'Go wherever I fucking want!'

James sighed and sat back. The poet was a woman in her forties, with a mass of frizzy grey hair, heavy glasses and sandals. She was speaking barely louder than a whisper.

'I trusted you.
I trusted you.
And I scream
and I scream
in silence
and you don't listen.
And I scream
and I scream
and no one hears.
You don't hear
my pain.
No one hears
my pain.'

Another drunken shout from the bar, and a chorus of shushes from the crowd. 'Whatsamatter,' came the drunken voice, 'am I in church, or what? Thought it was a *bar*.'

James pulled up his T-shirt to wipe his forehead. His eyes were stinging with sweat. There was a commotion behind him as people began to reason with the drunk.

The poet was still reciting.
'Thursday brings the swelling
moon-tide, the great sluice walls
open, the womb dissolving
into a red sea, opening,
innocence
dissolved.'

He blinked at the stage and noticed a tall figure to one side, leaning against it, a young man in sort of New England casual clothes, beside the massive speakers. James smiled: De Courcy.

The young man stood with one hand against the speaker and one hand on his hip, his head leaning forward into the light, tilted up towards the poet, rapture on his face. James stifled a giggle. De Courcy's short hair was slicked back, shiny black in the aurora of spotlight, his pointy chin neatly shaved. His baby-blue polo shirt had a little white laurel logo twinkling over the left breast; his khaki canvas trousers were pressed to a knife-edge. A yellow cashmere pullover was knotted around his neck. James craned his neck, but he couldn't see the shoes.

The man's expression, visible to all the tables close to the stage, was one of total concentration and sympathy.

James had seen De Courcy dressed as a farmer on a trip to a cottage, with a baseball cap and a plaid jacket; he had seen him dancing in Cuban drag. He had grown a moustache for his short-lived job at a bank. But never had James seen a performance quite as convincing, quite as deeply *felt*, as this one.

He tried to wave, alarming the poet in the midst of a denunciation. She stopped whispering for a moment and shaded her eyes from the spotlight. Squinting at the audience, whispered, 'Am I out of time?'

De Courcy looked around, frowning sternly. He couldn't see James.

A faint demurral was heard from Dick, in darkness at the bar.

'Could we have quiet please?' said De Courcy to the audience.

'Well,' she whispered, 'I guess I'll just read one more.' She hesitated. 'I've never read this one in public before.' Her bottom lip appeared to quaver. 'And this may be quite difficult for me.'

The audience rustled, giving up a few embarrassed, encouraging murmurs.

'Well, here goes.' The poet took a deep breath. You could feel the bravery coming off the stage; you could just *smell* the bravery.
'*I hide*
in the bathroom,
the pad a white
marshmallow cookie

26

stained with red jam,
listening to his
breathing outside,
the guilty womb's
collapse ...'

James tuned out instantly, sitting back. He looked at his watch, then scanned the crowd again, trying to guess which white-haired guy in a plaid shirt might be Boben.

'I'm *asking,'* shouted the drunk, 'if this is a *church,* or WHAT!'

Bravely, the poet continued. Some fifteen minutes later, she was still describing her early life, which had been, James had to concede, unquestionably unpleasant, and he had considered in detail every German sandal and Nicaraguan shoulder bag in his line of vision, and finally decided that he had only seconds in which to rudely stand and leave before his mulchy shoes actually putrefied and turned to liquid sewage, when suddenly he found that he was looking right into the gaze of the leather-jacket woman, who had turned to look at the commotion and caught his eye instead, and that she was smiling at him and he was smiling back.

It only lasted a fraction of a second before she looked away. James continued smiling at her neck as a constellation of equally dramatic truths flared in his head simultaneously, like a meteor shower: (a) she had a gold ring dramatically piercing the middle of her swollen lower lip (b) it *was* the same one as at the Pursuit opening (c) she couldn't be older than twenty-five (d) she had very pale skin and enormous dark eyes (e) she had smiled at him (f) her cropped T-shirt was very tight (g) she had smiled at him unprovoked (h) she was quite fantastically perfectly featured (i) she had now smiled at him *twice.*

James looked around, grinning idiotically at all the sad people. He felt very compassionate towards them. He began to hum *Eleanor Rigby.* A grey-haired woman frowned at him. He nodded at her benignly, grinning, just as the poet burst into tears.

There was nervous applause, in which James participated energetically, even adding a loud whistle. 'Right on,' he shouted. 'Good going!'

He kept thinking of that ring in her lip. The sight of it had given him goosebumps.

There were only three more poems (all about the poet's father, whom she apparently still loved and thought about from time to time) before she shuffled off, sniffling bravely. And then Dick came back on, his nose only imperceptibly redder, and announced that there had been news that Ludwig Boben's flight had been delayed, but that he was on his way, and they expected him in the next set. In the meantime, there would be a short break.

In the mass stretching and groaning that followed, James rose briskly. He tried to push his way through the damp backs to the bar, catching sight of De Courcy's polo shirt, his sleek head floating serenely above all others; he was moving towards James, carrying high two misty bottles of beer. 'Hey!' James yelled, waving. The bottles looked so cold they made him salivate. 'Over here!'

De Courcy smiled back, weaving neatly through the bodies. 'I thought,' he said in his slow, soft voice, as he drew up, 'You might be here. And I thought. You might have worked up a kind of.' His lips barely moved as he spoke. 'Sympathetic thirst.'

'Jesus,' said James throatily, clutching at the bottle. It was icy, wet with condensation. He sucked deeply on it and the cold reached into his belly. He drank so quickly the alcohol stung his throat.

When he had stopped, panting, he said, 'Jesus' again, and put the bottle to his forehead. 'Jesus Christ. Thanks.'

'Thirsty work, compassion,' said De Courcy.

James laughed to hear him, remembering how he always sounded exhausted or drugged.

'I was feeling positively ... parched by the time she reached adolescence. It's the sadness.' His eyelids lazily, slowly closed. 'That does it to you.'

James sputtered, laughing. 'Jesus. Good to see you. How the hell have you been?

'I see you share my sympathies,' De Courcy continued, 'although I must admit it surprises me to find you here – not of course meaning to question your compassion, but I wouldn't have thought it was really your *line*, this sort of thing?'

James drained his beer. 'No it absolutely fucking is not. I'm supposed to interview this poet or novelist or Renaissance fucking Man for *Reams and Reams*, the publishing mag. This poet who isn't here. The only poet who isn't here.' He was scanning the shoulders, looking for the shock of the leather-jacket woman's hair and pale face. She had disappeared. He turned to De Courcy. 'So what the hell are you doing here?'

De Courcy raised his neat eyebrows and smiled by turning down the corners of his mouth. 'I liiike ...'

James wondered how long he could stretch the word.

'To keep up with the. Arts.'

James snorted.

'And I had the feeling you might be here. I see from you recent pub ... from your recent *oeuvre* that your area of expertise now includes literature.'

James smiled. 'Jesus, it's good to see you.'

'And you.'

'Long time, hey? What ...' He hesitated. This was always a delicate question with De Courcy. 'What exactly are you ... how are you filling your days, these days? Besides keeping up with the arts?'

De Courcy sighed. 'Well. I have school, of course.'

'School? You're back in school? Doing what?'

De Courcy looked at him as if surprised. 'Well, art history, of course. You knew that.'

'Well, I knew you started a degree a few years back that you never got around to finishing ...'

'Well, I'm back at it now,' said De Courcy quickly. 'I was always enthusiastic, I just had an awful load of emotional stress that year.' He dropped his voice. 'That was the year of Julio, if you recall.'

'I recall.'

'Well, anyway, I'm very enthusiastic about it now. I'm back into it with.' His voice grew very quiet; he closed his teeth. 'Abandon.'

James smiled. 'Well, that's great. That's terrific. Full time and everything?'

'No, not full time. I couldn't quite manage full time, I'm too busy.'

'Uh-huh. How many courses?'

De Courcy held up one finger. 'For the moment.'

'Full course or half course?'

'Half. But I'm taking it spread over two terms. So the workload is lighter.'

James nodded gravely. 'Great. Congratulations. Where are you living?'

'Oh. Too *funny*.' De Courcy's jaw was closed again; the words emerged as if from death. 'I have the nicest new place. And,' he added casually, 'I'm living with a girl.'

'A girl?'

'You think I'm incapable of living with women.'

'Yes.'

'Well. I'm not *living* with her living with her. But I do like her. She's delightful. She's hilarious. She's from a place in Cape Breton, Nova Scotia, called Meat Cove, and she's actually called Fiona.'

'Fiona from Meat Cove. Terrific.'

'No, you'd love her. I'll have to arrange a meeting. She's actually quite sweet. She does nursing or physiotherapy or something. And she has the most unbelievably textbook boyfriend, I call him Big Gulp, he looks like Judd Hardbird, seriously –'

'Judd Hardbird,' murmured James. 'Why is everyone –'

'His real name is Buck, can you believe it.' There was no question in the sentence. 'No, it's true. It's absolutely true. And they don't find it funny at all. He's unbelievable. He plays hockey and he studies kinesiology which is what they call phys ed now ... and he's always slapping me on the back and telling me it's great how some people are in the arts, because we really need the arts in a healthy economy. And ...' De Courcy's voice grew deep. 'And he's about six four and all muscle and thigh and ...' His fingers fluttered. 'And *chunk*, you know?'

'Ahh,' said James.

'He's like a great big sentient steak,' said De Courcy in his lowest voice. 'Two hundred pounds of hot steak.'

James laughed. 'And do he and Fiona have any idea about ...'

'Probably not. I don't think Buck wants to know.' He was

looking around the room, frowning very slightly. 'And you. I must say, congratulations, I can't open a paper without seeing your byline. I see your aesthetic pronouncements on every possible subject in which aesthetics could *possibly* have a role.'

James was searching again, narrowing his eyes, looking for the flash of leather. He saw the two tall girls again, and tried to smile, but they turned away coldly.

'And I love your drolleries on restaurants,' said de Courcy, 'although I wonder how many catch the irony.'

'There's no irony,' said James distractedly, 'it's –'

And there she was, coming right towards them: the pale face and almost exaggeratedly large eyes. She seemed to have materialized from nowhere.

James smiled again, automatically, planting his feet widely enough to withstand the shock wave of pierced lip, thigh-high tights, tight top, exposed belly and navel piercing – another little gold stabbing, sprouting from the round belly like a worm, surrounded by a tattooed ring, a Celtic snake motif. She was wearing heavy motorcycle boots.

'Yikes,' said James weakly.

De Courcy was watching him closely. 'Well well well,' he said.

'Listen, do you know who that is? I see her everywhere.'

De Courcy was shaking his head dolefully. 'What did I tell you. Nothing but the beautiful and famous for our aesthetician, our arbiter of the aesthetic.'

'You do?'

'I'm surprised you don't. She lives in the Bomb Factory, you know that new –'

'The Bomb Factory!'

'It was an old munitions –'

'I know,' said James, 'what it is.' He drank a half a bottle of beer. '*Edge* ran a story on it. I wanted to do it but they wouldn't give it to me. But I know the whole story. Architect from Miami, new breed of loft dweller, new urban blah blah.' He considered this for a moment. 'I've never been inside it.'

'Look, there's Guntar Nettel.'

'The Bomb Factory,' said James. 'Is she –'

'He's teaching again. That business of the infantilists' magazine seems to have been forgotten. He's a theorist now, you know.'

James lost sight of the girl for a second. 'Oh?' he said absently. 'What kind of theorist?'

'The worst kind,' murmured De Courcy. 'A *prancing* theorist.'

There was a silence, and James realized that De Courcy was staring at him through narrowed eyes. De Courcy said suddenly, 'And she works for all the magazines you write for.'

'So she is a photographer?'

'She's not a photographer, she's *the* photographer. That's Nicola Lickson.'

'Nicola Lickson!' He tried to quash the exclamation mark at the end, but it came out. He peered after her, narrowing his eyes, trying to hide the exclamation marks in them. He saw her leaning against the bar, laughing with the two tall girls. Of course she would know them. 'So that's Nicola Lickson,' he said nonchalantly. 'You know, she shot my piece on new hallucinogens in *Edge*. She invented that whole cartoon reptile look, remember that? Last year? Or brought it here anyway. Then everybody was doing it for a while.'

'And she designed the inside of Control, and did the video footage for the monitors, and she shoots that TV show about fashion, and now she's doing art videos.'

James looked up at him in exhaustion. 'You're amazing. How do you know all that stuff? *I'm* supposed to know that stuff.'

De Courcy shrugged. 'I know you are.'

James blinked at the women at the bar. 'Nicola Lickson.' He cleared his throat. 'Of course she would live in – I'd love to see a place in there.'

'Oh dear,' said De Courcy.

'Why? You know her?'

De Courcy shook his head. 'No no.'

'What are you getting at?'

'Well, I'd just be careful, that's all. I think she's known to be a little. Wild.'

'Wild,' said James slowly. 'Well, I can see that. I have no problem with that.'

De Courcy smiled grimly and was silent.

James looked at his watch again, rubbed a hand over his sweaty face. 'Where the fuck is this writer?' The crowd was beginning to thin out. 'I have to pee.'

As he entered the urine-smelling corridor where the toilets and the telephone were, he almost bumped into the three women in damp cotton sundresses waiting outside the closed toilet door in obvious discomfort; they looked clammy. They looked at him with panic, as if he would step in front of them. Smiling pacifically, James took his place.

He noticed he was next to the telephone, and remembered the restaurant copy he had faxed off that afternoon. He found a quarter and called his machine.

'James,' said his landlord's voice, 'where are you? Please return my messages. It's urgent, I'm –'

James skipped to the next message. He was surprised; Franco was rarely so insistent about a simple bounced cheque. He assumed that was all it was – the rent cheque would, indeed, inevitably have bounced – and the problem would be resolved the instant James deposited the bloody *Dental Week* cheque he had been expecting for weeks. So there was really no need to call him back until he got it, when he could assure Franco that the money was in the bank. Still, he resolved to call Franco back immediately, or soon, possibly even the next day. Politeness counts, he thought, even if there was nothing he could do about the money.

The next message was his mother, just reminding him of his promise to come up to Munich the following week for his brother's graduation from law school.

He made his clubbed seal face, peering out of the corridor to see if any sad poet had taken the stage. Not yet. The women in the toilet queue were talking about restaurants. 'When he was at Swindle,' said one, 'he used to do a really fabulous kimchee-sorghum pancake with the deer hearts.'

He really had to pee.

The next beep came.

'James,' said Julian from *Edge*, rather more briskly than usual, 'small problem here with your restaurant copy, could you call me

as soon as you can, tonight if possible? We're already in production. I'll be here till late, ten or eleven at least. Are you there?
Hello?'

He looked at his watch: eleven-thirty. He sighed and called
Edge.

Julian was a little calmer by the time he got to the phone. 'Oh,
James, thanks for calling. Nothing serious, just a little hole I need
filling. Just a minute while I find it.'

While keys clacked, James considered graphically various
means of filling Julian's little hole.

'Okay. Here it is. We lost an inch of the Celeb-O-Meter after the
lawyers got uptight about lawsuits, so we can fill it with Food. If
you just came up with another paragraph about Chimera, that
would be great. About an inch. Maybe forty, fifty words.'

'Fifty words about what?' said James. 'Anything in particular, or
you just need random words?'

'Well,' said Julian, unfazed, 'I think you could use a little more
about the actual food. I mean you've got lots of sociology here, but
we want to know what you ate. But listen, don't worry about it
right now. Think about it carefully, fax it to me tomorrow.'

'Tomorrow?' James considered. He absolutely had to do the
Boben piece tomorrow, and get started on the *Dental Week* thing.
'Uh, no, Julian, that's okay. Listen. I'm going to give you the paragraph right now. You ready? Read me the last line, before where
you want to put this in.'

Julian read, 'Plus amusingly proletarian tempura onions. Nice,
that. I like that.'

'Okay. Write this down. You ready?' James closed his eyes, tried
not to hear the washroom-queue conversation.

'I like it for the kimchee alone,' said one languidly. 'I could die
for good kimchee.'

Another poet had begun to read; his amplified voice echoed in
the corridor.

'My father was killed
in the Holocaust.'

James focused. 'Okay,' he said. He cleared his throat. His eyes
still closed tightly, he recited, 'More entertaining, comma, at least,

comma, is the rather languid potato soup, comma, in which a drift of latticed leeks meandering gently into a thicket of chervil overlays...' He hesitated. 'A pleasingly bashful vichyssoise, comma.' He stopped. He couldn't remember a single other dish.

'It was a sort of a Thai-Greek thing,' said one of the women next to him, 'with mashed potato and apple.'

'Apple?' said another. 'How post-modern.'

James said, 'Echoing with distant notes of apple.' He opened his eyes. 'Now read that back to me.'

Julian did.

'Okay, no, I have notes twice. Strike distant notes. Put distant hues. Distant hues of apple. No. Wait a minute.'

'Endless cattle wagons,' read the poet,

'endless wagons of death,

moving inexorably to the room,

the place of death

from which there is no

escape.'

A roar of flushing came from the toilet; the queue shuffled forward.

'A distant tinkle,' said James. 'A distant tinkle of apple. How's that?'

'Wonderful. Thanks, James.'

James hung up, smiling. He was pleased with distant tinkle. Distant tinkle was good. He looked with longing at the closed toilet door. Someone had found a way ahead of him in the line.

'They separated me from my mother,' droned the poet,

'my sister,

my brother,

no, I cried,

don't take my brother.'

James rushed down the corridor, hoping the Holocaust poet was Boben; he knew that Boben had once published a long narrative poem about Dieppe.

He emerged into the club. The guy on the stage was also bearded, but didn't look like the pictures James had seen. Besides, Boben had never lived in Europe.

The pinball machine was still blaring its touch-tone overture.
'*Father,*
mother,
brother,
Sister,' said the poet,
'*uncle,*
aunt,
cousins,
second cousins.'
'Catch me, baby,' burped the pinball machine.
'*My mother's*
brother's
family,
his wife's
family.'
Nicola Lickson's seat was empty. There was an empty seat beside hers. James hesitated, bursting; the queue might be shorter now, and the Holocaust guy would probably be interminable anyway.
'*One small flower,*' whispered the bearded poet,
'*here in the dry grass,*
the long flat factory buildings,
now deserted but ever silent monuments,
one small red flower
in the desert,
of continuing.
Thank you.'
A ripple of applause as he clambered down. James clapped away. Too late to head back to the washroom now: the next reader could be Boben.

He scanned the crowd for Nicola's hair. He was already beginning to call her that. Nicola.

Dick was back at the mike. 'Thank you, Al. Well.' Long pause. 'Bad news, I'm afraid.' James looked at his watch. 'I'm afraid Mr Boben was not at the airport after all, he appears to have missed his flight –'

There was an enormous scraping of chairs as the matted

audience, a herd of something nearly extinct, something like
mastodons, slowly changing direction, began to gather their bags.

Dick almost shouted above the stamping, 'As you may or may
not have heard or, ah, learned, today, Mr Boben was just awarded a
prestigious prize, one of Western Canada's most, ah –'

James rubbed his eyes. He would have to call *Reams* first thing
in the morning. He crossed his ankles, thinking of the washroom.

'Coveted, I suppose, awards for literary fiction, the *Prairie
Afternoon* Responsible Fiction Award, so perhaps Mr Boben is
celebrating, and I, ah, for one, don't blame him. Anyway, all this to
say that our evening is now unfortunately at an –'

The stereo system snarled to life, and Dick's voice vanished.
James watched the herding around the one exit for a moment,
then turned back towards the toilets.

And there, standing right behind him, was Nicola Lickson, her
hands on her hips and her lips slightly parted. He recoiled.

'Hi,' she said, smiling. 'Excuse me, but you're James Willing,
aren't you?'

James opened his mouth and closed it again. Then he said, 'I
guess so, yes. Hi.'

'I just wanted you to know that I really love your restaurant
column, and your stuff on music and all.'

'Oh!' said James, his eyes opening wide. He opened his mouth
again, wordless. The language sector of his hard disk was spinning,
inaccessible. He smiled, forcing himself to keep his gaze rigidly on
her eyes and not on the Celtic snake tattoo on her belly. Finally,
he said, 'Thank you.'

'Well, I mean not everything, but I really think it's important
that some people really say what they think about things.' She
was standing with her legs planted firmly apart, caressing her belly
and its little ring with one hand.

He cast a quick glance down and up again. 'I never say what I
think about things,' he said weakly.

She laughed. 'No, I'm sure you don't.'

He wasn't sure why, but he laughed too.

'I mean,' she said, one finger toying with the ring, the other
running through her hair, 'I think it's unfair that people call you a

prick and stuff, although you are sometimes, because it's really important that someone is willing –'

'Who calls me a prick?'

'Listen, I just say I think it's great that we have someone who is willing to be honest.'

'Oh. Thank you.'

'I'm Nicola.' She was still staring straight at his eyes.

'Oh, yes, sorry,' said James, sticking out his hand. 'Hi. I know, actually, who you are. And I should say that I really admire your work too.' He crossed his ankles, trying not to upset his bladder by breathing too deeply. 'You shot a piece of mine for *Edge*.'

'Did I? Really? What piece?'

'On drugs. New hallucinogens.'

'Oh yes! You wrote that? Cool!' She frowned for a second, glancing around her. 'I don't always read the bylines.' She looked up at him with a small smile. 'You know how it is.'

'I don't always know who the photographer is either.'

'Where did you get your nose done? I like it.'

James's hand went instinctively to his wimpy little ring, embarrassed that Nicola could probably tell how new it was. He shrugged. 'Franz at the Penal Colony, of course. Like everybody.'

She touched her own nose. 'He did this. But I go to Dr Moreau's now.' Gently, both her hands floated down her front to her belly.

James stared helplessly at the piercing. 'Listen,' he said quickly, 'just stay here for a second, okay, because I really have to –'

'So tell me this one thing I've always wanted to know. When you go to those restaurants, does the magazine pay for your whole meal?'

James looked over her shoulder at the toilet door. 'Oh yes. Of course. Everything. In fact, it pays for a couple of meals.'

'You mean you take people and their food is paid for too?'

'Well, you didn't think I ate all that myself, did you?'

'That's incredible,' she said. 'That's incredible. That is like an ideal job. You are so *lucky*. You are so lucky. You just go out and have a great time and then write about it and you get all these great meals!' She moved her face closer to his and her eyes narrowed slightly. Her voice dropped. 'Just how did you get this gig, anyway?'

'Oh, that's a long story. But it's not quite as simple as that, anyway. The writing part, I mean.'

'Did you go to cooking school?'

'Ah. No.'

Her face was still close to his. He could smell patchouli and cigarettes. 'Did you ever work in a restaurant?'

James puffed out his cheeks. 'No. Listen, hang on one second and I'll –'

'So how many nights a week do you eat out?'

'Oh, too many. Maybe three or four.'

'Three or four! Wow, that is rough. That is really rough.'

'Well, you know –' He tried to chuckle. 'It does get a little tiring.'

'Oh, give me a break!'

James winced as the swishing of the dishwashing machine tweaked him with images of shimmering waterfalls and great spouting cascading – 'I guess,' he said with effort, 'it's probably a little like always being out at nightclubs. You must get a little tired sometimes?'

She tilted her head and frowned, as if considering. Then she said, 'I'm moving more into video now.'

'Video? I heard that. Cool. Congratulations. What kind of video?'

'Oh, you know. *Independent* video.'

'Right.'

'I've just released a video that's kind of a women's issues film. There's a screening party Wednesday. You're welcome to come if –'

'Oh, thanks,' said James, leaning on the wall and trying to relax his abdomen. 'I'll certainly try to make it. What's it about?'

'Well, that's hard to say.'

'Of course.' James nodded. He had been to independent video screenings before.

'I guess it's mostly about women's relationships to power tools, you know, there are a lot of images of power tools in it.'

'Fly,' said James. 'Interesting. I'd love to see it.'

'And menstruation. I guess.'

'Of course.'

She nodded, playing with the next navel ring again.

James looked away.

'All my friends are interviewed on it while they're bleeding. Just something I always wanted to do.' Then, quickly, she said, 'So, what else are you working on?'

He glanced over her shoulder at the toilet door. 'Oh, a number of things. Are you in a rush, because I'll just be –'

'Yeah, I am actually,' she said, glancing around. She picked up her tiny knapsack. 'I've got to cover this party at Questing Beast. Are you going?'

James nodded, as if to show that he knew all about Questing Beast, which he had never heard of.

But an idea had just come to him.

He pretended to yawn, then said, while looking at his watch, 'No, I'd better get home. I'm so busy this week. I've got to do Ritchie LeBlanc's new place sometime, and then –'

'You mean Mirage?' said Nicola sharply. 'His *new* new place?'

'Yeah, it's kind of a drag because it has to be in by Friday, and then I've got –'

'Wow,' said Nicola. 'Wow, you are lucky. You are so lucky. Mirage. I've heard all about it. I've never tasted – I mean I had some stuff at his first place, back when he was at that café at King and Dufferin, so I mean I have an idea what it's like, but that was years ago, and – so that's brand new, right, the one with all that new steelwork in the design and –'

'Oh, yes,' said James as casually as he could, 'there's a great – a fly, a *phat* steel staircase rising up three stories in the centre of the room, all that stuff. But it's silly, really, the prices are ridiculous. I could never afford it if it wasn't paid for.'

'I bet.' She looked away for a second, then said, 'Well, wow, terrific. Have a good time. Tell me what it's like, and all. I envy you.' She pushed hair away from her forehead, and waited.

'Thanks,' said James. *Red leader*, he said to his helmet microphone, *I have a target lock*. 'Well, it was nice to meet you, maybe I'll run into you at some opening.' He gave it a second more, just to maximize impact, then fired. 'Listen, if you're really interested in seeing Mirage, I'm always looking for dining partners.'

She looked up quickly. 'What, you mean to go with you?'

James shrugged. 'Sure. I can't eat all that stuff myself. I don't have a date for this one, so if you have any free time ...'

'Oh my *God*,' said Nicola, her face opening up. 'I'd love to.'

James kept his face nonchalant. *Fox one, hit confirmed, Red four disengaging.* She was almost jumping. It was like watching an Iraqi baby-milk factory disintegrate under your sights.

She quickly regained control of her face, dropping the smile back into an icy void. 'Sure,' she said. 'I'd love to see it. I mean if you're serious, I really would.'

'Terrific,' said James, now letting loose his own grin. Magnanimous in victory, he said, 'I'd love to take you. What are you doing this week?'

'Well, my screening is Wednesday.'

'Screening?'

'Of my video, that I told you about, the one on menstruation?'

'Oh, right, of course. Wednesday? Well, I could make it Tuesday or Thursday.'

'I tell you what.' She was back in full control now, glancing around and looking bored. 'I would love you to see this video. And you might really enjoy the people at the screening, I think they're *so* cool. I'll come to Mirage with you if you check out my film.'

He closed his eyes for what he hoped was an imperceptible second. 'Sure,' he said, 'I'd love to.'

Then there was the fumbling for pens and scraps of paper for phone numbers, and he had agreed to call her on Wednesday and leave a message with her roommates so she would remember to call him back – 'And make them *promise* they'll give me the message,' she said, 'don't be afraid to be mean with them' – and he stumbled towards the unbelievably open door of the washroom.

When he emerged into the largely empty room as if into bright sunshine, De Courcy was waiting for him at the bar. 'Glass of wine?'

'I'm kind of zoned, you know, better crash. Have to get up early tomorrow. What do you have?'

'Half a bottle of Les Ormes du Pez '89. And a largely untouched Oregon pinôt noir.'

'Jesus Christ. Sure. I can't stay up late, though.'

'You'll get to meet Fiona.'

'I absolutely can not stay up late.'

'Of course not,' murmured De Courcy, pointing his silver cigarette case towards the door, 'of course not.'

James paid for the cab. De Courcy had already disappeared into a narrow path between two buildings, softly singing *'Parigi, o cara'*. James got out and peered down it into blackness. Five or six boys in baseball caps watched him from the corner, spitting occasionally on the sidewalk. The lane was between two dark shops, Açores Travel and Viseu Tax Accountant and Dry Cleaning, which had a sign in the window reading, 'We speak English.'

He walked carefully down the alley, both arms extended in front of him, past a sign in orange letters which said, 'NO TRESPASTING BEWARE OF ROTTEN DOG'. A spotlight flashed on him and he started. The lane led into a black courtyard. Blank brick walls went three stories up on either side of him.

'It's motion activated,' came De Courcy's voice ahead of him. 'Come on.'

There was barking and the scrabbling of nails on gravel as two dogs surged from nowhere, teeth bared, running at him. James froze.

'Ignore the dogs,' came De Courcy's distant voice.

James had taken in that one was brown and one black and the brown one had a spiked collar when he turned to run, but De Courcy's voice stopped him again.

'Don't run! *Don't run!'*

James stopped and the dogs stopped, snarling and growling at his feet. One was wagging its tail.

'They're called Gilligan and Tisha,' yelled De Courcy, apparently from somewhere above him.

'Hi Gilligan,' said James. His voice came out squeaky. 'Hi Tisha.' Gingerly, he stepped around them. They followed him down the lane, sniffing and bumping against his ankles, into a dogshit-smelling courtyard. There was a thumping of bass from somewhere. James bumped against a motorcycle.

'Up the fire escape,' said De Courcy.

Feeling along a wall with his fingers, James found the fire
escape ladder which was almost vertical; he climbed it and came
onto De Courcy's balcony.

'My deck,' said De Courcy, standing under a light near the door.
There were three old bicycles, a hillock of garbage bags, a bulky
standing radio from the 1950s and an armless stone Virgin. 'You
have to admire Jennifer.'

'Who?'

'Jennifer the virgin.'

'Jennifer the stone virgin.'

'I named her after someone I knew at Queen's.'

'I admire her,' said James, breathing hard. He pulled up his T-
shirt to mop his face. 'God in a latrine, what a virgin.'

'Now you may come in.'

As he jingled keys, another door onto the balcony swung open.
A burst of light, and a silhouette, swinging a weapon. It stepped
forward as a tiny woman in a yellow terrycloth bathrobe, holding a
broom in both hands like a weapon. 'Who is that!' she shouted,
waving the broom handle and narrowly missing James, who
stepped back. Her hair was grey and in curlers. '*Who is that!*' Her
accent was foreign.

'Elsie!' said De Courcy warmly, opening his arms wide.

'*Misser Decoosie!*' she yelled, still swinging.

'Yes, Elsie, it's me,' said De Courcy, also stepping back. 'It's
okay, Elsie. It's only me. And a friend.'

She put the broom down and glared at James. 'Who your friend?'

James coughed.

'This is my good friend James Willing, Elsie. This is my landlady, James.'

'Hello,' said James.

She turned to De Courcy and held out a bony finger. 'Are you
drunk?'

'Drunk? Elsie!'

'I hope you are not drunk. I tell you last time.' The accent was
Eastern European, possibly Polish. 'Last time I say, Andrew, the
next time I catch you like this –'

'Ah,' said De Courcy, 'but you see, you're mixing me up with

44

Andrew. I'm not Andrew. Andrew is in 2C, remember? Underneath you. I'm Piers. Piers De Courcy, remember?'

Elsie's face dissolved into uncertainty. 'You are not Andrew?'

'No. Andrew is downstairs. I'm Piers.'

She breathed heavily, staring down at her broom. Finally, she
said, 'Oh yes.' She shook her head. 'I am sorry, Misser Decoosie.
That Andrew, he is always drunk. And I tell him last time –'

'Oh, I know, Elsie. I know. It's quite all right. Did you enjoy the
muffins?'

She looked up. 'You gave me that muffins?'

'Yes. Yesterday. That my wife made.'

'Oh, the muffins your wife make?'

'That's right.'

'Oh yes.' But she was already moving back inside. 'You tell her
thank you. How is your wife?' She was closing the door.

'She's fine, thanks, Elsie, good night.' The door slammed.

James exhaled. 'Jesus Christ.'

'Sorry about that. She's all right, actually, you just have to
know how to deal with her. I must say it's a little ...' He sighed.
'*Tiring*, though, her confusing me with Andrew. He is always
drunk. But there you are.' He was still fumbling with keys. 'I
make her muffins every now and then, from a mix, and tell her my
wife made them.'

'Fiona?'

De Courcy nodded. 'It's easier in Elsie's buildings if you're married.'

'Her buildings, plural?'

'She owns most of the neighbourhood, so it's best to keep on
her sunny side. She's a honey, really. *Voilà*.' The door swung open.

In the kitchen was a strong girl with two red pigtails. She was
smoking and reading a textbook. There was an empty beer bottle
on the table. De Courcy kissed her on the forehead. 'This is my
old, old friend James,' he said, 'James, Fiona. How is it tonight? Do
we have art?'

Fiona nodded, squinting as she sucked on her cigarette. Her
breath held, she said, 'Jesus fuck.' She exhaled at length. 'Do we
have art.'

A voice boomed, distorted and echoing. It seemed to come from all around them. *'I breathe,'* it boomed. *'I transmit.'*

James glanced around wildly, looking for a stereo speaker. 'Fuck was that?'

De Courcy sighed. 'Acton, guy who lives upstairs. You'll have to meet him. Excuse me a minute.' He disappeared.

The voice reverberated again. *'I am imprisoned. I transmit.'* A glass rattled on a shelf.

Fiona thumped the seat of the chair next to her with her fist, beaming at James. 'Sit yourself down, Jamie. I'm so happy to meet you, finally. Percy has told me so much about you. You want a beer?'

'He has?' This surprised James a little. And he was pretty sure De Courcy was not keen on being called Percy.

'Oh you bet your furry little ass.' She slammed a beer bottle in front of him.

'I breathe,' came Acton's voice from upstairs, liquid like the voice of a ghost in a film. *'I transmit.'*

'Jesus holy purple mother of Christ,' exhaled Fiona. 'There she blows again. Like clockwork at midnight. We should publish a schedule.'

'What's he doing?' said James.

'Anguish,' said the voice, slow and regular. *'Liberty. Anguish.'*

'Is he okay?'

'Oh, you can bet your logans he's okay. He's happy as a clam up there. Stupid as my arms, but happy as a clam.' She expertly smoked the last centimetre in her butt. 'You're taking a long time with that beer, Jimmy, you need a hand or what?'

'Liberty,' came the ethereal voice. *'Liberty. Liberty.'*

'He's probably tied himself up again,' said Fiona, reaching for the broom. Without removing the butt from between her lips, she poked the ceiling with the handle. 'We'll have to go and let him out by the end of it.'

'He ties himself up?'

Fiona was pounding vigorously. Her teeth clenched to hold the butt, she shouted, 'He locks himself into this tramsitter box he built out of old video cassette boxes.'

46

'I see.'

Fiona pounded some more, and the voice stopped.

James cleared his throat. 'And why, why exactly does he do that?'

'Oh it's art. I heard all about it, don't worry. You will too. Acton told me. He said it's the prison of mass culture. And he's o-*ppressed*, see. Which means he's really feeling mad, Percy explained to me. And if he's really feeling mad, you know, like, more *o-ppressed* than usual, he clips himself up with computer cables and D-rings, and sometimes he can't get out. Except it's hard to know if he's really yelling for help or if it's just part of his act.'

She put down the broom and helped herself to James's beer. 'Fuck me clean. I marvel. I just fucking marvel. My uncle in Big Tracadie used to lock himself in the salting shed. I guess he wasn't too much of a performance artist, no. I imagine.' She sighed and sat again, lighting a new cigarette. 'That's on my mother's side, he wasn't really my uncle. My mother's cousin, really, my grandmother's brother's son, the Boutilier side from Tracadie Landing. All those Tracadie Landing people are crazy. Although most of them left in eighty-seven – was it eighty-seven? No. Wait a minute.' She was staring at something past James's shoulder, frowning. She took a deep drag.

James glanced briefly behind him to see a blank wall.

Fiona shook her head and announced, 'Nope. I tell a lie. Couldn't have been eighty-seven because that was the year Jimmy MacDonald married the Arsenault girl, and they hadn't even built the farm until –'

'*I breathe,*' came Acton's voice, '*I transmit.*'

'I hope,' said De Courcy shrilly, entering with a corkscrew held aloft, 'that you're not spoiling your palate with beer.'

'Oh spare me,' muttered Fiona.

'Would you like to see the place?'

'Sure.' James rose.

He followed through the purple living room ('Grape jelly,' murmured De Courcy), the charcoal corridor with the signed Kandinsky print ('A very large run, though,' said De Courcy sadly), the

ochre bathroom and Fiona's room, plain white, hung with Blue
Jays pennants and a poster of a windsurfer. De Courcy's room was
deep red, hung with wrought-iron sconces. Above his curlicued
black lacquered desk ('Japanned papier-mâché,' he whispered,
'eighteenth century') there was a rack for glasses like those that
hang over bars. Long-stemmed crystal and bulbous brandy snifters
upside down in neat rows.

De Courcy sat at the desk on what appeared to be a Regency
dining-room chair; James sank onto an Arts and Crafts sofa. 'Now,'
said De Courcy, opening desk drawers. 'Where shall we begin.'

Each drawer held two bottles of wine. 'Red on the right, white
on the left, champagne and rosé in the top middle, theoretically,
although we drank the champagne last night and actually I *detest*
rosé, it just makes a nice aesthetic bridge, something about that
that I can't – ah. Here it is.'

He held up the bottle, ruby in the lamplight. James nodded, past
reading the label. Seated comfortably, De Courcy reached a long
arm up to the rack above the desk and detached two glasses.

'I didn't know you went to Queen's,' said James, as De Courcy
cut off the lead wrapper.

'What?'

'On the deck. You said the virgin reminded you –'

'Oh yes. I did. For a year. The year before I came here, before we
met.' De Courcy eased out the cork and scrutinized it, frowning.

'The year we met was your first year here? No kidding.'

'Certainly. We met at a Trinity College dean's list wine-and-
cheese. Remember?'

'I remember. We were both crashing. I wasn't even at Trinity. I
was doing my bee muz at Vic. I was following some girl there.'

'You do the honours,' said De Courcy, pouring James a splash. 'I
remember her well.'

'Do you? I don't.'

'Of course I do. Blythe Reynolds. A very rich girl.'

'Blythe Reynolds. What a name.' James tasted. His eyes popped
open. 'Jesus Christ.'

'I take it that's okay.' De Courcy filled the glasses. 'Unfortunately, this is the eighty-eight. The eighty-nine was the main

event, apparently, epic and stuff, all big cannons and opera.' He tasted, and spent a minute contorting his face at the ceiling.

James sipped again. The wine tasted like cream and raisins and blood. The red walls shimmered in the candlelight.

There was a large and hideous jug sitting on a side table: its surface was inlaid with a pattern of bright enamels representing either a tree or a nude. It was mostly green and red, the colours separated by black lines, as if stained glass. 'Fuck *is* that?'

De Courcy was still concentrating on the ceiling. Slowly, he brought his unfocused eyes down to James. 'Chocolate,' he breathed. 'And pencil lead.'

James nodded. 'I noticed chocolate. I mean I thought so too.' He sipped again. 'Very sexy. Fuck is that jug thing?'

'*Sexy* I'm not sure about.' De Courcy was puckering his cheeks, swilling the wine. 'Elegance, refinement, yes. But a certain repression, a certain austerity, a coldness in the veneer. Silk blouses and pearls.'

James grunted. 'Tweed suits.'

'Perhaps.' De Courcy focused on the jug, and whispered something in French.

'What?'

'Cloisonné. French Second Empire. Hideous, of course, but a very fine example.'

'Cloisonné,' said James, as French as he could. 'I like that. I like that word.'

'So do I. Perhaps it's the word I like best. It just kind of *drips*, doesn't it?'

'Yes. With what, exactly?'

De Courcy shrugged, frowning. 'With.... ambiguity, I suppose.'

They drank in silence for a moment. Then De Courcy said, 'I have the most appalling faux-gold mirror in the closet that I got just because it was ormolu. *Ormolu*. Makes me shiver.'

'*Ormolu*.' James's body was humming with the wine now. 'But silk stockings too,' he said. 'Under the tweed. Possibly even a garter belt.' He was thinking about Nicola Lickson again.

'I BREATHE,' boomed the ghost voice through the walls, 'I TRANSMIT.'

'Does this go on all the time?'

De Courcy sighed. 'We should be pleased, you know, to have such immediate access to the making of culture.'

'Is he serious about this? He performs it?'

'Acton has not yet had a show,' said De Courcy solemnly, 'but he made thirty thousand dollars in grants last year. He has explained to the agencies about the necessity of a tranquil gestation period. He doesn't want to rush it. He doesn't want to just put any old thing out. That's what he told me. Any old thing.'

James began to giggle. Feedback-like screeches began to surround Acton's voice.

'He's building up for a big show,' said De Courcy, beginning to giggle as well, 'he told me possibly in the next three years. He said that. In the next *three years*. Apparently those are the conditions of his grant. But he's not worried, he says, about such a tight deadline.' De Courcy was laughing hard now, snorting as he tried to speak and wiping his eyes. 'He's not worried because he says,' De Courcy gasped, 'he says ...'

James was laughing uncontrollably now.

'He says they're flexible.' De Courcy had tears on his cheeks.

James was coughing and spilling his wine, his sober voice telling him as if from a great distance that anything was going to be funny from now on.

'*I am a battlefield*,' moaned Acton, and James dissolved completely.

'I am glad,' said De Courcy with difficulty, 'I am glad they are at least flexible on that one issue.'

This too James found too hilarious, and it took him some minutes to recover. His diaphragm was hurting.

In the subsequent silence, he said, 'Dec, what are you living on?'

De Courcy's eyes flickered at him for a moment, then found the ceiling again. 'The seventy-nine was apparently the great authoritative Les Ormes du Pez. My Great-uncle Edmond says it was the most instructive wine of his life. A quiet voice of reason, he said, whimsical, patient, tolerant of human foibles, attentive to the poignancy of the mundane.'

'A sort of retired, unnoticed novelist of a wine.'

'Exactly. He said its critical neglect was one of the great
tragedies of late twentieth-century journalism. My Great-aunt
Sophia says he died of it.'

'Of wine?'

'Of bitterness.'

James sat back, listening to the electronic aviary noises of
Acton's equipment, all bleeps and hisses. At length he said, 'Dec?'

As if with great fatigue, De Courcy said, 'You know my arrange-
ment.'

'Your uncle in Verona?'

'He's in Rimini now.'

'Uncle from the Batarelli side, not the De Courcy side?'

'He's not really my uncle.' De Courcy was speaking quietly.
'He's just the man my brother used to live with.'

'You have a brother?'

'No. He died three years ago. Just after you and I shared a place.'

'Oh.' James put down his glass. There was a whirring of tape
noise. 'I didn't know.'

'It's all right. I hadn't spoken to him for some time. He was on
my father's side in my whole leaving home thing.' De Courcy's
manner had changed. He was sitting still, his shoulders hunched,
speaking without any accent. 'Then Henry put me through art
school, and he still ...'

'Supports you.'

De Courcy shrugged.

There was a silence.

Then he said, 'All I have to do is visit him twice a year. That's
where I go every Christmas. I tell everyone I'm in Montreal, but
I'm not. And I don't go to any cottage in Muskoka.' He shivered
slightly.

'Well, that's okay. Rimini's on the Adriatic, isn't it?'

'Oh, he has a beautiful place. Condo on the beachfront, house in
the hills, everything.'

'Well, shit,' said James uneasily. 'That's not bad, then, eh? Free
trip to the beach every year? Must be a blast.'

De Courcy was silent.

'Isn't it?'

He shrugged. Then he said, 'No. Actually. It's not.' He took three large gulps of wine.

James looked away. He held up his glass to a candle. The wine was almost black in the glass until you held it up to the light, and then it was not like blood as usually described, James thought, but more like something artificial like nail polish. But ruby was still good. It was, in fact, the colour of a ruby.

To break the silence, James said, 'What did your brother die of?'

De Courcy stood up.

'Now,' he said, 'I have a surprise for you.'

He opened a closet and began throwing out deck shoes and polo shirts. James turned his attention to a stack of J. Crew catalogues, neatly arranged by month beside the stack of L.L. Beans. 'I get Undergear,' he said, 'you know Undergear? It's a little more sexy than this stuff.'

'Fag wear,' shouted De Courcy from the back of the closet. 'Tacky. Can't stand it.'

'How did you hook up with Fiona?'

'Oh, it was her place. I answered an ad.'

'And you changed it like this? Did she object?'

'I don't think she minded.'

'If you don't mind my asking, you seem to be doing okay, financially, I mean what with Henry and all. Why do you need a room-mate?'

'I can't stand living alone. Here it is.' De Courcy withdrew his head and a hard black case the length of a tennis racket. 'And actually I'm not doing really *that* well. I tend to spend too much. Such as at an auction downtown, last week.' He presented the case to James.

James opened it cautiously, then stared. His fingers caressed the contents professionally. 'It's an alto,' he murmured. 'It's quite old, too, did you know that?'

'They told me that, yes,' said De Courcy, swinging one khaki leg over the other on an uncomfortable-looking modernist chair. 'Which is funny, isn't it, because they didn't start reconstructing these until quite recently, did they?'

'Well,' said James, lifting out the narrow wooden pipe, 'there was a brief surge of interest in the nineteenth century. It went along with medievalism in architecture, you know, all that Merrie England stuff. But, ah...' He paused, distracted by a carved emblem near the reed cap. 'This one is quite elaborate. It may have been somebody's hobby, you know, somebody built it himself. Or herself. So it could be recent. Or it could even be Victorian. Those are quite rare, almost as rare as the real thing, which would date from about, well, before the recorders of the eighteenth.' He looked up at De Courcy in surprise. 'You must have spent a wad on it.'

De Courcy reddened and smiled.

James put it to his lips and blew a buzzy note. It was deep and woody. 'Nice,' he said. He blew again, harder.

'Goodness,' said De Courcy, 'I had no idea they were so loud.'

'Oh, they have to be loud.' James was sweating again, from exertion. 'They were meant to be played outdoors. Often from towers set up just for musicians, you know, for street festivals and stuff.' He blasted the bass notes of a saltarello.

'Good Christ,' said De Courcy, covering his ears. 'You'll disturb Acton.'

'Disturb Acton! Now there's something I wouldn't want to do.' James finished the saltarello. 'It's lovely,' he announced. 'Thank you, Dec.' He trumpeted some more, tapping his feet. There was a pounding of broom handles from above and below. 'Oops,' said James, breathing hard.

Fiona was pounding on the bedroom door, yelling, 'Jumpin' dynes, what do you got in there, a cow in labour or my Aunt Marion after Thanksgiving dinner or what?'

'It's all right,' called De Courcy. 'It's music. Come in and hear it.'

Fiona opened the door. 'I don't need to come *in* to hear it, my son. Hear it from the friggin Beaches. Now what the Jesus H. is that?'

James had put the shawm at his side on the sofa, and was sheepishly trying to cover it with his arm.

'This,' said De Courcy with a leering smile, 'is James's secret passion. His little fetish. Isn't it James?'

53

'Not Renaissance specifically,' said James, knowing his face was the colour of the walls. 'Music generally. Actually, I play the violin.'

Standing in the doorway, Fiona folded her freckled arms and shook her head. 'Yup,' she said in a long intake of breath. 'Yup. All we friggin needed. More friggin *art*. Why is it that all art has to sound like a pig's fart? You ever heard a pig's fart, Percy?'

'I don't think so, Fiona.'

'Sounds like that. But not as loud. But fiddling, *fiddling's* not bad – why didn't you say you could fiddle?'

'I –'

'I knew Bryden McBride, in Meat Cove.'

James and De Courcy looked blank.

'You didn't know he was from Meat Cove? And he used to teach at the Gaelic College, before he became mister most famous quiff fiddler in the world. Gay as a two-dollar bill.'

'As a two-dollar bill?'

Fiona blew James a kiss, which startled him, and shut the door again, still laughing.

'She's a darling,' said De Courcy. 'I have no idea who Bryden McBride is.'

'It's okay if she knows, isn't it? I mean, she doesn't really hang around with the same crowd or anything, right? She doesn't know anyone in magazines?'

De Courcy laughed. 'I am so amused by this embarrassment. When are you going to come out?'

'Yeah, big talk.'

De Courcy's laughter subsided.

'Look,' said James, 'you don't know how it is. It would kill my image if this came out. It would kill my career. You know what classical music buffs *look* like?'

'Tell me.'

James considered, sipping. 'At the last meeting of the Munich Renaissance Circle –'

'Munich? When were you in Munich?'

'Munich Ont. I grew up there. My parents live there. Remember?'

'Yes, sorry, I do. Munich Ont. How fascinating. Could you arrange a visit for me?'

James snorted. 'I *don't* think so. There's nothing in Munich you would like. In fact there's nothing in Munich. It's not really you. Well, except for the music department at Luther which is strangely good. That's why people go there from all over the country, well, from elsewhere anyway, and it's why I had a good teacher when I was a kid. Anyway. Professor Senninger is in the group. He breeds dogs, for shows. Dogs everywhere. In cages in the living room, barking.'

'In the living room?'

James nodded. 'We rehearse in the study. His wife who plays a massive great bombard makes some kind of vile salad with green aspic jelly stuff and Frederick Barnabus, he's a Jungian shrink, always drinks too much and there's a poor mousy woman called Amberlynn Snetsinger who cries in the bathroom and –'

'*Dio mio*,' said De Courcy, 'it sounds entertaining, but not really your kind of scene. *You're* the snob. How do you – why do you –'

'I love it,' said James shortly. He felt himself blushing again, and stuck his nose into his wine. 'No, the Renaissance thing is just a joke. It's easier to play, too. You can pick up the wind instruments fairly quickly. They're all basically recorders. The violin, though ...'

'You don't play it any more, do you?'

'No.'

'Why not?'

'No good at it.'

There was a silence, interrupted by some grating and hissing noises from Acton's apartment.

'The violin,' said James, 'is incredibly sensitive. It's like a very beautiful and very neurotic girlfriend. All you want to do is ... is get on her good side. You know? Or, no, it's not even a girlfriend. It's more like a clitoris.'

De Courcy didn't laugh. He was listening very solemnly.

'I mean, you touch it wrong and your hand gets slapped away. I don't know what I'm trying to say. And the object itself is so well designed. I think it's beautiful just to look at. It's something that's evolved over about two hundred years, and now it's almost perfect. It's the most perfect, I think, really, the most perfectly evolved human artifact.'

De Courcy raised his eyebrows. 'Another drop?' He poured, and then asked, 'So James. You haven't explained *why* you stopped.'

James sighed. 'Oh, I just, I don't know.'

'For me, James. I'd like to know.'

'Okay. First I didn't get into the master's program in Chicago, or into any of the big performance schools, after my bee muz. You remember I came here after doing one year at Luther. They thought I was pretty great there, so I guess I did too. I got a letter from someone at Vic, seen me in recital, thought I would be better off here, blah blah, got a scholarship, finished off here. Things were a lot more difficult here. That's the thing about the violin. You can never get good enough. Then I thought I had it made when I got into the Atlantic Symphony. That was about a year after you and I lived together. I remember telling you about it, when I saw you somewhere.'

'Possibly. Tell me again.' De Courcy was staring straight at James, rather sternly, James thought.

'Nothing to tell. They didn't renew me after a season. And it kind of went out of me after that.' James paused. 'And Dumbrowsky died that year.'

'Dumbrowsky?'

James took some more wine. 'He was my teacher. He was very old when he took me on, when I was a kid. He heard me play in one of those Kiwanis festival things when I was, I guess I was only about eight or nine, and he wrote –'

'I have no idea what you're talking about when you degenerate into your small-town dialect.'

'Oh, Kiwanis, you mean? Sorry. It's one of those service clubs, like Rotary or Kinsmen or whatever. I think. All I know is for some reason they're into promoting music. So all these towns have this annual music competition for kids in the school music programs, with a million categories, you know, piccolo, age nine-ten, oboe, age eleven-twelve, you know. Everybody gets a prize. It's

56

actually quite a bizarre thing. You get all these recent immigrant parents, so proud their kids are integrating so well, these tiny Asian girls in ribbons and shiny shoes and party dresses up on the stage playing Chopin nocturnes, this music totally subversive, I mean just dripping with sex, everybody beaming and clapping.' James chuckled. 'Bizarre. Totally bizarre. I always used to feel that if they knew anything about Chopin at all, I mean Chopin personally, how weird he was, how totally dissipated, I mean the guy never weighed more than a hundred pounds, they'd be horrified. And if they understood the music at all.... I had this friend, in high school, this girl, we never went out, but it was always sort of under the surface, who got quite good at the piano. And her parents –'

'What was her name?' said De Courcy softly.

'Alison. Alison. She got quite good. It's quite a musical town, you see, because of the music department at MLC and this festival. We used to see sad Eastern European percussionists bewildered in the malls on Saturday mornings. Anyway, this girl's parents, who were Lutherans, paid for her to have lessons with quite a good teacher, and before you knew it she was doing quite a bit of modern stuff. You know, they often start you out now with Stravinsky or Hindemith easy pieces, just because they're easy, not because of the socialist theory behind it. They don't tell the parents about that. So before you knew it she was playing these very bizarre Kabalevsky preludes and stuff, and the parents, I always wonder what they thought of it. I mean they couldn't really have been *listening* to it, because they wouldn't have approved of it. I mean Kabalevsky was a genuine Stalinist, for Christ's sake. And everybody's very proud of little Alison and nobody understands the first thing about it. I mean think of the equivalent of modernist music in visual art. Cubism, abstraction, what not. They would have *hated* it.' James, who had been speaking with some volume and at increasing speed, realized that his forehead was running with sweat again, and sat back. He sipped the luscious wine.

'Back to you,' prodded De Courcy. 'What about this teacher.'

James puffed out his cheeks. He spoke more softly, 'He was very good to me. He taught me for free, for several years.'

'Who was he?'

'He was one of these profs at MLC. He was in their string quartet, too. He came here from Austria, in nineteen thirty-five.'

De Courcy's eyebrows shot up again. 'That was clever.'

'Yes, it was, wasn't it? He rather thought so in nineteen thirty-eight.'

'But Canada. Christ.'

'No, he didn't come here first. He was in New York, then Montreal. Anyway. He was quite an institution when he was here. He saw me play in one of these Kiwanis competitions and he wrote a letter to my parents, asking if they would let me come and see him twice a week.'

'Really? So you were a child prodigy kind of thing. Like a schizophrenic in a movie. How glamorous.'

'Yes, for a bit. It ended up being every day.'

'Nice fellow,' said De Courcy, raising his eyebrows.

'Yes. He took quite an interest in me. He got me into the university orchestra, and then a little quartet.'

There was a long pause in the room, now filled with deeper disco bass, and Acton's occasional wail.

'So, you were ...' said De Courcy, and hesitated.

'Hmm?'

'You were close.'

'Yes. Very. I was very close to him. He was very stern, but ... kind of a father figure, I guess.'

'So it was love.'

James snorted. 'A kind of love, yes.'

'A kind of love.'

They were silent for a long time, both holding their glasses up to the light.

Then De Courcy said softly, 'And after he died you had no one to push you.'

'Oh, it wouldn't have made any difference. I had decided at that point I didn't have it. Now I haven't practised for so long I've lost it.'

'But you were very good in school, weren't you? Couldn't you teach, or –'

'Don't want to teach. Let's talk about something else.'

'No. What do you like about it?'

'What do I *like* about it?' James leaned forward, almost spilling his wine. 'What do I *like*? I don't *like* it, it's, it's *everything*. It's as if – some of the music I like, I think it's so good that I can't imagine humans ever wrote it. I don't know where it came from. When I first played in that sextet in school you saw me in, that Brahms sextet, I wasn't even first violin, it was the most difficult and complex thing I had ever seen. I couldn't imagine how we were ever going to – and that was just Brahms, mushy romantic Brahms with predictable tunes and everything. The Ravel quartets are even more complicated.'

'Why don't you compose?'

James shrugged. 'Tried it. Composed a lot. Have a whole file full of … no good at that either.'

De Courcy's eyebrows convulsed again. James pretended not to notice. He turned to look at the cloisonné jug. He caressed the ceramic panels with his fingertips.

He took some more wine and said, 'And besides. No one's interested.'

Acton's rumblings had disappeared. The apartment was almost silent, vibrating only to the deep bass of a car stereo in the courtyard. The glasses in De Courcy's rack rattled.

De Courcy said, 'All a big waste of time, I guess.'

'Yes,' said James with some force. 'Yes, it is. Think about it. Have you ever been with someone, been talking to someone, and you hear a piece of music in a commercial or on a radio or in a movie, and they say, oh, that's so pretty, what is this? And it's like the "Ode to Joy" from Beethoven's Ninth, or "Für Elise", or the toreador song from *Carmen* or something and they just haven't a clue. They know they've heard it before, but they have no idea who wrote it or in what century even. They can't tell if it's baroque or romantic or –'

'But James,' said De Courcy gently, 'of course people are uneducated peasants, we know that. It doesn't make any –'

'No no no no. I'm not talking about uneducated peasants. I'm talking about highly educated, middle-class people. People I went to school with who are doing PHDs in so-called English which means so-called cultural theory, you know, I mean people who could at least recognize that "to be or not to be" comes from *Hamlet* and that the Parthenon is in Greece, you know, I mean these are the equivalents, right, of the "Ode to Joy", right? I mean if you can recognize a Picasso or a Renoir, which most of these people can, then you'd think you'd know the "Ode to Joy", right? But they don't. It's this huge gap. Somewhere along the line the schools stopped teaching it to us. I don't know why. It's as if they stopped teaching literature or art history all of a sudden and nobody noticed and nobody says anything. Because it doesn't matter any more. It's the past and it's over, so it's dead, who cares.'

'How did you learn?'

'Dumbrowsky,' said James, and as he said it he felt himself subsiding. 'Dumbrowsky,' he said again, more softly. 'I used to go over to his house every day after school and listen to records. He had all these old vinyl discs.' The wine was warm in his mouth, and he felt suddenly close to tears.

De Courcy was smiling at him. 'You've never told me about all this. Even when we lived together. I thought you were just interested in ... in girls and restaurants. I can't believe you keep it all a secret, James. I mean there are people who would find all this interesting. I'm sure women, I'm sure there are women who would find it all so romantic –'

James snorted. 'What do you know about what women find romantic?'

De Courcy was silent.

'Joke,' said James.

De Courcy pursed his lips. His jaw was tight.

'Sorry,' said James. 'I just meant –'

'What I meant was that I find it romantic. I find it fascinating.' De Courcy's voice softened. 'I'm *trying* to be *nice*, James.'

'I know. Sorry.' Then, awkwardly, 'Thank you.'

'I find *you* fascinating.'

James cleared his throat. He knew he shouldn't be uncomfortable with this conversation, but he couldn't help it. 'Thank you. But you're ...' He cleared his throat again. 'You're different.'

'Yes, I am.' De Courcy placed his hands regally on the arms of his chair and looked at the ceiling.

James was silent for a long time. Then he said, 'Anyway. You see what I mean. I am deep down, fundamentally, basically uncool.'

De Courcy nodded, chewing on wine. 'How did you get cool, James?'

'Have I never told you the story?'

'I've never got it out of you. It's one of your secrets, like the violin.'

'It's a funny story.'

'I would be delighted to hear it.'

James held up his empty glass. 'This is broken.'

De Courcy turned back to the wine desk. He opened a drawer on the right. 'Well. Perhaps something heavier.'

'Are you hungry?' said James. 'Maybe pizza?'

De Courcy was opening, pouring, swirling, tasting, murmuring, 'Sort of an ecclesiastical neo-Burgundy.'

'Could we order one? I haven't eaten.'

De Courcy was filling his glass. 'It's a sort of an Oregon cult leader, this wine. Flashy and smooth on the outside, well-dressed, a dark and brutal core.'

James blinked. The candles shimmered. The wine tasted like tar. The thumping bass from the alley was strangely lulling, and reminded him of a little Spanish song called 'Tres Morillas', which he began to hum. He was getting sleepy.

'Well?' said De Courcy.

'*Tres morillas*,' sang James.

'How exactly did you begin as a restaurant critic?'

James took a deep draught of wine and sluiced it through his teeth. He put his head back on the sofa and said, 'I was working as a waiter at the Montenegro, and –'

'At the Monte*negro*. I can see why you didn't tell me this before. The horror.'

'Oh yes, I was there for a year and a half at least, hated it, didn't know what else to do, I'd got kicked out of the symphony –'

'Your contract wasn't renewed. You weren't kicked out. You're so hard on yourself, James.'

'Yeah.' James drank more wine. 'Anyway, I thought I might try my hand at composing or something, actually I wrote a little string trio the first year, but I really didn't stick at it, I was just goofing around. I didn't have any plans.'

'As now.'

'As now. So one night there's this sad little man. Very thin, weedy guy in a grey suit. Actually not old, only around thirty, but balding, glasses, just sitting alone with all this tons of food he'd ordered. He had all this marinated shrimp and a soup and these horrible eggplant things I used to have to – anyway, I knew he'd ordered a main course to come, and he couldn't even finish this stuff, he was just sitting there incredibly sad looking at it. He kept sighing and looking at it. I thought he was going to cry. The place is really dead, so I come over and I say, can I take that away? You didn't like it? And he laughs this tired laugh and he says, very soft-spoken, I don't care, I just don't care any more. And for some reason I take an interest in this guy and start talking to him. And it turns out he's Jacob Feldman. You remember that name?'

'Feldman. The critic.'

'He worked for years at the *Globe*, he had a column in *Connoisseur* – I only found this out afterwards, because I didn't know anything about these things, I wasn't interested in food. I'm still not. Anyway. I said I expected a food critic to be fat and bearded and fifty, and he said maybe that's why he wasn't cut out to be a food critic. He was being a little crazy. The guy put his head in his hands and said that he didn't know why he was confiding in me, he was on the edge, and he just couldn't go on. He said he wanted to stay home and eat baked beans on toast in front of a video one night. He said his readers were the stupidest people in the country, made worse by the fact that they had gobs of money, and that they were obsessed with food because it was the easiest thing for anyone to understand. Something like that. The point was it was all bogus and he was bored and he had this review to write the next day for *Epicure* – it doesn't exist any more, remember, you used to get it with the *Star*? Anyway, I went off to do some other tables, and when it was all cleared out he was still sitting there trying to eat his main course, and we chatted again, and he found out what I did, and he seemed really interested in music. He said he wished he could do something a little more serious, like collecting stamps. I think that's what he wanted to do. So he asks me, you can write, right? And I say, well, I went to university, and he says, that's all I mean, you can write English, right, you can write a sentence? That's all you need.'

'So he offered you his job.'

'Right then and there. He made me write down everything he had eaten and told me what to say about it. He said I had to write it the next day and he would call his editor and tell him to expect it and that he was recommending me. He said he wouldn't say how we met, and the editor would have no choice anyway, because he had to run it on Saturday.'

'So you became Jacob Feldman.'

'I had nothing to lose. It was just a joke at first. The first column even ran under his name. No one knew the difference. After a while I convinced the editor that I could do it and they started running my name. Then *Epicure* folded, and I had a book of tears I could take to *Edge*, and that's how I started there. Julian really liked me because I hated everything, so next thing I knew it was night clubs and fashion and dance music and ...'

'What happened to the critic?'

'No idea. Never saw his name in print again. I imagine he's happily writing novels somewhere, or doing something productive, like numismatism. He got out,' said James gloomily.

'But you got in.'

James sighed. 'You really don't think Fiona will tell anyone, do you?'

'What?'

'You know. About the music.'

De Courcy's eyelids drooped. 'What the hell are you so afraid of? I think people will think it's impressive.'

'Impressive!' James almost shouted. 'Impressive! I might as well go and tell them I play Myst eight hours a day or subscribe to a, some fucking *font* magazine, *Typeface World* or something, or I have an impressive collection of *X-Files* tapes or, or –'

'I think you should tell Nicola. It'll probably excite her.

Modernist violin music. It's the kinkiest thing she'll ever have heard of.'

James stood up, and the room tilted. He steadied himself on a wrought-iron side table. 'You wouldn't. You wouldn't dare …' His thesaurus files were crashing, access denied. 'Squeal on me.'

'Squeal? My dear,' said De Courcy, with immense fatigue, 'I never *squeal*.' He sipped and looked at the ceiling. 'Besides, you're wrong. That's not what makes you uncool.'

James looked up, too. 'What does, then?'

De Courcy sighed. 'Nicola …'

'Yes.'

He was shaking his head. 'I know all about Nicola.'

'No you don't. You haven't even met her.'

Weakly, expiring, De Courcy breathed, 'I have foreseen and foresuffered all.'

'Ah.'

'Nicola … the difference between you and Nicola is that she doesn't know *why* she likes things. She can't explain it. As soon as you start explaining things you're out of …'

'Out of the Bomb Factory.'

'Precisely. And explaining things. Is what you do. Only too well.'

James sighed. 'Well. I'll have to find that out myself. Listen, just don't get involved, okay?'

'Are *you* going to get involved?'

'Oh.' James fell back into the sofa. 'I don't know. I'm not too good at that. I mean, longer than …'

'I know.' De Courcy was flipping through the phone book. 'What do you want on it?'

'What do you mean, you know?'

'You haven't had a girlfriend for as long as I've known you.'

'I've had girlfriends. You know it. You remember that girl, Polish girl or something, black hair –'

'There are fourteen pages of pizza delivery. I know you've got *laid*. I mean a relationship that lasted more than a week. You know. The way grown-up people establish these sort of primary relationships in which they see each other a lot and exclude –'

'What, and drive a minivan and promote Montessori schools? No. No, I haven't done that.'

'You don't have to get married to be in a relationship. A girlfriend. Going steady. You know about that? Or don't you?'

'I've had girlfriends.'

'When?'

'At school.'

'So about five years ago.' De Courcy picked up the phone. 'Well, you should think about that.'

'Would you stop being so goddam *significant*. About what?'

'About what it means that you are incapable of –'

'Oh Christ, afraid of commitment, I know, arrested adolescent, I read the magazines, Peter Pan syndrome, I know, there comes a time when a man must stop playing around and accept his family responsibilities, do his duty to –'

'It's ringing. What do you want on it?'

James closed his eyes. 'Cheese,' he decided. 'Process cheese food. Make sure it has it.'

'Not any old pizza,' agreed De Courcy, dialling.

'No sir,' James mumbled. His eyes were closing. Behind his eye-lids was a warm red light, and the flash of silver rings and Nicola Lickson's thighs. 'Not any old pizza,' he murmured. 'Too cool. Too cool.'

■ CHAPTER FOUR

A wrecking ball, perhaps, slamming at the side of the house, or Serb artillery dangerously close outside, or just cathedral doors shutting one after another in a long corridor – something was waking James up. There were needles in his cheek, which revealed themselves to be the steely fibres of the woollen carpet he was lying on, prone. He opened his eyes to see the toe of a boot and dusty wainscoting. He realized his arm was pinned under him, that he had been asleep on it for some time, and decided to postpone further movement. The slamming began again and his brain rattled in his skull. He pictured it rocking about, withered, brown, wrinkled as a walnut. He opened his mouth and closed it again with a sound of rustling paper.

Whatever was banging was close by, sending tremors through the floor. He rolled over and attempted a moan. Fiona's chin came into view, upside down. She was standing over him, a grim smile on her face, her hands on her hips. 'Good morning, Jimmy,' she bellowed.

James put his hands over his eyes.

'Mind if I get through here? Time to take a dump. Major dump.'

James rolled out of the doorway to the bathroom. The door closed behind her. Slowly, he sat up, taking care to protect his walnut from unnecessary rattling.

Bang bang bang. He squinted into the kitchen and saw a giant bouncing a basketball on the linoleum. The giant had to bend his head to fit under the ceiling. He wore a sweatsuit and puffy basketball shoes and was concentrating on the basketball, which ricocheted up and down from his hand to the floor in a vicious straight line, as if on a string.

James stood and shuffled towards him. 'Hi,' he said, entering the kitchen.

'Hey,' said the giant, mercifully tucking the ball under his arm. 'James.' He held out his hand. 'You do look like Judd Hardbird.'

'Judd Hardbird?' said the giant, pumping James's hand, 'you think?'

'Does *that* feel better.' Fiona had entered, bellowing. 'How do you spell relief? D-U-M-P. Load of bricks off my mind. So you met Cud.'

She ruffled the giant's red hair.

'Don't *call* me that.'

'Had a good sleep, Jimmy? Jesus H. *Crapper* you guys were toasted last night. Wasted? I imagine. I imagine you want some orange juice. Couldn't stop you bleating on that god-damn horn, sounded like a barnyard. What the hell you call that thing Jimmy?'

James had been wincing and shading his eyes against the volume of this speech. 'You know, Fiona,' he said, 'I kind of prefer James, actually.'

'Well lah-di-dah excuse me for living.' She pointed a finger and cocked thumb at him like a gun, and fired. 'Okey dokey, smoky. *James.*'

'It's an old-fashioned musical instrument. It's a copy of a thing they used to play in the middle ages, called a –'

'*He* thinks,' yelled Buck, 'I look like Judd Hardbird.'

'Sweetheart, Cud darling, you couldn't look like a movie star even if you closed you mouth once in a while. His ree-tarded brother, maybe.'

'He – this guy –'

'James here is a reporter,' Fiona yelled.

'Oh yeah,' said Buck, beginning to bounce the ball again, even while seated. 'What, are oh bee?'

James had a swimming sensation. 'What?' Everyone seemed to be yelling this morning.

'I know a guy's a reporter for the are oh bee. You'd think those guys would rake in the coin but they don't, you know?'

'The Report on Business,' said James. 'Right. Actually he would probably make more than I do.'

'Is that right? Weird me out,' said Buck. Fiona was up and clanking metallic objects together at the sink, humming. Buck said, 'What, you're not getting enough work, or what? I guess with the economy the way it is there's not much to report on, with the

stock market dead like that, except maybe currency. Currency's
the way to go, believe me. Just sell Canadian dollars and keep selling 'em. Make a mint. I'm from London,' he added, helpfully,
'London Ontario.'

James said, 'It's funny, you remind me of my brother.'

'Older brother or younger?'

'Older.'

'Uh-huh.' Buck nodded, satisfied.

'So are you in the financial business?' said James.

'No no no no no. I'm in school. Kinesiology.'

'Thanks,' said James to Fiona, who had poured him a tumbler of
orange juice. He sucked it back.

'He's a professional jock,' said Fiona. 'When he graduates he's
going to get paid for being a jock, arncha, Bonk?'

'Don't *call* me that.' Buck turned to James and said with hau-
teur, 'It's not *quite* that simple.' He recited so James could hear
the capitals, 'Kinesiology is the Study of Movement. It's not phys
ed like it used to be. There's a whole lot more science now. It *is* a
science. It's a Bachelor of Science I'll be getting.'

'So you can coach high-school basketball,' said Fiona. 'I think
that's terrific, Bucky, I really do.'

'Actually,' said James, 'I do kind of arts and entertainment
reporting.' He stood to get more orange juice, then stood in the
window, looking down into the courtyard. The motorcycles, the
two dogs lying in the heat, the brown turds in the gravel. A gang of
brawny squirrels who looked about ready to ask you for a cigarette. The air was still grey.

'Is that right?' said Buck. He held the basketball tight, 'Arts.
You know, I have no problem with that.'

'I'm glad to hear that,' said James.

'No, really. No problem at all. Most people don't realize how
the arts contribute to the economy.'

Some of the windows in the other buildings were boarded up. A
pile of green garbage bags, a cloud of flies. A gate led into an alleyway where boys in baseball caps were leaning against garage doors.

'What economy?' murmured James.

'You know, one of those musicals employs five hundred people, and then you get all the increased business in the restaurants and stuff. *Americans* come up to see that stuff.'

James poured another glass.

'As long as the community values are respected,' announced Buck. 'I mean obviously you have to watch out for the stuff that's against community values.' He looked at James and frowned. 'But I guess as a reporter you don't have to mix with a lot of that.'

'With what?' said James feebly. He was on his third orange juice and concentrating on feeling his insides expand again.

'Well, all the homosexuality in the arts.'

'No,' said James. 'Luckily, I don't.'

He raised his eyebrows at Fiona, who rolled her eyes quickly.

'I mean if the arts only appeal to a minority, and if they offend community values, then *quite* frankly I don't see why they should get our support.'

'Well,' said James quietly, 'the thing is, they don't really get our support now, do they? The government no longer supports them and nobody goes to see them. So you needn't worry about them.'

'Well, the only thing I worry about is the children, really. I mean they shouldn't be exposed to some of that stuff.'

'What stuff exactly?' said James.

'Well, I mean like all those paintings of kiddie porn and stuff like that. I mean, excuse me, call me ignorant, but I just have to condone that stuff.'

'You what?'

'I do,' said Buck emphatically, beginning his bouncing again. 'I'm sorry, but I condone it.'

James stifled a giggle.

Fiona was yawning, oblivious.

'Well,' said James, 'that's your right.'

'Exactly. That's my perog-adif.' Buck stood up and nearly hit his head on the ceiling. 'Call me a homophile, maybe I am, and maybe that's a crime these days, but I just have to say it. I can't stand that stuff, it weirds me out, and I can't accept it. I'm a homophile.'

'You be who you are, Buck,' said James, pretending to cough. 'Nothing wrong with who you are, Buck. Say it loud and say it proud.'

'That's right,' said Buck, smiling widely. 'Glad to meet you, man.' He held out his hand again and James shook it again, heartily.

When he had retrieved his hand, he looked at his watch and felt a grip on his insides. He bit the inside of his cheek. This was something he did to himself instead of biting his nails; it left him with rough ridges inside his mouth which he would play with his tongue and which would encourage further chewing to tidy up, which would make it worse. It was James's equivalent of anorexia: he ate himself.

Find Boben, call *Dental Week* and ask for more time. Call landlord. He said, 'I'd better get going.'

'Us too, wha, Bunny Rabbit? You going to make that practice or what, hey, Judd?' Fiona stood up.

'Should ice my knee,' said Buck.

'Should try massage,' said Fiona, going to the freezer. 'I've been going to the massage students' clinic. Oh my *lord* what a turn-on.'

'A turn-on?' said James.

'Doesn't take much,' said Buck in a low voice.

Fiona was crouching down to wrap a clean dishcloth around Buck's knee. She applied the bag of ice.

James was surprised to feel himself blushing. He looked more carefully at Fiona's sturdy body. Her frizzy red ponytails bounced by her ears. She wore tight jeans and a loose T-shirt that said, 'Rehabs Do It Better.' Her arms were freckled. There was no making out the landscape under the T-shirt, but the strong thighs held his attention for a few seconds.

She stood up. 'Now don't frig with it, for Christ's sake.' Buck blew out his cheeks.

She sat at the table and lit a cigarette. Buck was frowning at the paper. With effort, James took his eyes off Fiona's thighs.

'Fucking frogs,' said Buck, folding the paper. 'Fucking frogs again, looking for special treatment.'

Outside, James breathed in a mouthful of heat. He looked around, shading his eyes. He realized exactly where he was, and that his house was only a few blocks away. He began to walk slowly. There were piles of green plastic bags in every front yard buttressing fire hydrants, most with holes already torn in them by the animals. Hovering clouds of flies, and the deep seismic pounding of disco bass.

It was perhaps garbage day again, although they were always changing the day of garbage collection and the labyrinthine rules of recycling collection. James had read the strict injunctions about the alternating weeks of blue box (glass and plastic) and the mysterious, sacred grey box (paper and cardboard excluding newspaper and, in fact, cardboard – indeed excluding, apparently, everything). So he understood why nobody in this neighbourhood knew which day was garbage day any more. It was always garbage day. James tried to hold his breath as he passed each mound and its sweet cloud of bad meat, old fruit, feces. He could feel the stink clinging to him like mist.

Ahead of him was a squat car with black windows. Its doors were open so the world could enjoy its stereo. It was the epicentre of the bass James had been feeling through the pavement for half a block. Three teenage boys leaned against it. James looked bravely right at them, and recognized one from his own street. Usually they were in front of his own building.

They stopped swearing for a moment to stare at him.

'Boys,' said James as he approached, nodding.

They frowned at this. The one in the white undershirt studied his bicep and its clever tattoo of a wizard, flexing ruminatively. The fattest one, the only one with a shirt and his baseball cap on frontwards, turned back to the car. 'Anyway,' he said to the assembly, 'I told him he was a fat shit and he can pick my ass.'

James was already past. The booming dimmed a little as he moved away, along the line of parked cars radiating heat.

He turned the corner and slowed. He had always admired the architecture here, ornate and vertical. There were children playing in the concrete squares before each house, fenced in by wrought iron, grandmothers in black watching from the verandas. A smell of grilling sardines. It was not unpleasant. It was peaceful. He noticed as he had not noticed before that several of the houses had gardens tight with roses. He permitted himself some deeper breaths. He stopped before a narrow house with a trellis covering its entire front wall, right up to the attic window, wound with bright red blooms. The grandmother on the porch smiled at him, fanning herself. He smiled back and told her she had a lovely garden. He moved on, passing a beautiful raven-haired fourteen-year-old (at whom he also smiled but who did not smile back) and a short man of indeterminate age in a T-shirt that read, 'Azoreans Do It Better.'

He came to the top of his street and heard a jackhammer pounding and stopped. He pictured his dim room, the walls vibrating with jackhammer, the red light on the answering machine.

He turned south and headed for the Revitalization Zone.

You had to walk along Queen past three blocks of mental hospital. It was the biggest in the country and the sidewalks were always interesting. At Ossington a man said to him, 'Come here, English, come here English bastard,' and at Dovercourt a woman said, 'You took my baby, you bastard, you fuck.' She was in stiletto heels and velvet leggings.

You walked down Dovercourt and it curved around between two vacant lots and then the city just ended. James loved this moment when the city went quiet and distant: on either side of him were piles of rubble, just piles of crushed cinderblocks, and the cracked concrete floors of factories which had disappeared. There was a stencilled sign hanging on a chain-link fence which read 'LIBERTY'. In the far distance were the hazy office towers, looking like a foreign place. Just beyond the tracks, the raised expressway roared audibly, with its billboards flashing Sony and Nikon. Between the expressway and the vacant lots were the remaining factory buildings, with some of their painted signs still intact, Johnson Carpet and Williams Machinery.

James slipped through a fence and onto the railway tracks. He had never seen a train on them, and there were weeds. You could see the backs of warehouse buildings from here, with grafittied gang names and abandoned shopping carts. James had been coming here for his walk every day since the beginning of the heat wave. Aside from the hiss of the expressway, it was quiet.

He crossed King Street and headed for the building whose faded lettering read, 'MURRAY TEXTILE'. The streets were deserted. All the buildings had tall leaded windows, and they had once manufactured buttons and mattresses and tractors, which was a culture James could not imagine. Now those which had not been destroyed sat empty or housed airy design studios and digital print labs; they had varnished hardwood floors and stripped beams and secretaries in catsuits. Murray Textile was now one of those: James could see ceiling fans spinning against white ceilings, the shadow of ferns in the windows.

He looked around and realized he could no longer pretend to himself that he didn't know why he had chosen to walk around here when he had so much to do. He was looking for the Bomb Factory. He wanted to see where Nicola lived.

The building across the street had a billboard on its roof, advertising apparently nothing but sex itself: an implausibly built young woman smiled down at him, baring her cleavage to the sun and smog of ten city blocks. James squinted at this for some seconds: she appeared to be in a desert and wearing a fur coat over nothing else, which was incongruous in the heat; then he realized she was in snow or an ice field, which seemed even stranger. The letters on the billboard said, 'THE COLD COMES: AUGUST 2.'

A block farther on, towards the expressway, he found what he was looking for. A newly renovated factory, obviously a residence. He crossed the street to look at it.

Part of the brick had been replaced, seamlessly, with new brick in the same colour, which he knew would have to have been imported or made specially. There was some still nineteenth-century lettering visible around the top floor: FERGUSON and MUNITIONS. A faded mural on one side encouraged the buying of Victory Bonds. Half of the façade had been plastered over in salmon, a modernist arc that included the doorway and its awning or portico, a triangular piece of concrete which jutted from the wall and bore the words 'THE BOMB FACTORY' in a cool font, a sort of London underground deco thing with letters cut from steel.

James stood under the awning and admired the halogen lights studding its underside. Through the glass door he saw the dim shapes of the empty steel lobby, the retro fifties pomo sofas

snaking around the walls like a clever joke. There were buzzers on
the outside marked with no names, only numbers, and a slot for a
security card above a steady red electronic eye. James smiled up
into the video camera, and backed off. He admired the oddly
spaced windows in the top floors, scattered among the original
Victorian openings; he saw just the green tops of shrubs and trees
swaying above the walled rooftop decks. He walked around to one
side and saw the fortified entrance to the underground parking
garage, a maze of fenced decks sprouting from the side wall.

It was strange that anyone wanted to live here, out of walking
distance from a supermarket or dry cleaner or cinema or anything
but the mental hospital and the hookers. If you could afford one of
these spaces you could afford a house in a subdivision, with your
own strip mall nearby with plenty of parking and your own security guards limiting the neighbourhood's undesirables.

These people weren't like that: they did post-production, they
were Design Associates, computer animators. There would be
over-forties with their antique Coke machines and their Ducati
motorcycles in the process of being restored on the living room
floor, sure. But there would also be young people, couples who had
made it in website packaging or cigar bars or glossy new-media
magazines about pop stars. Death-babe photographers.

Nicola, the Ebola babe.

James wiped the sweat from his face. There was a thundering
and the ground shook as a commuter train passed over the end of
the street. The building was shuttered and smugly silent, as if pretending to sleep. The video camera watched him stonily; it gave
nothing away.

He tried to imagine her apartment: no old Coke machine, for
sure, but computers and graffiti and Regency divans. Wrought iron
coffee tables and heavy gold curtains and sconces and a DJ with
dreadlocks asleep on the couch. It would be half-finished, with a
stack of drywall in the entrance hall that everyone was just used
to stepping over.

But it wasn't the decor so much that made him sad – because
he realized, suddenly, that he was sad, lonely, standing out here in
the heat next to the empty lot under the billboard of massive

cleavage and the train roaring past and the video camera staring at him – it was that Nicola would have *just* her close friends in there, people she smoked strong DuMauriers with and slapped in the face, and they made just enough money and they lived in a plane above the verbal, who had never read what James wrote and didn't care, who hadn't read *anything* and didn't care.

Which was silly to worry about or envy or even think about. He strode away towards the streetcar, kicking stones. On the corner there was a woman in a miniskirt, teetering on her heels. She smiled at him. He looked away from her legs and almost walked right into a flutter of teenage girls, all bare skin and bra straps. They passed him and he stopped for a second and closed his eyes.

The heat did not abate.

Sweat ran over his eyelids. He opened his eyes and the blurry image which came to him was the billboard a block away, the huge female body like a Stalinist icon. He hunched his shoulders and waited for the streetcar, derided by the wild hair, the snowy field, the snowy skin.

He got off at the bottom of his street and heard the jackhammer again. He walked towards his house and it grew louder.

And then he stopped and his heart started hammering as well.

His house was completely changed. There was a truck pulled up on the front lawn and a bulldozer next to it, already starting to tear at the sod. Workmen moved in and out. An upper window – his living-room window – was wide open, the frame already removed, and objects were flying out of it.

James yelped and ran towards it.

A bright blue Mazda Miyata cut him off by driving onto the sidewalk. James attempted to leap over the opening door and hurtled into the cologned and fleshy mass of Franco Giardini, his landlord.

'I tried to call you!' Franco shouted. 'I told you it was urgent. The place has been sold for months. *Months.* These are the new owners, renovating. You don't open your letters, you don't answer my calls –'

Running into the house, James yelled, 'Tell them to stop chucking my stuff.'

'They'll stop for one minute,' Franco called after him, 'one minute, Jimmy, that's all you get. I tried to warn you.'

Past a guy with a sledgehammer in the hallway. The plaster was
coming down in apocalyptic clouds. James ran upstairs and into
his apartment. His bedding and clothes were in a pile in the
middle of the living-room floor; a dwarfish man in hard hat and
boots and a gleeful smile was tossing books out the open window.

'Stop it!' screamed James.

The man looked disappointed, but stopped. James made it into
the bedroom just in time to see the bed get heaved out the
sledgehammer-widened window. He dove onto the now revealed
violin case, lying under a veil of plaster dust. *Everybody stop!*
Stop for just one second!' He hauled himself off the case – coura-
geous sergeant falls on grenade to save platoon – and opened it.
Okay.

Three bemused workmen had gathered in the doorway of his
bedroom. They watched as he carefully disconnected the computer, killed the answering machine's blinking little blind eye,
unhooked his framed posters. He made eight or ten trips up and
down the disintegrating stairs and enlisted a workman to help and
soon had his belongings, including his desk and chair – the bed
was toast – stacked on the sidewalk. A crowd of children and
black-wrapped mothers had gathered along the wrought-iron
fences to watch. Also a knot of the baseball-cap boys folding their
arms, wide-eyed, looking hungrily from Franco Giardini to James.

Clenching and unclenching his fists, James approached the blue
Miyata. Franco was leaning against it, talking on the cellphone,
wearing dark glasses and a linen jacket. Even in the heat he had
his black mock turtleneck under it, shiny leather shoes.

A foot from him, lifting a fist to shoulder level, James paused to
size him up. They were about the same age, but James was
definitely taller, and had his steel-capped drill boots to Franco's
loafers. But the boy entrepreneur carried a weight under his croco-
dile belt, a heft to his shoulders and forearms.

There was also his litigious mind to consider. James's image
before the court during future legal actions. Things like assault
charges.

CHAPTER FOUR

James's vision was blurry with sweat, his shirt sucking to him. The boys crowded closer, silent for once in their excitement, chewing gum with much open-mouthed concentration. Never had James seen any of them exhibit so much pleasure.

Franco calmly folded up the phone and turned to him. He put up the palm of his hand. 'Now James, listen. You don't have a case.'

James lifted his fist again, and Franco recoiled.

'I wasn't going to let them trash your stuff,' said Franco, 'I came to stop that.'

'Like fuck you did.'

There was an approving chortle from a Cro-Magnon in a heavy Raptors jacket. He spat near Franco's foot. James glanced at him for a second, distracted by the unbelievable discomfort of such a jacket on such a day.

'James, it's out of my hands now, it has been for some time. I gave you your legal notice two months ago, the guys downstairs from you were out two weeks ago, maybe you didn't even notice, listen, this area, this area is up and coming now. I didn't have a choice.'

There was a slamming of car doors. A bubbly yellow jeep, squashed high and short and perky like a toy helicopter, some sort of urban adventure vehicle designed exclusively for carrying Mozart-listening babies to and from farmers' markets, had pulled onto the sidewalk, and a woman got out. She had dark glasses and dyed blond-grey hair (why? thought James, why dye your hair grey?) and another linen suit and canvas espadrilles that made James, inexplicably, want to vomit on them.

He wasn't thinking clearly.

Perhaps he just wanted to vomit.

'Gabby,' said Franco, 'Gabby, how's it coming?'

'That depends, Franco, on if all the junk's out of the house. I see you're still working on that. I told you, Franco, I wanted it all gone *today*.'

James stepped in front of her. 'Are you the new landlord?'

'Yes I am. Do you own all this junk?' She took off her sunglasses, and he saw the diamond ring neatly twined with a

wedding band, the worried eyes, the narrow mouth, all of which
for some reason indicated to James membership in that class of
successful and nearly intelligent people which included publicists
and marketers and real estate agents and which was the one class
of people James loathed most in the world.

He took a deep breath. He opened his mouth and closed it again.
And then what came out of his mouth, slowly, was, 'Those. Shoes.'

'What?'

'Those shoes.' He pointed.

She looked down at them with a blank face.

'Do you know how ridiculous you look in those frumpy shoes?
Do you know how dated they look? Do you?'

Now she looked up at him with her mouth open, and he turned
and pushed Franco against the blue car. 'Give me your phone.'

Franco handed it over. The woman was still staring at her shoes
as if hypnotized. James walked past her and sat with the phone on
his crumpled and very clearly stained futon at the far end of his
caravan. He righted a standard lamp which had fallen across the
sidewalk, and picked up his silly Mexican sombrero with its fringe
of dangling pompoms. He stared at it for a second. He hadn't
known where it was for some time. He hung it on the standard
lamp, and leaned against an upturned drawer which was spilling
socks and underwear onto the concrete. Lying on the sidewalk was
an old toque bearing the emblem of the Munich Dachshunds
Hockey Club. He kicked it back into the drawer with his foot as
he dialled.

De Courcy was still asleep; Fiona woke him up.

'Hi Teemu,' said James. 'It's me, Esa.'

De Courcy coughed. 'Hello Esa. Congratulations on the hat
trick against Chicago. And on making the all-star game again. Are
you going back to Helsinki for Christmas?'

'Okay. Listen. Here's the story.' James sighed. He wasn't sure
how to explain his predicament. 'Okay. The story is this.' He
paused again. 'What I want to know is, are you and Cathy Tru-
bashnik going to wear skirts to school tomorrow? Because if you
and Cathy do, I will. And we won't tell Jennifer Seifert and she'll
be like *faced*.'

'Oh yeah *right*,' said De Courcy. 'Like last time Cathy Trubash-nik promised me she would wear a skirt and I was like promise promise and she was like oh yeah and then she shows up in like jeans and I'm like *two-face*. She is such a two-faced, backstabbing *bitch*.'

James laughed. There was a commotion between Franco Giardini and the new landlord. He couldn't believe he was laughing. He stopped laughing and said, 'Okay. Seriously. I have a little problem.'

He explained the problem. De Courcy said, 'How unfortunate,' and 'Of course you can stay here,' and agreed to call a rental company for a van right away, and that was that.

He hung up in time to see a chainsaw go through a window frame like butter.

It wasn't until the next day, amid the sierras of books and picture frames and crusty socks and jokey gift key rings heaped into the back room of De Courcy's apartment, that he plugged his answering machine in again and heard the message from *Edge*.

'James,' said Julian's voice – yesterday morning? the evening of the day before? – 'something rather exciting has come up for you, someone from New York – you'd better call me, I'll explain, but she wants to get a hold of you right away. It could be fun. Where are you? Hello?'

James piled his early-eighties computer components into a mountain in one corner, and dug a trench in the clothing to sit in. He called Julian.

'Well, I hope you're going to be grateful to me, you snob,' said his editor, 'because I am doing you a mondo favour. I could have had this work myself, and I turned it down. I want you to know that.'

James grunted, crouching, the phone held by chin and shoulder, ploughing books into ridges along the walls.

'Well.' There was a pause and a snapping as Julian lit his cigarette. 'Chick from *Glitter* in New York calls me – you know *Glitter*?'

'Of course I know *Glitter*.' James stopped moving and sank into a bog of sweaters. 'You mean *Glitter* the glossy, with the tits on the cover?'

'Stars, I think, is what we call them, James. Celebrities. And as it happens they have Judd Hardbird on this one, the one I told you about.'

'Never heard of him.'

'Yes you have, because I offered you a review of the film, which you turned down obviously without even thinking about or listening to, which is fine, because that's what we expect of you, but now listen. Remember *Breaking the Ice*, the Arctic scientists and natives movie? It's busting all the box records, it's going to be nominated for eighteen hundred Oscars, Hardbird's going to be on the cover of *Glitter* and *GQ* and *Vanity Fair* and god knows what else, and this chick, I'll give you her phone number, okay, her name's Maya Lipschitz, write this down –'

'Julian,' said James, 'thanks, but no thanks, I told you I can't do this Hollywood movie stuff, besides –'

'No no no no no no. Listen. That's not it. They have people doing the star profile and all that stuff, they wouldn't give you that anyway. She wants something on a Canadian guy she says is going to be very big, a guy called Ludwig Boben. You know him? You ever heard of a Ludwig Boben?'

'*What?*' James stood straight up. '*What?* She wants – Julian, Ludwig Boben is a Prairie poet. Are you sure she was with the real *Glitter?*'

'I'm sure because I looked up the number before I called her back.'

'Now just go over this slowly with me, like I'm a moron: what does this have to do with the Arctic movie?'

Julian took a second to exhale smoke. 'This is what's cool. I admire these New York people, I really do.'

James smiled. 'Yes, Julian, I know you do.' There was a startling screech of ripping steel outside the tiny air vent that served as the sewing room's window: white noise from a garden radio, searching for stations.

'Maya has a lead on this Paris designer who's doing Arctic fashions now. Like based on Inuit designs.'

'God help us,' said James perfunctorily.

'Except she said Eskimo, of course, isn't that cute?'

'Cute, yes. I don't get it.'

'There's also a product spin off, too, from the film, all these *Breaking the Ice* games and plastic snowshoes and what not. They're running a story on the designer to tie in to all the Northern stuff. You get it?'

'They're creating a trend.'

'They get a lot of help from the movie's distributor, if you understand what I mean, and the publicists they need and all that, if they do everything they can to make Northern hip.'

James lay back on the cushion of stale clothing, kicking the walls of his foxhole higher with his boots. Something hard jabbed his side: a squash racket. 'So they're looking for Northern subject matter for the books section.'

'Exactly. Canada's suddenly hip. A profile, with photographs. They heard about the big prize he just won, she said she heard it was like the country's biggest honour – is that true?'

The radio outside had ceased searching for static and had settled on a massively orchestrated version of 'My Way' in Portuguese, the radio's capacity so distended it sounded about to disintegrate, to grate itself to death. James closed his eyes and laughed. 'Julian, the prize she's referring to is a mention in a minuscule Prairie magazine. There were only about five writers submitted for the damn thing, and they all know each other and judged the editors' books last year and so on. It's like an in-house employee-of-the-month poster.'

'She said it was worth fifty grand.'

James laughed harder. 'A couple extra zeros. Someone got the decimal point wrong. Five hundred, homes.'

'Well, maybe it's best if she doesn't know that. If you want the piece. She asked me and I said I was too busy, and besides I've never heard of the guy. And she said she really wanted him and she had heard he was like a big star up here – that's what she said, "up there" – and that he's kind of a recluse, and, you know, time to bring him to the attention of a wider audience and all that. Do you *know* how many readers they have?'

'No, how many?'

'Well, neither do I, but it's in the millions. It's maybe five times ours. Money, James, money. Big break for you. Once you're in that New York loop you get more work and more work.'

James considered this: it was true. He sang with the radio, '*And now I face, the final curtain.*' He added, in his best Portuguese, 'Esh mizh zhmizh vnizh-maaa…. So you gave her my name?'

'I said you were a literary expert and knew his work well and just interviewed him. Didn't you?'

'No. But I will.'

'Well, listen, say that you have. They're under a pretty tight deadline.'

James stuffed his tongue under his lower lip, dropped his jaw, rolled his eyes up into his head and scrunched his head into his shoulders, hoping to thus resemble one of the teenagers lounging in the alley outside. 'Ub cuss dey ur.'

'Sorry?'

'Of course they are.' James unbuckled his mouth but kept his shoulders hunched in what he deemed was persuasive Neanderthal tension. He stood up and began to jump about the room, dragging his knuckles on the floor-like terrain. 'What am I?'

He chattered and screeched.

'I don't know,' said Julian, unperturbed.

'Australopithecus. Early man. Of course they're under a tight deadline. Of course. Okay. I'll do it.'

'You *have* to do it.'

James found a deep New England voice. 'I am not a numbah,' he declaimed, 'I am a free man.'

'Oh, she wants us to recommend a photographer up here to do him, too; cheaper than them flying one up.'

James was silent for a moment. Finally he said, 'Curiouser and curiouser.'

He got through to Maya Lipschitz at *Glitter* almost immediately; the piece must be important.

'Oh ter*rific!*' she cooed. 'I am so *happy* you'll do it for us! Julian faxed us through some of your articles, and I'm just so impressed, I'm sure you're perfect for it. Now.'

Her voice changed as she went through the instructions, the details of the contract – scene plus description of the guy (romantic, right? He's pretty rugged-looking?) plus brief bio plus review of the new book plus summing up of the political situation up there and a brief rundown of Canadian history to put people in the picture, 1,000 words max, $1,000 U.S., two weeks tops, sign both copies of the contract I'm couriering and fax one back – became harder, louder, slower, more American. James imagined he was talking to one of the female detectives on a cop show.

'Book him,' he said, when she was finished.

'I'm saary?'

'Terrific. Now, the most important question is, how to I get to where he is? I mean, if he's not willing to come to Toronto for this, are you going to fly me out West?'

'What? Out West?'

'Doesn't he live out West?'

'I thought he lived near you – Taranto, right?'

'That's Otranto,' said James, 'Castle of.'

'What was that?'

'Yes, I'm in Toronto but Boben –'

'Just a minute, I've got a press release from his agent here. I was calling Taranto because I thought – here it is: 16 Willowdale Crescent, Burlington. Burlington. Isn't that near Taranto?'

'Burlington?' James felt his features loosening, sliding around his face, gelling into one big, coherent, radioactive smile. 'Boben lives in Burlington?'

'Says here, 16 Willowdale –'

James interrupted her with laughter. He rolled back onto his shoulders and flailed his legs in the air. 'Burlington! Boben lives in Burlington! I love it! I absolutely love it!'

'Isn't that near you?'

James gathered his limbs and facial features and smoothed them down and sat upright again. 'Yes, yeah, not exactly close to me, but I can get there. It's about an hour from here, but there's a commuter train. It's this suburb town for commuters to two big industrial centres, here and a place called Hamilton, which – never mind, it's just funny that Boben lives there. I pictured him in a log cabin in the bush. I *knew* it.'

Now Maya Lipschitz sounded worried. 'You mean – you think he might not be rugged enough? We thought his publisher sounded – what was the publisher's name?' James heard a frantic crackling of papers and snapping of cigarette lighter.

'I think he's with Pussy Hollow now,' he said, 'which is out West. He used to be with Fern Arbour, and Elrond for a while, before they both folded.'

'Here it is: Pussy Hollow Books, that right? Well, that's pretty good, right, it's rural and all?'

'Well ...' James wondered how rural she would consider downtown Regina. 'Sure. Sure it is. Rural enough for our purposes.'

'And he is a recluse and everything, right?'

'Well, he's certainly hard to find. He's hard to get an interview with, that's for sure. I don't think he's in the best of health.' *Owing to about a forty and a half of Canadian Club a day,* James didn't say. 'I haven't seen him in public for some years.'

'So maybe you could use that, James, I mean build that up, you know, here he is this national icon and everyone is dying to know the face behind the name, you know what I mean? And you're the one who's got behind the mask, know what I mean, like this is an exclusive thing, right?'

'Right.'

'You have interviewed him before, right?'

'Oh, absolutely.'

'Good.'

Then there was the question of the photographer. James put her mind to rest immediately: Nicola Lickson was without question the most sought-after, the *edgiest* – Maya might have seen her work in *Random*? No? – and would be eager to do whatever James suggested; he promised to have Nicola's portfolio into the Fedex van before nightfall. And Maya gave him the number of the publicist who was to help set up a meeting.

James hung up and stood up, looping his thumbs in his belt. He narrowed his eyes and turned down the corners of his mouth. 'You and me, pal, we're goin' downtown, and then you're goin to the big house for a very lawng toime.' He wheeled to the air vent, now spewing a toxic blast of Gypsy Kings. He pointed and growled, 'You are goin' down. I don't care who you know, I don't care who your daddy is, whose dick you're suckin awn: You. Are. Goin. Down.' He expanded his chest, and yelled, 'Book him.'

He had to mine deeply and methodically for the scrap of paper bearing Nicola Lickson's number.

After seventeen minutes, he found it in his wallet, in his pocket.

He pictured the phone – sleek and cordless? or jokey, kitsch, shape of a hamburger or cartoon character? – on some purple velvet divan, or stuck to a welded metal sculpture, wax-splattered from candelabra made from bicycle parts, the phone now ringing, possibly muffled covered by the frayed ends of a great red-and-gold theatre curtain now adapted to the curled wrought-iron rods over the expanse of plate-glass window, in the dim, cool, apartment behind the cold, sealed, salmon, sand-blasted, electronic-eyed façade of the Bomb Factory.

For exactly two hours and seven minutes, sitting on a kitchen chair before his computer, set up on a card table in the tiny sewing room, James had been listening to the Portuguese radio, enough time to have heard the most popular easy-listening hits twice, in one case three times. The 'My Way' cover had resurfaced, inexplicably, twice. He was beginning to decipher the ads, as well, the one that ended with the long, screamed '*Gôôôôôl!*' probably being for a sporting goods store ('O casa do *futebol!*'), not to be confused with the one for the auto body shop (which also ended in '*Gôôôôôl!*').

He'd written on his computer screen, 'DENTAL WEEK PIECE,' then underneath that, 'NOTES', and underneath that, '1. humour.'

He typed, 'bossa nova,' and sat back.

There didn't seem to be any oxygen left in the room.

His clothes were at least stacked against one wall, the books against another. He had slept the night before on a single mattress De Courcy had found in the garage. He had set up the computer. He had no idea what the temperature was outside, but he couldn't imagine it to be any hotter, even in the sun, than in this box. It seemed to be hotter than yesterday, and the day before. He stared with hostility at the odd little air vent that was both salvation and nemesis: it was the source of oxygen and noise. The hysterical radio must be just outside, possibly against the outer base of this very wall. At least it drowned out Acton's reverberant lamentations from upstairs.

He got up and wiped his face and stepped into the corridor. Fiona was sitting in the purple living room, her legs in sweatpants tucked under her, on a vast and sagging sofa, smoking. She was reading another fat textbook, or possibly the same one.

'Hey,' she said, 'heard about your big break.'

'Yeah.' James stood at a window and looked down into the alleyway. There was the usual thicket of boys, gathered closely and talking. 'Problem is, she won't return my calls.'

'Who won't? The editor?'

'Editor?'

'Of the magazine. I thought it was this New York –'

'Oh, that, yes, sorry, *that* break. Yes. Well, that's going smoothly, actually, I called the guy's, the poet's publisher's publicist, and she said I'd be getting this phone call –'

'So which break were you talking about?'

The vibrating floorboards told them a mammoth plodding creature or car was approaching, oozing down the alley, probably, towards them, a car equipped with the usual stereo. The windows rattled. It was like listening to the earth's heartbeat. There it was, slowly rounding the corner, squat, small and utterly black, its windows tinted black, the bumper sheathed in black vinyl – except for the fluorescent decals on the hood: a bright pink Tasmanian Devil with a barbell between its teeth. James watched with interest as the boys widened the circle to accept the car. It drove among them and one of them leaned into the window, which rolled down slowly.

'Do you have a girlfriend?' asked Fiona.

'Nope.' Being almost directly above the car, he couldn't see the face in the open window. The teenager leaning into it, one hand on the roof, one hand on the door, was chatting, smiling, nodding, the stereo still booming. They must be really yelling at each other. 'I asked this girl if she wanted to do the photography for this piece. Could be a big break for her. But she won't return my calls. She'd better do it fast or they'll get Julian to recommend someone else.' He was speaking almost to himself; Fiona wouldn't know who Julian was. The boy leaning in the car window reached into his pocket and handed something into the interior blackness. James turned away from the scene. 'Anyway, Boben, the writer, this guy I'm supposed to be writing on, is supposed to call me tonight at nine, and I'll set up an interview. He's incredibly difficult to get a hold of. They wouldn't give me his number. I gave this phone number. So if you don't mind, please don't plan any phone calls around then.'

'No problem, babe, I'll be out. Going out with Buck's hockey team. Big date.'

James sat on an angular black chair that immediately began sawing at his back. 'Jesus Christ this chair is uncomfortable.'

'Oh, don't sit in that. That's not real.'

'What do you mean it's not real?'

'It's not real. It's not a real chair.'

'Ah. I see. An illusory chair. Possibly sent by an evil demon to confuse my senses.'

'No, I mean it wasn't built as a chair. It was built for some play or something he was in. It's a hoojamathingy. He brought all this stuff in here when he painted all these colours.'

'De Courcy was in a play?'

Her reply was swallowed in the booming bass as the car outside revved and turned in the alley. James went back to the window to watch. The black windows were sealed up again, the car creeping away. The bass gradually receded, and the boys resumed their lounging positions against the garage doors. The graffiti on the doors read, 'Loco Christie Posse'.

'Prop,' he said. 'It's a prop. Fiona, have you noticed that a car comes up this alleyway about every fifteen or twenty minutes, and the guy in it talks to the guys down here, and then it leaves again?'

Fiona didn't look up from her textbook. 'They're just teenagers. Friends.'

'So they're just greeting each other.'

'Yeah. They're all unemployed and dropouts and they have nothing better to do.'

James nodded. 'Friends. Except it's always a *different* car. Plus, they also seem to be trading something. You know, *exchanging* something.'

She shrugged. 'Maybe they have like a common interest.'

'Like baseball cards.'

'Yeah. Baseball cards. Comics.' But the corner of her mouth was smiling. She looked up at him and winked.

James laughed and sat in the unbearable chair again and suddenly found himself asking, 'Fiona, how long have you been going out with Buck?'

'Just a couple of years. One and a half, I guess.'

'He's younger than you, right?'

'Oh yeah. He's only twenty-two. He's a baby.'

'I was a little shocked by that stuff about gays, you know, gays and the arts?'

'Oh,' said Fiona, closing the book with a snap, 'Buck doesn't know what he's talking about. Don't mind him. He thinks he has to impress people with big ideas sometimes.' She was lighting a new cigarette.

James cleared his throat. 'Why ... why exactly do you go out with him?'

'Why do I go out with him? Jimmy, have you ever gone to bed with a twenty-two-year-old? I mean – okay, I guess it's different for guys, but believe me, for me it's worth it.'

'The sex.'

'The sex! Great sex. I mean great sex. Like a friggin' tornado, holy flying fathers, those guys never stop. I mean it may not last too long, the first time, but then they just get right back at –'

'Okay,' said James, rising, 'okay, I got it. I got it.'

'You asked.'

'I did. I know I did.' He reached across her for the phone. 'I'm going to try that chick again.' He dialled Nicola's number, which he now knew. He listened to the phone ringing in the Bomb Factory.

Another tinny radio reared up under the window, this one even louder.

'Jesus CHRIST,' said Fiona, snapping the book shut. 'It's getting too much even for me. That's missus fucking Pimentel again, can't even fucking hear it she's so deaf. I've asked her to turn it down a million fucking times. What a fucking maggot head, what a *cock* brain.'

James heard Nicola's message for the fourth time and then hung up.

'I'm going outside,' said Fiona. 'I'll talk to her fucking husband. Fucking guy doesn't know shit from shinola, but at least he wears the boots, know what I'm saying? She's just a g.d. poopynose.'

She left James standing in the middle of the purple living room. He said, 'Poopynose?'

Immediately he heard the shouting. Mr Pimentel had come out

onto his back stoop across the alleyway in his undershirt and was standing – James saw from the window – protectively before Mrs Pimentel and waving his arms, and Fiona was waving her arms. They were separated from the thugs by a garage, but a couple of the boys had opened the gate to the narrow garden, to watch. One, in Bulls cap and baggy jeans, was bow-legging his way up the garden path. James thought: son: and he quickly opened the kitchen door and ran down the fire escape.

He had been wrong about the temperature: it was hotter in the sun.

Mrs Pimentel was flattening the air before her with down-turned palms, the referee's signal for 'incomplete pass', shaking her head emphatically and saying, perfectly comprehensibly and without a foreign accent, 'No English. No English.'

'Listen,' said Fiona, 'you know god-damn well what I'm saying. I'm your frigging neighbour, all right? And I've asked you politely, about a trillion times now –'

'Musica,' said Mrs Pimentel, from behind Mr Pimentel, who folded his arms. 'Only musica, no English musica, Portugues musica.'

Mr Pimentel grunted and frowned. His moustache twitched. His chin was unshaven and his eyes were red. His mouth opened as if he was going to speak but he just looked balefully from James to Fiona. He looked tired and deeply depressed. James felt a little sorry for him.

Now the baseball-cap boy had drawn up, his hands in his pockets. He stepped up onto the concrete steps of the Pimentel's back porch, in between James and Mr Pimentel, and said, to James, 'What's your problem.'

'Our problem's not with you,' said James, adding unconvincingly, 'man.'

'It's with you too,' said Fiona, 'with your god-damn stereos pounding all day long while we're trying to do our homework.'

James winced at 'homework.' He put a hand on her shoulder, murmuring, 'Fiona –'

'Our problem is with the noise, constant, all day long frigging noise you people seem to –'

'Fiona,' said James, 'Cool it. Listen, we don't mean to be impolite –'

'You're talking to my mother. You're talking to my friggin' *mother* here.' The boy's hands were still in his pockets.

'Listen,' said Fiona, her fists on her hips, 'if it doesn't stop I'm calling the police. I've had it with this.'

'Police!' yelled Mrs Pimentel, 'give me a break! Give me a break! It is daytime! Three o'clock in the afternoon! I can play music! There is no law against music!'

'Yes, actually there is,' said James, 'that's the problem. And maybe this would be the quickest way to solve it, just to call the police.'

Mr Pimentel's sweaty brow furrowed and he swung towards his wife, his mouth open wider. Consternation, but no words.

'How many years you live here?' said Mrs Pimentel, folding her arms over her heaving apron.

'Me?' said Fiona. 'Where? Here? Or in this country?'

'Whoa,' said James, sucking in his breath.

'On this street.'

'Two years,' said Fiona, 'but I've lived in this city for –'

'Seventeen years,' said Mrs Pimentel. 'Seventeen years I live on this street. This street Portuguese street. This music Portuguese music.' And she swirled around and dived into the house, slamming the screen door behind her.

Mr Pimentel looked back at James and Fiona in utter confusion and apparent anguish. He looked about to cry.

'Look,' said James, applying pressure to Fiona's shoulder, 'we're not going to solve this this way.'

'What about you, bud?' said the son, pushing his face into James's. 'How long you been here?'

'Me?' James squared his shoulders and lifted his chin. He was a good foot taller than Mr Pimentel and his son, but he didn't at all like the girth and hairiness of the combined sets of forearms. 'I've just moved in. Name's James.' He held out his hand.

Mr Pimentel turned and lumbered into the house.

The boy pushed his face closer, to within an inch of James's. 'You a friend of the French guy? The faggot? You his pal?'

James held his gaze.

The boy whispered, 'Faggot,' and quickly moved back.

He was ambling towards his garage when Fiona said, 'What did he say to you?'

'Never mind,' said James, 'let's go back inside.'

'Hey cock head!' called Fiona after the boy.

He stopped and turned, his face crinkled against the sunlight. 'What?'

'You are a shit brain, you know that? You are a poop mouth bum face –'

James grabbed both her arms and yanked her towards the fire escape, saying, 'Shut up. Fiona. Shut up.' He dragged her all the way up to the apartment and locked the door behind her. The boy had shrugged and slumped away.

Fiona rushed to the open window and yelled out of it, 'Turd eyes! Bugger ears!'

James sank into the bog-like sofa, breathing hard. 'Terrific,' he said, 'terrific. All we needed. A fucking gang war.'

'*Cunt neck!*'

De Courcy shuffled in, in a red silk dressing gown. 'Good morning.' He went into the kitchen and put his head in the fridge.

Fiona left the window, red-faced, and sat with James.

'You know,' said James, 'they kind of have a point, about the noise. I mean it is their street really. Those are their values, you know, they don't mind noise all day long, it's normal to them. Their other neighbours don't mind. We're the minority. We're the foreigners, come to impose our values.'

'Jimmy, I am no foreigner.'

'Fiona, there's a sign in the window of the travel agent below us that says, We speak English.'

'So? They damn well should speak English, shouldn't they?'

James sighed. 'I'm only saying that they've been playing their radios outside for seventeen years here. No wonder they're a little bit confused by us. Hey, homes, had a nice sleep, did you?'

De Courcy came back in with his orange juice. He was already shaved, his hair was combed and slicked back. 'Yes. Thank you.'

'Weren't disturbed by any noise, were you, homes?'

'No.'

'Good. Well, I'm glad you got up before nightfall anyway.'

'Why?'

'Never – oh shit. Fuck.' James stood up. He was staring at the answering machine, the blinking little red eye.

'What?'

'There's a message.' James fell on the machine, jabbed the button. It whirred and snapped. 'Fuck. Fuck fuck fuck. There was a call when we were outside. I missed it.'

The rewinding took forever. The machine whirred and whirred. James tapped his feet and chewed on the inside of his cheek. Then, after an endless Morse code of clicks and pops and crunches, Nicola Lickson's voice came on. 'Hey, James.' There were voices and laughter in the background. 'Nice to hear from you. Sorry it took me so long to get back to you, but –' There was a screech and a crash, and Nicola giggled and said something indistinguishable to someone else. 'Anyway, I'm still on for Thursday night, and I'd love to hear about whatever this big project is you're talking about, now, I'm going out again and I won't be reachable this afternoon –' Another hoot, and gritty music came on at her end. She had to shout over it. 'But I guess you can tell me about it at the screening tonight, it starts at seven-thirty and we're meeting for a drink at seven, it's at the Pig and Mallet, which is kind of a scream, it's so tacky, it's a blast, and it was cheap to rent the room, anyway, it's at the corner of ...'

James scrambled for pen and paper. He had to replay the whole message to get it right. He erased the machine and sat on the couch, staring at the paper. It was a corner in the east end, near a famous strip bar and a housing project. 'Fuck,' he said. 'It better be over by nine. I have to be here at nine for that fucking ...'

Both outdoor radios were roaring at full volume, and another car stereo arrived in the alleyway. De Courcy put two of the fake chairs together, sat in one comfortably and put his feet in the other. He opened the newspaper. James noticed that his toenails were painted a dark metallic green.

He closed his eyes and tried not to think about the corner of Gerrard and Parliament, the Pig and Mallet Pub.

'People, excuse me, *hello*, people, could I have your attention please? People?' The enormous screenwriter was standing unnoticed at the bar, sandwiched between two incandescent screens: one, above her shoulder, which showed a curling match in progress, another, at her elbow, the spinning fruit icons of video gambling. She wore a white T-shirt with a brown stain over the left breast, and, unfortunately, walking shorts. She had short hair and glasses.

The actor talking to James paid no attention. He said, 'But I'm moving into video more, now.'

'That right.' James looked around. The audience for the video screening, easily distinguished from the regular clientele by their quilted vests and riveted workpants, their heavy boots and ironic pink suits, was corralled up against the pool tables, which were in use by men with long hair and plaid jackets and moustaches. The place was packed. There was a row of old men in baseball caps at the bar, coughing in concert, and a waitress who had apparently come to work one day in 1975 and never left, not stepped outside once since then. There was a large screen set up behind the pool tables, but it was not clear how it was going to be seen unless the pool players – all apparently at the end of a long day of community service – ceased playing pool. The idea had been, Nicola had fleetingly explained to him, to rent the back room (or rather, as she said it, the Back Room), but that had fallen through because no one could find the key, so they had set up the screen in the main bar, and now everyone was waiting, rather frightened. Nicola had been swallowed by a group of women with crew cuts; James could just see the magenta blur bobbing above them. He had lost De Courcy, who had come along enthusiastically costumed (after much consultation with Fiona) for the Pig and Mallet, in Schooner Beer baseball cap and windbreaker. James looked at his watch: quarter to eight.

'So I'm taking this course in video production,' said the actor, 'at Cable 10, the community cable channel. It's really cool, you can sign up for this course and learn the technical stuff and it's free.'

'Really?' said James, turning back to him. 'That *is* cool. Why is it free?'

'Oh, it's *ongoing*,' said the actor. 'It's ongoing.'

'Ah.'

'Excuse me,' said a woman in a tight top, 'you're James Willing, aren't you?'

'That prick?' said James. 'I tell you, that guy is a *sexist*.'

'I don't think so.'

'You don't?'

'No. I admire people who write. I'm a writer myself.'

'Really?' James did his best to smile and look at her face so as not to look at her breasts, and he was noticing that she had perfect skin and dark lipstick, and feeling guilty about being more interested in that than in any writing she had done or might do in the future. With reluctance he said, 'What kind of writing?'

'Oh, fiction, you know, and ... you know.'

James nodded. *And what? You know what?*

'Actually, I wanted to talk to you because I just love talking about books. You know I'm just a book *addict*, I'm a total *junkie*.'

James nodded and smiled and looked at her breasts again.

'And I just heard this writer interviewed on the radio, and I just saw you and I thought, you would *love* her, she was so, I don't know.'

'Who was it?'

The woman frowned. 'That's the thing. I can't remember her name. But she was so cool. You would have loved her. She was talking about –'

'Do you remember the name of the book?'

'Oh.' Her face wrinkled again. 'Shit. I did hear it. But.'

'Hello!' whimpered the screenwriter, 'people?'

'Looks as if we're going to start,' said James. He was staring at one of the baseball caps at the bar and thinking that it belonged to an unusually young man, one who was not even coughing, and then realizing that it was in fact De Courcy, chatting breezily with a crusty regular in a Legion jacket, who was pointing at the TV and the curling. De Courcy was nodding and asking questions.

The roar in the bar seemed to increase as the screenwriter made her announcement, which faded in and out of James's hearing like a radio station on a car trip. She clutched a square of paper, and made no effort to raise her voice above the crowd. 'First, I want to thank you all very very *very* much for coming, because this is the kind of project you ...'

James saw Nicola detach herself from the cluster and come towards him, smiling. He smiled back hugely. She had two small gold boxing gloves draped around her neck by the laces: her purse. Just before reaching him, she banked and dove between two tall men in tight leather coats, humorously unfashionable coats. They were probably models: unshaven, cropped heads, dark glasses in the darkness. James was close enough to see one of them pat her hip and graze her cheek with his abrasive chin, close enough to hear him murmur in a deep and velvety voice, 'Nicky. Enjoying it. Enjoying it.'

She disappeared.

'And I want to apologize for the change in venue,' the screenwriter was saying, 'but if we can just get everyone's cooperation when we do the screening, and we get a little quiet, that would be just ...'

James stomach glurped. He hadn't eaten since lunch. There was a microwave behind the bar, with a plastic blackboard over it and things like wings and fries scrawled on it in fluorescent marker. He began to push his way towards it.

'Anyway,' squeaked the screenwriter, 'what happened was that we kind of lost access at the last minute to the place where we were going to screen it, so we've left a note on the door there, redirecting people to come here, and so we're going to have to wait a while to make sure everyone makes it. Also this VCR doesn't seem to be working, so we've got another one on the way here in the truck, so, anyway, what this means is that the screening is now scheduled for eight, instead of six-thirty. So in the meantime, please enjoy yourself and have a drink and order some food ...'

James wedged himself between De Courcy and the next man.

'Hey, Jim,' said De Courcy in his deep straight voice, still rather languid. 'Want you to meet my man Harry here –'

'Larry,' croaked the old man, eyeing James and his nose ring with a fearful and pained frown.

'Larry is explaining to me how curling works. I never had a chance to learn, myself, being from the east coast, we don't do much curling there.'

'Now, which east coast is that?' said James.

'Is that right, eh?' wheezed the old man. 'What part of the east coast you from?'

'Rimini,' muttered James.

'What's that?'

'I'm from Cape Breton,' said De Courcy, 'place called Meat Cove.'

'That right?' said the old man, 'I got a brother settled in Dartmouth.'

'Dartmouth, eh?' said De Courcy. 'Cheers. You all right for draft? Larry is from Thunder Bay.'

James asked the waitress, 'I guess there's no table service?'

'Oh,' said the waitress, frowning and looking around. 'Well, there is, normally. Kimberley should be out there.'

James turned and looked around. 'But she's not?'

'FREDDY!' bellowed the waitress towards the flap covering the hole to the kitchen. 'FREDD-EEE! Where's Kimberley?'

Eyes appeared at the slot. 'Had to go to the drugstore,' said a male voice.

The waitress turned back to James. 'Oh. She had to go to the drugstore.'

'So I guess there's no table service,' said James. 'Okay. So could you order me a –'

'But there is normally.'

'Right. Could you order me one personal pizza, please, and another –'

'Well I don't do the food, normally. Kimberley takes food orders.'

There was a soft hand on his shoulder, and he turned his nose into Nicola's face. 'Sorry. Hi.'

'Hey.' Her hand lingered on his shoulder. The touch of her cheek and hair burned on his nose. She smelled of incense. 'Having fun?'

'Oh, yeah, yes, sure, well, actually, I'm a little bit tense, because I'm going to have to go soon, and I'm not sure if I can –'

She pulled back her hand. The gold boxing gloves swayed against her hip. 'You're not going to go before the screening?'

'Well, I hope not, no, but I absolutely have to be home for this phone call, and actually this is what I had to talk to you about –'

'Do you know,' said De Courcy, turning his back on Larry from Thunder Bay and slipping back into his expiring voice, 'that the frantic sweeping actually has a physical effect on the path of the block, which is called a rock. I always thought they did it for exercise. How do you do?' He extended a hand to Nicola, smiling wanly. He had taken his Schooner Beer cap off, and his eyes were half closed.

'Piers De Courcy,' said James, 'my friend.'

Nicola squinted at the screen. 'Is that curling?'

'Always a rock, here,' murmured De Courcy. 'Anything made of stone is a rock, which always confuses me.'

'What?'

'I was always taught that a stone was something you could pick up, a rock something you sat on, whereas here a rock is anything made of stone. You throw rocks, here, for example, not stones: let him who has not sinned cast the first *rock* suggests above average strength.'

'Are you English?'

James sighed. Quickly, to forestall the explanation that De Courcy would not hesitate to produce, he said, 'De Co – Piers went to an English school. Nicola, can I talk to you for a second about –'

'I *love* England,' said Nicola. 'Where in England?' She moved between James and De Courcy and put a hand on the bar.

'Oh, it wasn't in England,' said De Courcy, now leaning back against the bar and spreading his arms out along it. He was still smiling; he looked very handsome. 'There was one in Siena, and one in Deauville, which is in the north of France, and –'

'*Wow*,' said Nicola. 'James, that's – are you okay?' She had turned to catch him making his dying beluga whale face at De Courcy.

James coughed. 'Fine, fine, listen, I *have* to talk to you. It's very important.'

'Ok-*ay*!' she said sharply.

De Courcy raised his eyebrows. 'It's been a pleasure to meet you, Miss Lickson.' He held out his hand. She blushed and smiled. James gritted his teeth. The old man was tugging on De Courcy's sleeve and gargling at him. 'Something exciting happening in the game?' De Courcy picked up his draft and turned back to the screen.

'Sorry to have to do this right now,' James began, 'I know you're distracted, but this really exciting break has come up for both of us, and I managed to swing it so that you –'

'Nicky.' Another deep-voiced man at her side. 'Nicky. Enjoying it.'

She squealed and kissed the man and introduced him to James and to another guy, this one slim and black, with widely flared trousers and bleached blond hair in tiny dreadlocks like stumps. 'Nigel,' she said, throwing her arms around his neck. '*Nigel!*'

'Baby.' He held his hands parallel to the floor, his fingertips stretched out on either side of Nicola's waist.

'Your nail polish still wet?' said James.

Nigel didn't hear; Nicola was kissing him at length on the lips. When she had finished, Nigel said, 'Well. I am now happy. I am under a ray of sunshine and *you* –' He waved his shiny nails at the rest of the world. 'May be under clouds and rain, I am *all* sunshine.' He giggled and snorted; they all giggled and snorted. He turned to the deep-voice man. 'Peter. Long time.'

'Long time. Good to see you.' They hugged.

'How's it going? You've *moved*, right? Where you living? We should get together.'

'Hey, absolutely. Absolutely.'

'Listen,' said Nigel, 'give me your card. You have a card, right?'

'Oh, absolutely,' said Peter. 'If I have any left. Hang on.' He unslung his knapsack. 'I think in here …'

'Oh, listen, it's no problem,' said Nigel, 'just write it ...'

'No no no no no,' said Peter, 'it's right here. Sure I have a. Couple left. Maybe in my other.' He checked all his pockets, all the flaps of the knapsack.

'Nicola,' said James.

'Here you go!' said Peter. He handed a card to Nigel. 'Knew I had one left.'

'Phew,' said James.

'Hey, thanks babe,' said Nigel, looking at the card. 'Thanks. I'll call you.'

'Absolutely,' said Peter. 'Now, listen, though, that card, that's not the right address, right?'

Nigel paused. 'It's not?'

'Well, I've moved, right?'

'Oh yeah.'

'So the address has changed. And the number.'

'Oh.'

'I'll write down the new number for you. If you have a pen.'

'A pen?'

James felt his new HelioPoint rollerball shifting uneasily in his back pocket: $12.99 for six at Business Depot, and he was down to two. One with him, one buried somewhere in the landfill of his new room.

'Anyone have a pen?'

James jammed his fists in his pockets and stared at the floor.

'Nicky, you have a pen? No? Maybe this guy at the bar ...'

James felt the pen glowing in his pocket, the top of it doubtless protruding, visible.

'People?' quavered the screenwriter's voice, 'it looks like we're going to start.'

'Angie, you have a pen?'

'Here,' said James, holding out the pen to Peter. 'I need it back.'

The lights dimmed. The big TV screen lit up. The country music on the bar's system did not diminish, and the pool players did not stop shouting and whooping, and the curling wasn't switched off, but louder music was now coming from the big screen. Murky, orchestral.

The film began with an image of the sea, grey and turgid, a wide horizon, and a woman's voice saying, 'When I was a little girl, my mother used to say to me, when you grow up, you can be anything you want, a doctor, a lawyer, an astronaut ...'

The images changed: a tricycle on a lawn, a swing, a box of tampons, a man in a lab coat, the sea, a whirring planesaw, a hand with painted red nails. Other voices were gradually superimposed; most seemed to be other women recalling their childhoods. There were more and more images of drills and jackhammers, and then one of the voices added was moaning in pain or ecstasy.

James looked up at the screen with the curling for a few minutes, but that was no better.

'And I would swing in that swing every day, until she would call me in for lunch, and I remember the sound of her voice and the smell of grilled cheese sandwiches and Campbell's tomato soup ...'

He looked at his watch: eight-fifteen. And then the image on the screen had changed, and James was staring intently. It was a slow pan over a graceful neck and shoulder, a woman's naked shoulder, muscular and pale, a few wisps of red hair on it.

James tensed and leaned forward.

The camera panned down the woman's back, and James was disappointed to see that it was not naked but shrink-wrapped in a white leotard, almost diaphanous, spaghetti straps on the shoulders. The camera drew back as the woman started dancing, and of course it was Nicola.

The noise in the room softened. Even some of the pool players turned to watch this part. Only the row of old men sat fixed on their beers or on the curling.

She was dancing in slow motion, of course, in a white room, just your standard sort of expressive modern dance, with arms and hair flailing and head swaying and legs kicking out, the kind of dance James didn't know enough about to judge, but he knew she was at least pretty good. De Courcy hadn't said anything about dance. And he knew he found it extraordinarily beautiful. The white thing was a full body catsuit, and she had bare feet. Every time her chest whirled in front of the lens the two dark bumps of nipples appeared, maddeningly brief. But it was the feet that James found transfixing, the bare feet and the slim waist, writhing, and the sad music. It wasn't bad, really. It was kind of lulling.

You could see the shadow of pubic hair, too, slipping in and out of sight as if airbrushed. And then James noticed something strange: a stain at the crotch, a red stain. She was bleeding.

The segment only lasted a few seconds, not long enough for the patch to spread. It was subtle. But in the images that followed – sanders, saws, nail guns – James was longing to see the red blur again, in slow motion, between the images of sea. He felt sad and full.

He looked over at Nicola, whose face was carefully blank. She didn't look at him.

At nine-thirty he was tripping up the dark fire escape to the apartment; he had left De Courcy playing pool with some of the regulars and the black guy called Nigel. He fumbled with the key in full view of Elsie the landlady's twitching lace curtain. He banged his knee against a chair in the kitchen. Through the doorway to the dark living room he could see the red gleam of the answering machine's LED, blinking.

Swearing, he stumbled over to it, almost falling on the basketball, and hit the button. There were two messages: the first from *Glitter* wondering if he'd found the photographer and if she had couriered her book to them yet.

After the next beep, there was a pause, the sound of heavy breathing, a grunt and an incoherent word. It sounded like, 'sodomy', but it couldn't have been that. It sounded uncertain and drunk.

The answering machine's synthesized voice told him that this message had been left at 'Nine. Oh. Seven. P.M.' He sighed and sank onto the sofa: it was like a waterbed.

He'd finally got his personal pan pizza, in the roar of congratulations after the screening, and burned his tongue on it. And he had cornered Nicola and congratulated her and threw the *Glitter* thing at her and she'd pretended to be nonchalant, but he knew she was excited. She said no, she'd never worked for *Glitter* before, and she promised to Fedex some of her work to them the next morning. 'You were beautiful,' he remembered saying, rather too intently, 'really beautiful.' And she had kissed him quickly on the cheek before he left.

'Kafka!' he yelled in the dark apartment. His voice died instantly in the humid air.

At least they were still on for the restaurant.

He rubbed his eyes. The apartment was dead quiet, aside from some soothing disco bass rumbling somewhere down the street, and airless. The sweet smell of garbage hung in the doorways. He saw Nicola's body again, in the video, the vertebrae and muscled back, the bumps of nipples in the gauzy fabric, the damp stain at the crotch. He drew in his breath sharply and suddenly felt like crying.

There was a screech of feedback from above, and Acton's ghostly voice boomed out: 'Technology. Transmission. I exist.'

James laughed weakly. He patted his back pocket. He had never got his pen back.

'I can get you an edit pack,' yelled the woman into the cellphone, 'which is the short pulls minus the rollup and the debrief.'

James tried to listen to Nicola, who had just said, 'I danced as a teenager.'

'And that's the best I can do on VHS,' yelled the woman.

James turned to look at her. She was at the next table, alone, except for her laptop and her phone and three different sizes of bottled water. She was about twenty-five. 'I mean I can't fuck around for hours in the archive. Jesus fucking Christ. Hold on. Hello? David! David fucking McLaren, at fucking last. Listen. I have had *enough* of this service. I am switching back to Systel, I am going to talk to whoever signed the contract with you, David, I am going to move *mountains* to get us off your fucking service. It's always a problem, David, *always*, I never had situations like this with TelWeb –'

'Sorry?' said James.

'I danced as a teenager. But I wasn't into the whole body image thing. I remember standing at the barre doing pliés, we were all in a row, and I was watching the girl in front of me, she had this brown stain start to spread down the back of her leg, and then she had to go off the bathroom to shit, because she'd taken too many laxatives. It was like common, nobody said a thing. The bath-rooms always smelled of puke.' Carefully, using her fork like a fine scalpel, Nicola severed a camouflage of crispy leek, pronged a nub of black truffle, pulled it out from its entanglement, and put it in her mouth. She closed her eyes.

James looked down and tried to concentrate on his soup, a shi-itake venison consommé. He couldn't eat, but he reached for his notebook. The music, highly orchestrated pop from the sixties, a male singer booming *baby baby*, Wayne Newton or Tom Jones or someone, though cleverly ironic, was far too loud.

'I don't care if you build a fucking transmitter in my back yard,

David, it's not going to be enough, I have had enough of this service, I am *walking*.'

Nicola swallowed and said, 'I'm glad I got out of dance. I didn't want to have to go on worrying about my body. I never had the right body, anyway.' She took another large gulp of her second Cajun martini. The hot pepper in the glass wriggled as she slammed it down. She wiped her lips with the back of her hand.

'You didn't?' James looked, with some pain, at her cleavage. She was in a sort of goth getup, a long black lace dress that clung to her like a chemical film, and under it visible black underwear which also appeared to be lace. The most painful part of it was that the superimposed filigrees didn't quite add up to opacity; nor were they simply see-through. Aureolae moved behind the floral shadows as maddeningly vague smudges, a sort of dark tormenting glow. As she had swung through the tables to meet him, forty minutes late, in her worn leather biker jacket, he had been unable to take his eyes off the shifting shadow at her groin. And then there was the almost obscenely low cut of the neck, scooping to cut off just the very tops of those smudges, now appearing as fine pink edges, rims, boundaries – and then – he just couldn't help enumerating all this in his head, again, was he sick? one of those beer-eyed guys in the Adult section? – then that incredibly long neck and the black velvet choker around it looking vaguely confining. She shook her head and the red ringlets, piled up and pinned, writhed. He managed to say, 'Your body looks perfect, to me. For dance, I mean.' His face boiled over. 'You're very slim.'

Her eyes were distant as she chewed. 'I didn't think they would be so salty.'

'No. That's the lamb reduction they're in. It is a little too salty. I've made a note of it.'

'How is yours?'

'Here, taste it.' He pushed his bowl towards her. He wasn't hungry: he never was when reviewing. He lost all hunger the moment his eyebrows locked over the riddle of the menu – *pan-seared à la, market fresh in juice of, forests of young blackened, ginger-puréed dusted by* – words whizzing around in his head. His stomach would knot up. Eating was about words, and words were work.

'Can you order me another martini?' she said, a little too loudly, 'I can't see the bitch from here.'

He scanned the room, frowning. 'I can't either. They all have better things to do around here.' Indeed, none of the legion of genetically engineered Alpha Babes who had sullenly taken orders and provided eight-dollar martinis – his was bright icy blue, shot up with the face-puckering antifreeze of curaçao – was visible, even hovering nakedly around the roaring table of the cable TV mogul or the frighteningly silent foursome of Arab gentlemen in linen suits who had attracted so much attention earlier. 'But you know, you should be drinking this wine.' He tapped the label of the white Burgundy. 'For one thing, because you've probably never had anything like it before, and for another because you can't taste anything when you're drinking that fire, it's fucking gasoline.' He reddened quickly, realizing that he had never sworn in her presence before. 'And it's going to disappear soon, I've ordered red for the mains. Whenever we get them.'

She gave an exaggerated pout, turning her black lips down, saddening her raccoon-painted eyes. 'I *love* martinis.' But she was pouring herself wine.

He watched her metallic green fingernails for a second, noting that they were exactly the same colour as De Courcy's toenails, and marvelled again at De Courcy's instincts for these things. He looked up, catching the silvery blur of their waitress's clingy crop top as she passed. 'Excuse me,' he said, trying to catch her eye. 'Excuse me.'

She turned with a pleading expression. 'I'll be with you in one –'

'Could we have another Cajun martini,' he said quickly, 'and is there any way to get this music turned down at all? It's very loud where we are, I can hardly hear my –'

'You don't like the music?' said the waitress with a mysterious smile. She appeared to be looking over James's shoulder at something ironically amusing. She was rubbing one foot against her leg and scribbling something on her pad simultaneously; she appeared to have too much energy or be nervous. It was a sort of hyperacceleration James was familiar with from similar restaurants, and he became aware of a cloud of worry forming somewhere in his head. He checked the eyes and her pupils were indeed troublingly tiny. 'It's *Tom Jones*,' she said with excitement.

'Yes, I thought it was. And no, I don't like it. But it is too loud, don't you think?'

'Oh but it's a *scream*!' she said, and took off like a top.

'Oh boy,' said James. He dropped his gaze to Nicola's ankles, crossed on one side of the table, just in his line of vision. Her legs were bare, but the ankles were crossed with black velvet ribbons, part of the clunky platform shoes with their diving arches. They were almost like point shoes, turning her feet into flying buttresses. Next to them, on the floor, was her purse: a hard box, covered in black velvet, in the shape of a coffin, shoulder strap attached, a cross embroidered on its lid. 'I didn't know you were into the goth thing. Do you read the vampire books and all?'

She almost choked on the soup. 'Oh *god* no. Well, I mean, I did, once, like everybody, when you're younger.'

James nodded, never having opened a vampire book in his life.

'Oh, you mean my purse? I just thought it was cute. I thought it was, you know ...'

A scream, thought James.

'A *scream*.'

There was a shout from the open kitchen, behind Nicola's head, and James bent his neck to look. No one seemed to be manning the twelve burners behind the mosaic wall separating kitchen from cavernous dining room; their blue flames roared. There were a couple of pans sitting on them, clouds of steam or perhaps smoke gathering above them. James looked around the room: the blue banquette that undulated along one side, packed with grey-blond hair and the red faces of people who didn't just live in buildings like the Bomb Factory but actually *owned* them; the great aquarium above it, then the deconstructed wall, the plasterwork just ending twenty feet above them, giving way to girders and cables and cinderblocks. The huge rusted girder overhead that just stopped half way across the room, in imitation of a bridge blasted by a retreating army. The whole room bore these carefully constructed signs of devastation, as if bravely continuing operation after an earthquake or nuclear attack. The bar, another wavy wall of ceramic and glass mosaic, just crumbled at one end: the servers had to step over the rubble to get behind it.

The other side of the room was a sort of Renaissance-Baroque classicism, with Ionian columns painted gold stretching up to the hangar-like ceiling, heavy red curtains suspended between them: they hid the plate glass windows and the passersby who would otherwise be staring in as if watching a live telecast. James had, in fact, been filmed by a television camera on stepping up to the front door, just after two mohawked punks had asked him for change, one of them coolly adding, 'To buy drugs.' James had given him a buck.

He looked again at the art on the far wall: a series of vast canvases, each of which bore splashes of paint and large stencilled words. 'DON'T BELIEVE WHAT I TELL YOU', shouted one in red paint. 'I AM NOT A FREE AGENT', said another. James's favourite was an unpainted canvas, bare except for the large stick-on letters, 'BATTERIES NOT INCLUDED'.

He and Nicola had possibly the worst table, in the shadow of the steel staircase that rose, apparently unsupported, three stories in the centre of the room. The guy who had seated them, Mister Mambo King, a doleful model with slicked hair and a black nylon T-shirt stretched across his pecs, had not left his post at the bar when James had entered, chatting with the Alpha Babes while James sweated in his wrinkled jacket and tie, looking around, for a full five minutes. When James had gone in search of his own table, the guy had darted like a snake, stayed him with a hand on the shoulder, handed him two menus and jammed him under the staircase, his back to the door and his head touching the steel. Now the guy had disappeared too. Another muffled shout from behind the kitchen.

'You know who my childhood icon was?' said Nicola. 'For the way she looked, I mean. Cruella de Ville, in –'

'*A Hundred and One Dalmations!* Me too!' James laughed. '*Me too!*'

'Wasn't she just the sexiest? She was scary and she had the coolest dresses and she scared the *shit* out of me when she chucked things in the fire and laughed, remember, didn't she throw something on the fire –'

'It was this huge raging fire, I remember that. Didn't she throw a glass or something that made the fire rear up again, frighteningly high? I'll have to rent that sometime, see it again.'

'Good idea. Let's rent it.' She was smiling, blotches of red on her face from excitement.

James felt a warmth rushing to his groin at the sound of 'Let's.' He looked down at his soup. 'I wish they'd clear these plates. It's been about an hour since they arrived.' The kitchen was still abandoned, but the Mambo King was back on the bar, talking intensely into a cellular phone. 'What did you think of the soup?'

She took another slow mouthful, contemplated it as it went down, her eyes lifted up to the splintered beams high above them. James watched her lips and her throat. Finally, she said, 'God. I like it.'

'I do too. Intense mushroom, intense venison, good and clear. I'd add a drop of lemon juice myself.'

'There's something like a little bit sweet, maybe booze ...'

'Very good. I think it's sherry. In fact I'm sure it's sherry. Just a little nauseous hint, very subtle.' He was already seeing words glowing on a screen, rearranging them. 'I would say it's real Spanish sherry, very dry, probably fino. *Christ* this music is driving me *crazy.*'

She leaned back and gave him another of what he had begun labelling her *mysterious* looks, her eyes half closed. 'How *did* you learn to do this?'

He laughed. 'Oh, I just ... learned, I guess. On the job.'

'How? How did you start?' She leaned forward, put her chin on her hand.

He sighed. 'It's a long story.' The warning lights on his cockpit dashboard, his Head Up Display, began to flash. It was really too early to let her in on this story. Danger. Warning.

She waited, opening her eyes wide, and he felt as if his body was about to open up in a wide gash down his torso, that everything was about to come sloshing out at her. 'It's not that interesting.'

She said nothing, twirling a strand of hair around her finger and smiling faintly.

He sighed again. 'Actually, it's kind of a funny story. I was working in a restaurant.' *Low altitude, pull out, jettison fuel.* 'As a bartender, actually.' *Abort, pull out, eject, eject now* ... 'Tell me something. You live in the Bomb Factory, right?'

'Uh-huh.'

'Well, I've always wondered what it's like in there. I kind of think I would like to live in a space like that.'

She shrugged. 'It's great. I guess.'

'Yes? Tell me about it. How do you have your apartment?'

'Well, it's cool. It's a cool space.' She went back to her soup.

'Yes.' James was drumming his fingers on the table. 'Describe it to me.'

'Well. I have this huge –'

'FUCK YOU!' yelled a high-pitched and quavering voice quite near them. They both flinched: Nicola swivelled to see the kitchen; James half rose to see over her shoulder. A young, ponytailed man was striding the length of the bar, on their side, struggling with the buttons on his kitchen whites, apparently trying to tear them off, screaming, 'Don't you ever, ever, *ever* talk to me like that, you fucking prima donna *bitch!*' Under the halogen lights, tears flashed on his face.

In the sudden silence, thirty tablefuls of computer animators, talk-show hosts, senior publicists and CEOs of small software companies jerked their necks to get a view of the kitchen. In the entrance to a corridor – a glowing glass-studded corridor leading to god knows what sprawling aquatic lounge, dim pool-table annex, science-fiction toilets, row of Italian-designed telephones – stood another young man in kitchen whites and mad eyes, his ponytail covered by a red kerchief. He had rings in his nose and ears and eyebrows and clutched something brown and glistening and possibly organic.

'That's him,' whispered James, 'that's Ritchie.'

'That's Ritchie LeBlanc? *Cool.*' She gripped the back of her chair with both hands, knocking her martini into her truffles. James gritted his teeth briefly, but it wasn't as distracting as watching Ritchie LeBlanc pursue the young sous-chef towards the front door.

'*Cry baby!*' yelled the chef, waving the wet thing in the air over his head in a wide circle. It was a piece of meat, cooked meat, spraying fat; he appeared to have it by some appendage. The tables of entertainment lawyers and dating agency directors near the bar ducked and shrieked. 'TAKE A PILL, GIRLFRIEND!' he bellowed, and the thing flew out of his hands: it splatted against the now slamming frosted-glass door and stuck for a second before slowly sliding to the floor, leaving a shiny trail. It was a roasted capon or duck, minus one leg.

James's heart was pounding. Nicola was giggling and hiccuping and pounding her fists on the back of her chair. The man with the host-like job had grabbed Ritchie LeBlanc's wrists and pinned him against the wall, talking low and intense to him. One of LeBlanc's hands still clutched the torn leg of the bird where he had held it; the host-like man swatted it to the floor, hissing. Two other sous-chefs rushed out and wrestled LeBlanc back down the corridor.

'Terrific,' said James, sitting down, 'another hour before they get this straightened out, another hour before we get our mains.'

The open kitchen was filling up again with white jackets, shouting and fussing around over burned things and dousing small flames. A waitress had wrapped the projectile fowl in a cloth and was removing it; another wiped the glass door.

Nicola poured herself a too-full glass of Puligny-Montrachet and drank it off in a full twelve seconds of gulping.

'Whoa,' said James. 'That's about fifteen bucks' worth of wine you just took on in that glass.'

'Well, you get it free, don't you?' She knocked over a second glass, and James began to wonder if the blotches on her pale skin were just due to excitement.

'Save room for the Barolo, is what I mean.' He stood up and waved at a waitress, but everyone else in the room was doing the same.

'He looked really mad. That guy must have really pissed him off.'

'It doesn't take a lot to piss one off if one has been chain-snorting cocaine for twenty-four hours or possibly longer.' James felt suddenly articulate. He was speaking with warmth, twisting his napkin around his knuckles. He wanted to tear it to shreds.

'Did you notice the tremor on the fantasy babe who almost dropped your martini, the way she talked really fast? Look at those sous-chefs, look at them wave their arms. They're wired. This whole place is coked up to cracking. Why do you think this fuck-awful music is so loud? Everything is just cranked up to their pace.'

'Did you think she was a babe?'

'I ... here she is.'

And indeed she was, trying to pass them unnoticed at least, looking highly displeased. Her blond neo-sixties beehive was coming undone, and she tugged at the wisps as if to rip them out.

'Excuse me,' said James, still standing, 'excuse me, I know you heard me.'

She turned and scowled. 'I'll be with you in one minute, okay?'

James sat. 'Like fuck she will.' He was no longer worried about swearing before Nicola.

'I heard that,' said the blonde, standing over them.

'Good,' said James. 'I was wondering if we could have our –'

'Look, I don't need this, okay?' said the waitress. 'I really don't need assholes being rude to me right now.'

James was formulating a suitably outraged and caustic response when Nicola stood up too, swaying perceptibly, her face bright red. A coldness in James's belly told him something bad was going to happen. She said, 'Do you know who you're talking to?'

'*Nicola*,' he said sharply.

'We could *close* your restaurant, if we wanted to,' said Nicola.

James stood up, put a hand on her shoulder. 'Nicola. Please.'

'Oh could you?' said the waitress sarcastically. But she was looking closely at James.

'No we couldn't,' said James. 'Forget it.'

Nicola sat violently, pouting again.

'She means that if you treat all your patrons rudely, then they won't come back, and that could –'

'What I *mean*,' said Nicola, 'is that you never know who you're serving, they could be a –'

'Anyone at all,' said James, 'exactly. Now, could we at least have the second wine, even if the mains aren't ready, and perhaps some bread.'

The waitress had closed her mouth tightly and folded her arms, flicking her eyes between James and Nicola. She now opened her mouth, hesitated, and snapped it shut again. She gathered up their dishes at speed, audibly cracking one, and sped off.

'Nicola, you remember what I said about being incognito? It's very important.'

'Oh, I know, James.' She bowed her head. 'I'm sorry, I couldn't help it. I couldn't stand that bitch. I couldn't resist letting her know who's boss.'

At the bar, the waitress was tête-à-tête with the Mambo King, their eyes frequently directed to James's table. Mambo King was nodding grimly and unfolding the cellphone again.

'Shit,' said James.

'What?'

'Nothing. I think I've lost my cover. It's not a big deal.'

Nicola turned to watch the staff gather around the Mambo King, who had produced a clipboard holding many pages. He was turning the pages quickly and the three waitresses were watching each page: the pages appeared to be blown-up photographs.

'Yup,' said James. 'They've got me.'

Nicola looked back at him, subdued. 'I'm sorry, James. That was stupid of me.'

'Never mind. Happens all the time.' He sighed, and resisted an urge to put his head in his hands and moan. His brain was swimming with curaçao martini and it was now 9:30 p.m. without food. 'If they've got me, then the fun starts now. Nothing to do but sit back and enjoy it.'

'I feel stupid.'

'Forget it.'

'No, really.' She reached out a hand and touched James's. 'I'll make it up to you.'

'Excuse me,' said a deep and unctuous voice. A wave of citrusy cologne. Mambo King with his slicked-back hair was leaning over their table, smiling. 'I just wanted to check that everything was okay.'

'Yes, fine,' said James.

Nicola stared at the tablecloth, her face now entirely red.

'I'm *terribly* sorry about the delay, and that embarrassing scene.'

'Quite all right.'

A waitress had arrived with a tray, and placed two flutes of something fizzy in front of James and Nicola. James cast a quick glance around the room and noticed that a lot of eyes were now on him, including several pairs from the TV mogul's table.

'Just to make up for any discomfort, we'd like to offer you some complimentary glasses of champagne while you wait.'

'Thank you,' muttered James, his fingers tapping on the table. 'Very kind.'

Nicola had already picked hers up and gulped at it.

'It's a wine we don't often serve by the glass,' said the host in an even deeper voice, 'but I'd like to know what you think of it. It's a Billecart-Salmon *brut zéro* from 1986, which you may think sounds a little old for a champagne –'

'No no no.'

'– but which is one of those rare vintages which has proved durable.'

'Quite unnecessary,' mumbled James.

'We find it complements even the more serious dishes.'

'Yes.' James was watching Nicola, who was now halfway through hers. There were still two waitresses hovering, as if waiting for the host's next command. 'All we really want are our main courses.'

'Of course, and again I apologize for that little outburst in the kitchen. This is one of the things you can expect when working with an Artist.' He let James have the full effect of the majuscule. 'Artists are temperamental. And we think it's worth the wait for what they produce, because it's quite different from what you can expect from –'

'Yes,' said James, 'of course, thank you.'

'Thank *you*, sir. Anyway, there will be no further delays. The sous-chefs, who are all hand-picked and trained by Mr LeBlanc, have received their instructions from him and are preparing your main courses as we speak.'

'You mean Ritchie – Mr LeBlanc's not doing them himself?'

The host glanced around quickly, then lowered himself further to speak into James's ear. 'You needn't worry,' he hissed, *'I've locked him in the walk-in fridge.'*

'Excellent,' said James, 'I guess.'

'If there's anything else you need, don't hesitate to ask me personally.'

'Thank you.'

'Thank *you* sir.' And the host strode off, followed by the two waitresses and ignoring the frenzied hand-waving and finger-snapping of the TV mogul and the Arab foursome and various cosmetic surgeons and sports commentators, all of whom punctuated their gestures with curious and unabashedly irritated stares at James and Nicola.

'That was good,' said Nicola, slamming down the empty champagne flute and licking her lips.

'Yikes,' said James.

■ CHAPTER NINE

The night air had reached some intermediary stage between gas and solid, something like what James imagined ectoplasm to be. It smelled of cheese and automobile exhaust. There were still roaring cars and people shouting at each other on the street, even though it was past midnight. Nicola waited for him on the sidewalk while he carefully negotiated the four steps down. She was giggling, one hand to her mouth.

'How did you get down so fast,' he said, 'on those shoes?'

'I think I flew.' She flapped her hands and stepped into the street, where a large jeep or van swerved around her, horn blaring.

James grabbed her shoulder and pulled her back. 'Whoa,' he said, 'I think you and I are going to have to be a little careful getting home.'

She held tight to his hand as he guided her a few yards from the restaurant door, successfully avoiding death in three or four other forms, including a large transvestite prostitute who chose the moment they were passing to keel over towards them in unconsciousness or despair. Having successfully righted her/him, James's jacket coming into contact with quantities of beige pancake makeup, they continued towards a brightly lit corner, with a vague plan forming in James's mind to hail a taxi and accompany Nicola to her apartment, where he would in gentlemanly fashion ascertain her safe entrance and nobly flee.

Nicola let go of his hand to dance a little pirouette and sing a tune in a high but surprisingly assured voice. Then suddenly she disappeared. James stood for a second or two staring at the black segment of wall she had been in front of, aware of nothing but the fact that decisions and insights seemed to be taking an unusual time to come to him, before moving forward to check it out. He more or less quickly determined that the black wall was in fact a hole or alleyway between buildings, and the sound of her laughter confirmed that she had slipped into it.

He called her name while walking into the alley – towards, it now appeared, some kind of abandoned parking lot – with his hands stretched out in front of him as radar. His shoes squelched in something organic. 'Shit,' he said aloud. 'Nicky?' He hadn't yet called her that but thought that the time was right for crossing certain barriers. 'Nicky?'

There was a sudden liquid sound alarmingly close to him, right next to him, in fact, a slurping or slobbering (or retching or voiding? he thought with fright), and then a belch and a gasp and a familiar giggle. He reached out and touched Nicola's hair; she was leaning against the wall. She grabbed his wrist with a wet hand and pulled him close to her and nuzzled her nose in his neck. Her whole face smelled of alcohol. There was something hard and cold between them, which she quickly freed and lifted to her lips: a bottle. There was the rushing liquid sound again, which must have indicated a second ago, as it did now, that she was drinking deeply from it.

'Have some,' she spluttered, when she had finished. She was gasping. She shoved the bottle in the direction of James's face and it hit him in the nose.

He pulled it from her. 'What is this? Where did you get this?' He was aware, as he spoke, that they were both now leaning against the wall, which seemed to be covered with more ecto-plasm, and that the shoulder of his jacket was noticeably damp, and that his hand was on her waist and her pelvis was closely locked to his and quite warm.

'I got it from the restaurant.'

'You stole it? How did you –'

'It fit in my purse, my coffin purse, it's just the right size for a bottle, I couldn't resist, when I went to the washroom there was nobody behind the bar, they were all yelling at each other in the –'

'Jesus Christ.'

'They'll never *notice* it.'

James pulled away and took a few steps, bottle in hand, towards the glow of a light in the parking lot. Nicola was making whining noises. Once he was in the arc of orange light he peered at the label. It said, in frighteningly large letters, 'GAJA,' and underneath

that, 'Barbaresco', and underneath that '1978.' He said, 'Holy.'
'Give me that.'

He stepped back to her side and she wrenched the bottle from him, then dropped it to the ground, where it smashed, splattering James's trousers. 'Smash!' she said quite loudly in his ear. 'There. No more trouble.' Her hands were at the back of his neck and his hands were around her waist, which was amazingly small and firm. Her lips were wet and soft, except for the smooth edge of the steel ring, which was not cold, as it looked, but as warm as her skin. James kissed her unrestrainedly for a few minutes, and she kissed him back, putting her tongue in his mouth and slipping her hand inside his jacket and caressing his back and chest. Their nose-rings clicked. He felt her nipples through her dress and his shirt and her belly against his belt buckle and her buttocks tense under his hand as she stood on her toes to reach him. It was far too exciting to stop. He brought his hand up to her front and cupped her breast and she quivered. She dropped her head to his shoulder and sighed.

He panted and blinked in the darkness, trying to regroup. Her hair was in his mouth, her heart beating under his hand. She wriggled and moaned and brought her lips up to his again.

'Listen,' she murmured, kissing him lightly and running her hands through his sweaty hair, 'we can't go back to my place.'

'Okay,' said James cheerily. 'No problem. I wasn't thinking –'

'It's just, there's a lot of, there's some bad karma there with me and, with me and, guys, you know?'

'No problem,' he said, uncomprehending.

'You know, it's just some bad energy that's going to take a while to, to dissipate.'

'Right. Good word. Excellent word.'

'What?'

'Dissipate.'

'What?'

'Leave it.'

'You think I'm not very smart, don't you?'

'*What?*'

'Well, it's just an ordinary word, you think it's impressive that a ditzy photographer has a normal vocabulary.'

'Well, yes.'

She dropped her head again.

He blew out his cheeks and felt repentant. 'I'm sorry if I –'

But she was giggling and kissing him again, making snuffling noises.

He let this happen for a few dazzling seconds and pulled away again. 'I understand,' he said, 'hesitation, you know, if there's some tension in your life or complication that makes you not want to rush into things, that's –'

'So we'll go to your place.'

'Oh. My place?' He thought fast about his mattress under the pile of clothes, about De Courcy and Fiona. And Buck. And Elsie. 'Well, no.'

He could see her eyes picking up the orange from the parking lot, shining at him in the darkness. 'No?'

'We can't. I'm sorry. I don't have a place right now.'

'What do you mean you don't have a place? You have a phone number.'

'Yeah, but, it's complicated, I'm staying with a friend –'

'You don't have your own room?'

'Sure I do,' he said, and regretted it. 'But –'

'What are you going to do, just leave me here?' There was something wavering in her voice which made James's insides go cold again.

'Of course not, we'll get in a cab, I'll take you back to your place, and I'll –'

'But I *can't go back to my place*.' She was definitely crying now.

'Why not?'

'I told you. It's complicated.'

'Oh boy.'

'Take me home with you.' She began rubbing his chest again and nibbling at his neck and hiccuping and crying, which was distracting.

'I'm sorry, Nicky, I'd love to, believe me, I'd really love to, but I can't, it's …' He stopped, wondering why exactly he couldn't take her home. Aside from the obvious awkwardness of presenting

Fiona and De Courcy – awaking them, in fact – with a visitor who looked and behaved like a climactic scene in a drive-in slasher movie (which was something he couldn't diplomatically explain to Nicola at the moment) he knew there was some other reason. He knew that he had repeatedly, even in his limited sexual experience, *proved* to himself that to sleep with very drunk people one didn't know very well, especially when very drunk oneself, was an extremely not good idea, but for the moment he couldn't remember what the proof was.

'Okay,' she said loudly, sobbing. She disengaged herself entirely, straightened her dress. 'I'll have to go to Etobicoke. I *hate* going there. Just take me to a subway.' She wiped at her eyes.

'Why on earth Etobicoke?'

'My mother's.'

He sighed, adding a twenty-five-dollar taxi ride onto his carefully scrutinized expense account. 'Okay. I'll get in a taxi with you.'

'No!' she almost shouted. 'Leave me alone!' She turned and took a great stride towards the street, but must have slipped, because there was a flapping of fabric and a screech.

'Nicky!' he shouted, trying to grab her before she toppled and collapsed with a bony thump at his feet. He crouched down and took her hand. She was on her knees.

'Ow,' she said, sounding genuine.

'Jesus. You fell in the broken glass. Are you okay?'

'Ow.'

He got her to her feet and they hobbled together out to the street, where she sat on the curb with cars passing inches from her. He sat with her and studied her knees, which were cut, but not badly. There didn't appear to be any glass in the cuts, just concrete and oil and blood. Her tights were torn up and bloody.

'I'll be fine,' she was saying, 'I don't need you to come with me. Take me to the nearest subway.'

He hailed a cab which would have killed her had he not stepped in front of it, waving his arms. He loaded her into it and tried to get in beside her but she pushed him out. The Rastafarian cabbie slowly turned to stare at her from under a bushel of dreadlocks. He said nothing for a few seconds.

'I don't *want* you to come with me.'

'Okay. That's okay. It's going to cost a lot, though, do you have the –'

'I'm taking the subway.'

'No, you're not. Here, here's forty bucks, okay, just take it, now give him an address.'

She folded her arms and sniffled.

'All I need,' said the cabbie in a gentle voice, 'is an address.'

She shook her head.

'Don't you know the address?'

'Just take me to the *subway*.'

Wearily, the cabbie looked at James, who was leaning in the open door, and said softly, 'She can't take the subway alone, mon.'

James sighed. He looked at Nicola, who was looking up at him. Her raccoon-like eye makeup was striping her cheeks in tear-tracks. Her lipstick was smeared. Her tights were ripped up and there was blood running down her shins. In a faint, high, teary voice, she said, 'Take care of me.'

He got in the cab, shut the door and gave the cabbie De Courcy's address.

The fire escape presented some difficulty, but he removed her shoes at the bottom, where she began to sing again, and then half carried her most of the way. She was fairly quiet until the very top, where she burst into a particularly raucous chorus – '*It's the* SPRING *and I'm in* LOVE ...' – and Elsie's light snapped on. He cursed and shushed her while he searched for his keys, but Elsie didn't appear; perhaps she was still searching for her housecoat when James shouldered the door open and dragged Nicola inside and slammed it behind her.

De Courcy was sitting alone at the kitchen table, staring straight ahead, his arms folded. The overhead light was on. He looked up at James and Nicola blandly, a question rather than surprise on his face. He looked pale and thin in the harsh light.

'Sorry, Dec.'

'For what?' Without rising, De Courcy held out a hand to Nicola. 'Nice to see you again, Miss Lickson.'

'Nice to see *you*.' She stumbled and sat heavily on De Courcy's lap. '*So FLY away LOVE, bring me blah BLAH boo* ...'

'Nicky, shhh, there are people sleeping.'

'Had a good dinner?' said De Courcy as if from a distance.

James realized he was holding Nicola's shoes. He put them on a chair. He noticed the bottle of bourbon on the table, the single glass. 'Working late? You okay?'

De Courcy said nothing, grimacing under Nicola's shifting weight. She slid off him and climbed onto a chair, where she stood, singing, '*Bring you baaaack, to my HEAART* ...'

'I'll make some tea,' said James, reddening. 'I think we have to calm down a little here.' He began opening cupboard doors. 'What did you do tonight?'

'*I'm an inVISible STAR in the NIGHT of your boom boom BOOM* –'

'Whoa!' said De Courcy.

James turned quickly to see him leap up; Nicola was standing on the table, her arms outstretched like an airplane, teetering on the edge. '*To my heaaart!*'

He rushed forward; the two of them caught her as she fell.

'Whoo!' she said, without much effort, when they had seated her again.

'Look,' said James, 'maybe we'll skip the tea. I'd better get her to bed.'

'Whatever,' said De Courcy dreamily, pouring himself another whisky.

'I'm going to sleep on the couch, if that's okay with you. She can have my room.' He hesitated. 'Dec?'

'Whatever.'

'This way, ma'am.' He took Nicola's hand and she followed him docilely into the dark living room, where she immediately sank onto the sofa.

'Come on Nicola,' said James gently, kneeling in front of her, 'you're waking everybody up, and you need to sleep. Please. Let's get you cleaned up, they probably have some stuff for your cuts in the bathroom –'

'My tights are ripped.'

'Yes. Take them off, and come into the bathroom and I'll put
some –'

'You have to give me a hand.' She raised her left leg straight out
in front of her, the toe pointed like a dancer's, and put her ankle on
his shoulder. Her toes brushed his cheek. She pulled up her skirt
to get at a stocking-top; he had a quick glimpse of shadowy thigh
and lace, a gust of perfume and body heat. Her ankle was warm
and solid on his shoulder. His body was reacting. He watched as
she rolled down one stocking to the knee; she winced as it reached
the ground-up skin. He reached out to help her get it past the
lacerated area, pulling it gently away from the skin as she moaned
a little.

When he had peeled off the stocking from her foot and thrown
it aside, she extended that leg and put the ankle on his other
shoulder. For a second he was caught there, his neck between her
ankles as if in some kind of wrestling grip. She giggled again, and
he couldn't help laughing too. Then she dropped the left leg to the
floor so they could work on that stocking.

When they had carefully peeled that off he sat still for a second,
her bare leg still cocked on his shoulder and his hand on the ankle,
feeling the pulse in it. He circled the other ankle with his other
hand.

He could just make out her eyes in the dim room, half closed
but looking straight at him. She was breathing rapidly. Abruptly,
he pushed off the leg and stood up. 'Come on in the bathroom.
We'll get that cleaned up.'

Sighing dramatically, she followed him into the brightness. He
made her sit on the rim of the bathtub with her dress hiked up and
he fussed with clean facecloths and water and mercurochrome and
Band-aids. She made no effort to help him, humming instead, but
not too loud.

He took her into his room and closed the door behind him in
case she started singing again. Once he had cleared a path to the
mattress and the clothes off it, she pushed past him and stood on
it.

'Okay,' he said, his hand on the doorknob, 'if there's anything
you need ...'

He stopped, because she was undoing the buttons all the way down the front of the dress. Her hair had come loose and was all over her shoulders and the tops of her breasts. In a faint voice, he said, 'Please don't do that.'

She pulled the dress open and it fell to the floor. The underwear's diaphanous qualities were no longer in question. Nothing was any longer in question. Tearing off his tie, he stepped towards her.

She stopped him with a foot on his chest. She had a strange smile. 'Aren't you going to seduce me?'

'Oh, boy, this isn't one of those master-slave things, is it?'

'*Oh*,' she said, taking the tie from his hands, 'well if you're *into* it, why didn't you tell me?'

'I'm not.'

She looped the tie around his neck and yanked it towards her. 'Not what? A master? Or a slave?' She jerked it again and he lost his balance and toppled forward; she fell onto his head and they collapsed at the centre of the bed.

'Ow,' he said, under her. Something had twinged in his neck as he went down; he twisted it now and a sharp stab went from his shoulder to his ear. 'Ow.'

'What happened?' She had him on his back now, was straddling him.

'I think I hurt my neck.'

She dropped her head to kiss his neck. Her hair swamped his face. 'Feel better?'

'I think.' He shifted his head again. 'Ow.'

She was unbuttoning his shirt. Her hair was tickling his nose. 'Let me know,' she said, her hands massaging his chest, 'if I hurt you.'

But he didn't.

'How long do you have to keep it on?'

'Just two weeks,' said James, turning stiffly from the waist to pick up his coffee mug. 'It's just a pulled muscle.'

Fiona eyed him suspiciously. 'How *exactly* did you do it?'

'I told you.' He wasn't looking at her. 'I was going down the fire escape in the morning and I tripped on –'

'Oh, yeah. Couldn't say butter if your mouth was full of it.'

'What?'

'It was the night the foghorn was here, wasn't it?'

'No, as I *said*, it was the next morning – the who?'

'The foghorn. The banshee. The screamer. Jam bottle Jesus but she's got a set of lungs on her. Or else you've got something damn special, Jimmy, some thundering technique you should think of patenting, because jumping *dynes*, you'd think she was at some amusement park, like on a roller coaster, or at least giving *birth*, Jimmy, wow, it was –'

'I'm sorry about that,' he muttered, his face burning.

'Don't be sorry, Jimmy, be proud. I was impressed. I wish I'd seen her. I didn't get a glimpse. Percy says she has hair like toxic waste.'

'Does he?'

'And you're sure it was the morning after, eh? Because I heard a hell of a lot of thumping and hollering, I thought, *holy*, someone's going to get hurt.'

He stood up and grimaced: the brace garotted him every time he moved. 'Look, I know it seems very funny, but it was a hell of a drag, let me tell you, spending the day in emergency. Four hours I waited. *Four hours.*'

'I know, Jimmy, I'm sorry.' She chuckled. 'I didn't mean to laugh,' she said, and laughed harder. 'Reminds me of the time we had to take Bucky's friend in after we went to the Load of Mischief on Atlantic Night and he got in a scrap and he got his lower lip bitten off.'

'Bitten off? Really?'

'Well, not entirely. Half of it. It was Wayne Arsenault, he can get crazy. It was a lucky thing, too, Buck found the rest on the ground, *damn* lucky thing, it just looked like a bit of bacon rind or chicken guts or a slug or something, it had dirt all over it because this was in the parking lot –'

'Ow. It hurts to laugh. Don't.'

'– but Bucky saw it right away and put it in his pocket and took it to the hospital so they could sew it back on.' Fiona sat back and laughed violently. 'But by the time we got there Bucky'd forgot he had it, he was reading a magazine in the waiting room, and he just remembered after they wheeled Donny in and he ran after them yelling HEY! HEY! and waving the thing in the air like a, like a ...' She was coughing and wheezing now, with tears in her eyes.

'Ow. Ow. Don't.'

'... Like a piece of bait.' She hacked and cried and spat. 'Ex*cuse* me. But you gotta laugh in this world. You just have to laugh.'

James did laugh, painfully, for some seconds.

'I'll have to take you there, one night.'

'Where? To emergency?'

'The Load. It's out in Downsview, but it's like a home away from home for people from back home, every Thursday anyway, with music and all, and everybody sings "Barrett's Privateers" and "The Island" and all, and we all have a good cry. It's a hoot.'

'If no one bites your lip off.'

'JESUS FUCK!' yelled Fiona, standing up and knocking her chair over. 'There she goes *again*, I've called the police *three times* now and do you think they'd as much as knock on her door?' She ran to the window that looked down into Mrs Pimentel's garden and began to talk obscenely to Mrs Pimentel and her extended family, quite loudly, James thought.

He said, 'I suppose they might be tied up with crack dealers and murderers and that sort of thing. Noise complaints in the middle of the day in this neighbourhood ...'

The phone rang, adding an interesting sort of bleating texture to the blanket or cloud of two car alarms, two hissing radio stations and more than one car stereo that enveloped them – a blanket that had been recently embroidered with the addition of construction noise, the hammering and powersawing connected to one of the garages in the alley, which had neatly burned down a few days before. James leaped onto the phone, stiff-necked and grimacing, and yelled, 'Hello?'

But it was only Buck for Fiona. As she took it there was a Gestapo-like rapping at the door. James raised himself and staggered over. He opened it, but there was no one on the deck. He looked around for a second, stepped forward to look at the fire escape, and tripped over a person standing right in front of him. 'Oh, hello, Elsie,' he said, reaching down and righting her, 'sorry.'

The landlady, in a brown-and-yellow tracksuit which might once have been a variant of white, was breathing heavily, patting down her hair and staring up at him with an expression James had only ever seen in televised professional wrestling. Her eyes were a good three feet lower than his; he felt like kneeling, as you would talk to a child, but thought better of it when she barked in a strong voice, 'Who are you?'

'I'm James, James Willing, a friend of De Courcy, of Piers, remember? He mentioned to you I would be –'

'I see the girls you are bringing home.' She was shaking her head and waving a scaly finger.

'Ah. Yes. Well that was –'

'You no live here, you no pay rent, you make this place a *whore house.*' She pronounced the last two words with great distinctness, perhaps the result of some practice.

James opened his mouth and closed it again, collecting all his effort for resisting and erasing any of the forceful words that were rapidly presenting themselves for his immediate use.

'She is *drunk,*' continued Elsie with the same careful enunciation, 'and she dress like a *strips tease.*'

He opened his mouth again, having settled on a particularly pungent phrase, when he felt a hand on his shoulder.

'Good morning, Elsie,' said De Courcy. 'Lovely day. How are you?'

'Your friend bring home *girls.*'

'Is he? Oh, that must be his sister. Did you meet her? Charming girl. She's a –'

'She is *drunk*, I can't believe she make it up the stairs, she is falling down and yelling and screaming and –'

'She wasn't yelling and screaming *then*,' said James, in the spirit of frankness.

De Courcy squeezed his shoulder. 'She's a doctor, you know, Elsie. She works such long hours at the hospital. She must have been very tired.'

'A doctor?' Elsie's expression changed to one of confusion. 'A doctor?' she repeated, more weakly.

'Oh, yes, a specialist.'

'That young girls is a doctor?'

'There are many young girls like her, you know, these days, who are doctors,' said De Courcy. 'My friend James is very proud of her.'

'Oh yes,' said James.

'James is a doctor too,' said De Courcy, patting James's back.

James winced, having bitten an extra-large chunk off the inside of his cheek.

'You are doctor?' said Elsie, blinking.

'Now, about the rent,' continued De Courcy quickly, 'as I mentioned to you, James will be staying here for a few days longer, and so we'll add a small surcharge to the rent this month – say, twenty-five dollars? Just in case there is any inconvenience to you, you know, having all these extra people about.'

'Oh no,' she said, waving her arms in the same incomplete-pass gesture James had observed Mrs Pimentel make, 'no extra trouble, no no no no. A doctor.' She took James's hands in hers, and looked up at him with shining eyes. 'Doctor, you like perogies?'

'Do I like perogies?' said James, who had once caused a small hurricane of letters to the editor of *Edge* by writing that mucus-like gobs made entirely of soft white dough and soft white cheese were an acceptable substitute for food only in extreme cases of famine, drought or Polishness. 'I *love* perogies.'

'Good,' said Elsie, turning away and scurrying towards her door. 'I bring you perogies.'

'Thank you, Elsie,' said De Courcy, going back inside.

James stood for a second on the deck, breathing in the noise. He

129

squinted up at an area in the sky which was more yellow-white than brown-grey, vaguely circular in shape, indicating the location of the sun. It throbbed, a great oozing perogy in the sky.

Elsie was fumbling with her lock. She stopped and turned back towards James. Something clouded her face: the wrestler's expression, as if she remembered something. 'If she comes back,' she said throatily, 'I come out with *baseball bat*.' She disappeared into her apartment. James heard the snapping and slamming of numerous bolts.

He let out a large breath and went back inside. When he came into the living room, De Courcy was commentating. 'TROUBLE WITH THE NHL THESE DAYS,' he yelled, 'ALL THESE EURO-PEANS, TAKE A GUY LIKE SUNDIN — AND I WAS SAYING THIS LAST NIGHT, YOU REMEMBER, I'M THE ONLY GUY WHO SAYS THIS, YOU REMEMBER BACK IN CHICAGO —'

'Dec.' James slumped on the sofa beside Fiona. 'Did anybody call —'

'TALK ABOUT INTERFERENCE, NASLUND, I REMEMBER THE DAYS WHEN NASLUND AND ALL THOSE OTHER SWEDISH GUYS — WE HAVE SOME TAPE HERE, OKAY, ROLL THE TAPE, ROLL THE TAPE, OKAY, NOW WATCH NASLUND HERE, AND I WAS SAYING THIS BEFORE ...' He subsided suddenly and sat in the fake chair. 'What?'

'I'm waiting for that phone call from Boben's agent.'

'A cottage,' said De Courcy. 'That's what we need. Dock, lake, woods. You know anyone?'

James shook his head. 'I used to. My parents do.'

'There must be someone we can bug. How about Cruella? She have rich friends?'

'Who?' said James innocently.

'Your imaginative friend. Dear little Nicky. Nicky the Knife. Nicola Fear.'

'I don't know.'

'I'm going to call some people. I'm going to get on the phone.'

'No, you're not, as soon as Fiona's off I have to ...' James trailed off, noticing something. 'Why are you dressed like that?'

De Courcy looked down at his ensemble as if surprised. He

wore a denim shirt, unbuttoned, over a white T-shirt, and tight
jeans and heavy work boots, unlaced. 'What?'

'You look like one of my brother's friends, or a telephone repair-
man.'

'You think?' He grinned, and stood up, looping his thumbs in
his belt. 'Thank you, ma'am.' He began to dance, a sort of strip-
tease dance, with much pelvic thrusting and wiggling and jutting
of bum.

James giggled, because De Courcy was frowning and sticking
his tongue out the side of his mouth like a five-year-old in deep
concentration. Then he began to chant, '*Everybody* wuhks in the
*unner*ground c'mon *dance* to the *house*,' but then he was out of
breath so he had to stop. 'What do you think?'

'Buck says I should call the city,' said Fiona, hanging up. 'Noise
control bylaw people. He says they're the toughest.' She pulled the
ratty telephone book out from under the sofa. 'So how's the training going, Percy?'

'That's a good idea,' said James. 'They might send threatening
letters and things. What training?'

'I'm going to go for it,' said De Courcy. 'I joined the Y –'

'Again,' said James.

De Courcy closed his mouth.

'Sorry. Go on.'

'Haven't you heard?' said Fiona. 'Blue Collar Hunk of the year.
Right here.'

De Courcy was picking at the remains of his blue nail polish.
'Have to get this off, though.'

'Have you never seen it?'

'Seen what?'

'You should watch Janni Bolo more.'

'That's like the housewives' show?'

'I doubt she, I doubt they would be pleased to hear you call it
that.'

'Oh *no*,' said James with a warmth that surprised even him and
hurt his neck a little, 'I wouldn't want to offend the host or *producers* on the *Janni Bolo* show, I wouldn't want to malign the
intelligent viewers who happen to have nothing else to do with

their mornings than watch the Blue Collar Hunk of the Year Competition – I assume that's what we're talking about, is it, a competition you're going to enter? – because they're not all housewives, no, some of them are unemployed pseudo-students who would be better off buying a porn magazine but are too shy or embarrassed or uptight to –' James broke off because De Courcy had gone pale and taut and was looking away. 'I suppose you think it's a scream,' he said more gently.

'No I don't,' said De Courcy quietly. 'They look gorgeous and they have rock-hard muscles and I want to be one.' He left the room.

'It's true,' said Fiona. 'They come on the show and the studio audience goes wild. They dress up like construction guys, with boots and hard hats and all, and you get to see a little video of them at work, like one of them was an Italian baker and all through his video he keeps grinning at the camera and saying, 'Nobody has better buns,' and all the chicks scream and stuff. And then they come into the studio and do a little dance and take off their shirts, and then you vote. Some of them are babes.'

James sighed deeply. He closed his mouth and turned down the corners, then he half closed his eyes and blew out his cheeks, hoping for a general flattening effect. Then he made a glurping sound with his mouth, as if blowing bubbles. 'What am I?' he said, and glurped again.

'What?'

'No, wait.' He closed his eyes entirely and stretched his mouth farther, attempting to create jowls. He hunched his shoulders so his jowls puffed over the rim of his neck brace. 'Okay, now.'

'I don't know. What are you?'

'Dead grouper.'

'Dead what?'

'Grouper. It's a kind of fish. No, no, wait, better ...' He worked on the jowls more. 'Okay. Now what am I?'

'I give up.'

'Moribund Politburo member.'

'Moriwhat?'

'Never mind.' He opened his eyes and sighed again. He wished the phone would ring. Boben had never called back; now his agent was trying to set up the interview. And he felt bad about De Courcy. 'What's he going to do about his accent? For this competition?'

'Oh, I'm giving him lessons. I'm trying to get him to say, "*Thet little stir-fry*".'

James laughed. 'Has he really been working out?'

'Almost every day.'

'I suppose I should have noticed. And I should have thanked him for saving me with Elsie.'

'He's actually getting some definition.'

'*De Courcy*? Lord, what is the world coming to.'

'Buck's been showing him some exercises.'

'Aha.' James smiled. 'Okay, what's this?' He puckered his lips and turned his nose up.

The phone rang. 'That'll be Buck again,' said Fiona, holding out her hand for the receiver.

'Faster pussycat,' said James into the phone.

There was a pause. 'Excuse me?' A woman's voice.

'Sorry about that, it's James Willing here. Hello?'

'Oh, Mr Willing, I'm glad to have got hold of you. I've managed to set up that interview with Mr Boben. He wants you to come and visit him at his home.'

'In Burlington?'

'Yes, in Burlington.' She paused. 'Is that a problem for you?'

'No, I just wanted to hear you say it.' James grinned at Fiona.

'I'm sorry?'

'Never mind. When and where?'

She gave him the details – this Saturday, one o'clock – and the directions.

James hung up. 'Kill kill,' he said quietly, 'you ditz. Kill kill is the line.' He dialled Nicola's number.

■ CHAPTER ELEVEN

'Exit off North Service Road, god help us. Sounds scenic, doesn't it? North Service road. You'd think he would live in a place with no road at all, a house called Atakatuk. Agogagog. Or at least Haliburton House, Champlain House …'

'The Cedars,' said Nicola, her silver boot on the dashboard.

'Yeah, The Cedars. No, The Birches. Shit, is that the exit?'

'Wait.' She unfolded the map on her lap.

'Too late now.' James tried to relax his grip on the wheel. All three westbound lanes were travelling at a hundred and twenty kilometres an hour, with a good five feet between each bumper. He was in the middle lane, a truck like a high-rise on either side and in front and behind, a sort of high-speed canyon. He couldn't see the signs until he was underneath them. Turning his head was a problem with the brace on. 'Air conditioning okay?'

'No. Too much. Okay, we're fine, it's not for a while. You better start to change lanes though.'

'Terrific. Change lanes. I don't really have that option.' He fumbled with the controls on the air conditioning with a certain disappointment. It wasn't often he got to drive a car, let alone a sort of rocket ship with air-locks and computers like this one; he wanted to use the air conditioning. It had put his stressed Visa card well and truly over its limit, but no one seemed to have checked, and he was sure he could invoice *Glitter* for it before the bill came in. Although he should perhaps have checked that too.

He glanced over at Nicola, who now had both silver boots on the dash, her silver miniskirt so high as to be non-existent. He was uneasy about this outfit: the boots lacing up to the knee, the thigh-high white stockings, the cropped T-shirt with the word 'Baby' in pink. It was pretty obvious that Nicola hadn't been to Burlington or any place like it for a while, perhaps ever. He postponed thinking about how she would appear to a sixty-year-old Canadian writer.

'So you think this guy is any good?' she said.

'Good?' James chewed on the inside of his cheek. 'Good.' He sighed. 'You know … it's hard to explain, but it's not really about that. These guys.'

'What guys?'

He made circling gestures in the air. 'Things have changed now. You may be too young to remember. Nowadays you can win big contracts and even awards and prize money if you write big fat books about starving people in other parts of the world, or the Holocaust or something. You know.'

'You mean like novels?'

'Yeah. Novels are like movies now. They can't be about things here.' He waved out the window.

'I can't say I read them much,' Nicola murmured, turning to the window. The power lines rose and dipped along the side of the highway.

'No. Neither do I. Apparently lots of people do. Anyway. It didn't use to be like that. It used to be that you could get a lot of recognition by writing about Canada, as long as it was about small towns and nature.'

'Really?'

'Yeah. You could have canoes and the prairies or, also, sad women, very sad women who were fat or whose husbands had left them or something. There was a lady who wrote about fucking a bear, which was like a union with the land. There was a lady who wrote about mystical experiences she had at a cottage in northern Ontario. I was never sure what that was about. They were very important at one time, very stern and important. I had to study them in school. Anyway, he was one of them. He concentrated on the prairies. He wrote a lot of books about the prairies, with a lot of native names, and wise native people, like there's a young boy with an Ojibway grandmother who will teach him the ways of the forest, sort of thing, and there's a lot of history, like a lot of the Riel rebellion for example.'

'The what?'

'History. And there's a lot of disaster, on the prairies, like people having to rebuild their sod houses after floods and so on.'

They drove on the humming highway for a while.

Then Nicola said, 'So you haven't answered my question.'

'What question?'

'Do you think he's any *good*?'

'Oh. The thing is…. it's not, it doesn't matter. Its about our history. It's *important*. So it doesn't matter if I think it's good or not.'

'Okay. So it doesn't matter. So I'm asking you. What you think. Do. You. Think. It's. *Good*.' She slapped her bare thigh.

James paused for a long moment. He was nosing ahead of a transport truck, preparing to slip back into its lane. He was getting the hang of the rocket. It glided smoothly across lanes. He accelerated, decelerated, felt he was cutting through highway like a ship with a sharp prow. The competing lanes fell away on either side. He said, 'There's one Boben book, I think it's *Cold Season*, or maybe it's *Comfort of Winter*, which ends with the line, "a story which Canadians must never tire of telling." What do you think of that line? A story which Canadians must never tire of telling.'

She shrugged. 'I have no idea.'

'I'll tell you what you think of it. You don't give a shit. I'll tell you what I think of it. I don't give a shit either. But I also think it's the worst bullshit I've ever heard. I think,' he said, accelerating, 'that Ludwig Boben is a fucking asshole.'

'That's it,' said Nicola, pointing, 'North Service Road, quick.'

Sixteen Willowdale Crescent was a bungalow with a driveway and an attached garage; it looked much like the house James had grown up in. He helped Nicola unload the tripod and metal boxes, which possibly contained lights, although he didn't like to ask, and carried her large bag up the curved path to the front door. He rang, and heard barking. He couldn't see through the frosted glass on the diamond pane. They waited for some seconds and he began to sweat tidally. He felt embarrassed by the thick wad of the brace around his neck. He could hear a lawnmower in the distance. There were no cars on the street.

The door opened and a dog barked at them, held by a small woman with short grey hair and glasses with purple plastic frames who said, 'Hi, hello, hello, come in,' without looking at them. She wore stretchy purple slacks and a sweatshirt with a frog on it. They came into the hallway, which smelled of cooking and had clear plastic non-slip runners over the carpet. There was a green soapstone sculpture on a side table, a hunter and a seal. There was a television playing loudly in another room. James recognized the screaming of "The Price Is Right". At least it was cool inside. The dog plunged its snout into James's crotch.

'Ookpik!' said the woman, 'Ookpik, stop it! He's all right, really, just friendly. *Aren't* you a naughty dog?' She bent, pulling the dog's head towards her by the ears. 'Aren't you a naughty dog? Yes? Yes you *are! Yes*! Yes you *are*! Would you mind taking your shoes off?'

'Well,' said Nicola. She was looking down at her platform boots.

'Of course,' said James, bending.

'These are kind of hard to get off,' said Nicola, 'and I need them for height. When I'm shooting.'

'Oh,' said the woman. She released the dog and put one hand to her mouth. Her eyes were darting towards the TV room and back. 'Well. *You're* the photographer?'

James busied himself with his shoes, bending stiffly from the waist so as not to twist his neck.

'May I look around?' said Nicola, pushing Ookpik away. The dog was particularly interested in what was under her skirt.

'It's just that ...' Mrs Boben started to move towards the kitchen, clutching both hands together at the level of her throat, and hesitated in the doorway. She was looking at the silver boots and the plastic mats. 'Ookie, come here. He's in the den.' She fingered the collar on her sweatshirt, shook her head as if to clear it of hovering insects, then turned and disappeared into the kitchen. 'I've made some chili for lunch,' she called.

Nicola screwed up her face. '*Lunch*!'

James whispered, 'Listen, we'll have to eat it if she's gone to the–'

'Fuck *off*, dog.' She booted Ookpik deftly and hard in the centre of the chest, and he fell over, righted himself and began barking again.

Mrs Boben's face reappeared in the doorway. 'Would you like lunch first?'

'Oh, you needn't have done that,' said James. 'That's very kind. Perhaps we should get the interview over with first.'

Nicola was opening the metal boxes and unrolling orange electrical cord, throwing warning glances at Ookpik, who was edging closer. 'Could you show me where the outlets are?'

'Outlets?' said Mrs Boben faintly, her eyes wide.

'We'll find them,' said James. 'Mr Boben is in there?' He pointed to the doorway where the television seemed to be loudest.

She nodded. 'He's in the den.' She appeared to be backing up. 'If he gives you any trouble, you give me a shout.' She disappeared.

James raised his eyebrows at Nicola.

'Trouble?' she whispered.

'I have no idea.' He walked towards the den and stood in the doorway. Boben was asleep in an easy chair facing the TV. His face was red, his mouth open. There was a thread of saliva between his open lips. He had a grey beard and wispy grey hair. He wore a cardigan and slippers. James said as loudly as he could without shouting, 'Hello, Mr Boben.' He walked closer. 'Mr Boben?'

Nicola giggled. She began setting up lights.

James touched him lightly on the arm, then shook his shoulder. There was a half-full bottle of rye on the side table, and a glass with cloudy fingerprints or lip prints. James looked around the room: more soapstone, some big prints that looked like totem pole designs, bold black and white lines, birds with big beaks. James wanted to call them Inuit but realized with a surge of panic that he didn't really know it they were Inuit or what. He had a vague memory of school trips to art galleries where they had seen Haida art. Perhaps they were Haida. He should find out more about this stuff if he was going to do more Canadian writers. There was a bright print like a cartoon for children over the mantelpiece; it showed, in solid colours with black outlines, natives of some sort in parkas with fur-lined hoods on a snowy plain, making igloos. There were strips of colour in the sky that were probably the northern lights. And there was a large framed pen-and-ink drawing of a shed and some fishermen that was boldly signed 'Blackwood'.

He walked into the kitchen and said, 'Excuse me, but I can't seem to wake him up.'

'Turn the TV off.'

James went back into the den. Before touching the TV he got close to the cartoon-print and read the signature: Ted Harrison. 'Shit,' he said softly, 'Don't know about that, either.' One of the bird drawings was signed, 'Morrisseau'. He knew that one. He turned the sound down on the TV.

Boben's eyes jerked open. 'What the fuck?' he said in a clear voice.

'Hi. I'm here for the interview, James Willing? This is Nicola Lickson, the photographer.'

'Oh yeah,' said Boben, struggling to rise, then sinking back into the chair. His eyes narrowed as he took in Nicola. She smiled and he smiled back.

James pulled up another chair. He took out his tape recorder and put it on the side table. He consulted his notebook. 'First, thanks so much for agreeing to an interview, Mr Boben.'

Boben said nothing. He squinted, apparently trying to focus on Nicola, who was bending, her back to them.

'It's kind of a big break for both of us, since *Glitter* is usually not –'

'Call me Don,' said Boben distractedly. He whistled faintly. James glimpsed at Nicola, bending over a silver box, her bum in the air. The skirt had risen to reveal a bunched triangle of white underwear. Boben clucked his tongue.

'Don? I thought your first name was Ludwig?'

The writer waved a hand. 'Nobody calls me that. May I offer you a drink?' he said in his strong actory voice. He was looking at Nicola.

'No, thanks,' said James.

'Yes, please,' said Nicola, studying a light meter. 'Could you sit up a little, please? Turn this way.'

James had to go to the kitchen for more glasses. When he returned, Boben appeared to have fallen asleep again.

'Prop his head up, would you?' said Nicola.

'For Christ's sake. Let's do the interview first, okay?' He poured them two small whiskies. 'Mr Boben? Don?'

Boben's eyes opened startlingly. 'She's cute, isn't she? I bet she'd …' He hissed suddenly, like a cat. '*Momma*.'

'Sorry. Let's begin with your childhood, and then your early career. You were born near Medicine Hat in –'

Boben picked up the remote control and started changing channels. 'Jays game somewhere here.'

James looked at the TV. He waited for a moment. 'Jays haven't been quite the same without Molitor, eh? And Alomar.'

Boben jerked his eyes towards him. He appeared surprised at what he saw; the eyes widened, then narrowed again, as if he were seeing James for the first time. 'What d'you do to your neck?'

'Oh,' said James. 'Nothing. I fell on a staircase, outside my apartment, where I'm staying, there's this very steep ...'

Boben wasn't listening.

'I was saying, the Jays haven't been quite the same, without –'

'Never the same,' muttered the old man, his voice losing its stagy qualities. '*I've* never been the same.'

'No? Since what?'

Nicola came closer to the chair, holding the camera in her hands, snapping quickly. As she bent forward, the scoop neck of her T-shirt fell away from the tops of her breasts. Boben and James both took in the lacy top of her bra.

Boben, alarmingly, began flicking his tongue in and out at her, flecking his beard with spittle. He was also wiggling his eyebrows up and down, rapidly. For a second, James thought he was having some kind of seizure, then he realized it was some kind of panting-like-a-dog act. Then, suddenly, he sat up and roared, 'You call that a skirt? Call it a hairband, more like.' He reached out and caught the hem of her skirt, but Nicola slapped his hand away without pausing. 'Remember that?' he said to James, subsiding. 'Hairbands and, what do you call ...' His voice grew indistinct, his eyelids fluttered. 'Those skirts and sweaters, sets, sweater sets. And you had shiny shoes and ...'

'Could you put your chin in your hands?' said Nicola.

'Nicky, please, we have to concentrate on the interview right now. It's too distracting.'

She sighed. 'It's no good anyway. I'm going to have to turn on the lights.'

James turned back to Boben, who had found the baseball game.

He cleared his throat. 'Okay. Let's talk about the last book. When exactly did you write it?'

Boben laughed raspingly. 'My last book! Nineteen seventy-four. I think.'

'I mean the new one. *Fields of Glass.*'

The laugh again. Boben reached a shaky hand down for his glass. 'Around there, I think.'

James paused. 'I'm not sure I follow you. You wrote *Fields of Glass*, your last book, in nineteen seventy-four?'

'I have no idea. Around there somewhere.'

James glanced at Nicola, who was fiddling with a crackling sheet of blue plastic.

'That fellow in Regina,' muttered Boben, 'fellow with the long hair?'

'I'm not sure,' said James. 'This fellow –'

'Publisher. Wanted a new book. I said I haven't written any-thing since…. Jesus Christ, now, look at all the signs around the boards. You ever wonder why they have those company names all over the boards?'

James looked at the baseball game. 'I think they're advertising.'

Boben took a jerky sip from his glass.

'So this publisher asked if you had anything new, and you said you had this book –'

'Advertising, eh? I remember this one advertisement, it must have been in the sixties or maybe even earlier. You wouldn't even have been born yet, eh sweetheart? They used to wear their skirts short then, too. So short you could –'

'Listen,' said James. 'So you had this book lying around? That you hadn't published yet? And the fellow was Ron McCormack, from Outbuilding Press, in Regina?'

'I had it lying around. Sure. They never wanted it back when I was at … I never liked it, really. So he fixed it up again and away you go. I hear it's got a lot of attention.' Boben drained his glass, fumbled for the bottle.

James refilled his glass, handed it to him and sat back, puffing out his cheeks. He checked his tape recorder. 'So *Fields of Glass* isn't really your most recent book. You must have finished it before you wrote –' He checked his notebook. '*The Owl Man*. And *Blizzard*.'

'Soap, I think it was. Or some disgusting stuff.'

'What?'

'The advertisement. I think it was soap, but I remember it was called Lyril. Remember that? What a name! Lyril! I remember the girl, too, pretty girl, reminds me of....' He was struggling to get up, his hands scrabbling on the fabric of the armchair. His mouth was open and he was looking at Nicola. James didn't help him up.

'Here we go,' she said. *Phuf* and the lights came on; the television went off. 'Oops.'

'Come here a second, sweetheart,' said Boben, heaving to his feet.

Mrs Boben called from a distance, 'Did something happen to the power?'

Nicola had her back to them, hands on her hips, considering the lights. Boben lurched towards her.

'Nicky.' James stood up.

Boben grabbed a fistful of her skirt and yanked it up and she whirled around. 'Hey!' She stepped backwards and Boben tripped over a cord and fell heavily, bringing down a light.

'All right,' said Mrs Boben, in the doorway. 'All right, dear.' She and James helped him up and they got him back in his chair, everyone breathing heavily.

'Bulb's gone,' said Nicola, kneeling.

'He doesn't know what he's doing,' said Mrs Boben softly.

'I can see that,' said James, less softly.

'You come and talk to me after,' said the wife. 'I'll give you all the information.' She disappeared again.

James pulled his chair even closer to Boben and sat. He studied the face, the network of capillaries. The writer was now truly asleep or unconscious. James's skin itched under the neck brace. He worked a finger under it and scratched. He said, 'Mr Boben. Don. My tape recorder is still running. You're telling me you haven't written anything since the mid-seventies, and you are now in an alcoholic stupor most of the time, is that correct?'

Boben grunted; his hand fluttered.

'Would you agree that most of your work is simple-minded and sentimental?'

He got another grunt, and Nicola giggled.

'And that you are now a complete has-been and washup? Thank you. Now, Mr Boben, *Don*, Donny, I would like to ask you something very important. Pay attention.'

'James, maybe you could put his hands together on his chest, and prop his head up, tilt it upwards. Then even if his eyes are closed it looks like he's thinking.'

James arranged the hands, and crouched behind the chair, one hand on the back of Boben's head. The neck was dry and scaly.

'Tuck your foot in,' said Nicola, 'it's showing. Head down.'

James made himself small and held his breath, while Nicola took a series of shots of the contemplative writer. With his fingertips straining, James tilted the heavy head to one side and then to the other, as Nicola directed. His hand grew tired, supporting the weight of the head, and his legs and neck were crampy, scrunched behind the chair. His own head was pressed into the nubbly back of the chair, which smelled of bacon and cigarettes. He suppressed a sneeze. The more he held Boben's scaly head, the more he had the unpleasant sensation that his fingers were dislodging flakes, and that the flakes might be falling, behind the chair, onto his own head. But he couldn't look up, because Nicola kept shouting, 'I can still *see* you!' And also because he was afraid he would get some in the eye.

'That should do it.' She began packing up.

James let the head loll and stood up. He brushed himself off and shook out his legs. 'Now.' He sat beside him again and said intently, 'Now. My question is. And my tape recorder is still running. Do you or do you not think the Toronto Maple Leafs have a shot at the playoffs?'

Boben's head started; his eyes and hands fluttered. 'Leafs!' he shouted. 'Leafs haven't been the same without Gilmour!' His eyes grew wide as he remembered Nicola, now standing with her back to them, and then, unfortunately, bending again. Boben's eyes were narrowing again, his lips working as if he were concentrating on saying something else. 'Sweaters,' he mumbled. Then, excitedly, 'Twin sets! That's what it was, the sweater sets. And skirts ...'

Nicola was backing up towards them, coiling a length of electrical cord. Her platform boot caught a loop of wire.

'Nicky!' called James, but it was too late; she had fallen square into Boben's lap.

'Uff,' he said.

'Oop,' she said, swatting his hand off her bare thigh. 'Sorry.'

'Don't go,' he whined. She was off him, standing, brushing at herself as if covered in lint. James couldn't avoid the impression that she was covered in dandruff.

Boben was still stretching his trembling hand out towards her. His voice had gone low and throaty again. 'So short, sweetheart –'

'You done?' said James.

'Yup,' said Nicola, flouncing away.

'So short, you could see a ... little string if they had a ...' The scaly head fell forward.

'I would say he's trying to understand the vastness of the natural environment,' said Mrs Boben, clearing her throat. She took a quick drag on her cigarette, a sip at her Coke. 'And ... put, to fathom the unfathomable. Put, he's trying to reconnect to the vastness that dominates our collective imagination.' She took another drag.

James scribbled this in his notebook. He looked up at Nicola, dreamily chewing chili and staring at the fridge magnets, then out the window at the bird feeder, the thermometer. They were in the kitchen. Boben was asleep again, in the other room; he had not budged from his chair. 'Would you say that Elias Mariner represents your rejection, I mean the author's rejection, of the mundane? I mean the daily routine of the city and so on, the lack of romance in his suburban origin, and so on?'

'Yes, of course Mariner is the author, or the way the author would like to be. Don would say ...'

Another long drag, her eyes on the ceiling.

'Don would say, Mariner is like me in that we both see ourselves as apart, as resisting. There are very few men left who refuse to participate in the relentless ... who are truly independently minded, and not afraid to ... of a truly passionate spirituality, inspired by nature.' She paused, cleared her throat and said, 'Mariner is my way of breaking free of the tyranny of the Eurocentric mindset, from the tyranny of the overpass and the television. Would you like some more chili?'

James was scribbling furiously. 'Thank you, Mrs Boben. Thank you very much.'

James wrote for three days in his little room. At the end of the first day he took his neck brace off because it was too hot and itchy. Nicola didn't call, and he didn't call her.

His rural roots evident in his choice of dwelling, sternly apart from the cellphones and breakfast meetings of urban. Steadfastly refusing the shrill hurly burly of. Framed by the majestic landscapes of David Black-wood. Of Ted Harrison. Or Whatsit Kurelek (*CHECK*). Framed by the spirituality of Norval Morrisseau and the mystery of native ritual objects, the artist contemplatively

He refused to drink wine with De Courcy, who was at the gym most of the time anyway. He called the police twice, when taking breaks, to complain about the noise from the neigh-bours. The police said they would 'swing by' if they had a car available.

After long silence. The writer remains undisturbed by. Unexcited by the massive hype apparently provoked by sheer public adulation of. Boben's placid. Boben's contemplative. Boben's serene indifference to. Boben's profound calm in the face of searching media attention is not unlike majesty.

He allowed himself a pizza slice every four hours. His neck ached, and he grew used to not turning his head much. Buck and Fiona came and went, bouncing basketballs. On the second after-noon he heard Fiona's whimper in the room next door, long breathy gasps, then a series of high 'ohs'. He put on his head-phones and turned up the volume.

Are there still places on earth where community? Where the twin strands of community and individualism are inextricably? Can one not see traces of the writer's Germanic roots in the fierce discipline of Lars Thormund, the hero of? Boben admits, 'Elias Mariner is like me in that we both see ourselves as apart, as resisting.' 'The tyranny of the television and the overpass.'

He wrote three drafts, which shrank from 5,000 to 1,200 words. He called City Hall and asked about noise bylaws, and they agreed to send him a formal complaint form.

It was near seven o'clock on the Tuesday. He wrote,

As if the injunction, 'A story Canadians should never tire of telling,' were directed, mantra-like, at the story-teller himself. A story-teller we will never tire of hearing.

He hit save and stood up. He yelled, 'Book him!', and winced at the pain in his back.

He ran a spell-check, adding the words 'mantra', 'yuppified,' 'zingy', 'deconstructionist', 'unforgivingly', 'brutalist' and 'élitism' to the computer's lexicon. He turned on the printer, hit print, and it began shuddering and spewing with the grating screech that always made him feel intense relief and sleepiness.

He hit his forehead three times on the doorjamb, enough to feel it but not really hard. He spun an imaginary turntable with each hand and chanted, 'I'm a hard-core D.J., hard-core crew! Whistle posse, CAN WE HAVE SOME NOISE IN THE HOUSE!'

He called Nicola and left a message.

Hey, Nicola, it's James, just wondering, ah, how's it going, how's the developing coming, I'm just about to fax the piece off, tomorrow morning I'll fax it off, so I'm just wondering if you're done, if you've arranged a courier and all that. So, ah, give me a call, give me a call one way or the other. Hope everything's okay. Okay. Okay then. Call me as soon as you can, okay? I like to be sure of everything, you know. Okay. Bye.

He peeled off his T-shirt and unrolled a new one from his bag. He put on deodorant and went into the hall, stretching. His neck

burned and his arms had pins and needles. He slowly rotated his
head with a crunching sound in his ears. His vision seemed unusually sharp, as if everything in the house was outlined in fine black.
He felt sleepy and jumpy and thirsty. He stood for a long time at
the kitchen window, looking at the courtyard, listening to the
printer ratcheting out paper. A single image was forming in his
head, like a slow rendering in pixels. It was of a overwide and over-
tall and cold glass with mist on it and an amber liquid striated
with very, very, very fine bubbles within.

The door opened and Buck and Fiona brought themselves and
their clothing and their equipment in with much sound and movement and olfactory texture.

'A spectacular melding of,' muttered James, watching. 'A
sense-dazzling array of.'

'How you doing, man?' said Buck, pumping his hand.

'Jimmy, are you ready?' She unloaded a fluorescent knapsack
full of slab-like books and a pair of rollerblades onto the table.

He had to think for a moment. 'Fiona,' he said finally, 'I. Am.
Ready.'

'Good.'

'Right on,' said Buck, kicking his gym bag into the living room.
'WHOO-EE!' He swung his U-lock at the end of his arm.

'I'll take a quick shower,' said Fiona.

James watched Buck weighing the bicycle lock in his hand, and
asked, 'What am I ready for?'

'You know,' said Buck, raising the lock up to his eye level, 'you
could really hurt someone with this.'

'Yes, you could.'

'*Really* fucking hurt someone.'

'Yup.' James rubbed his eyes. 'Where are you going?'

'Where are *you* going? Where are *we* going, more like. What
night is it, James?'

James thought for a moment. 'Tuesday.'

'And what night is Tuesday night?'

'Buck, this is way too difficult for me right now.'

'Only the most funnest night of the week,' called Fiona, slamming the bathroom door.

'Tuesday night,' said Buck, 'at the Load of Mischief, is a load of a party.'

'Oh, is tonight, is this the Maritime thing?'

'Atlantic night at the Load of Mischief, and you don't want to be a herman and stay home.' Buck lowered his voice. 'Hooters R Us.'

'What?'

'Hooterville.' Buck was throwing the lock in the air and catching it. 'It's like seventy percent female. It's like every homesick nurse and dental assistant and legal secretary ever left Bumfuck Newfoundland to look for a husband up here goes to Atlantic Night, to listen to "The Island" and have a good cry. It's total hooterville.'

James smiled. 'I thought you weren't single, Buck.'

'Hey, I can look, can't I? And you ...'

James thought for a minute, about making a last-ditch effort to avoid getting extremely drunk immediately. He was leaving the next day for Munich. 'I don't know. I should take a nap, get something to eat.'

'You can eat there. Wings, discs, everything.'

James thought with nausea about another pizza. 'I don't think so, Buck. I don't really know the songs or anything, and I don't know if I want to go all the way to Downsview and –'

Buck leaned his face close. 'No, listen, you do not want to miss this, man. We're talking wall-to-wall *fuck*.'

'Well, you know, legal secretaries aren't really my...' He trailed off. He would have to get up early for the bus, reread the article before he faxed it. 'I shouldn't, really.'

'What a herman. What a fucking howie. You are a dorb, you know that? You are a total dorboid. You rot my bag.'

Fiona was singing in the shower, '*Step we gaily on we go, heel for heel and toe for toe ...*'

'Do I have time to take a shower after her?'

'Don't bother. Stinks in the Load anyway.'

James dozed in the back of Buck's blue Chevette. He leaned his head on the back speaker under the McMaster University decal on the rear window, so that the letters were shadows on his face in the setting sun. When he opened his eyes he saw highways, over-passes, long factory outlets. He closed them again.

They were stopped in a vast parking lot full of cars. Fiona and Buck were slamming the car doors and yelling at him to get out. They were walking towards another long warehouse with blank walls, some kind of corrugated white material, broken up only by a doorway and a sign. There was already a queue.

Inside was dark and cool and smelled of beer. It sprawled as far as James could see, descending to dance floors and secondary bars all around. There were television monitors everywhere, each showing a different sport, and long bars with rows of draft levers. There were a few wagon-wheel chandeliers left from some previous incarnation, and new fishing nets on the walls with cork floaters. They had to get past a monolithic bouncer in a green T-shirt that said 'the LOAD of MISCHIEF' and had a shamrock and a thistle on it, who asked them all for ID, including James, and then through a crush around a similarly mammoth red-haired waiter in a similar T-shirt, who held a vast tray packed with full glasses of beer. A lot of guys yelled, 'Hey, Cud!' at Buck and hit him on the back and he hit them back. Everyone was holding up fingers to say how many beers they wanted. Buck pushed his way through and handed Fiona four and James four and came away with four himself. They carried these, spilling, to a table where Buck arranged his in a straight line pointing from his right hand to the centre of the table. Fiona did the same.

'I can't drink four,' said James. There were girls with long hair and tight T-shirts everywhere.

'Cheers,' said Fiona. 'Fasten your seatbelts. There's Maureen McKendrick, that's Tommy's sister. MAUREEEN!'

Buck nudged him. 'What I tell you.'

'CUD, MAN!'

'Don-NEE!'

The beer was icy. 'Phew,' said James. 'That one went fast. Shall we order some wings?'

'Wings suck here.'

'Do they rot your bag?'
'Order a disc. I'll get it.'
'No more pizza.'
'It's the only thing. Get Ceri over. CERI!'
'How are you *now*?' said Maureen. She wore a very tight white T-shirt.
'I am *great*,' said James.
'Race you,' said Buck, lifting his glass.

Then James was standing in the washroom at the urinal, leaning his forehead against the cool wall. When he had finished urinating, which seemed to be about half an hour later, he pulled back and read the graffiti.

> *We ARE the NuTTers From MONCtoN!*
> *Karma Coma*
> *More bandwidth to the backbone!*
> *Tina has a big* (something scratched out).

Under this someone had written: *How wuold you 'know'?* He wondered what Tina had that was big. Then he peered closely at a line written in clear capitals: *GO HOME DAD, YOU'RE DRUNK.*
He shivered. The air conditioning was too high in the washroom. He realized he was alone at the row of urinals. He fished out his last HelioPoint and wrote on the wall, *My heart aches and a drowsy numbness*
He heard the door swing open and he stuffed his pen away.

The band didn't start till late. James had to lean very close to Maureen to hear her once they started playing, especially since Buck and Fiona were singing at their table and pounding their beer glasses. 'Until they stopped calling it Human Resources,' Maureen was saying. 'Now they call it Restructuring.' She shrugged. 'But I'm happier at the Commerce than I was at Scotiabank. I travel around, do all the downsizing at all the branches.'
'The department of restructuring,' said James. 'The department of perestroika. At the Bank of Commerce.' He was watching two

girls with long brown hair dance. They had thin summer dresses and black parade boots with heavy white socks and they were laughing and swinging each other around and their hair was flying. It made him sad for some reason, and then he thought of the girls he had gone to high school with whom he had had such desperate crushes on and this made him sad too. Then he thought of Nicola and how silent she had suddenly become during their strange night together. After he'd finally got her to lie down and relax and stop twisting his arm or pulling his hair. And she'd gone limp and let him come inside her and then she had stiffened up and gone silent. He bit deeply into the inside of his cheek.

'Well,' said Maureen, 'you are different, that's for sure. Oh, I love this one.' She rocked her head back and forth and sang, *'When the boys of Killybegs come rolling home ...'*

James turned to the guy with the plaid shirt and the funny voice who had joined them. 'Cheers, Timmy.'

'Cheers bud, forget your name,' said Timmy, and they drank.

'James,' said James. 'And this is Maureen. She's from Inverness, and has a very tight shirt on.'

'I know Maureen,' said Timmy. 'I grew up with her. In fact, we used to be married.'

'Timmy. Timmy.' James pounded him on the back a couple of times, as he had seen Buck do. 'You're the one in diapers, right?'

'Yupper.'

'Big time diapers, like Huggies or Pampers or something. You're the marketing guy in diapers, am I right?'

'Absolutely right.' Timmy grinned and tugged on his red beard. He had a high-pitched voice and was probably gay, although it seemed strange in here.

'Mind like a steel trap,' said James, tapping his temple. 'I remember everything Maureen has ever said.' He glanced again at her T-shirt and thought again of Nicola and the two girls dancing and didn't know what he wanted. 'She's the star of the County Down. The belle of Belfast City. Well, Timmy. You've come a long way from Inverness. *There'll be singin' in the town, when the boys of Killybegs come rolling home.'*

'I have, at that,' said Timmy softly. He was looking down at his beer.

'So have I, Timmy, so have I. That makes two of us. Would you believe I'm off to Munich tomorrow?'

'That right?'

'Munich Ont, though, Timmy. Munich Ont. All alone. And what will await me on my return?'

'Cheers.'

'Cheers.' James drank and rotated his head and noted that he felt no pain and that his neck was apparently healed, and then thought for a moment about diapers. 'So you're responsible for all those offensively, I mean *offensively* perky, ads with cute kids being funny and choosing their –'

'No, no,' said Timmy, wagging a finger sternly. 'That's Huggies. Huggies is upbeat fun. We're Pampers.'

'Oh. So what are Pampers?'

'Pampers are cleaner –'

'*Oh the year was seventeen seventy eight*,' roared Buck and Fiona together, standing up and knocking over two glasses.

'What?' yelled James at Timmy.

'I said, cleaner dryer babies of loving confident moms.'

'That's what you are?'

'We are cleaner dryer babies.'

'Cleaner dryer babies,' yelled James, lifting his glass.

'Of loving confident moms.'

'Right.'

'Cheers.'

'Come on, Jimmy,' yelled Fiona, pulling on his arm, 'time to dance.'

It was about half an hour later that the fight started. James didn't see it, even though he was right there on the dance floor, having found that he could sing at least the chorus of 'Out on the Myra'; he was in fact next to Buck and the guy, another plaid shirt: all of a sudden there were bouncers all around them, pulling the two of them apart and carrying them out. Fiona followed, bellowing and tugging on the arm of the one who was dragging Buck, and he kept brushing her off, like an insect, until he got angry and grabbed her too and dumped both of them in the parking lot.

By the time James had pushed through the crowd and got outside, Buck and the plaid-shirt guy were hugging and laughing. Buck had tears on his face and a bloody nose. 'Jesus H. Christ Tommy McCormack you son of a bitch,' he was yelling, 'you slugged me so fast I didn't have time to see it, but I got one good shot in before I went down.'

Tommy McCormack was laughing hard and loud, wiping at his mouth.

'I love you, Tommy McCormack, you filthy bastard!' Buck yelled, and they hugged again.

Fiona was sitting on a curb, singing, *'We are an island, a rock in the stream ...'*

James breathed in the polluted night air. There was a roar of highway nearby. He looked up and saw that most of the light in the parking lot was reflected from a huge white billboard with a row of spotlights under it: Alicia Montgomery's mammoth cleavage on a sea of snow. THE COLD COMES, said the billboard, in letters five feet high, AUGUST 2.

'I know,' muttered James.

His left knee began to tremble and he knew he had to sit down immediately. He sat heavily next to Fiona, who looked at him with shining eyes.

'I get all emotional,' she said in a choked voice.

James tried to smile, then put his head between his knees. There was a pain like a knife in his neck. He resolved to wear the brace all the next week.

'What's the matter with you? Jimmy, whatever is bugging you, drop it. Just relax. Have a little fun.'

He looked up, at Buck and Tommy and Maureen and Timmy, who had now come out and were all singing *'We are an island'* in the parking lot, under the billboard. He realized he had no idea where they were.

'I'm not very good,' said James hoarsely, 'at having fun.'

It wasn't until eight o'clock the next evening that he made it to
the bus station. He sat in a row of moulded plastic chairs, between
two old men with plastic bags and newspapers, in the hot sooty-
metal smell of bus exhaust. He tried not to breathe too deeply. In
his hair and clothes and lungs was invisible carbon monoxide like
evil spirits. There was a student sitting across from him, a girl, her
tight blond ponytail and maroon team jacket with the MLC logo
indicating that she was on her way to Munich too, to Martin
Luther College. But nobody would look at anyone else.

He put on his headphones and switched on the soundtrack. A
violin played: Shostakovich. It screeched and shuddered. For the
trip, he had this and a new Tavener choral piece and an old but
particularly violent techno collection that included pieces from
the notorious Deathrave CD; if you really couldn't concentrate on
anything, this would get your attention.

There was a bus at eight-fifteen. He had a feeling that if he
could just survive the next fifteen minutes, that if he could find
something to do with his brain until then, something to fill it
with or cover it with like White-Out, a Block command, delete
button, wipedisk C colon backslash all dot all, or just an *off*
switch, or failing that some all-absorbing activity such as simultaneous eating, music and masturbation – and still he had a feeling
that maybe even that wouldn't distract him now, maybe it had to
be out-and-out violence, maybe nothing short of vigorous and life-
threatening boxing would enable him to survive these next fifteen
minutes, for if he was left alone with himself and whatever disease
he seemed to have caught, apparently cholera and rabies at once,
with his twitching legs and parched throat and desire to pee and
shit and vomit, and with *this smell*, he simply would not survive.
He would be cast into a perpetual and infinite purgatory of this
seat in this bus station. If he could make it to the boarding of the
bus everything would be okay, would be calm and clear thought

and possibly even sleep from then on. Lasting, indeed, the rest of his life.

He wasn't wearing his neck brace but he had it in his bag and promised himself he would wear it in Munich.

He picked up his paperback, the last of the Bobens he had assigned to himself (*A Chair on the Porch: Selected Poems 1965–1976*) and realized with relief that he no longer had to finish it. He put it down and then realized with less relief that he had no other book to read. And then, with a recurrence of the panic and need for boxing, realized, as he had realized several times over the past year or maybe even two years, that he had not read a book in about three months and had less and less of a desire to read books, ever, and he wondered again what this meant and whether any complex intellectual casuistry – the modern consciousness more prone to emotional connections? more adept at analysing images? – could possibly be constructed to explain this as a good thing.

The violin was jangling him; he turned it off.

He waggled his foot and felt with his tongue the frayed strands of flesh dangling off the inside of his cheek. The MLU girl had crossed her legs and was resolutely staring just over his left shoulder. She must have realized he was staring at her, because she pulled out a novel with raised silver type on the cover.

James had no idea what had become of his day. He'd done a read-through of the piece and made a few changes and called Nicola again and left another message and faxed it to New York and now it was eight o'clock.

His mother had been warned of the delay and would be bravely waiting for him at the Munich end. The ceremony was tomorrow, so at least he'd have a good night's sleep tonight.

He refused to accept the possibility that he was worried about Nicola's untraceability and the progress of the photographs. Since she was always like that. And everything was probably fine.

It was dusk when the bus pulled out, late. James got a window seat. Once they were on the expressway, the wide and dark landscape became a grid of orange lights: highways, parking lots, stretching to the horizon in every direction. The traffic slowed as they passed another billboard for *Breaking the Ice*; James found his head almost level with the deep, shadowed valley between the enormous breasts. He was so close he could see the separate dots of colour that made up the photograph. Only if he blurred his focus could he see the buttery expanse of colour as recognizable curves. He turned up the Shostakovich again and searched his bag for his flask. That was one thing, at least, he had done today: fill up the flask with the last of De Courcy's Scotch. He had left him a note.

The factories and warehouses passed, long, flat windowless buildings, all in the same corrugated white material. Miles of parking lots, the same signs in every strip mall: McDonald's, Petsworld, Adults Only Video. Occasionally there would be a Lighting Unlimited or an Arby's, but on the horizon, approaching, would always be a McDonald's, a Petsworld and an Adults Only. He turned off the overhead light and sat in darkness. The whisky numbed his tongue. He tried to listen to the Shostakovich but it was too difficult; he couldn't concentrate.

He switched it off and slid in the techno tape. The hammering began in his ears. 'Skyscraper,' droned a voice over the booming, 'I love you.'

He watched the flashes, reflections of the orange highway lights, slipping the length of the cars in the other lanes. They drew alongside then dropped away. The bus itself was studded with orange lights. James saw them reflected in the windows of the trucks that seemed to float beside them.

'I'm invisible,' chanted the voice, 'I'm invisible.'

Occasionally, there were strip malls with vast, windowless bars, shuttered bunkers with glowing signs that said, JIMMY'S SALOON GIRLS GIRLS GIRLS or IGUANA ROADHOUSE EXOTIC DANCERS. They had large neon cactuses or cowboy hats. And then there was McDonald's, Petsworld and Adults Only.

He turned up the beat. It was accelerating now, overlaid with drum patterns and pierced with sirens. He closed his eyes and felt the whisky creeping through his veins. He pictured great shifting planes of metal and translucent fibreglass, scraping and sparking against each other. His breathing slowed. He was the bus, soaring down the highway, pinned to its one track like a spark along a wire. The metal boomed.

Closer to Munich he opened his eyes. The signs were more idiosyncratic along this highway. They passed a lot stacked with lengths of huge pipe, steel and concrete, and the sign, JUST PIPE. A brightly lit supermarket called Food Galaxy. A brightly lit restaurant called MegaBite. Rows of new brick houses with garages, mud around them: Freehold Towne Houses. Software Depot. About Bedrooms.

He stepped onto the asphalt of the Munich bus station and smelled the same hot concrete and cigarette smell, but also a distant hint of mown lawns and barbecue lighter. (A distant tinkle, he thought.) Waiting for his bag to be unloaded, he watched the girls waiting for their city buses, in cut-off jeans. Bare legs at night always excited him. They smoked cigarettes and pushed each other and pretended not to notice him.

The bus driver said to him, 'Arthur?'

'No. James.'

The man stared. He was overweight and needed a shave. His eyes looked as if he had been driving all night. He raised his hand and James recoiled: for a second he thought he was going to get slugged. 'No, no. Arthur. You going on to Arthur? Or Fergus?' He was pointing at a bus.

'Ah. No. Thank you.'

The driver shuffled off, shaking his head.

James picked up his bag. The woman behind the ticket window was watching him, her face totally blank.

His mother waited outside. When he was in the car, she said, 'Do they serve liquor on the buses, now, too?'

He said, 'So Kurt's home?'

'No, Kurt's out with the Senninger boy, I think, and Brenda, of course.'

They drove through the few square blocks of abandoned warehouses and nineteenth-century family factories which had once been downtown Munich. Names were still legible across the tops of the factories: Rumple Felt Mfg; Krupp Footwear. There was a banner hung across the deserted main street: it said, 'Welcome to the Munich Multicultural Festival.' It seemed to have been up for a long time, for it was full of holes. Then they drove through a subdivision called Woodcrest Village and then to their own subdivision, Sherwood Park. James didn't see a single person on the street anywhere, not even dog-walkers, except for a convenience store clerk smoking a cigarette in the bright glare outside the Dutch Boy Shopette.

They pulled into the driveway of the house James had grown up in and James saw his father in a circle of light on the front lawn. He was kneeling, his head close to the grass and his bum in the air. He wore shorts, and his legs were white. His bald patch glowed; the spotlight was over the garage door. James called to him as he opened the car door, but his father only grunted. He seemed to be scrabbling at something in the grass.

James hauled his bag out and stepped onto the lawn. There was a distant hum of lawnmower, maybe two blocks away, a smell of green. His father jerked his head up and waved frantically at a patch before him. 'Watch that, that's just seeded. And careful of the edging.'

'What are you doing?'

Mr Willing hauled himself up, patting at his grass-imprinted knees. His face was red with exertion. He held a small ruler in his hand. 'Just measuring. I tell Georg to keep it exactly two point five centimetres, but there are patches where it varies. I'll have to speak to him.' He waved at the far edge of the lawn. 'Burnt patches over there, too, I think it's some kind of fungus, from having leaves on it too long. I told him.'

His mother was walking up the path of coloured paving stones. 'You know, Jamie, Georg talks through his hat sometimes, he tried to tell us it was snow damage. And I said you can't tell me about lawns.'

James shook his head. 'Mom, if he thinks he can tell you something about lawns, then he's got another think coming. Who is Georg?'

'You know Georg,' said his father with irritation. 'The lawn man. You know Georg.'

'Don't think I do.' James shouldered his bag and made for the front door.

'Yes you do,' said his mother, 'he's Arthur and Joanne's son.'

'Don't think I know Arthur and Joanne, Mom, but it doesn't matter.'

She opened the door for him. 'You know Arthur and Joanne, Arthur and Joanne Winterson.'

'Winterson. No, Mom, I don't. Honestly.'

'Now you're going to take your shoes off, aren't you?'

'They're clean, Mom, they're fine.'

'Please take them off, Jamie.'

'They're fine, Mom, they're dry, I've just been in a bus and a car.' He took a few dangerous strides towards the kitchen, dragging his bag. He didn't know what it was about this conversation that made him so irritated.

'We all take our shoes off. Everyone takes their shoes off.'

He stopped and turned to her. 'You see, Mom, the problem is that I plan my outfit. These are not running shoes. They are Italian leather sandals. I don't wear them as a kind of all-purpose utility suit, the way Kurt does. I wear them because I like them. They are a part of my outfit. If I take them off –'

'For heaven's sake, Jamie, it's just us, I don't know who you're –'

'– if I take them off I will be in bare feet, and I don't like walking around in bare feet, especially at my advanced age, twenty-eight if you recall.' The week of Boben and day of bus was seeping out of him now; he could feel it pooling on the carpet, all in the direction of his mother. He couldn't stop it. 'An age at which you had, if you recall, two children and a house. And a car. Or did you already have two cars?' He stopped pacing and took a deep breath. His mother was watching him, her arms folded. He put a knuckle to his cheek to move some gnawable inner meat, then stooped to unfasten his sandals.

'Thank you,' said his mother. She went into the kitchen. He began to haul his bag down the stairs to his basement bedroom.

Her voice came floating down to him, calmly and faint. 'We didn't have two cars for *many* many years.'

He saw Kurt at breakfast. There was some tension over coffee, because their mother had 'forgotten' that James liked real coffee and had neglected to pick it up on her last trip to Woodcrest Plaza, and was calling Dad at the office to make plans for exchanging cars to make an exceptional trip, despite James's protestations and assurances that instant was fine or even tea and that no one need drive anywhere just for coffee. Kurt came in in his sunburned way and said, 'Hey,' and put a hand on James's shoulder. 'Thanks for coming in.'

'No problem. Feels good to be finished?'

'Well, I've been finished for a while. Looking forward to articling now. I've got a possibility in London.'

'Good. Excellent.' There was a silence as James stirred his instant coffee. Kurt poured himself a half-litre of orange juice and drank it without pause. James noticed he was wearing his rubber-toed rock-climbing shoes.

They could hear their mother on the phone in the next room. 'No, Brenda needs Kurt's car for lifesaving, and Kurt's taking mine to his wall this afternoon, so if he drives me to your parking lot –'

James said, 'So what kind of law will it be, again?'

'Well, everything at first. But commercial, you know, corporate, ultimately, I hope.'

'Uh-huh.' James tasted the coffee and made his gored pit bull face. He controlled himself and said, 'Well that's good. And how is Brenda?'

'Great. Excellent. She's interning in Orangeville, so we'll be apart for a while, but it's a short drive.'

'Excellent.' James reached for the Coffee Mate. Kurt was standing up, staring into the garden with yearning, stretching his calves by doing toe-raises and scooping cereal into his mouth in quarter-pound loads.

After a masticatory pause, Kurt cleared his throat and said, 'So how are you doing?'

'Fine. Fine. Excellent. Just finished an article for a big deal magazine. New York. Pretty big deal.'

'Excellent. Which one?'

'Called *Glitter*.'

Kurt shook his head. 'Don't know it.'

'No.' James sighed and pushed his coffee away.

'How's your love life?'

'Oh.' James hesitated. He pictured Nicola in her goth gear, the lace underwear. He pictured Brenda. 'Nothing ... nothing new.'

'Huh. Too bad.' Kurt's eyes raced over the garden as if scanning for prey. 'You'll find someone.'

Their mother entered, talking. 'Well. Kurt, Dad has my car at work, so if you can drive me later to his parking lot, I can pick it up and go to Variety, Brenda can take yours to lifesaving, and you can take the van to the wall, and James can maybe take the Honda later to Megadose.'

James didn't know what any of these words meant. 'What the hell are you talking about?'

'James, watch your language.'

'What?'

'Brenda's doing her NLS trials this week,' said Kurt. 'Pain in the butt, you have to recertify every year.'

'Uh-huh. And what's your wall?'

'Oh, I'm climbing up at the Rockwood gym. They have a lot of good surfaces.'

James smiled. 'High?'

'Oh yeah. The biggest one is sixty, seventy feet. Plus overhangs, face climbs, there's a cave for bouldering problems, you name it.'

'Any really ...' James tried to remember the code. 'Pumpy climbs, or are they all –'

'Mostly scrambly, but you can get really big air if you want to. Geoffy Bauer took a whipper last week, broke his wrist.'

'Really,' said James. 'He deck?' He could feel his language atrophying into Kurtspeak as if bent by magnetic field.

'Big time. I thought I was going to too. I was second for him, and we were hauling a pig, for practice, you know. I was gripped. He was trying to on-site this one wall, you know, try it without a beta.'

'Right.'

'So I was giving him the sequence as we went, like, you know, go for the hueco there, toe the flake just below it, crank down real hard with your right foot on the sloper, you know, kind of stuff. And we came to this really led-out part, like, if you peel here you're going to get a lot of air-time, and I said just don't peel here, man, whatever you do, and he kind of got stuck. So I'm just like breathe it out, man, trying to relax him, remember to straight-arm it, stuff like that. I'm going, *just roll up to the sloper and send it*, but he got sewing-machine leg, you know when your leg starts to shake? That's when he slipped.'

James whistled.

'He's okay though. We got him back up there pulling plastic before his cast was off.'

'Excellent. Now.' James turned back to his mother. 'Variety I take it is the Variety World supermarket. I've got that. Megadose, however, sounds vaguely threatening, Mom, and I'm not sure if I want to go there.'

'What?' said his mother, writing out a list. 'Oh, all right then. I thought you might all want a video tonight.'

'Ah. Ahah. Fine.'

The ceremony wasn't until the next day. James went for a walk after breakfast along the railway tracks. They were overgrown with weeds, lined with brick factory buildings, all empty. The air was humid and silent except for the distant lawnmower – the same one? – and the high-tension buzz of cicadas, fading in and out like passing trucks. He didn't see anyone anywhere, but kept passing through the aroma of barbecue lighter fluid.

He emerged, already damp, from one siding at the parking lot of the Woodcrest Plaza. He looked at the cars in the parking lot and thought about going back the way he had come, and then he saw the great sign that proclaimed the five thousand square feet of Megadose Video, and he realized he had nothing at all to do that afternoon or evening except watch videos that Kurt and Brenda found acceptable, such as those that concerned the beautiful wives of rich men in jeopardy from attractive but dangerous mobsters, or

scientists stumbling upon unproven cures for fatally ill children
and convincing the grey-haired establishment to believe them, or
crisp young military men in courtrooms being grilled by steely but
sensual female lawyers ... he made a note to begin writing all
three of these screenplays, and walked through the grey haze on
the grey asphalt to the automatic doors.

He shivered on entering the air-conditioning.

He browsed through Action and Martial Arts and then Drama,
which was where he discovered all three of his screenplay ideas
already packaged, and then Comedy, and then Wild Comedy,
which was like comedy but with bikinis, and found himself looking instead at one of the clerks, a teenage girl in shorts, as she bent
over a stack of cassette cases. She had long brown legs. As he did
this he realized someone quite close to him, on the other side of
the Wild Comedy rack, was looking at him, and turned to see her,
between *Goofballs VIII* and *Warty's Party III*, as she turned away,
flicking light brown hair. He saw her print sundress move behind
the rack, and more brown legs. She was pushing a pram down the
aisle. He rounded the corner to see her. Her back was to him, but
there was something familiar about the long, straight hair, the
suntanned arms and shoulders. She turned to look at him and
smiled.

He said, 'Alison?'

'I thought it was you. Visiting?'

'Kurt's graduating.' He smiled at her and moved forward, but
she didn't seem to want to kiss him. He had forgotten that they
never did that in high school, that kissing was a Toronto affecta-
tion. So he looked at her. She was thinner but no older, just suntanned and half naked in the cotton dress; he kept his eyes on her
thin shoulders just a second too long. He bent to the contents of
the pram, a small boy with blue eyes like hers, who frowned up at
him with deep suspicion and hostility. 'Hi,' murmured James. He
looked up at her. 'Holy fuck, Allie.'

She frowned and whispered. 'James. Baby.'

'Oh. Yeah. Sorry.' He stood up. 'I just mean wow. When did this
happen?'

'He's two next month.' She was smiling as if amused at him.

'He's Jeremy. Say hi to James.'

'Hi, Jeremy.' James tried to smile. The boy twisted his face up in defiance. The contortions were impressive, simultaneously evincing pain, fear, hatred and smug condescension, which James knew was no easy feat; he tried to make a mental picture of it for future reference. 'He's beautiful.' He had noticed, when looking down, that Alison wore ugly sandals.

'I got married three years ago.'

'Who to?'

'Jan Reglar.'

'Jan Reglar? No kidding? Wow.' He felt himself blushing and wasn't sure why. Perhaps because he had no picture of Jan Reglar other than as lugging golf clubs around a green all summer, tall and blond. His facial features were a blur. 'Cool,' said James. He turned to the documentary rack. *Nostradamus' Predictions. Death from the Deep.* 'How is Jan?'

'Oh he's fine. Fine. I think.'

He glanced at her.

'We're not together any more.'

'Oh. That's too bad.' He tried to look sympathetic, but she shrugged. She seemed to be staring at him very seriously, looking very pretty and pure and grave. He said, 'I mean, I'm sorry to hear that. I guess.'

She laughed quickly and fully. 'Oh, James.'

'What?'

'You're so funny.' She was smiling and wrinkling her eyes, and in that he saw the first traces of crows' feet in the suntanned skin, and he felt bad for noticing it, as he had felt bad for noticing the sandals.

'Look,' he said, 'have you got the videos you want? Because I'm not going to get anything. We could get a coffee?'

They talked all the way across the parking lot and into the mall, where they found a Grabba Java and sat down. Her divorce hadn't quite happened yet, but it was going to. She was working part-time as a legal secretary in town; she liked it, she felt lucky to have it, and lucky to have Jeremy, who did, she admitted, limit her social life somewhat, but he was worth it.

'How?' asked James innocently, staring at Jeremy, who stared back at him.

'How?'

'I mean in what way?'

'In what way is it worth it to have a *child*? Well, James ...' She glanced around the concourse with alarm in her eyes, as if afraid someone could have heard him. James glanced too: the mall was empty. 'It's worth it in every way. Children are such a ... they're so wonderful. Don't you ever ...'

'I guess not. They frighten me, I guess.'

'Oh. That's too bad.'

'Perhaps. I don't know.'

'Oh *James*. I'd forgotten what a *prick* you can be.'

James suddenly felt too tired to even smile. His sandalled feet were chilling in the air-conditioning.

She said, 'You learn so much from children. They're just a constant ... they're just a constant wonder.' She looked down at her coffee and James knew she was turning red. 'You haven't changed.'

'No. I guess not. Sorry if I seemed rude. I just like to talk about things.'

She looked back up and smiled genuinely. 'I know,' she said softly. 'You always did.'

'I'm getting cold. You want to walk for a while?'

They walked down Ridgeview very slowly in the heat. There was no one on the sidewalk. James scrutinized every passing car to see if there was actually a human driver. Alison asked him what he was doing and where he lived and said it must be very exciting, although she wondered how he could stand living with so many people and having no privacy. She had never lived with anyone besides a girl she shared an apartment with in her first year at MLC, which had not worked out, and Jan, of course. She was less impressed by the *Glitter* thing than he had hoped she would be, and James realized that she took it for granted that he was writing for American magazines, that she even expected it of him.

'So what does Jan do?'

'Oh, still insurance. He's in his dad's firm, Reglar Garamond. Carl Hentgen is there, too.'

166

'Really? Haven't seen him for a while, either.' He tried to picture Carl's face and found that it was a blur, too; they all were,
Carl and Jan and Dave Carmichael and Hobie Horst and all those
guys, all the guys he had known through Kurt. He couldn't
remember a single face. For a second he couldn't picture Kurt's
face, either.

'Dave Carmichael's a lawyer, works in Hamilton. He married
Jackie Mitchell, and he's a partner now.'

'Jackie Mitchell, eh?'

'Uh-huh. And she's doing really well, in real estate.'

'Good for her.' James could hear his voice flattening into the
tone he used when talking to his mother, a series of reassuring
murmurs like the hum of equipment, beeps, homing signals that
indicate the line of communication is functioning, messages
received.

'Now Dave *Morgan*, he's done really well, he was a G.P. in
Woodstock for a while, then he did a specialty in Community
Medicine, and now he's up North –'

'Cool.'

'Yes, says he loves it up there. Jannie Meissner did medicine
too, now she's ...'

James tuned out. He kept his eyes on the tanned backs of her
hands, pushing the pram. He had a quick vision of her family's
dining room, in high school, one day after school, watching her
play. She had been quite good at Debussy, of all things.

'... and they have a cottage near Midland.'

'Uh-huh,' he said quickly. 'Do you still play?'

'Play?'

'Do you still play the piano?'

'Oh.' She shrugged. 'A little.'

'You used to be so good.'

'I had to stop for a while, when I had Jeremy. I don't have a
piano, either. But I've started practising again, the Dunlops let me
go over there to use theirs, you remember the Dunlops?'

'Nope.'

'Sure you do. Remember Jamie Dunlop, and he has an older sister Rebecca, she married –'

'Nope. Nope. Nope. I promise you. I don't.'

'Oh.' She glanced timidly at him, then looked down. They walked a bit in silence.

'Anyway,' he said, 'that's great that you're playing again. I'd love to hear you.' He was thinking of Debussy. 'It was very difficult, that music. I always thought your parents didn't understand what you were getting into.'

She didn't seem to be listening. 'That's strange,' she said suddenly.

'What is?'

She was shaking her head. 'You must remember Jamie. He was in your year, and he used to go out with Heather –'

'Listen,' said James through gritted teeth. 'It is possible, indeed likely, that I once met or even knew a Jamie Dunlop. But I promise you I don't remember him. I assure you. I do not. Please believe me. Okay?'

'Okay.'

James exhaled. 'So what do you play now? I mean any particular period, or –'

'All kinds. Schumann, some Debussy. I've been working on a funny little Stravinsky easy pieces thing.'

'*Really*?' He stared at her, her brown legs, the sullen child, the plain brown hair loose on her shoulders. He tried to picture her in her curling gear, the hair held back with a barrette, a pleated skirt and a crested windbreaker. A skip with frizzed hair, who chewed gum. And listened to her playing Debussy. The girl with the flaxen hair. 'The girl with the flaxen hair,' he said.

She laughed. 'Yes.'

He laughed deeply. 'Someone who understands a music joke!'

She said, 'And I *love* Chopin. Don't you just love Chopin?'

'Indeed I do. Although I would never admit it in the city.'

'Because it's too romantic and mushy. Not cool.'

'Yes,' he said, impressed.

'Couldn't have all that emotion in the city.'

'Nope. I could admit to liking Milhaud and Poulenc and Hoenegger, if anyone knew who they were.'

'But you do like them.'

'Very much. Almost more than Debussy, in fact often more than Debussy, who wallows a bit. I don't like a wallower.'

'No wallowers for James.'

'Nope. Whereas the six are cynical about emotion. They're elegant. They're like dandy composers, very playful, very urbane. You know Poulenc used to ... anyway. You don't want a lecture.'

'No, I'm interested.'

'You are?'

'Actually, I'm more interested in your playing. Don't think you're going to get off without talking about the violin.'

'Oh, that. I don't play any more.'

'You were much better than me,' said Alison firmly. 'You used to play really intellectual stuff, like Schoenberg and Scriabin and stuff.'

James smiled. He had forgotten that she would know these names. They fell out of her onto the sidewalk in front of the abandoned Bock Carpet factory, and vanished. Her ugly sandals. He said, 'Schoenberg only when I had to. Scriabin's another matter. Yes, though. I like Scriabin. I like him....' He breathed deeply in the thick air, feeling suddenly emotional about Scriabin. 'I like him a *lot*.'

They walked in silence for a while. Then she said, 'You guys were always so interesting. I remember you and Finn and Anthony Friedrich talking like that all the time.'

'Uh-huh.' He felt embarrassed now.

But she had slowed her pace, was smiling at him. 'You guys,' she said, shaking her head, 'you and Finn and Anthony. Everyone knew you three were different. Everyone knew you guys would go on to do ... neat things, I don't know, special things.'

'Everyone knew we were different, all right.'

'You guys are so talented. We all could see it. Do you still see them?'

'No, we're all in different cities. We write sometimes.'

'See, I knew you guys would all go away and make it. So where is Anthony?'

'Well, he did very well in art school, and now he's in Manhattan. Painting. But things aren't –'

'See! You see! I can't even imagine going out there and –'

'He's also a heroin addict and he lives in hostels.'

She shook her head proudly. 'Well, I don't know how you guys do it. I really don't know how you manage.'

'Me neither.'

'And Finn?'

'Well, Finn really is something of a success story.' James suppressed a giggle. 'Maybe the only one of us. He's … he's a … he's without question the best-known drag queen in Edmonton. He's quite famous, really.'

She nodded admiringly. 'You see. I always knew you guys had … I'm so proud of you guys.'

He didn't know what to say to this, so he just looked down at her ugly sandals. Her legs were amazingly pretty, though. He hadn't remembered her having such legs, so long and smooth and brown. She had to stop and bend again and he looked at the fine short blond hairs on the back of her neck. Something stirred in his belly. He looked away. 'You're nice, Allie,' he said faintly.

As if she hadn't heard, she said, 'I'd better get him home. He's getting cranky.'

He walked her to the corner of Rosemount and Mitchell. 'Well,' he said.

'How long are you in town for?'

'Well, just until the day after tomorrow. But tomorrow is the ceremony and …' He thought of the long evening ahead, the videos. 'Listen, would you like to get together later on? Maybe there's somewhere we could go for a drink? My parents don't drink at all and I find it kind of….' He gave a nervous laugh.

Jeremy wailed.

'Or, oh, yeah, you have to find a sitter and –'

'That's no problem. There's a girl downstairs who would love to.'

'Oh,' said James. 'Well. Great.'

She smiled at him intently and crossed her arms over her breasts, forcing them to swell up a little over the neck of her dress. He felt the sweat beading on his forehead. 'Okay,' he said. 'Okay.'

He got home and paced the empty house. He didn't read the three notes his mother had left him about the timing of supper and exchange of cars. He didn't know why, but he wanted to call Nicola. He picked up the phone and dialled. He stared at the back lawn, the neat brown plastic compost box, the bird feeder, as he listened to the bleep that signalled the phone ringing in the empty or crowded or ugly or beautiful interior of the Bomb Factory. This time he couldn't picture it at all.

Hi, Nicky, it's me again. Could you call me? I'm getting kind of worried. Reassure me that the photos have gone off. Just let me know that everything's okay. No big deal. Please call me. It's James.

■ CHAPTER FOURTEEN

There were two pubs they could go to: Alison preferred J.J. McCoy's, in the Sablewood Mall, where the students went, because she had been going there ever since she was under age and it was very relaxed but clean, which meant that it was decorated like a gymnasium and the waiters and waitresses all wore identical red polo shirts and black Bermuda shorts, which was kind of fun. James preferred the place where 'older people' went, the absurdly Tudor, half-timbered segment of the Bayview Plaza strip mall, the Hog and Porker, where there was a torn floral carpet and dart boards and British beers on tap, despite the confrontational conversations that were unavoidably to be heard in a variety of colonial accents from short men in dandruffy V-neck pullovers with crests on the breast. Anything was better than J.J. McCoy's, where James had a fear of running into Jan Reglar and Carl Hentgen and Hobie Horst and Dave McNamara and not recognizing one of them.

So they sat at a dark wood table amid a crowd of standing men and talked, at first, about curling, which Alison apparently pursued with some local success in the winter. She wore a different but very similar linen zundress with thin straps, and a citrony perfume that James breathed in with the euphoric feeling that it was oxygen, something nutritious and purifying. They drank fat pints of Harp and Kilkenny Cream, which seemed to have the same effect. She seemed to have no problem keeping up with him.

'So how do you do it?' she said. 'You just call up these magazines and ask them if you can write an article? Do you come up with the idea or do they?'

'Sometimes I do. You start out that way, pitching ideas. Then they start coming to you. It's more interesting if it's your idea, but usually they're not interested in interesting ideas. It usually has to be something about a celebrity.'

'So you started out just, like approaching people, cold?'

'I guess. Yes.'

'And some of them turned you down?'

'Most of them turned me down. They still do.' He shrugged. 'You sell one in three, one in five.'

She shook her head with that same defeated look. 'Wow. That's incredible. I couldn't do that. I hate selling myself. I get so embarrassed. It's like you have to ... I don't know, go out on a limb.'

'Yes, you do.'

'PATTERSON! PATTERSON'S N.B.G. IN THE SCRUM!' shouted the man standing next to their table. 'New Cardiff's best against our second fifteen!' he roared. The accent was Scottish. He was short and red-faced, and his V-neck was navy. He was poking the other man, whose V-neck was red, with a stubby finger and spilling beer. 'And McCarthy will still show you! McCarthy and Davies will take Patterson on any bloody day, mate, any bloody fine day.'

'New Cardiff, no, mate,' said the other, an Australian. 'Bloody New Hamburg, maybe.'

'Getting the work isn't the worst part,' said James. 'It's doing it.'

'I have a hard time writing,' she said.

'Of course you do. Everyone does. I do. I'm sure John bloody Updike does. It's awful.'

'Why do you do it?'

'Oh, to make money.'

'Is that all?'

James took a gulp of beer. He knew there was some other reason. 'And I guess because....' He couldn't remember what it was. He knew it was because at one time he had had an interest in words and writing and music and saw them as somehow linked. He tried to dredge up some excitement, some line of a poem or book that had excited him.

'And enchors awye!' shouted the Australian next to them. 'You know what I'm saying? Not a care in the world! Get away from it all, you know? Creck a few tubes, throw some shrimp on the barbie, enchors awye!'

'It's just a skill,' said James, 'that I learned and I spent a lot of time doing and so I'm good at it. Of course you're not as good at it as I am, I spend all day doing it. I'm no good at....' He tried to remember something Alison was good at. 'Curling. Or reading actuarial tables. I'm like a – it's like being a piano tuner or a ... or a backhoe operator – which is much more difficult, by the way, have you ever seen a backhoe operator scooping dirt out of a hole, you know, on a construction site? It's just incredibly difficult and you've got about sixteen levers in front of you and they manipulate them so gracefully, it's beautiful and I'm sure I could never do it.'

'Is that what you want to be?' said Alison.

'Yes. Yes I would. A good one. It would be better than.... That's all writing is. It's just a specialized skill. That's all it is.' He realized his voice had risen and he was clenching his beer tightly. 'Music, though. Music is something else.'

'Why don't you write about music?'

'McCarthy on the lineout,' sputtered a South African directly above them. 'And buggerall gets by Williams, those big bolshie hookers from Guelph front of the scrum –'

'Listen,' said James, 'you want to get out of here? Walk a bit?'

The parking lot felt even stuffier. It had rained, water evaporating on the hot asphalt. The air was still misty. Cars roared along Lord Durham Boulevard. They walked towards it.

'You should still play, you know,' she said.

'No. I've given up. For good. You get to a certain level and then if you're not really good you don't want to do it. I don't want to do it as a hobby or something. I'm very competitive.'

'You should compose. You know enough about it.'

James was silent. They walked on the bank of the highway, past the parking lots of Foodland and Adults Only. Alison took off her shoes and walked in the wet grass verge.

'Really,' he said, 'I just like to talk about it. I like to talk about Scriabin.' He laughed nervously.

'I find that interesting,' she said, seriously. 'I've never ... I never really understood it. Even when I had to play it.'

'Scriabin? Oh, no one does. That's what's so exciting.'

She laughed.

'No, seriously, he was a nut, he was a loony. I think he was kind of an idiot savant. He was *trying* to write Romantic music and got bogged down in experimentation because he just couldn't get it to sound right. He ended up with this sort of proto-modernism by *accident*. I think, anyway. I have no way of proving it.'

He wondered where they were going to end up. At the Kaiser Wilhelm Community Centre, perhaps. There was a park there, and benches. He watched her feet glistening in the grass, thinking of Scriabin. 'Anyway, it's very polite of you to listen to me.'

'*I like it*. Tell me more.'

The glow of Kaiser Wilhelm Park loomed. The floodlights were on all night in the baseball diamond in the summer. The mist held the light like a cloud over the community centre. They crossed the highway, and walked down the grass in the centre of the boulevard towards it. James talked about music. He talked about monody and polyphony in the Renaissance, and about Beethoven's fixation with Napoleon, and about how some feminists thought Beethoven was patriarchal. He told the story of Prokofiev dying, composing in the hospital under the bedclothes with a flashlight, defying the nurses who had forbidden him mental exertion. 'Oh, and I was going to tell you about Poulenc,' he said, now talking very rapidly. 'He used to tour the provinces, playing his own music on the piano, and he hated leaving Paris so much he would finish every show with a little song he would sing about how wonderful it was to be leaving the *morose* countryside for pretty Paris, and they would all applaud him making fun of them. I think that's kind of cool. *Ah, la charmante chose,*' he sang, '*quitter un pays morose, pour Paris, Paris joli.*'

'Why don't you write about it?'

'Write about it? Where?'

'I don't know. In magazines.'

He gave a short laugh. 'That's a nice idea, but no one would publish it. Maybe if there was a TV show or a movie you could tie it to. There are no celebrities involved.'

'Sure there are. There are beautiful violinists and crazy conductors and –'

'No, no, I mean actors. Celebrities basically means actors. Sorry. I didn't explain that.'

'Oh. Well that's silly, isn't it.'

They were walking the length of the chain-link fence around the Kaiser Wilhelm Memorial Pool. There was a smell of chlorine, and a blue light rising from the water. The floodlights were off, the underwater lights still on. 'Why is it closed?' he said. 'It's still hot.'

'It closes at nine forty-five.'

'Why? We could swim.'

'It closes at nine forty-five because it always has.'

He glanced at her and saw that she was smiling. He almost grabbed her hand, but didn't.

She said, 'We still could. I'm sweating.'

James swallowed. 'The gate is locked.'

They rounded a corner and came to the brick lifeguards' building, where the fence ended. There was a buzz of orange sodium lamps: one patch of the concrete around the pool, in front of the building, was bright. Alison pointed to the handholds. 'We could hop it, no problem.'

James wiped sweat from his forehead. He was thinking about what underwear he was wearing. 'You think?' He looked around. The grounds and buildings were deserted.

'If you wanted a swim, we could. When I was at MLC, we used to do it all the time.'

He remembered the underwear: rather tattered Jockeys. He wished he had had just one more beer.

'Come on,' she said, her face suddenly close to his. 'It's a blast.'

He looked at her and wondered what underwear she was wearing. He had noted a strand of plain white bra earlier. 'Sure. Let's.'

She scrambled up, wedging her toes onto the struts that joined the fence to the wall. She moved quickly and smoothly, like an athlete. James glimpsed a flash of white as she swung a leg over at the top; her hair was outlined in a blast of orange light and she dropped to the concrete on the other side.

'Cool,' said James, climbing.

It wasn't quite so easy for him; he had a moment of breathless uncertainty at the top, with one leg on either side of the fence and his balance going, but he managed an undignified drop. He panted on the wet concrete; his neck hurt. 'Ow,' he said, rubbing it.

'You hurt yourself?' She was whispering.

'No. I mean yes, before. Old war wound.'

They stood together on the dark concrete without moving. He could smell her lemony perfume or soap. Then she turned to the water, moved to the shadows under the diving tower. He followed her, suddenly feeling chilly. He didn't know how he was just going to casually take his clothes off. He didn't think he could do it.

She quickly pulled her dress over her head. He could hardly see her in the darkness, just a flash of white underwear as she ran for the water and slipped in noiselessly.

He kicked his shoes off, pulled off his shirt and shorts, and walked to the edge, where he sat in a puddle with his feet in the water. It was lukewarm. His tattered Jockeys were already soaked. She was bobbing a few feet away, sputtering. 'Come *on*,' she said.

He heaved himself in and the water was suddenly cold. He sank as deep as he could, keeping his eyes open in the blue glow. The chlorine stung them. When he needed air he rose to the top and burst the surface, gasping. He looked around for Alison; she was at the other end of the pool, swimming in a straight line with precise strokes. She seemed to be doing lengths.

He splashed about a bit on his back, staring up at the dome of orange light over the complex. He felt clean and cool and energetic. He rubbed his body with his hands as if to clean the sweat off it. Alison swam back, and they found themselves clinging to the side in the shadow under the diving tower. She was about two yards from him. 'This is great,' he said. 'Really great. What a good idea.'

'Uh-huh.'

She seemed to be waiting for him to move over to her but he couldn't. He couldn't even look at her. He kept scanning the fence for guards. He pictured them in helmets, with guard dogs, maybe gas masks. Instead, there was a buzzing of bugs, the cars swishing past on the boulevard.

There was a rushing of water as she hauled herself out. He watched her sit on the side and shiver, water running off her dim skin. Her breasts were small, her shoulders strong, her waist thick.

He pulled himself out too and shivered on the side. She stood and walked to her clothes; he followed her. They put them on in silence.

'Well,' he said, 'that was fun.'

He took a step closer to her but she bent over and began wringing out her hair like a towel, so he backed off. When she had finished she said, 'Okay?' and walked briskly to the fence where they had climbed over, picking at her wet dress.

James followed her with the sick feeling that he had missed the moment, that he should have kissed her in the pool. His T-shirt was soaked and clung to him like seaweed.

They clambered over and walked slowly down the path to the park, James behind and watching her hips move under the slick fabric. He stopped shivering and instantly began to sweat again.

Action, he decided, was called for. He snapped his cockpit hood shut and said into his helmet microphone, *Red leader, I'm going to engage.* He tightened his fists as if gripping two joysticks – one throttle, one for rockets, the red buttons the revolving machine guns – and moved alongside her. *Red four,* came the answer in his headset, *rrroger that, we are go for engagement. Keep tight formation and your eyes open, buddy.*

The back of his hand brushed hers and she didn't pull it away.

He took her hand.

The fingers were cool and loose.

He tried relaxing a little more and put his arm around her waist; she leaned her head against his shoulder. He exhaled with huge relief; he felt like shouting. *Red leader,* he said into his radio, *we have contact.*

He chuckled. He could hear the joyous crackle of static. *Outstanding, red four, outstanding.*

'What?' said Alison.

'What?'

'You were whispering something.'

'Was I?' James cleared his throat. 'Nothing. Let's sit down.'

They sat on a damp bench. He kissed her cheek and eventually worked his way to her mouth, and after a few minutes had a cold and damp breast in his hand, which was not unexciting. She had her hands on his neck and her tongue in his mouth. His body was stirring. He ran his hands over her thighs and under the skirt.

They pulled apart, both giggling a little.

'Nice to see you again,' she said.

'God, yes,' said James. He thought for a second and said, 'I'm leaving the day after tomorrow.'

'Mmmm.' She kissed him again. 'It's too bad.'

'Yes.'

His palm and fingers were on the inside of her thigh. He tried to think about the bus back, the hot bus station. The messages on his answering machine.

'What are you going to do when you get back?'

He made a hissing noise between his teeth. 'Run around. Try to find someone who I'm supposed to be working with. Then I'll probably fight with an editor. I need a place to live. Panic. Be hot. I'm going to talk to the police again about a noise complaint. It will all be very exciting.'

'I often think about moving there.'

'To the city? Yes?'

'I mean, it's fine here, but it's not very exciting. I need a little spice in my life.'

'No you don't.' James listened to the crickets, the humming highway. He felt a faint pulse under his hand. He moved it higher up the thigh, until he felt an edge of damp cotton. 'It is fine here. I don't know why you'd want to leave.'

After a while she stood up and said she should get home. They walked a mile along Lord Durham and then through the leafy, empty streets of Woodcrest. There were sprinklers buzzing, even at night. They didn't see anyone on the sidewalk. James kept his arm around her waist or shoulders the whole way, aware of their shared chlorine smell.

On the doorstep of her apartment building, on the drab corner of King and Prince, she said, 'Do you want to come up?'

He had been waiting for this, and thinking about it. 'Um, no,

179

actually.' He coughed chlorine. He wanted to take this away and hold it for a while; he didn't want it to get more complicated. He put his hands on her hips and said softly, 'I don't think that would be a good idea. I'm leaving, and the baby, and ...'

She turned down the corners of her mouth. 'We could just have tea.'

'Yeah. I don't think I could just have tea.' He smiled.

'Uh-huh.'

'I think I should go now. But I'd like to see you again. Before I go.'

'Well, if you have the ceremony and the party tomorrow night, and you're leaving the next day –'

'I don't have to leave the next day. I can stay another day.' He said this before he realized he wanted to.

'You can?'

He chewed his cheek. 'I think I can.' He still hadn't begun the *Dental Week* piece; he had to find an apartment; there would be changes required from *Glitter*, fact-checking problems. Maybe problems with the photographs. He thought of Nicola.

There was a distant rushing sound and wail, the rattle and horn of a passing freight train on the invisible tracks the other side of King. It was a sound that had put him to sleep as a child. 'I can stay a few more days.'

He kissed her for a long time and then said goodbye and walked home through the deserted streets, whistling first a trilly Chopin waltz and then the really plonky part from Prokofiev's *Romeo and Juliet*.

'And I put it to you, ladies and gentlemen, that we are looking at a true paradigm shift.'

It occurred to James that he had never, not once in his life, fallen asleep involuntarily. Not on a train, during a slow movie, reading in a warm library. He had trouble enough falling asleep in darkness, horizontal, in silence. He couldn't imagine it. Certainly, he had made conscious decisions in libraries, pushed the book away with a vague shake of the head intended to signify regret to possible observers, folded his arms and succumbed to the laminated particleboard – and even then he had been half conscious of it being a romantic gesture, one of reckless living that didn't suit him, as if you should really have a shaved head and be called Raoul to do such a thing. (Of course he had been proud of it for the same reason, as of his nose-ring, and subconsciously hoped for notice.) Fine, but never had he woken, disoriented, with no memory of the descent, the book open on his lap.

'And I would point to the continued expansion of such departments as Business Communication, Community Marketing, and the new faculty of Medical Insurance....'

He had a twanging envy of the type of person who could do so (most people, it appeared), and also a disdain and a pity for them. He couldn't believe how insensitive, how elephantine their senses, how slowly their neurons must be firing. He meant, how could you fall asleep in the dead centre of the sound and the light and the narrative of a *movie* without being pretty well comatose to start with?

Not that he hadn't tried. How he had tried. In buses to New Munich, in hospital waiting rooms, at wedding receptions, in plays about child abuse, he wished keenly for that turgidity of mind which he so despised in normal people. He yearned for stupidity. And how he yearned for it now.

'We're in the business, ladies and gentlemen, of service

*delivery. The students, and the corporations that will eventually
employ them, are our clients, and the service, or product if you
will, is learning. Excellence in learning is ...'*

He had heard, of course, about the great marathon orations of
the Athenian Areopagus, the length of theatrical entertainments
in Elizabethan England, and had always piously wished for such
seriousness in contemporary life. Apparently the Jefferson-Lincoln
debate had lasted some eight hours, with an unchangingly huge,
entranced audience; now, there was real democracy, real intellectual life. And there had been iron-man musical concerts at the end
of the nineteenth century, jammed with proletarian crowds laden
with provisions to last them through assorted jaunty Rossini
warmups and murky Brahms entrées before digesting a couple of
epic Beethoven symphonies followed by four hours of seismic
Mahler – and he had found that impressive. The indoctrination
sessions of the Cold War Eastern bloc had been endured by massed
peasants, as here, for periods several times as long as this, with
speeches about the euphoria of increased production lasting for
days. And they had stood it.

Still he could not imagine any form of public ceremony or
entertainment in history that could ever have been longer than
this.

'Looking forward to the twenty-first century,' said the next guy
on the podium, *'in an increasingly globalized marketplace ...'*

James pulled the shirt away from his chest; it made a sucking
noise. His father's breathing was growing slower beside him, his
mother's perfume growing more intense. With his tongue, he
explored the dunes and fissured riverbeds of his mouth, listening
to his tonsils crackling like kindling as his jaw opened and closed.
He mouthed the word for water in as many languages as he knew
– *agua, aqua, wasser, eau* – making his raft-of-the-Medusa face. He
surveyed the heads beneath him – he was high in the gymnasium's
bleachers – looking for white plastic jewellery. He had never seen
this until today and had so far counted three pairs of earrings –
plain opaque glossy smooth white plastic hemispheres, like buttons – and four bangles. Generally, they accompanied white patent
pumps. He wouldn't have been able to imagine it until he saw it.

Now he tried to imagine the aesthetic it connected to; for it must have been associated with some glamour in someone's mind at one time; the romance of science fiction, perhaps? The hard white armour of the Imperial Stormtroopers, the patriotic efficiency of the *Enterprise*'s bridge? He shook his head. Too far-fetched. It represented something simpler, something domestic: lawn furniture. That's what it was. The colour and texture of patio chairs. He snorted, and then pretended to cough. The women were wearing references to patio chairs.

'Facing ever new challenges and new communications techno-logies ...'

James tried to find Kurt's head again, in the banks of graduands that faced the audience. He was distracted for a minute by a not unpretty face with straight brown hair; it reminded him of Alison. She had her hair pulled back on top, leaving the sides down: a style that always jolted James's psyche back into fourth grade, filling him with the same yearning and inadequacy that he used to feel sitting beside queenly Beth Webster in her shiny mary-janes and white knee socks. The only time he had ever seen this hairstyle in the city was when he had watched women's curling on TV while tasting an eighty-three Palmer that De Courcy had bought at auction. It occurred to James that Alison curled, and probably did the same Beth Webster thing with her straight brown hair as this girl did, sliding down the ice with her black kilt swaying and her jaw locked and concentration in her blue eyes.

He smiled: it was a pretty image, and a somehow relaxing thought. Whatever curling was, it wasn't stressful. He closed his eyes and tried to picture himself with a curler girlfriend. He would drive a Ford Windstar van and they would watch a video every Friday night, of the kind that Kurt and Brenda watched, and go to a wedding every Saturday. Eventually he would learn to curl himself. And eventually they would begin to talk about having children. They wouldn't have too much sex, which was okay, because sex was stressful anyway. He resolved to think seriously about this.

'Because as long as we input back into the community, the ongoing pursuit of excellence ...'

He opened his eyes, feeling refreshed, and quickly saw the glossy top of Kurt's hair, not far behind the curler girl. James grinned. The head was slumped forward, the eyes closed, asleep.

Hans Willing didn't care for restaurants much, he often said; he didn't see the point in wasting all that time and money, and it was so much easier and cheaper to eat what your wife cooked for you at home. Furthermore, you always got what you wanted there, what you needed, nothing fancy or too spicy, and you always knew what you were getting. It was for this reason that when occasions such as weddings, graduations or funerals required a restaurant outing – as they required uncomfortable shirts and ties and the endurance of speeches – Mr Willing relied on a place he at least knew, a place where no surprises would be pulled on you, the Passages Dining Room at the Howard Johnson's. (Even when he was travelling, he would drive some miles out of his way to the security of a Howard Johnson's; although the names of the dining rooms varied – from Signatures and the Harmony Lounge in the big ones to Alfie Q's and the Greenhouse Café in the university towns – you could always rely on them, he said, though he never made it exactly clear for what.)

Joy Willing spent much of her time at these outings trying to put Dad at ease by reassuring him that he could eat various menu items and it would be fine, occasionally going so far as to suggest that he might enjoy them; this was not always relaxing for the assembled group.

This time the group included Kurt and Brenda and James and Kurt's friend Dave whose family was out West. On entering Passages, James made a note of the entrance to the adjoining Horizons Lounge, and steered the family to a proximal table; he had a feeling that, although his father would tensely and grimly order a celebratory bottle of wine for the six of them (an event that, like a reference to sex or someone's colostomy bag, brought averted eyes and shuffling of feet from everyone else), supplemental alcohol and a brief change of decor would not be unwelcome at key junctures in the meal.

'What most people don't realize about Ontario wine,' said his father once they were seated, 'is that it's regarded outside Canada as among the finest wine in the world.'

James brought a knuckle to his cheek and brought a pad of frayed flesh in line with his molars. He would not get into this discussion; he was not going to. He chewed with concentration.

He noticed Dave from out West glancing at him with raised eyebrows. But it was Brenda, fucking stupid Brenda of course, who couldn't resist. 'Well, I'm not sure it's the finest in the *world*, Mr Willing,' she said with her cute laugh. 'It's still got a long way to go against *California* wines, you know.'

'Now, you see, this is exactly what I'm, exactly what people don't realize,' said Mr Willing, bringing his fingertips together. 'What you don't know is that Ontario wines have been winning international wine tasting competitions, over in Europe and France and everywhere, and the wines in those competitions include French and Italian wines. Like our Ontario ice-wine has won *gold* medals –'

'Dad,' said James, releasing his dental hold on his cheek, 'those competitions are only entered by people with new products. The famous vineyards don't enter them, so your Ontario wine is going up against a new Bulgarian wine and a new New York State wine and no wonder they ...' He relented, seeing his father's drooping face, the rearranging of cutlery around the table. 'Anyway, some Ontario wines are very....' He trailed off, cursing himself. 'Nice. Very nice.'

There were a few moments of silence.

'Dave,' said Kurt, 'I was thinking of trying sky-surfing.'

After the first course – James had a shrimp cocktail – and his one glass of wine, he made his first trip to the washroom with a murmured excuse. He slipped unnoticed, he thought, into the Horizons Lounge, and sat at the bar, where a white-haired bartender in a white jacket and black tie said, 'Good evening, sir, what can I get for you tonight?'

James smiled widely at him. He wanted to lean forward and shake his hand. 'Good evening to *you*,' he said with unaccustomed warmth. 'Let's see. I just have a second.' He made a show of consulting his watch. He scanned the glowing bottles, the low padded swivel chairs around the room, their seventies rocket-ship design. There was a piano, mercifully unattended, and a sign on it with a picture of a dark-haired man in a ruffled dress shirt. 'Anton Magyar,' it read, 'Piano stylings, 5-7 p.m.'

James smiled, appreciating *piano stylings* for its playful ambiguity. When he was with his curler girl, they would come here every fourth Friday to sing along with Anton. He turned back to the bar, suddenly wanting an old-fashioned drink, something with a Cary Grant sound to it, something this guy would know how to mix perfectly, something you had to shake, something you would call a *cocktail*. A martini, a manhattan, a Tom Collins. He wasn't exactly sure what a manhattan was, but the sound was right. He wanted something manly. 'How about a highball,' he said with relish, and repeated it. 'A *highball*.'

'Certainly, sir.'

'Thank you.'

'But what those sky-surfing guys are really into now,' Dave was saying, 'is the Wind Weapon. You know?'

'Exactly,' said Kurt, 'Wind Weapons are excellent.'

'No,' said James, 'I don't know.'

'Windsurfer sail's fixed, like rigid, like aluminum or something, so you build up speed, you really start hauling, and you just flip the thing up over your head and it turns into a wing, the whole thing turns into a hang-glider, and you just take off. Hardcore.'

'It rocks,' said Kurt, 'you can really haul. It's like psycho how fast.'

'Excuse me,' said James.

'Are you all right?' said his mother.

'Upset tummy,' murmured James to her. 'Sorry.'

His father said, 'Well, if you people would learn that nothing is free in this world, and a little hard work never hurt anyone. When I think of how your mother and I first managed it, two growing boys, nickel-and-diming it the whole way –'

'Are we going to order another bottle?' said James.

'*Another* bottle?'

'I'm always having ideas for magazine articles you could write, Jamie,' said his mother. 'There are so many interesting things in this area that I'm sure people in Toronto would be ... would be interested in.'

'Uh-huh.'

'The trick is,' Kurt was saying to Dave, 'it's a new kind of universal joint, you can lock it, so your board doesn't go spazzy on you, it's an alloy too.'

'Titanium?' said Dave.

'How about for one of those travel magazines, like *Byways!*' said his mother, toying with her fillet of sole and tartar sauce. 'Because there's a story here that's just *crying out* to be written.'

James focused on her through one glass of wine, one highball, one martini (with olive!), and one manhattan, which he had found to be sweet and faintly nauseating. 'What?'

'Well, there's a bed-and-breakfast here that's really special. It's really unusual. It's Bonnie Hausen's place. It's a renovated girls' school, but you wouldn't believe how pretty it is. It's really gorgeous, with a garden with the most beautiful rambling rose, and hedges, and those wooden archways for creepers, what do you call them?'

'What archways?' said his father.

'There's a word for them,' said Brenda, 'I *know* it.'

'What, like a summerhouse?'

'No, no, just an arch, like a doorway –'

'Gazebo,' announced Kurt.

James was staring at the dark passageway, now glowing like a highway tunnel or nightclub entrance, to the Horizons Lounge. 'Pergolas,' he said.

'Is that it? Well, anyway, it's so beautiful because the guests can sit in the garden and read on the lovely little wrought-iron benches, that are all painted white, and the food is really wonderful. You get a full breakfast with home-made pancakes, bacon, fresh syrup –'

'So it's a bed-and-breakfast, Mom. What's so special about it?'

'Well, this is the thing. It's the people who stay there who are unusual.'

'Yes?' said James with something distantly resembling hope. He had a sudden vision of Nicola in her silver skirt.

'Some very important people stay there. Bonnie won't call it a bed-and-breakfast. She says it's a "Home Away from Home for Transient Executives". Isn't that cute? Because, you see, the guests are all in town for job interviews at the college, or the hospital, or for lectures or what have you. We ran into the most interesting people there.'

James sat back, sighing. 'Uh-huh.'

'There was one fellow, quite old now, retired, who used to be the *president of Anheissen Life*!'

'Really.'

'Yes! And we met that one man – what was his name, Dad? – that very nice man who was an ophthalmologist, who had been brought in by the hospital to give a lecture!' His mother put down her knife and fork to beam at him over her glasses.

'Ophthalmologist giving a lecture, hey?' James gave a low whistle. He looked around the room. 'Is there a payphone in here? Because I should phone this one in right away, or else someone else, maybe someone in New York, is going to grab this scoop. I mean, I'm thinking *cover story*!'

His mother stopped smiling and looked down at her plate. 'James,' she said, 'don't be smart.'

He realized she looked old, and he felt a wave of sadness and appreciation for her and said, 'I'm sorry, Mom. I was just … I know you're trying to help.'

There was a moment of silence at the table and James looked down at his New York striploin with asparagus tips and felt about to vomit with guilt. He thought of Alison and how much nicer he would become if he spent more time with her, and suddenly wanted to and knew he was not going back to the city right away. He rose, excusing himself again and gaining knowing and immediately sympathetic glances from his mother, so that was all right, and moved towards the tunnel. This time, he was thinking, *Harvey Wallbanger*.

He called her at her office the next morning, as soon as his father was at work and his mother at her Walking Group. Kurt was still asleep, having gone on to J.J. McCoy's with Dave and Brenda after dinner. She was giggly on the phone, said she couldn't talk. He told her he wasn't leaving right away, and she asked him to come over to her house after work. He hung up with his heart pounding. Then, without really knowing why, he dialled De Courcy's number.

'Control,' said De Courcy.

'Chaos. I guess. Hi.'

'Hel-*lo*, warty.' De Courcy's voice was as languid as James had ever heard it, as if he were anaesthetized. 'Mister world traveller. Why are you calling home? Do you need money?'

'No, I'm fine, actually.'

'How are the highways?'

'Skyscraper,' said James, 'I love you.'

'Is it really awful? Listen. Just think, when you're having your next decaffeinated instant coffee and listening to another decaffeinated conversation about siding and drywall –'

'Foodworld in Woodcrest Village versus Foodland in Sablewood Plaza.'

'Exactly, when you're there, and you just think you won't make it, then just think about those polar explorers who have to eat each other, is it polar explorers or –'

'I think that's rugby players crashed in the Andes, but anyway, it's not so bad.'

'Now I know what you're thinking,' said De Courcy in a gravelly voice, 'you're wondering, did he fire *five* shots just now, or *six*?'

James smiled and said, 'And to tell you the truth, in all the confusion, I kind of lost track myself.'

'But seeing as this is a forty-four magnum –'

'The most powerful handgun in the world –'

'And will blow your head *clean off* –'

'Okay, listen,' said James.

De Courcy was silent and James could tell he was irritated at having his skit interrupted.

'Listen, it's *not so bad.*'

'Oh.'

'And I think I'm going to stay a couple more days.'

'What *can* you be talking about?'

'I'm going to stay a couple more days. I need it. I like the quiet. I'm just going to relax.'

'Wait a minute. You're going to relax in your parents' house in New Munich, which is the place you've often referred to as the least sexy place on earth ... wait a minute. Is there something happening there?'

'What do you mean, happening?'

'James. Have you met someone? One of those delightful doctor women with Fair Isle jerseys and a golden retriever? Are you keeping something from me?'

James writhed. 'No.' He couldn't think of anything else to say. 'Of course not.'

'I see. Well I guess the question you have to ask yourself is –' He was in his hoarse voice again. 'Is, do I feel lucky? Well do ya, *punk*?'

James sighed. He didn't know what embarrassment or sense of propriety was keeping him from telling De Courcy, but he couldn't. 'I just feel I need the break. I'm watching a lot of videos, you know ... hey, has Nicola called my machine? Have you heard a message?'

'I wouldn't know. But I don't think so. Message from *Glitter*, though, they want to talk to you.'

'Fuck.' He kicked the kitchen cupboard. 'Fuck it, though. I'm on holiday for a few days. I'll deal with them when I come back. How's your quest for a cottage going?'

'Not bad. A few leads.' De Courcy was using his quiet voice, which meant his feelings had been hurt and which was irritating as hell to James.

'Well, then,' said James briskly. 'See you later in the week.'

'Okay. Goodbye.'

They hung up.

'Well that was fucking strange,' said James in the silence of the kitchen. He didn't even try Nicola again.

■ CHAPTER FIFTEEN

When he met Alison that evening, she was in another sundress with bare arms. She opened the door and put her bare arms around his neck and kissed him on the mouth. He could smell sun on her skin and wine on her breath, and his body expanded like a sponge.

■ CHAPTER SIXTEEN

He left her place after noon the next morning, a Saturday. He walked very slowly through the haze along Lord Durham, then past the shops that always seemed to be closed in Bayridge Village, the dim Italian Family Restaurant, the mirrored insurance office, the Video Plus. He didn't mind the heat or how sticky he was or how bizarre it was that there was never anybody on a street that appeared to be commercial in intent; he walked slowly, without thinking of anything much, occasionally humming the passacaille from the Ravel piano trio. His body felt delightful – he didn't know in what way, exactly; it was just that he didn't seem to *mind* his body as much this morning. As if it were natural.

He stepped up to his parents' door, whistling, hearing his sandals squelch, and fully intending to remove them without bitterness once inside. He pushed open the door and heard voices.

He came to the doorway of the living room and opened his mouth. De Courcy was sitting in an armchair with a bottle of wine in front of him, and James's mother and his father were sitting in chairs on either side of him, and everybody was laughing and everybody had a glass of red wine.

An expression of Fiona's came to James. 'Holy smiling dancing smoking –'

'Aha,' said De Courcy, softly, rising. 'The return.'

'What the hell –'

'You really surprised us, James,' said his father, heaving to his feet. 'Piers tells us you invited him a week ago, and I think it was a darn nice surprise.'

'We're always telling him to ask his friends when he comes up,' said his mother, beaming, 'and we've heard so much about you.'

'You didn't warn me you had an early morning appointment,' said De Courcy reproachfully. 'I would have arrived later. I should have remembered you're such a one for long morning walks.' His smile was wicked.

James was still staring at the wine in their glasses. He made a stifled hissing noise, as if trying to scream in a dream.

'You didn't tell us Piers was in *medicine*,' said Mrs Willing, her voice all potpourri and cinnamon buns.

'And you didn't warn me you'd suddenly taken to wine at lunch. If I'd known I'd have been drinking myself –'

'Oh,' said De Courcy, 'I didn't realize your father was such a connoisseur – we got into a little chat about the last Ontario harvest, and I happened to have brought a present of a couple of bottles of my own recent favourite, a little Canon-Fronsac I bought through Van Plixéville – one of these futures deals, I split a case with Alex – and I managed to persuade your parents –'

'I figured why not?' said his father. 'It's the weekend.'

'Why not live a little?' said his mother.

'And it's actually not at all bad,' said his father, picking up his glass. 'Not at all bad.'

'I'm so glad you like it,' said De Courcy. 'As I said, it's a little young still –'

'Not at all,' muttered Mr Willing, 'not at all.'

'But I find that adds to its charm, especially in summer, don't you think? James?'

James stared from one smiling face to the other. 'What have you done with my family?'

'Would you like to try some?' De Courcy was already handing him the glass. James took it without thinking, and drained half of it before realizing it was fantastic.

'Easy,' said De Courcy softly.

James gave him his strongest glare. It was all he could do to refrain from clubbing him with a porcelain figurine. His fury grew as he took in De Courcy's khaki shorts, his sober green polo shirt, the deck shoes. He had done his best to look like one of Kurt's friends, but one of the nice ones, one of the marryable ones, and De Courcy's best was a sophisticated one. Everything about his appearance and manner was a reproach and an example to glib, inscrutable and probably dissipated city life as exemplified by a nose-ring, and by the T-shirt that James was now wearing, the one that read, 'FORT' on the front and 'DA' on the back.

James could just see his polite arrival, polite surprise, easy self-introduction, would have commented on the lawn, known a thing or two about gutters – replayed the whole rosily charming assault in his head with sickness and admiration. It was like watching one of those nature shows about innocuous-looking sea anenomes and vapidly wandering fish. 'Well,' he said, still glaring, 'I hope you're all settled in?'

'Actually, I haven't taken my bags down yet, or is it up?' De Courcy looked shyly at Mrs Willing, who sprang up, suddenly nervous.

'Oh, I'm so sorry, I haven't shown you to your room yet – it's just a guest room, of course, but we'll get some towels in there for you –'

'Oh please,' said De Courcy, waving his hands, 'please don't go to any trouble, I have no need for –'

'I'll do it, Mom,' said James, taking De Courcy's elbow as firmly as he could, which was firmly. 'I'll show *Piers* to his room.'

In the basement, he relaxed his grip and spun De Courcy around. 'Now listen.'

'*Ow,*' said De Courcy in a high voice, rubbing his elbow. 'There's no need to get *violent*. I thought you'd be *pleased*.'

'Listen. Bravo. Excellent timing. I'm impressed. And now there's nothing I can do to get rid of you. But listen –'

'You're *not* pleased to see me!'

'What are you doing here?'

'Well, you sounded so bored, and I thought you might need some company. But I take it you've found some company.'

James sighed. He knew he was defeated. 'Yes, I have.'

'Well I can't wait to meet her.' De Courcy picked up his bag and floated into the guest room.

They went back to the Horizons Lounge that evening, at James's insistence. Alison was nervous and quiet at first, but De Courcy so showered her with interested questions about children and childbirth and local schools – he knew about the Whole Language debate, personally saw no problem with some combination of that

and more conventional phonics – interspersed with repeated com-
pliments on her ugly earrings ('I'm sorry, I know I'm repeating
myself, but I just can't stop looking at them – where did you say,
again?') and peppered with casual references to his various amusing and adorable family members of various cities of Europe – that
within a half hour she was giggling and red-faced and describing
the hilarious pranks she and her girlfriends used to get up to when
they were teenagers.

James sank into silence, drinking a string of manhattans, which
he had decided he liked despite or because of their medicinal
sweetness.

'You *didn't!*' roared De Courcy. 'But what did your brother say?'

James listened to Alison hiccuping her way through the stolen
cigarettes on the skiing holiday and the dirty magazines at the cottage and felt embarrassment rising like a hangover, and simultaneous guilt for his embarrassment and anger at De Courcy for
inducing it. He glanced at her breasts, now hidden under a loose T-
shirt that said Run for Life!, trying to revive his desire, and then at
her legs and the ugly sandals, and felt it seeping out of him; it was
like trying to cling to a pleasant dream that slips away as you wake.

She drove them home, talking all the way; De Courcy smoothly
bagged the front seat and made no effort to leave them alone at
any point. Even when the car stopped in front of the Willings'
house, De Courcy waited majestically for James to get out before
he said good night and thank you to Alison. James leaned his head
through the window to ask her if she wanted him to stay, if she
wanted him to come over later, but De Courcy was standing so
close to him on the sidewalk that he would have heard everything
and again James was embarrassed. And anyway, he was tired, and
suddenly wanted to sleep alone, and so he murmured good night to
Alison's rather surprised face.

In the entrance hall, De Courcy said, 'Well, she's charming.
Absolutely charming. I congratulate you.'

James just smiled grimly. He felt very little.

'Now,' said De Courcy, spreading the map on the kitchen table,
'after the famous Rope, Cord and Twine Museum, which I can't

wait to see, we have the whole afternoon, and your mother tells me that the *most* Mennonite – Mennonitical? – towns are in fact the furthest away, but –' He raised an ironical finger, smiling conspiratorially at Mrs Willing, who was sitting as close to the edge of the breakfast nook's bench as anatomically possible and smiling almost hysterically; indeed, she let escape a brief girlish giggle. '*But*, and it's an important but, James, the drive to Wurst through New Frankfurt and this place Bierschwein, if that really is its name, will also permit us a view of the incomparable Meyer Flats *and* some apparently unparalleled antique seeking along the way, and –' (another fraternal aside to his mother) 'James knows how seriously I adore antiques. *Sooo –*'

('Oh do you?' said his mother with helpless love.)

'Sooo –'

'You're sure Alison wants to come?'

'I called her while you were still asleep –' (a weary but tolerant look at Mrs Willing, instantly returned) '– and she seemed delighted.'

'Well, why don't you take her alone then?'

'James,' said his mother darkly.

'No, seriously, I'm really not keen on the Rope and Straw Museum, or whatever it's called, or the Meyer Flats, Dec, they're just *fields*, for ... Look. Seriously. I should think of getting back to the city. But I don't mean to stop you, I mean you should take Alison if she's interested, and you should go too, Mom, if you're so keen. You don't need me.'

'But Jamie, your friend has only just got here!'

'That's all right,' said De Courcy quietly, rolling up the map, 'it was just an idea.'

When they were alone, De Courcy said, 'What, bored with her already?'

James was standing at the doors to the garden, staring at the birdfeeder and chewing on the inside of his cheek. He had one knuckle up to his face. 'Has *Glitter* called again?'

'Oh yes, several times. I thought you didn't want to hear about that.'

'Shit.' He had already moved to the phone. 'What's your code?'

He hesitated before dialling. He pictured the stifling apartment, the dirty dishes, the red light on the machine, flashing hysterically under one of Buck's socks and a psychology textbook. The booming bass. He closed his eyes and hung up. Best to keep all that separate. 'I can't deal with it here,' he announced. 'I have to go back.'

'What about –'

'I'll go over there now and say goodbye to her.' He drained his coffee and walked into the hall for his sandals. De Courcy followed him. 'Alone.'

'Of course. Won't she be terribly upset?'

'I don't know.'

'You can easily come back any time you want, of course.'

'Listen, you stay a few days if you want to spend time with her.'

'Well ...' De Courcy looked at his watch, frowning. 'There are one or two things I should be.... What time are you leaving?'

'There's a bus at eight forty-five.'

'I'll just come with you, then.'

'Yes.'

'You know, I think you're right to go back and deal with this *Glitter* thing. By far the wisest choice.'

James found the phone and dialled Nicola's number.

Hey, me again, James. Did I leave my parents' number last time? Listen, if there's any problem, any holdup for any reason, we can work it out, whatever it is. Don't be afraid to call me, whatever it is. Call me anyway, right away, okay? Okay then. Bye. Talk to you soon. Bye.

James was home by seven to do the difficult thing he had to do. The last hour with Alison had been total distraction, facing it; the inside of his mouth was trench warfare. His father would have been home for half an hour, already eaten. He stopped in the cool entrance hall, smelling himself. He wished he had had time to shower. Alison had been rather cold, at first. Then forgiving, then passionate, then sad. He closed his eyes tightly as if it could prevent him thinking about his awkwardness at the door. 'In a few weeks, maybe. When this whole *Glitter* thing is done. And maybe by then I'll have my own apartment, so you can come and stay with me. Anyway, I'll call you.' He had kept looking at his watch, despite himself. He winced.

He kicked off his sandals and walked into the den where his father and De Courcy were watching TV. There was a clatter of dishes and 'As It Happens' from the kitchen. De Courcy sprang to his feet. 'I really tried valiantly to impose myself on the dishwashing process, but the defences were impregnable. Your mother is a fortress of self-sacrifice.'

'Oh,' chuckled Mr Willing, 'there's no getting past her to do those dishes. She won't let any old stranger's hands on them.'

'Dad,' said James, 'we kind of have to rush, if we're going to get that nine o'clock bus, and so do you think we could talk now? Remember I said I wanted to ask you –'

'I'll pack my bag,' said De Courcy, disappearing.

James sat in his empty chair.

'What can I do you for?' said his father, without taking his eyes off the TV.

James took a deep breath. He wished he didn't have to go through the preamble to the obvious. 'Well, it's just that I was wondering if, see, this *Glitter* thing has been a big break for me and I'll be getting, probably be getting a fairly large cheque at the end of it, the thing is they don't pay until –'

'How much do you need?'

'Well, it's just rent, really, which is coming up, and –'

'How much?'

'Three hundred is all I need to make rent, but if you happened to *have* five hundred I could pay you before the first of ...' A thousand, thought James, is what I need immediately just to stop the interest on my Visa from clicking inexorably and exponentially upwards as we speak, and then we'll worry about rent after that. He felt sick for asking in the first place and ashamed that he was too afraid to even request what he needed.

'Now what happened to that money you said you made from *Edge* last month?'

'Well, that wasn't really very much, Dad. You don't realize what rents are like in the city these days.'

Mr Willing sighed deeply. 'Well if living in the city is so expensive and it's so hard to find work there, then I don't know what the advantage of living in the city *is*.'

James was quiet: this was the part you just had to endure.

'I mean, I don't understand what, why you have to live such an extravagant lifestyle.'

James tried a tight chuckle. 'Well, Dad, it's not exactly extravagant, I live in a –'

'Your mother and I, when we were your age, we had two kids –'

'Yes, I –'

'And we never, ever ate out, we never, ever had a bottle of wine at dinner – you seem to just take that for granted! At dinner! We couldn't even imagine it! Except on special occasions, of course, and then it was a big deal!'

Well maybe if I had someone to cook for me, James didn't say. He said, 'I know, Dad, it's just that the kind of thing I write about requires me to –'

'I mean, you're at the stage of your career now where you just have to nickel-and-dime it, just like we did, you can't expect things to be handed to you on a platter. I know times are hard now, but you don't know hard times, my boy.' He was shaking his head. 'The first apartment we lived in ...'

After that, it was just a question of waiting and nodding.

His mother drove them to the bus station, reciting recipes to De Courcy all the way, who carefully wrote them in his notebook.

There was a bank machine there, where James deposited a cheque for five hundred dollars and withdrew a hundred, and they even had time for two quick Scotches at the tiny, smoky, desolate bar.

On the bus, they rationed themselves a teaspoonful every half hour – on the end of a plastic stir-stick – of the Iranian caviar De Courcy had brought all the way with him in a small jar in his Mountain Equipment Co-op bag.

■ CHAPTER SEVENTEEN

The first one was calm enough.

James, Maya Lipschitz here, just wondering what the story was with the photographs ...

Then a little edgy.

James, we can't get hold of Nicola, could you contact her for us pronto, if you don't mind, we're up against a deadline here. Now, about the story, I think it's a good start, but there's some major work that needs to be done, and I have a few, uh, questions ...

Then frank and open.

James, Maya, listen, call me as soon as you can. Analph is on this now and he's not happy James, he's not happy at all. Hello. Hello. Jesus. Hello, James? Where the hell are you? Okay. Call me.

James rubbed his eyes. He didn't listen to the next three. He waded through the air to the kitchen, where he pulled up the blinds on the courtyard, an activity similar to lifting the lid off a pot of stew. The air was almost misty with humidity. He stared for a moment at the gravel, the piles of garbage, the shifty squirrels. They were involved in a stare-down with a compost rat, shuffling around the bin's lid. The landlady's jaded dogs lay motionless but peripherally aware of the confrontation, like police in a doughnut shop. James tried to breathe through his mouth.

There was no orange juice or coffee or excavable bread; he drank some lukewarm water and turned with a whimper back to the phone. He dialled Nicola's number. No answer, but she had changed her message, which meant she had checked her machine. There was laughter and a beat behind her voice.

Hey, kids, get out of that Jell-O tree! Come on down here and leave me a message! And if this is Christian calling, talk to Yummola.

There was a screech, as if the tape had jammed, and then the beep. James did not shatter the phone against the bookshelf. He held it against his chest, which was thumping, and chewed on his cheek. 'Christian?' he said aloud, 'who the hell is Christian?' Then, after a second, '*Yummola?*'

He had to go and sift T-shirts – he settled on one with 'I refute you *thus*' in script – and chew on his cheek and bounce Buck's basketball for twenty minutes before he could call Maya Lipschitz.

He got her voice mail. He promised, speaking as quickly as he could, as if she could interrupt at any second and force him into dialogue, that he would track down Nicola and courier the photos today, and that he would be happy to do any changes Maya wanted on the piece, that she should just call him back here any time, and that he would be more than delighted to dent and irrevocably damage Maya's skull with the bicycle lock he was now waving around his head; he had already hung up by that point.

'Fuck you,' he shouted, in the thick air, 'Fuck off, fuck you, thank you, thank you very fucking much, New York City, fuck you.'

And even that didn't wake De Courcy up.

James filled another glass with water. He went into De Courcy's room and put it on the side table. He yanked open the paisley curtains. He shook the silk-pyjamaed shoulder. 'Listen, hello, is this on, consciousness, here we go, hell-LOW, okay?'

De Courcy was blinking and sitting up, opening and closing his mouth.

'Okay. Listen. Emergency. Concentrate.'

De Courcy noticed the water, extended a shaky hand towards the glass. James pulled it out of the way. He held the glass up in the air. 'In a second. Where does Nicola work?'

De Courcy put a hand to his throat and said in a cracking voice, 'Water.'

'In a second. One word and your problem is solved. Where does she work?'

'I have no idea,' said De Courcy faintly, and shrank under the sheet.

'Mmm-mmm,' said James, '*dolce, chiara, fresca aqua.* Clear creeks and brooks and waterfalls, dripping rain, glistening rock pools –'

De Courcy sat up. His face was white. 'This is the nastiest thing you have ever done to me.' He sank again.

'Think. You said she was doing something for TV.'

His voice came crackly from under the sheet, 'You are unspeakably unkind.'

'She was shooting a show on fashion or something, right?'

The body shifted.

'Right?'

Like a voice from a ghost, the words came: 'Cattle Call.'

James slammed the glass on the table, making sure to splash De Courcy a little, and rushed into the kitchen, where the old newspapers were stacked. He sifted until he found a guide to TV listings, then searched that until he found a reference to Cattle Call; Saturdays at eight on THC.

He hunted and trapped a phone book, under the bookshelf, and found the THC switchboard. He held for four full minutes before a harried female voice with noise in the background yelled, 'Cattle!'

'Hi, I'm looking for Nicola Lickson?'

'Nicola who? Jussec – Davey, *Davey*! You wanna put that over here please? I know, like, what-ever. What?'

'She's a director. Nicola.'

'Oh, no.'

There was a silence.

'No what? You don't know her? She's not there? Or she's not a director?' James had picked up Buck's basketball again, was holding it over his head as if about to throw it through the glass into the courtyard.

'Oh, yeah, I know her, but – oh my *god*!' She screamed. 'I don't *believe* it! Just one second.'

The phone was muffled.

'Are you okay?' said James, putting down the basketball.

After a few seconds the voice returned, breathless. 'Sorry about that. Someone just came in who I haven't seen for weeks and weeks and weeks and weeks and I just *had* to give him a hug.'

'Of course. Listen, I'm looking for Nicola Lickson, the director, and it's very –'

'Oh, well, see, we're not shooting this week. We don't shoot till Monday next.'

'So she's not around?'

'Well, she might be in tomorrow. I guess. *Sweetheart*! The purple rocks. Come over here right this second and kiss me.'

'Listen, this is very important. Please try to help me. Is there somewhere where you could leave a message for her? You do know who I'm talking about, don't you? Nicola, tall girl with dark hair, ring in her lip?'

'Oh of *course* I know Nicola, I work with her every day, she's a sweetheart.'

'I thought you weren't –' James clenched his jaw. 'Okay. So could you leave a message for her?'

'Well, see, I'm not sure.'

'You're not sure you could leave a message.'

'Well, see, I'm not here all the time, I'm a stylist. I don't know how I could ...'

'Ah,' said James, exhaling, 'a stylist. I see. I understand. Is there anyone else there who could help me?'

'Well Jannie's not in right now, but she's the one who could help you. You wanna call back in about an hour or two hours or like later on? Maybe tomorrow?'

'What-*ever*,' said James.

He burst into Fiona's room, where she was sleeping with Buck.

'What the flying jumping –'

'What the *fuck*, man –'

'Sorry, listen, it's an emergency, can I borrow your bike, Buck? Please?'

'James,' said Buck, 'you rot my bag, man. You really rot my bag.'

Buck's Hokatchi Black Fang Hypercube IV gleamed like a syringe. Every part was made of a different metallic substance and bore a different brand name in bright decals. It seemed to have two different sets of handlebars. It lived under a tarp *all the time* – this was vigorously stressed, even sleepy, by Buck – and bonded to the fence by two dangerous U's. After struggling and sweating with three different keys and dropping shackles and bolts into the dogshit, James clambered on and wedged his toes into the baskets, which seemed unforgivingly tight. He wobbled around the gravel, trying to understand the advantages of the different handlebar positions. It was slightly too large. His shoulders were lower than his hips.

He tested the narrow-profile caliper brakes, which bit into the alloy rims; the bike stalled with a shudder and he had to rip one foot out of the clip before he hit the ground. 'Sheee-yit,' he yelled. 'Red leader, we are go for launch.'

Elsie's head popped up over the deck's railing like a Punch puppet. 'You!' she yelled. 'That is your bicycle! You have no right to put against the fence! I wait and see who –''

James waved to her, shouted, 'Good morning, Elsie!' gesturing to his ears as if he couldn't hear, almost toppled again, decided on the lower handlebars, put his head down and careered into the alleyway.

'Last of the V-8s, Max,' he said, already breathless, 'get this baby out on the open road and – sorry, homes.' He swerved to avoid the black car's opening door and the squat thug emerging, regained the racing line within centimetres of a graffiti-ed garage door, and curved neatly into the busy street. He felt like a bullet. He rocketed between a streetcar and a moving van. 'Red leader,' he muttered, ratcheting through gears with both indexed shifters, 'we have liftoff.'

He stopped on the corner of a parking lot and looked at the expressway roaring over the next block, the vast billboards. He was panting and drenched and his stomach felt as if he had just consumed two packets of oatmeal. It was the big ad for *Breaking the Ice*, the vast cleavage in the sky, that told him where he was.

He found what was left of a chain-link fence a block away from the Bomb Factory, and began the process of hooking the bike to the corner post with its four locking components. It took him some minutes. He walked back to the glass doors and tried them: locked. He pressed every button on the buzzer panel. He waved and gestured pleadingly at the security camera.

There was no answer from the intercom panel.

He sat on the curb and waited.

No one came for two hours.

He got back on the bicycle. He rode towards downtown, rather aimlessly, thinking he might find the television studio, and then remembered that De Courcy had told him Nicola occasionally still went to a night club called the Agency, which was in an odd place, way up in gangland at Harbord and Ossington. It was too early for it to be open, but there might be a manager or something. He turned north.

The Agency had no sign, unless you counted the old neon above the tinted glass door that said 'BURGERS', which was camouflage. Then there was a small, hand-lettered sign beside the door reading,

> DRESS CODE
> No running shoes
> No rugby shirts
> No fucking nice sweaters
> (Make an *effort*, for fuck's sake)

Of course it was too early to be open. He pressed his face to the dark glass and cupped his hands around his eyes and made out some waitresses setting up behind the welded metal bars. He pounded, but they just shook their heads at him.

He drove around looking for a phone booth, and found himself in a shimmering field of heat beside Christie Pits. There were phones beside the Seven-Eleven parking lot, but there were large boys with no hair in each one.

He cycled east through thickening traffic until he was stuck at Bloor and Bathurst, in the glow of the enormous department store covered in light bulbs. He watched the patterns the bulbs made as they flashed. The store was closed, and there were street kids crouching in the doorways. They had rolled-up blankets and buckets. Their heads were shaved in odd patterns – except for one with red dreadlocks like Nicola's. In the white fluorescent light, they all looked very tired and underfed. There there was even a little dog curled on one of the mats.

James looked around for phone booths. The traffic began to move, and he rolled the Hypercube onto the sidewalk. He saw a phone booth across the street. The squeegee kids sat or lay on the sidewalk, against the illuminated glass. MEN'S LOUNGEWEAR, $15.99 AND UP, BARBECUE SET, $12.99, ASSORTED CANDIES, $2.99/BAG.

The sun was setting at the end of the long tunnel of Bloor Street, and the sky had taken on a pink glow. He watched one girl rummaging in her pathetic bag, her shoulder-blades making her skin look fragile. He saw her shallow breasts jiggle under the tank-top, and felt desire again. Actually, she looked beautiful in the unnatural light.

He crossed the street and waited at the phone. The swinging doors were missing from the booth. There was a girl on the phone, a teenager. She wore baggy jeans and had a bare midriff. She kept poking her head out of the booth and looking around the street, and James saw that she was crying, sobbing even, and that her eye makeup had run on her cheeks. She was saying, 'I don't have another quarter, so can you promise it's on its way?' Her voice was whiny and hiccuping.

James backed off a bit and looked at his watch.

'Sir? Sir' She was talking to him. 'Can you do me a favour?'

'I don't have any money.'

'I need a glass of water.' Her voice was so faint he looked at her more closely. Her face was clammy and pale, except for her forehead, which had been burned pink by the sun. She closed her eyes and for a second he thought she was going to vomit.

He glanced at the Swiss Chalet behind him. 'Okay,' he said. 'You should get out of the heat. Get into some air conditioning somewhere. Are you okay?'

She shook her head, still holding onto the receiver. 'No. I'm waiting for an ambulance. Do you see one?'

He looked up and down the wide street, the slowly shifting grid of fenders. 'No. Just a second.' He ran into the Swiss Chalet.

There were two punks with mohawks at the cash counter, waiting for someone to materialize behind it. James waited behind them for a minute. There didn't seem to be anybody working in the whole place. He shivered in the air conditioning. The Muzak breezed along. The punks were looking about, too. They had a glazed look. One of them had a T-shirt which read, 'WHERE'S THE FUCKING MONEY YOU OWE ME?'

'What's with all these pictures of like Heidi houses?' said one.

The other one squinted at the blown-up posters on the walls. 'Switzerland,' he announced.

'Why Switzerland?'

'It's a Swiss Chalet, right.'

James glimpsed movement through a hatch into the kitchen, and waved his arm at whatever it was.

'I don't get Switzerland,' said the first punk, as slowly as if in a dream. 'I mean it's never really turned me on, you know?'

'Yeah. It's not sexy.'

'Exactly. Switzerland's not sexy. Fuck Switzerland.'

'Fucking Swiss bastards. Fuck 'em.'

A teenage staffer emerged from the kitchen and James slipped in front of the punks. They didn't seem to notice. 'I need a bottle of plain water, to go, please,' he said, 'and a coffee, cream and sugar. I'm in a real rush.'

When he came out, she was sitting on the curb, doubled over. People were passing by. He sat next to her. 'Here,' he said, 'there's cream and sugar in that, you should drink it, and that's plain water.'

'I'm hemorrhaging,' she said, flatly, as if saying, 'I'm tired.'

'Oh.' He sat while she took ineffectual sips at her water and waited.

'Ow,' she said.

Finally he did see an ambulance, wading through the traffic many blocks away. He stood up and waved his arms. The cars slowly parted with shouts and honks.

It stopped next to them and the burly men got out very slowly. They hardly looked at the girl as they gestured for her to get in.

Once it had driven off, slowly, he had to lean against the brick wall of a bank for a second and regroup before he made his phone call. He felt sleepy. He very much desired a beer. He wiped his face with his T-shirt.

He held his breath and entered the phone booth. It was at least no hotter than outside, although there was urine. Dialling, he wondered how the urge would take you to piss in a phone booth. Say you were walking home from a bar or even if you lived on the street – countless dark alleys, parks, dumpsters, and you choose a brightly lit phone booth on the street where everyone can see you and it would spray and splash about and pool around your feet on the concrete.

'Fifth precinct.'

'What ya got for me, Jenkins?'

'Hair at Melonhead –'

'Of course,' murmured James.

'– talk to someone called Yummola –'

'Yumm-OLA!'

'– and she still hangs at the Agency sometimes.'

'Been there. Anyway. Excellent work.'

'Thank you. Ah, Buck's wondering about the –'

'A couple more hours. Tell him it's fine, I'm fine, tell him to take a cab if he needs to get anywhere, I'll pay for it. You're a fine cop, Jenkins, so –'

'BOOK HIM!' they yelled simultaneously, and hung up. De Courcy seemed to have forgotten the morning's outrage, and was enjoying the role of nerve centre.

James stepped back into the heat of the afternoon. 'Fuck

Switzerland,' he said aloud. 'Fucking Swiss bastards.' He wiped his face on his T-shirt and got back on the Hypercube.

'No, no, Dominic's at Fur, Synapse Wednesdays, and Fuzz, Mondays, Juan is McCatalepsis now, still drum and bass dub, you know.'

The door slammed behind James, but no one looked at him, or heard in the hammering beat.

'Any really hard stuff?' said the waif boy. 'Like nosebleed? Meth stuff?'

'No, no, some old jungle though, kind of retro jungle, not happy jungle, though, the whole thing is more like ambient and ice, ambient jungle, which is better than that whole illbient thing which is so over.' The woman looked to be about forty; she took a long drag on her cigarette and moved out from behind the counter so James could see the whole outfit: zebra-striped snakeskin flared jeans, bare belly, piercing, shiny plastic bra. She had bright metallic silver hair in dreadlocks like Nicola's. She looked at him briefly and turned away.

'Hi,' said James.

'McCatalepsis has a website now, it's kind of cool, it's just all black with clips from like the Dick Van Dyke show, you know, just occasionally, like whenever. You need a lot of bandwidth.'

'Hi,' he said again, this time to the waif boy, who had slumped into the orange fifties sofa and put his massive boots on the kidney-shaped coffee table. The thumping, backed by a humming like large bees and a random hissing, drilled into James's head and relaxed him a little: he could recognize it as new. 'Is that Yummola?' He shrugged towards the silver-haired woman who had moved back down the row of chairs to a client whose head oozed purple slime.

Waif boy put down his magazine (the oversized *Random*, James noted), and said, 'Hello?'

'Hi. I'm looking for Yummola.'

'She's with a client.'

James nodded. With a professional eye he took in the bright plastic chairs, the mutant female models, who were white, and the enormous male models, who were black, all chatting hysterically with the stylists. He took in the breast cleavage on the raven-haired one with the blow-dryer, the bum cleavage of the crop-headed one. He took in the German magazine whose name he didn't recognize, the flyers on the green and pink wall. One notice read simply, 'ICY', on a black-blue background, with a date. The music sounded like the nail-gun in the construction site next to De Courcy's apartment.

He was well aware that what he had just overheard was worth money at *Edge*. He would have to remember it, call Julian tomorrow, ask if anyone had covered ambient jungle at McCatalepsis yet. And had he heard about the website? He thought about ice and cat and crystal meth and suddenly felt tired and said, 'Fucking hell.'

'Do you have an appointment?' the waif boy said, knitting his brow. He had a tight lace shirt on, which was transparent. His peroxided hair hung in tufts on either side of his face, short else-where. James realized the boy had been concentrating on a reply since he had spoken.

'No, actually, I just have to chat with her. It's a social call.'

'She's right over there.'

James weaved through the models.

'She had a Marghiella coat that was like inside out,' yelled Yummola between puffs, 'Gaultier dress with the bare boobs, Demeulemeester waistcoat –'

'Hi,' said James, 'I'm James, I'm a friend of Nicola.'

'Hi James.' Yummola's face contorted and she squealed, '*Sweetheart!*' She was looking over his shoulder: he turned and saw the tall black man approaching, stooping to kiss the waif boy on the lips, embracing the stylist with breasts. James recognized him from Nicola's video screening. 'Well well well, the princess arrives when she wants to, are we worthy of you, darling? *Get* over here and gimme a kiss.'

The man rubbed himself against Yummola while the client strapped in the chair with plastic on his head twisted around to stroke him too.

'Listen,' said James, 'I'm in a kind of an urgent situation –'

'Sorry I'm a little late,' said the newcomer to Yummola's neck, still wrapped up with her. James dodged the curling iron in her hand as they spun.

'Would you happen to know where Nicola was?'

'You just get up or what?'

'Uh-huh. Still a little spacey.'

'Well, how was it, true love or what, big girl?'

All the stylists and all the clients were turned towards them, listening and smiling.

'Fabulous. It was fabulous. Spooky played all night and –'

'Spooky?' squealed a stylist, '*the* Spooky?'

'And we did K.'

'E and K or just K?'

'A little E.'

'There's no little E, girl,' said Yummola, turning back to her client. 'Now get to work.'

Everyone was laughing. The newcomer was taking his leather coat off.

'Hey, man,' said James, 'you know Nicola, right?'

'Nicola?'

'Nicola Nicky photographer Nicola, Lickson, I met you at her video screening?'

'Sure. How you doing?'

'Great, great, James, listen –'

'Hey James. Damon.' Damon was moving towards a back room.

'Was she at Spooky, where you were, last night?'

'Oh yeah.'

'Oh.' They were in the office.

Damon hung up his coat and looked in a ledger.

'Because I really have to find her. She has these photographs that this magazine needs.'

'Did you try Christian?' Damon turned and walked back out through the salon. James rushed behind. Damon greeted some people waiting on the couch and turned to the appointments book.

'Christian?' said James from the wrong side of the counter.

Damon looked up at him sharply.

James felt a distinct unease. 'No, I didn't.'

'Who did you say you were?'

'We were – we worked together on a magazine shoot. I wrote the piece.'

Damon's face relaxed slightly. 'Well, you should try Christian. Or just go to her place, he's staying there.'

'Uh-huh.' James wanted to sit down. 'I'll try there again. But I was there all day. Listen.' He felt weak. He hadn't eaten since breakfast and had two dollars and fifty cents in his pocket and the temperature was over thirty in the salon. Damon was looking at him and now not looking at all aggressive or distrustful. James had to confide in him. 'I have this emergency going on.'

'Okay.'

With a rush of relief like tears, James told him the story, about *Glitter* and the photographs and the phone calls. Damon listened. A tall girl with satin cigarette pants listened from the orange couch. James felt her eyes in his back.

'So if I could find the lab she uses, I could find out if she at least dropped the negs off for processing, and get them from them.'

'They won't give you someoneone else's negs without her permission.'

James wiped sweat from his eyelashes. 'It's worth a try.'

Damon smiled. 'All right. Look, you should just relax a little. This will all work out. She uses BGM at Atlantic.'

'Thank you, man. Thank you.' James turned for the door.

'Everything will be okay, man.'

'Thanks, Damon.' James paused with his hand on the door. 'Nicola and –'

'Angelica, I can take you now. What's that?'

'Christian.'

'Uh-huh?'

'Um.' James felt his face turning red. 'Was Christian there last night too?'

The girl rising from the couch put her hand to her mouth and tittered.

Damon looked away. 'I'm not sure, man.'

From the back of the salon, Yummola was shouting, 'Westwood bustle, silver plastic quilted Miyake –'

■ CHAPTER NINETEEN

He was vaguely aware that it was strange to be on the vast, exposed deck of a battleship under these rainclouds, dressed in nothing but shorts, but he knew there must be some good reason for his being there, such as perhaps Julian sending him, seeing as Julian was now watching him from the bridge which was also a television station, and besides, he was too distracted by the necessity of getting through the open French doors to question anything. The doors led to the captain's cabin, and had vines growing around them. Damon, the hairdresser from Splat, stuck his head out and said, 'Do you have a pass?'

'Of course not,' laughed James, holding up his violin, which had turned into a medieval instrument, a krummhorn. 'I have this.' He was trying to be jovial, which wasn't working. He grew shrill and shouted, 'Which should show you that it's extremely urgent, I have to call the President of the United States, he's depending on me.'

Damon looked scornful. Nicola's arms wrapped Damon's chest from behind, and her face appeared over his shoulder. She was nuzzling his neck. She looked briefly at James and said, 'You don't get in looking so ridiculous!'

Because James hadn't realized that he was in fact wearing a transparent lace goth dress, which was an extremely silly getup for the wet battleship – he had apparently been sitting in a puddle, too – and even more embarrassing now that he had an erection, poking it up like a tent, that all the hairdressers and the President and his parents were laughing at and pointing, at his cock and his krummhorn.

He woke and opened his eyes. He stared into blackness. A blinking red light slowly moving at great distance.

He was lying on his back and looking at a plane crossing the sky.

He reached out and felt gravel under his arms, which must be what was making his back so cold and uncomfortable. There was quite a strong breeze, which made him shiver. He sat up, wrapped his arms around himself. He was on a roof. The roof of the Bomb Factory.

He looked around. It was a flat roof covered in gravel. There was no other building as tall close by, so he stared off into the black sky. He stood up unsteadily and picked off some of the gravel that was stuck to his palms and the backs of his thighs. There were spots of sticky tar on his skin, too, which he rubbed at. The gravel was stuck to tar on the roof.

He rubbed his face and walked towards the edge of the roof. He looked out over the other warehouses. He saw the huge radio tower glowing in the distance like a middle finger, pinned with red lights, a white beam from its tip pointing straight up into the stars. James arched his neck to stare up at it. It appeared to curve over him. He wondered why. The office towers of downtown seemed very far away. He turned south towards the expressway, which was moving filaments of light. He could hear the swishing of trucks. The vast pixelboards for Canon and Sony spun and danced, the orange letters cohering and fragmenting again. Beyond the expressway was a charcoal mass: the lake. It looked like concrete in the darkness.

He turned towards where he imagined De Courcy's street to be, but it was too far to distinguish. There was a siren from the streets below, and a muffled bang that could have been a gunshot. He felt a little calmer now than he had when beginning the climb.

After being turned away like some kind of street person, which he supposed he now resembled, from BGM Labs, he had waited at the front door of the Bomb Factory, ringing buzzers at random. Then he had waited among some shrubs in a lane along one side of the building, staring up at what he thought were Nicola's windows on the top floor, which were lighted. He had yelled her name for a while. It had grown dark, and then he had noticed how the balconies all stuck out and were stacked asymmetrically, which presented advantages, and how almost all of them had apparently solid wooden trellises nailed to the wall, which could be climbed.

He couldn't quite remember what had prompted him to climb, or how he had made it from the ground to the first balcony, which was on the second floor. He remembered singing some of Fiona's Maritime songs as he climbed. He became aware of a burning sliver of pain along the inside of his thigh, which began to spread like fingers into his lower abdomen. He must have pulled something hoisting his leg up to that first balcony. He rolled his head around on his shoulders; aside from a little stiffness, it was holding up okay.

He was on the side of the building with the balconies now, directly over Nicola's windows. He was right over her balcony, could drop down onto it if he wanted, but decided against startling her like that. He wanted to know more about Christian first. If he lay on his belly and stuck his head over the side he would be able to look into her apartment, albeit upside down.

On the way up, he had looked into a very high-ceilinged, brightly lit room with bare walls. There were cardboard boxes in piles. The only object that had been unpacked was a monolithic television. In front of the television was a pile of flesh. It was a naked man in cowboy boots. He was fat and bald and his flesh quivered. It was hairless and mottled. He was pointing a remote control at the television. 'Home theatre,' James had said, giving the man the finger. Something about the cowboy boots had enraged him. He continued climbing. The man never looked up.

He sat on the edge of the roof with his legs over the side. There was a short parapet, about half a brick in height, around the edge of the roof, which was sheathed in aluminum, so it wasn't very comfortable. There was a gutter around the outside of the roof, too, a couple of inches lower than the parapet, which he rested his calves on.

He sighed. The gutter was cutting into his calves, so he stood up. He wondered why you would put a gutter around a flat roof. There was a rhythmic thudding in the air: he looked up to see a helicopter with flashing red lights arcing upwards across the expressway. 'Strange,' he said, in a television documentary voice. 'Strange and beautiful.'

It suddenly occurred to him that he had one thing, one small thing to feel grateful for: he had fallen asleep without trying. He giggled.

The cool breeze lifted his hair. He stretched his arms out wide and stood up, at the edge of the roof. 'Call me Raoul,' he said aloud. Then he remembered the fat man in cowboy boots and he laughed. He wondered if everyone in the Bomb Factory was naked. Maybe that was why no one answered their buzzers. He wondered if Nicola was naked, too. Just below him. He stopped laughing.

He stood motionless for a moment. Then he got to his knees on the sharp, clinging gravel, then gingerly lay on his front. He inched forward, making, he was sure, an avalanche sound below. He stuck his head over the short aluminium-sheathed parapet and looked into the gutter. He would have to push his whole chest out over the parapet and grab onto the gutter if he wanted to hang his head over the side.

The gutter was black with mud and rotting leaves. As he heaved his shoulders over the edge and grasped its sharp edges, he breathed in a lungful of its sewage smell. He wriggled his hips and legs forward and pushed his head further out. He looked down onto Nicola's balcony. There were dark circular shapes on it, also giving off vegetal smells. He made these out to be foreshortened shrubs in pots.

He wriggled further out and rested his elbows on the gutter. The parapet was cutting into his chest. He wondered briefly what was supporting the gutter, seeing as how there was no soffit on a flat roof. He hung his head down over the gutter.

The sliding glass doors were only a foot down from the roof. They were outlined in yellow light, covered on the inside by some kind of tapestry or blanket. A musical thumping emanated.

The tapestry curtain left a few inches of glass exposed, a lit band down one side. He twisted his head to see into it. He was breathing quite hard. The curtain twitched as if someone had bumped into it from behind and it came away even farther, to reveal a triangle of something or several things right up against the window. At first it looked like a jumble of fabric and something made of white plastic. It was hard to make out, upside down. There was a square of embroidered upholstery with part of a stuffed animal of some sort and a pallid object lying across it, which on second glance was not plastic but a fish with the skin removed. It had a wig attached to it.

James heaved forward a little farther, spreading both hands out along the gutter and putting all his weight on his wrists, as if he was doing pushups. He canted his head to one side and then to another, to try to make out what the upside-down stuffed animal was. He stared at the section of fish and decided it was not a fish but a plucked chicken. At that moment the fish or chicken object kicked at the curtain in a spasm, thus revealing itself to be a human limb or perhaps a section of torso, white flesh, hairless except for the wig part which must have been a tangle of actual human hair, short, curly body hair rather than head hair. The stuffed animal kicked as well; it appeared that these parts were intertwined limbs (or, again, torsos?) and that they were moving erratically and jerking at the curtain; the body parts must have been on some kind of divan or bed pushed up against the sliding doors.

The blood rushing to James's head was making him dizzy; he realized he was holding his breath as well. 'On this same divan or bed,' he grunted, hanging himself even further over. He began to be dimly conscious that one of those large, shrouded pieces of furniture at the back of his mind had shuffled forward when he wasn't looking: namely, the idea that if indeed Nicola was in the apartment and naked, as he had for some reason imagined, she might not be alone and naked, and that indeed the objects he was perceiving might well belong to her and to someone else, and that someone else might be this Christian.

He shoved this back. Nicola must often have different people in her apartment, including this Christian, who might simply be a friend, and these moving parts were not necessarily hers or his.

The jerking stuffed animal part was tubular in shape and covered not in fur but in a nubbly material like a sweater; it could have been an ankle in a sock. The plucked chicken with the wig moved out of sight; it could have been an armpit or a particularly skinny abdomen with pubic hair attached. It was impossible to tell whether it was male or female. Or indeed if there was more than one body involved. Whatever it or they were doing relied on rhythmic movement.

It was impossible for James not to consider that in a moment he was probably going to see Nicola naked and he wondered if he really wanted to. Seeing Nicola naked was always an unmitigatedly pleasurable experience, but now suddenly it was not. Nicola naked in the company of someone called Christian he most definitely did not want to see.

He lifted his thrumming head and shook it to stop it from thinking, but it was too late; before he could swat it away he was buzzed by the long-delayed question of what he was going to say to Nicola when he saw her, which led neatly into the question of how he would explain being upside down over her window and indeed of what the hell he was doing at all.

His head was about to explode. He tried to keep it up for a couple of minutes. He stared out at the skyline and began rehearsing things he would say to her.

Hey, Nicky.
Hey.
No, don't explain. I understand, whatever it is. You just got freaked out when you got all my messages. Now, I just need the negatives. You have the negatives? You remember those negatives?

His shoulders began shaking.

'Make no mistake, Mister Bond,' he said in a Russian accent, 'I want that microfilm. And I intend to get it.'

Then there was a sharp metallic crack like a beer can crumpling and he was falling through air, head first.

There were three major bumps, although he might have missed one; he counted specifically head, shoulder and knee. He did not know how long they had taken to occur. He seemed to be thinking slowly. His eyes were closed. There was a sharp line under his back, so he must be lying on his back. His legs were hanging over some object and not touching any ground-like surface. Something damp and light touched his cheek. One hand was clutching something sharp and cold, the other was tangled in a mass of something both soft and wiry. Gently, he tried to move his torso, and a needle of pain moved in his neck.

'Bother,' he said, and opened his eyes a slit, as if he could take in the scene by stages.

There was a band of light about two metres away from him, casting everything in a pale glow. He turned his attention to the thing touching his cheek, which was a small luminous pink sac with a velvet texture. It was striated with fine dark grooves or runnels. He pulled his head back and saw that the sac had a puckered and wrinkled opening that looked vaguely obscene. He focused on the opening and realized that the sac was a flower with pink petals which were closed. There were leaves with pointy edges all around his face. He stared up through the branches at the starless sky.

He struggled to free his hand from leaves and branches and sat up.

His legs were hanging over the edge of a wooden pot. He was sitting on a shrub with pink flowers. The light was from the gap in Nicola's curtain.

As he struggled to pull himself out of the pot, his neck seared him again. 'Bother,' he said stepping shakily onto the balcony floor. 'Curses.'

The curtain had been drawn, the door was sliding open.

'*James!*' said Nicola, 'Jesus *Christ* what are you *doing*, you fucking scared the –'

'Damn,' he said, unbending. His knees were shaking a little and he was breathing hard. 'It was so much better. I've gone and done it again. Damn and fuck. How are you?'

She wore a silk dressing gown. She backed up and looked over her shoulder. The curtain fell back over the doorway so he couldn't see anything of the apartment. 'James, I'm sorry about the –'

'You look lovely, I must say,' he panted. He stared at his right hand, which was firmly clutching a two-foot section of curved white aluminum. It was twisted and had jagged edges. He pointed it at himself. 'Sorry about my appearance. Haven't rested a lot lately. But I won't stay long.'

'I have to explain what –'

'Haven't got all day, babe.' He waved the section of gutter at her. His voice was hoarse. It seemed to James that somebody else was talking. Probably Raoul. 'You have those photographs? Or did you not have them developed? I'll just take the negs, then.' He held out his left hand.

'I took them to the lab this afternoon, so they should be ready by –'

'No you didn't. I already checked there. Look, let's not fuck around any more. Give me the negs and I'll do the rest.' He looked at his watch. 'Ultraprint is open till midnight. I can get them over in the next half hour and they can be done by tomorrow noon, I can get them off before five and they'll be in New York by nine the next day, and that might just save our asses, otherwise you and I never work for an American magazine again.'

She opened her mouth and closed it. Her face quivered. In a faint voice, she said, 'Just a second.'

He waited on the balcony, massaging his neck and looking out at the skyline. He picked some leaves out of his hair. He could make out the great orange letters sparkling across the biggest pixelboard on the Expressway. He squinted as they gelled into a phrase that slid sideways. THE... COLD... COMES... AUGUST 2. Then, as if exploding, the letters shattered. Their shards shimmered at random for a second, then started forming a pattern, a shape like a large fish, perhaps a whale. It undulated. James thought it was swimming. Then its top half rendered itself into a face with eyes and a big smile, and big wavy hair, and James realized it was a line-drawing imitation of Alicia Montgomery's image on the billboard poster. The centre of the pixelboard was her enormous cleavage, in stark yellow and black. The cleavage grew to fill the whole board. Against the black lake, he lost the edge of the board. The great yellow breasts were swelling out of nowhere into the night.

Nicola was behind him. 'Beautiful night,' he said, turning to face her.

She held out an envelope. 'Okay,' she said, 'look, I'm really sorry there was a delay, it's just that I've been under an awful lot of stress lately, with all this –'

'Forget it,' said James. 'Just forget it. Here, take this.' He held out his piece of gutter. She stared at it for a second and then dazedly took it. She handed him the envelope.

She examined the piece of metal, turned it over in her hands. Then she looked over the balcony. 'How did you get up here?'

'I climbed.' He wondered how he was going to get down. He had an urge to jump off the balcony and fly away like Batman.

'You had a bad fall.'

'Yes. Oh. By the way.' He turned and waved the envelope at the shrub. 'What is that?'

'What is what?'

'The plant.'

'The plant in the pot?'

'Yes.'

'What *is* it?' she said. 'What do you mean?'

'I mean,' said James patiently, 'what kind of plant is it?'

'That one?' She pointed the piece of metal at the pot.

'Yes.'

'That's a ... it's a hibiscus.'

'Hibiscus. I fell on it. I'm sorry. I think I damaged the hibiscus.'

'Oh.' She stared wide-eyed at the flattened shrub. There were pink petals scattered across the balcony. 'Oh. That's too bad.'

'I'm sorry. Anyway. I've got to go.'

'Oh. How are you going to get down?'

'Isn't there an elevator?'

'Oh.' Nicola looked behind her. 'Well, see, this isn't a really good time. For you to come in.'

James laughed. 'No problem.' He swung a leg over the balcony.

'James!'

'What?'

'You're not going to just ...'

'Well, see, Nicky, it's like this. If you won't let me through your apartment there's no other way I can ...'

'Oh. *Shit.*'

'It's no problem. I wouldn't want to put you out.'

'*Well,*' she said, defiant, 'if you had just warned me you were going to be –'

'Forget it. I wouldn't want to inconvenience you.'

'Oh, James, don't make me feel like a bitch. It's not fair,' she said, her voice going whiny. 'It's just that it's a really –'

'It's no problem. Really. See you.'

'James. Are you okay?'

'Yup. See you.' He put the envelope in his teeth. 'Shee ya,' he said again. He looked down and saw the balcony below, three yards down and about two yards over. He would have to leap sideways, which would mean a thump when he landed, which might attract attention from someone inside. He swung his other leg over and stood on the outer side of the railing, his toes wedged in between the railing and the balcony floor. There was quite a breeze, which should have frightened him. Instead, it made him want to attempt some kind of demonic laugh. But he couldn't because he had an envelope in his mouth. He looked down and planned his landing away from the potted shrubs on the next balcony.

As he kicked off he shouted, 'Whee!'

He felt air filling his T-shirt and then pain in his knees as he landed on the concrete of the balcony below. The envelope fell to the floor. The lights were off inside the condo. Through the reflective surface of the sliding glass doors he saw movement, then made out a figure: someone dressed as a Red Indian in war paint or perhaps as a camouflaged soldier. James started and ducked and so did the figure.

He was looking at his own reflection in the glass. He stood and approached himself. He had not realized that his face was smeared with mud. Rotten leaves from the gutter that he had plunged his nose into. No wonder Nicola had seemed a little frightened.

'James!' came her voice from above.

'It's easy,' he called up, 'when you know how.'

'Are you going down that way?'

'Yes.'

'Oh. Bye then.'

Light burst out of the glass doors before James; he froze in it. A woman in a terry-cloth dressing gown had walked into the great open space of her Bomb Factory condo and flipped the overhead light on. She had a towel wrapped around her head; she also had her back to James.

He looked wildly for escape. There was a wooden trellis running up the wall from the apartment below; if he climbed carefully over this balcony, he might be able to reach over and grab it or get a toe-hold on it by stretching his already stretched leg as far as possible. Slowly, so as not to attract attention from the woman inside, he bent his knees to pick up the envelope.

He had one leg over the railing when the woman turned her head towards him and James went hot and cold as they stared at each other.

It wasn't a woman at all.

It was some kind of reptile.

Involuntarily, James let out a hoarse bellow. He had almost let go of the railing and fallen.

She was either a reptile or she had a horrible deformity or disease that had led to a green scaly growth all over her face.

The woman jumped at James's shout, saw him half over her railing and screamed herself; her humanoid mouth opened wide.

In an instant, James realized what was wrong with her face. She had some kind of green facial treatment smeared on it, some kind of avocado-oatmeal mud pack. Hugely relieved, he waved. 'Don't worry!' he yelled at the glass. 'I'm on my way down!'

The woman screamed again, backing up, one hand closing the neck of her terrycloth dressing gown, the other reaching for a phone on a table.

James remembered his own mud-smeared face. 'Sorry!' he called, swinging his other leg over. 'I'm not myself!'

He decided against further explanation as the woman picked up the phone and began dialling. He put the envelope in his mouth and stretched his leg outward, feeling for the edge of the trellis with his toe. He found it, but couldn't swing his other leg over to it without letting go of the railing.

He stayed for a moment in this position, doing the splits between the railing and the trellis, reaching out with one hand to grab the edge of the trellis, which he finally did. There was a faint but recognizable *krik*, the sound of a match striking, as his fingernails scratched against the brick wall.

He said, '*Bugger*bum.'

It took a second of steeling himself to relinquish his toe-and-hand hold on the balcony. He swung all his weight onto the trellis, and began a careful descent. It was just like climbing down a ladder with tiny rungs, except that there were branches and leaves to get tangled in. The ladder creaked like old furniture.

'Home theatre,' he muttered. 'Home theatre indeed.'

There was a whining noise from above. He stopped and looked up, panting. The noise came down again: 'James?'

'Can't chat right now, babe,' he said at normal volume. She wouldn't hear him.

The trellis took him down two more storeys, and then began making a crackling sound.

'Hold on,' said James to the wood. 'One more floor.'

But the crackling became a snapping, and then a splintering. He realized he was leaning backwards at too great an angle. The trellis was coming away from the wall.

He dropped almost a full story into the black laneway. Luckily there were more shrubs there. Pieces of vine and trellis showered around him

He stood shakily. His knees were okay. Only his neck throbbed. He saw the light of the street a few yards away. His jaws were tightly clenched, and there was saliva dribbling from the sides of his mouth. This was because he was still holding the envelope in his teeth. He unclamped, and gently removed the envelope.

It was limp, damp, pocked with semicircular tooth-prints. He turned it over in his hands, breathing deeply.

He held the negatives.

There was a high-pitched voice from far above. 'James?'

He looked up.

'James?'

'Yes!' He looked way up at Nicola's silhouette, leaning over her balcony.

Faintly, her voice came down. 'Will you call me?'

'So,' said Maya Lipschitz. 'We speak at last.' Her voice was calm and enunciated, like a flight announcement at JFK, but as clear in his head as if she was standing right next to him and about to bite his ear. '*So.*'

'So,' said James, bent over. He was trying to untangle the phone extension cord from the kitchen chairs and table legs. He held three loops of it already in one hand, and had the phone trapped between ear and shoulder; if he could just free up five more feet he could make it into his room and close the door. De Courcy was playing Human League remixes in the living room, but was nowhere near. James could hear him singing along from his room, '*I was working as a waitress in a cocktail bar ...*'

'So. I've just had a moment to go over the piece, and –'

'Just now? What about the deadline?'

'Don't worry about the deadline. Anyway.'

'Uh-huh.' He yanked the remaining loop from behind the fridge and started kicking the mass towards his bedroom. 'So we had lots of time, really.'

'What? It's already been laid out, it goes to the printer tomorrow. Anyway. What we have here, James, I think, is a good start.'

'Okay.' He closed the door behind him and was trapped with his clothes. He kicked some out of the way and sat on his bed, where the disassembled pages of the first drafts of the article were scattered among the socks. He picked up the first page. 'Yes.'

'And the photos are great, by the way. Everyone's so happy with them we might even be going for a cover portrait.'

'A *cover*?'

'Well, when you have great art, you should use it. I've called Nicola to tell her we want to use her again, and she was so sweet on the phone, she's just charming, isn't she?'

'Oh yes.'

'Isn't she just a joy to work with?'

'Oh yes.'

'So, anyway, the piece is a good start, but it needs some work.'

'Okay.'

'Personally, I thought some of the stuff was great, of course, but Analph was not too happy about –'

'Analph?'

'Analph Betterave, the editor-in-chief.'

'Oh yes, of course,' said James, who had not looked at the mast-head. 'Analph.'

'He was questioning some of the stuff about Canada, you know, all the Canadian references?'

'Yes.'

'He didn't think it was really necessary.'

James paused, shuffling the papers in order. 'I'm not sure I follow you.'

'We cut all the stuff about Canada.'

'What stuff exactly? You mean the fact that Boben is Canadian?'

'Well, where someone's born is always important if it's a foreign place, somewhere exotic, but if the guy's born in Pittsburgh or Canada or, I don't know, it's not that exciting, right, especially if you're short on space to begin with, and that's another thing, we need to lose a few paragraphs. Also all the literary-analysis stuff can be cut down – remember, James, we're dealing with a personality profile here. People want to know about the man, what he's like, they're not going to want to read *poetry*.'

'Especially not from a poet.' James felt a flame of pain in his face and realized he had driven half a centimetre of tooth into his cheek. Wincing, he withdrew it, and said, 'And the fact that he only writes about Canada, that's not too important either, I suppose.'

'James, you have to think of our readers. They're from all over America, not the big cities, and they're from all walks of life. They're going to be very interested in this movie, you know –'

'*Breaking the Ice*.'

'*Breaking the Ice*, and so they're going to be interested in everything that's Alaska and stuff, but if you keep reminding them that that means *Canada*, then they might be a little frightened off.'

'Frightened off by – wait – Alaska,' said James, 'is part of –'

'Frankly,' said Maya with a slight briskness, 'our readers aren't interested in Canada. And we are *most* concerned with pleasing our readers. Right, James?'

James whistled.

'Right James?' This time the sharp edge was in the open.

He sighed. 'Right, Maya. So what do you want me to –'

'We don't have time for you to do a rewrite, we're right up against deadline. So what I've done is I've done an edit myself, and I'd like to fax it to you for your approval, do I have your fax number?'

James emerged into the living room. De Courcy was standing in front of the mirror, bare-chested and flexing. He wore nothing but tight jeans and workboots, which was strange. James stopped short. 'Don't mind me.'

'Oh, don't mind me,' said De Courcy. He was shiny with sweat and breathless. He turned to the stereo and rewound the tape. *'Don't you want me baby,'* he sang, wiggling his hips.

'Wow. You are looking impressive,' said James. De Courcy's arms and shoulders were bulbous, his chest swollen, his belly cut into cubes.

'You should see my favourites,' said De Courcy, contorting his torso in the mirror. 'Watch,' he said through a tight jaw. Veins bulged on his forehead. 'Obliques and serratus anteriors.'

'Wow. They look like little teeth under there. What's it all in aid of?'

De Courcy relaxed and put his hands on his hips as if dismayed. 'Blue Collar Hunk, remember?'

'Oh yes.'

'On Janni Bolo. You come out and dance to music of your choice, then the studio audience selects the hunk of the year.'

'When is it?'

'Next week. I'm a drywaller.'

'What's a drywaller?'

'It's someone who puts up the boards they use instead of walls in houses now.'

James slumped on the sofa. 'How did you find out about that?'

'I asked Buck for a word that was used in construction.'

'Don't they ask you for ID or anything? What about your accent?'

'Lord purple jumpin',' said De Courcy convincingly, '*you* are foolish as a *mitt*. I'm from Cape Breton. Fiona's been training me.'

'Well, good luck. What do you win?'

'Five hundred dollars.'

'That's not a lot for all this work. And what about your music? You're really going to play that?'

'Why not?'

'Well, it's not exactly – how to put this delicately – there could be more heterosexual music.'

De Courcy had opened his mouth, looking pained, when the phone rang. James answered.

There was a brief pause, then a 'Hi.'

'Nicola. What a pleasure.'

'Okay I just want to say one thing: I'm sorry I'm sorry I'm sorry.'

'Okay. It's all all right anyway.' He made his cokehead psychiatrist face at De Courcy, who had turned back to the mirror.

'I'm really sorry about everything, and I hope you're not still mad.'

'No, I'm not still mad.'

'Everything worked out in the end, didn't it?'

'Yes. They loved your photos. They hated my story.'

'Oh. Anyway, I was wondering if we could talk.'

'Sure.'

'I mean we have to meet.'

There was a beep in his ear. 'Just hang on one second, Nicola, I have a – hello?'

'James?'

'Alison! Hi!' He clenched his fists and jaw, arched his back, stretched his lips as wide as he could over his teeth, and rolled his eyes up into his head, thus achieving his electro-shock face. But De Courcy wasn't watching. 'Listen, can I call you right back? I have someone on the other –'

'Oh, it's okay, Jamie, I won't talk long, I just wanted to let you know that I'm coming into town – for a whole *week*!'

'You're –'

'Don't worry, I know that your place is too small for me and Jeremy to stay, so I've set it up with Jeff Bauer and Sandy, you remember them?'

'No. Listen, hang on one second, because –'

'No no no, I'll go, I'll call you when I get in. I can't *wait* to be in a city again.'

'What are – why are you –'

'Oh, Jennifer McClelland, remember her? She works in a law firm now, and she told me they had an opening for a paralegal, I sent my résumé in, and I have an interview next week! And, oh, and I have to tell you something, you'd be so proud of me, I just bought something you'd think was really cool.'

'Oh.' James's finger was poised above the link button.

'I bought these wild PVC pants. They're shiny and rubbery and tight. They're wild.'

'Wow. Okay. I have to go. Call me.'

They said goodbye and he said hello again to Nicola. She was still there. Her voice was small.

'Could we meet?' she said again.

James puffed out his cheeks like a blowfish.

De Courcy turned up the stereo. '*Now five years later on you've got the world at your feet ...*'

'Okay,' he said. 'Sure. Let's meet.'

The people next to him at the bar were talking about the last Loon Lake reading he'd been at, the one where he'd met Nicola. 'But that's the problem with all the fiction we're still hearing in Canada,' said one, the bearded one, 'it's still linear narrative. It's still the same old nineteenth-century tell the story, use a narrator, have characters with identities, it's shit, it's the same old bourgeois shit.'

The pale woman next to him nodded. They both wore grad student uniforms of jeans and fleece outdoor tops with bright brand names everywhere. She wore heavy German sandals; he wore leather deck shoes.

'There's a real place for the resurgence of an avant-garde in this country,' said the woman.

'It's bourgeois shit,' said the beard, 'narrative fiction is repressive.'

James noted the man's sports watch, all dials and buttons, waterproof to thirty fathoms, accurate to a billionth of a second: it said 'IRON MAN' on it. He wondered what they were doing in Splat. He raised his eyebrows at Carmen, the Asian bartender, but she was kissing someone. The place was too close to the Culture Corner, was the problem, so they came here after the readings. Probably *Next* or *Edge* had called it a literary café, and before you knew it the place was full of marathon-running post-structuralists.

'Another martini, James?' said Carmen.

'No, thanks, Carmen, I actually hate martinis. I don't know why I ordered it.'

'Because they look so pretty.'

'I guess so.' He breathed in a cloud of garlic and grilling meat and his body twitched. Behind him, in the open kitchen, Manuel was doing a special of quail and orange glaze; there was the odd *phuff* of a tablespoon of Grand Marnier catching fire, then the warm smell of burned sugar in the air.

James couldn't look at the passing plates without salivating. He looked at his watch: Nicola was only fifteen minutes late, so he had another twenty to kill. He pilfered another glance down Carmen's cleavage as she leaned over the ice sink. He caught a wave of her cinnamony perfume. Her shiny hair brushed her neck. The skin between her breasts was perfectly smooth, like a photograph. His heart, or something, jumped. He watched her glide away, her buttocks taut in the black plastic miniskirt, and felt the familiar vague pain or illness and wished Nicola would arrive.

On his other side, two people had big martinis. They were both dressed in steely grey. The woman was smoking a long cigarette. She said, 'And she's like, don't you think we should go with him? And I'm like, oh relax, we'll go visit him in the hospital tomorrow, come *on*, lighten up! Like what is she, Mother Teresa all of a sudden? Oh, by the way, I saw Geena Davis there.'

'What was she wearing?' said the man. James turned his head slightly to look at him. He had cropped hair and black plastic glasses. His martini was orange.

'Sweatpants. She was working out. Did you hear the Windermere burned down?'

'What a bummer,' said the man. 'Should we get some more tequila martinis?'

'Yes. Mother Teresa's supposed to be a fascist, anyway.'

'Mother Teresa? How do you know that?'

'Oh, it's common knowledge,' said the woman. She blew smoke towards James. 'It's this big thing that people know. You know, this whole thing that everybody knows.'

James swivelled on his stool to look at the open kitchen. Manuel was working with two sous-chefs, leaning over the mosaic counter, building teepees of quail breasts on bamboo skewers; one of them was patterning plates with red and ochre coulis. Manuel nodded at James, turning back to the three pans sizzling on the burners. James smiled and breathed in.

Manuel would say something to an assistant, pull three lamb chops off the grill without appearing to look at them, dump on a handful of tiger shrimp and shake two bubbling pans, in a second and a half. He had two cream sauces and a jus reducing on the stove, plus the grill, and he always moved smoothly. He never appeared to taste anything.

'How are you?' he called to James, flipping the shrimp and throwing a dash of salt into a pan with the other hand.

'I love watching you work,' said James. 'It's like watching an athlete.'

'Say artist,' said Manuel. 'I'd prefer it if you said artist.' There was a dazzling burst of flame, instantly subsiding.

James shrugged. 'I'm bored with that.' His eyes darted to a passing woman, in ponytails and a black lace dress, all pierced and tattooed. It wasn't Nicola. She squealed as she approached, threw her arms around a woman in a pink wool suit.

'Another beautiful mad girl,' said James to no one. He swirled the martini in his oversized glass. The gin on his lips tasted of headache. 'I love martini *glasses*,' he announced.

He glanced back at Carmen, who was still too beautiful to look at. The Mother Teresa couple had left his side and he could see the little guy who had been next to them, another little guy with short hair. He wore heavy round glasses and a black suit, and was writing something in a notebook on the bar, tiny marks. He had been bent over his book since James arrived; his beer was abandoned and flat next to him.

James arched his neck to look at the pages; the guy didn't appear to notice. He was writing frantically, making black dots. They were notes. The whole book was a score, and the guy was writing music.

'Wow,' said James, and the guy looked up. 'Sorry. I'm impressed that you write music. Are you composing something?'

'Yes.' The guy was covering the page with his hand. He reached for his beer. 'You read music?'

'Yes. How can you think in here? There's –' He gestured to the speakers above them, releasing toxic clouds of jazz into the air.

'I don't hear them. I guess I block it out.'

'Cool.'

'I hear my own music in my head.' The little guy looked down at his page and sighed.

James sighed too. The restaurant was suddenly too noisy, too smoky. The Grand Marnier smelled too sweet. The jazz picked at his ears. He thought about his violin and then thought about ordering another martini. 'I wish I could do that,' he said, before he turned back to Carmen. 'Baby,' he said.

'I really don't think that after Foucault,' said the bearded guy loudly, as if addressing a conference, 'you can think that the body even *exists*, given the fragmented and mediated perceptions we have of it, I mean we don't even have a self any more –'

'Wait a minute,' said the pale woman. 'My body doesn't exist?'

'We can no longer afford to think so.' And he downed his beer conclusively.

The woman was touching her arm. 'Wow.' She was feeling the bones and muscle, twisting her wrist under her sleeve. 'Cool.'

'Jesus fuck,' said James. He turned to the little guy, who was still composing. 'Do you know Richard Catherell?'

The composer put down his pen, smiling broadly. 'Of course I do.'

'Do you *love* him?'

The guy laughed. 'He's very talented.'

'Cheers. Sorry.' James had splashed a little gin on his sleeve. 'I never meet people who have heard of him. I never get to talk about, I never meet people who have any – Can I buy you a drink?'

'I –'

'Hello.'

James looked right into Nicola's neck. She was completely naked. Her neck was bare and smooth as Carmen's cleavage. He gulped. Then he understood that she was wearing something that made her appear naked, some kind of underwear or nightgown. Her hair was pinned up but disentangling. 'Hi,' he said. 'And you do, in fact, have a leather jacket on as well. I hadn't noticed.'

'What?' She uncoiled onto the stool next to him, which appeared to have been suddenly vacated.

'Hey,' said James, 'where'd he go?'

'Who? Are you okay?'

'Guy sitting there. I wanted to talk to him about …' Now he took in what she was wearing with a more conscious appreciation. The leather motorcycle jacket, as usual, over a yellow silk slip or camisole. It had tiny straps and was tight across her breasts and short on her legs. She wore heavy motorcycle boots. She was not wearing a bra. 'Hi.'

'Hi.'

'Drink?'

'Are you ready for a table now, James?' said Carmen, rather coldly, he thought.

'Yes, please.' He stood up and stood on the bearded grad student's foot. 'Oh, I'm sorry,' said James, 'did that hurt?'

'It's okay,' muttered the guy, hopping.

'It's funny that it hurts, doesn't it? I mean considering –'

'This way, James,' said long-haired Damien, waving a menu.

'This way,' said James, putting a hand in the small of Nicola's back. He could feel her vertebrae through the thin leather; it snaked as she moved. He caught a glimpse of Manuel, gently laying down a fillet of mahi-mahi and running his eyes over Nicola like a cold hand.

Damien led them to their booth, the best booth, back in the jungly part, the part Damien and Nigel had decorated with stick-on twigs that wrapped around the backs of booths and up the old warehouse pillars and around the wrought-iron sconces, like vines they had haphazardly seeded. It was all prickly and hidden in there.

They looked at each other across a blood-red cloth. Her nipples made bumps in the silk. James wanted to stroke them. 'So,' he said.

'How are you?'

'Terrific.' He was noting a glossy black head at the neighbouring booth, against the other wall, belonging to a woman with a shiny spandex top. There was nowhere to look tonight. He heard the woman's voice: she was saying, 'How many tequilas do they have here?'

Eight, he thought, *eight tequilas at Splat.* Then the guy she was with, a buzz-cut guy with sideburns and glasses that told everybody in the room he was from the Film Centre, said loudly, 'Eight. Eight tequilas at Splat.' James hated him.

Nicola said, 'Are you eating? I'm starving.'

'I would love to, but I don't have any money.' He was through trying to impress Nicola.

'I have money.' She picked up the menu. 'Red or white?'

James picked up his menu with a smile. 'The quails look good. And I like the Amarone, they have a private import licence for it, and – here he is, Damien, do you have any of the ninety Amarone left?'

'It's no longer on the list,' said Damien.

'I know it's not.'

Damien smiled. 'I might.'

'Thank you. So.' He looked at her. 'What's going on?'

'I just wanted to see you in a, you know, in a normal way.'

'Ah.'

'I just wanted to make sure we were still friends.'

'Oh.' James couldn't help listening to the woman across the

aisle, the one with the shiny hair. 'Anybody who tells you he can tell a difference between tequilas,' she was saying, 'is either a genuine Mexican peasant or he's *lying*.' James tilted his head to get a look at her. He had to concede they were an attractive couple. He said to Nicola, 'What do you mean, in a normal way?'

'I mean just go out, have fun.'

'Ah.' He wondered if the woman in the next booth was Sharon Wynne-Taglia, Julian's protégée, whom he had met once and who had looked something like that. 'So, there's nothing special you wanted to tell me?'

Nicola looked down at her menu. She was blushing in blotches. 'No.'

'I see.' James rubbed his head and looked at the menu. 'I guess I'll have the quails then. Here's the wine. Thank you, Damien.'

After he tasted it and they ordered and they drank two glasses each, quickly, before the quails arrived, James had stopped trying to peek at Sharon Wynne-Taglia and was looking at Nicola's lip-ring glinting in her flesh, her hair, her breasts under the fabric, her long neck. She was saying, 'Anyway, I heard her on the radio, talking about her new book, and I thought of you because I think you would really like her. I can't remember her name, but the book was about these people in a city, I think it was New York, or maybe Chicago –'

'Or maybe Minneapolis, who knows?'

'Maybe, something like that, anyway –'

'Do you remember the name of the book?'

She frowned. 'Oh. I'm so bad at that. Just a minute.'

James sensed activity in the neighbouring booth. He swivelled slightly. The Film Centre guy had put his hand over the beautiful Sharon Wynne-Taglia's on the tablecloth and they were both looking at it and full of tension. James was jealous. He gulped wine and looked back at Nicola. Her hand lay white and long on the red cloth.

'No, I can't remember, it was a woman, though, anyway, the lead character in this book, this guy, I can't remember his name ...'

James noticed a tuft of red hair under her arm and swallowed more wine. He wanted to undo her hair, smell it. He looked away. The jazz was frantic now; the air thick with Grand Marnier. The restaurant seemed to swirl and tilt. He didn't want to look at the shiny-haired woman and the Film Centre guy again. He put out his paw and placed it gently over Nicola's hand. She stopped talking and they both looked at their hands lying together. She smiled, and leaned towards him. He saw the metal ring coming from afar, and braced his lips to meet it.

'Phew,' said James.

She snuffled, working her nose between his jaw and neck. Her hair was over his chest. He was still breathing hard. They were lying tight together on his narrow mattress. 'How's your neck?'

'Ow.'

'It wasn't me this time.'

'No. You were very ...' He listened to the sirens and the stereos filtered through the air vent. Fiona and Buck were asleep next door; De Courcy was still up in his room. Occasionally James could hear his desk drawers opening and closing. He wondered if he had been listening to them.

A globe of sweat fell from his forehead onto hers. He shifted; his hand came away from her back with a sucking noise. Her shoulderblades glided like panes of glass. 'Nicola.'

'Hmmm.'

'Was that okay?'

Did she stiffen slightly? 'Yes. Of course.'

'Well, not of course.'

'What do you mean?'

'I mean sometimes ... some times are better than others. Or don't you find that?'

She turned her eyes up to him; they were wide and glistening. 'Was it no fun for you?'

'No no, of course it was, it's always – I was thinking more of you.'

'What do you mean?'

He cleared his throat. 'Nicky. Do you enjoy it?'

'With you?'

'With anyone.'

She was silent. And then shivering, and then a cooler drop on his chest told him that she was crying. He smoothed her hair and held her tighter. 'It's okay,' he said. 'It's okay.'

'I don't know,' she whimpered.

They lay for a while in the hot air until she stopped crying. Her ribs felt like wet knife-handles under his fingers. She said, 'It's just that I can't relax.'

'I know. I've noticed.'

A fresh drop fell. She said, 'I think I would if I felt that … that someone …'

James waited for the drops to stop. He stroked her hair, cupped a shallow breast with his palm. She didn't push his hand away as she had earlier.

'You'll think it's silly.'

'No. Go on.'

'If I thought that someone would stay with me. If it would last.'

'What would last? The sex?'

'No, no. I don't care about that. If I knew that the guy would be there afterwards and … take care of me.'

'You mean something permanent. Commitment.'

After a pause, she nodded, the mass of her hair shifting around him. 'Yes.'

'It sounds as if you want to get married. Why don't you get married?'

This provoked fresh tears. She quite convulsed on his chest. 'I would,' she choked, finally. 'I wanted to. I thought I might with …'

'With who?'

'I'm sorry.'

'For what? I knew there was someone else.'

'You're not upset?'

'No. No. Tell me. It's okay. I'm curious.'

'You don't know him.'

'This Christian guy?'

'How do you know his name?'

James chuckled. 'When I was looking for you that day…. It doesn't matter. Well. Doesn't Christian want to?'

'No.'

'I see. That's too bad. You'll find someone else though.' He patted her ribcage.

She nodded and sniffed. 'You're nice,' she said.

There was some shouting outside, and the snarling of fighting dogs. It faded.

'What does Christian do?' asked James.

'Don't be jealous.'

'I'm not. I'm just curious. What does he do?'

'He works.' She started stroking his chest, which was merely irritating in the heat.

'Works at what?'

'Shut up.'

'Come on. I'm interested.'

'He works for the government.'

'Okay. Come on. What does he do for the government.'

'He's a scientist.'

'A scientist. What kind.'

'It doesn't matter. Why do you care?'

'An engineer?'

'Yes. He works in a water purification plant.'

James could feel the laughter breaking on his face. He controlled it. 'You wanted to marry a guy in *sewage*?' He pretended to cough.

'He's very educated. He's a water quality engineer.'

The laugh broke; James shook. 'I'm sorry, Nicky. I didn't mean to laugh. I'm sorry. Don't cry. Don't cry. I'm not – I didn't laugh because I have anything against it, against what he does. Really. I admire people who do things like that. It's very impressive to me. It's just picturing you. I didn't picture you with a guy like that. That's all. It's not funny. I know. I think it's great. I think it's great for you. Seriously.' He stroked her hair. 'Don't cry.' He tangled his fingers in the ringlets. 'You have beautiful hair,' he said. He kissed her forehead. 'Don't cry.' He looked at his watch. It was 3:00 a.m. Soon she would fall asleep, and then he might, possibly, even, too, and then it would be morning and it would all be over.

'Phew,' said James. He was breathing hard. He rolled onto his back on the damp mattress. 'All that lifesaving makes you very athletic, Allie.'

She sat up and stretched. Her breasts glistened with sweat. They were fuller than Nicola's. 'Sorry I made so much noise,' she said, placing a flat palm on his chest.

'Oh, no one would hear it here,' he lied. He had heard De Courcy's plaintive door-slamming and tap-running just as she was approaching her crescendo. She seemed to have been shouting, 'Ouch, ouch,' but he wasn't sure, as he had had a T-shirt wrapped around his head. She hadn't given him much time to fully undress before she had straddled him.

Now he had the T-shirt off. He wished there were a breeze from somewhere. Or a window. The room grew smaller every day. He wondered how he had accumulated so many clothes.

'Ouch,' he said, as her fingers tweaked his nipple. She laughed, and reached for the other one. She squeezed it hard. 'Hey.'

She just laughed again, so he laughed too, though he wasn't sure why. He said, 'You're a very sensual person, Allie.'

'I surprise you, don't I?'

'Yes. Who would have known. All those kayaking sandals.'

'What?' She was still holding hard.

He kicked some clothes off the bottom of the bed as if he was going to rise, but she wouldn't let him go. He looked up at her and said, 'I guess ... I guess you must be pretty bored in New Munich.'

'Yes,' she said, with a strange smile. 'That's why I'm so glad I met you again. Now I've seen where you live and the people you hang around with and everything. I have a feeling you're not uptight about certain things.'

'Whoa,' said James. In one knee-cracking move, Alison had straddled him. She pinned his hands on either side with her palms. Her breasts swayed over his face. Her thighs gripped his sides.

'Stronger than you look,' he said.

She bent forward, smiling, so that his face was between her breasts. She was sliding her groin up and down him. He felt wet everywhere. He twisted his face to one side so he could breathe and gasped, 'Allie? I'm ... I'm not sure I can do it again. So soon.'

'*You*,' she said in an iron voice, 'don't have any choice in the matter.' She let go of one hand for a second and grabbed the T-shirt lying beside his head. She pulled his hands together on his chest and wrapped them with the shirt, which she began to knot up. James just watched. 'You are my slave, right?'

'Terrific,' he said. 'Here we go again.'

As soon as he perceived daylight under the crack of the door and as a halo around the air-vent, he crawled out of the bed, careful to touch her as little as possible. She grunted a little and curled into a ball, wrapping the sheet around her. He pulled on his boxers and padded into the kitchen, feeling the grit of dust under his bare feet. He yawned and drank a glass of water and sat looking at the court-yard. He would be able to sleep if he ate something, or maybe went outside and walked around, but he couldn't eat and he would have to go back into his room to dress. So he sat and waited for some-one to wake up. He realized it was almost quiet in the apartment: De Courcy asleep, Fiona and Buck absent, only a couple of radios already on in the courtyard, and some children shrieking that they were going to hurt each other on some balcony, and the traffic from the street, but he hardly heard that, and there was no deep bass anywhere.

So he sat and thought. He thought that when Alison woke up, he would give her breakfast, and he would direct her towards the apartment where she was staying, but he was not obliged to accompany her there, since it was daylight. And if she asked when they could see each other again, he would have to be honest and tell her that he did not want to see her again, at least not for a while. He put his head down on the table. It soothed his burning neck a little.

He wondered why he didn't want to see her again and decided that he didn't know. It wasn't that he would have to deal with a girlfriend with a small child, although there was that, too. It wasn't *just* that, anyway. And it wasn't that she was only now discovering the things that he had discovered five years earlier. Although it was that, too. It was perhaps that she was still Alison, even in PVC pants, and she was from Munich, even if she was trying to be Nicola, she would never be Nicola, and even if she managed to be Nicola, he didn't want Nicola, either.

He admitted that he was confused.

Perhaps he just didn't really want to get to know Alison.

A generator woke up grumpy in the neighbouring construction site: it must be later than he thought. They rarely started before eight. The machine grunted and popped. The nail gun started papping. Pap, pap, pappap.

He would have to tell Nicola the same thing: that they wouldn't see each other any more. Which was fine, really, it was easier for some reason.

After that, he was not sure what he was going to do.

By the time Alison had registered his absence from the bed and come looking for him, De Courcy had also woken up, and so had the bassmobiles, and the noise around had risen to its first crescendo, its midmorning plateau.

James was on the phone, standing and hopping in his boxer shorts. 'Yes,' he said as loudly as he could, 'I've already talked to Constable McManus, several times. I want to speak to someone higher up now. I want to speak to his supervisor. It's been weeks since my first complaint, I've written to City Hall, I haven't seen a single car come by here, and I want you to understand that this is a serious problem and I want to be taken seriously. Yes. Yes I understand that. And I want you to understand that my right to sleep and work in my own apartment is just as important as those things, and I'm sure my alderman would want to hear about this problem. I am not going to talk to Constable McManus again. Constable McManus has served his purpose. We have exhausted his function. All right. What's his name? Just a minute.' He scrambled for a paper and pencil. 'All right, go ahead. MacHenry, M-A-C-Henry, okay. Please do. I'll hold. And if I get cut off I will call you right back, okay? Your name is? Okay. MacInley. Thank you,

Officer MacInley. And – hang on one second, I want to tell you something important before I go on hold and get cut off, because I know that I *will* get cut off, because transferring calls is a myth, it doesn't work and it never has worked, so I will end up calling you back, but I just want you to understand something important, and that is that I am a reporter. I work for the media. All sorts of media, papers, magazines, TV, radio. And I can see a very interesting story shaping up here. Yes. Yes, yes I *am* trying to blackmail you. You better believe I'm trying to blackmail you. Arrest me if you want, it will make the story more interesting. Now go ahead and put me on hold and I'll get cut off and I'll call you back. Thank you.'

This went on for some time, during which Alison dressed and made coffee.

'*Mung* bean,' said James as he hung up. 'Fuck with me, man, fuck with me and you've got another fucking thought coming.'

'Thought?' said De Courcy, in his silk dressing gown.

'Good morning,' said Alison at the kitchen table.

'Hi. I think that actually did some good. I think I actually got through to them this time.' He went to the window and drummed with his palms on the windowsill. 'Fucking bastards,' he said to the courtyard at large. 'You fucking bastards.'

'I find the logic a little oblique,' said De Courcy without moving his lips, 'of fuck with me therefore another *thought*. Or perhaps it's merely the grammar that's dubious.'

'How's your neck?' said Alison.

'Fucking sore.'

'That's too bad,' she said. 'I'm sorry.'

'Transfer your call my ass,' said James, 'what a *fiction*.'

'Because if your neck is sore you won't be able to take me out to all the clubs I've been dying to see.'

James wheeled to look at her. 'Clubs?'

'Night clubs. The ones you write about. I'd love to see them. I want to meet all the models and photographers and –'

James coughed. 'Flying flanagan fuck.'

'What?'

'Allie, I don't want to go to clubs any more.'

'Oh.' She looked at him and her smile dropped. 'James? Are you okay?'

He turned back to staring at the courtyard. 'Where does your friend live?'

'What friend?'

'Jennifer, Janet, whatever. Where you're staying.'

In the end he offered to walk her there but she refused. She was quiet. No one said anything about the next time. He said goodbye and kissed her quickly and she didn't try to kiss him at length.

From the deck, he watched her skirt float down the alleyway. The floral pattern, her brown legs and those ghastly sandals looked not only out of place beside the green garbage bags but also suddenly vulnerable. He looked around for dogs or thumping automobiles but there were no dangers. It was just that the skirt and legs looked suddenly like Munich, like something from his childhood, like Beth Webster in knee socks, or perhaps like an image he had of Alison herself in high school. He wanted her to walk faster, to run. He wanted her away from the neighbourhood, away from where Nicola had been and De Courcy was. He wanted her out of there.

He was about to go back inside when Elsie's door cracked open and she bustled out in her yellow tracksuit and a storm of two dogs, who ran past him, down the fire escape stairs to the courtyard, where they gleefully dispersed the squirrels.

'Mister doctor,' she said, 'I been meaning to talk to you.'

'It's okay,' said James, 'she won't be coming back.'

'No, no, I don't mind with the girls, you do what you want with the girls. I have something for you.' She bustled back inside. James waited in the morning sun, feeling it sucking the last remaining moisture from his liver and kidneys and squeezing it out onto his skin.

There was a sudden barking and snarling and gravel-scattering from the courtyard, and a man's voice yelping, 'Hey hey HEY!' James rushed to the deck's railing and looked over: the postman.

243

He ran down the stairs. 'Gilligan!' he yelled, 'Tisha! Get off him!' He grabbed both collars and yanked. 'They're just playing. It's okay.'

The postman had already started to run, but sheepishly stopped and picked up his cap. 'Almost bit me,' he said in a high voice. He had a moustache and spindly legs in his shorts. 'I won't deliver mail here if there's dogs.'

'Well,' said James, 'sorry about that. They're not my dogs.' He squinted up at the deck; Elsie still had not emerged. 'Anyway. Do you have mail for us?'

'You hold the dogs.' The man made a wide turn around them and daintily deposited junk in all the courtyard's boxes; even a thin envelope, James noted with interest, in De Courcy's.

James waited until the man had scampered off, released the dogs to attack squirrels and rats, and picked up the envelope. It was addressed to him, James Willing, and was obviously junk, as it was from some probably fictitious organization called Williams Westwood Publishing, which probably wanted him to subscribe to a monthly series of romances at twenty dollars a month and win a million dollars. He almost threw it away but considered the fun of scratching the rubber off the boxes in the instant prize category, and took it upstairs.

Elsie's door was still open, and cooking smells were spreading: something that involved cabbage. On the deck he realized that he had heard of Williams Westwood before. That in fact it was the real corporation that owned *Glitter*.

He tore open the envelope. There was a cheque for one thousand u.s. dollars.

His heart began to beat. 'Well,' he said, looking up at the throbbing sun. 'Well well well.'

Elsie was standing beside him, holding a casserole. 'Doctor,' she said, breathless, 'I make you perogies.'

Inside, he put the casserole in the fridge and grabbed the pile of newspapers on the radiator. De Courcy picked up *Next* every week to read the personal ads. He opened this week's copy to the classified ads, apartments for rent. He found one that said, 'Quiet bach.,

Annex, $650+, immed.' He underlined the word *quiet*, and dialled.

De Courcy came home from the gym at about eight. James was waiting for him at the kitchen table. He had a bottle of Krug Brut in a bucket and a 1989 Montlabert breathing. He had two Partagas in tubes.

'What's going on?' De Courcy dropped his bag. His hair was still wet; his cheeks flushed.

'You look very handsome,' said James. 'Help me celebrate.'

'What?'

'I signed a lease this afternoon.'

'You what? On what?'

'A second-floor bachelor. It's perfect. It's at Borden and Harbord. It's beautiful. It's all white and there's no furniture or blinds or anything, but it's totally quiet. You wouldn't believe it, I was there for a full half-hour and there wasn't a peep, not a scratch or a thump. And you should see the little blond children around there, rolling around on three-wheelers like little CEOS, talking softly to one another about mergers. I didn't see a single drawing of blood, and I watched the playground for ten minutes, at lunchtime at that.' The cork popped.

De Courcy sat at the table. 'How could you afford it?'

'Got the cheque from *Glitter* today.'

'That was fast.'

'That,' said James, 'is American efficiency for you, yes sir, the old U.S.A., get up and go, pay the man, they said, pay the man. Don't you want any? Of course you do.' The bubbles prickled on his tongue. 'BOOK HIM! I took it right to the bank, yelled and screamed that it was the biggest corporation in the U.S.A. so they didn't put a hold on it, demanded to see a manager, who luckily was a woman, anyway, I smiled a lot and they didn't put a hold on it, cashed it right then and there, our dollar was gloriously weak, I walk out with close to fourteen hundred bucks cash, I see the apartment, put down first and last right there.' He cocked his finger at De Courcy and fired. 'Book him.'

'Well,' said De Courcy. 'Congratulations.'

'You don't seem very happy for me.'

De Courcy smiled. 'Of course I am. Cheers.'

'It's good, isn't it?'

'Interesting. Although I still stubbornly and perhaps pedantically prefer the Veuve myself.'

'Should we should eat something?' said De Courcy, an hour later. They were in his red bedroom, James sprawled next to the hideous cloisonné vase.

'Send out for pizza.'

'*Children of Satan*,' shrieked the air, a voice from all around them, '*Jezebel*!'

'Acton?'

De Courcy nodded. 'He's going to deconstruct the religious right. He told me.'

'*All red-haired women are Jezebels*!'

'You dial.' De Courcy tossed him the phone. 'So. What are you going to do now?'

'You mean career stuff? Or lovers?'

'Both.'

'Career stuff I'm not going to have. None. None at all. Lovers I don't know. I've made some mistakes recently.'

'Yes you have.' De Courcy was looking at him in a significant way that made James blush.

'They're just too tiring. Nicola wants to marry a water quality something engineer. Alison wants to go to the Agency and become a dominatrix or something. I never want to see those clubs again.'

'I would have thought you would be impressed by that. I mean, which would you prefer, a dominatrix or a curler?'

James was dialling and thinking. 'I'm not sure, to tell you the truth. The thing about Alison is ...' The ringing began at the other end. 'It's hard to explain, and I know this sounds really nasty, but Alison is only Alison in Munich. She looks different here. She looks out of place. And I don't want the same things here.'

'She shouldn't try to mix up the categories.'

James didn't answer this. 'And I mean, I know, sex is great, but it always gets complicated. It's – hey, Tak Sing, how you doing? It's the guys on Argyle here. Yep. The regular.'

'How are you going to pay the rent?' said De Courcy once James had hung up.

'I'm going to be a waiter. That's what I was before, it's much more appropriate for me than –'

'Before what?'

James sat upright and reached for the bottle. 'It's not special, I know,' he said, pouring, 'but it's the most expensive bottle the shitty little liquor store near here had, and I was lucky to get the last eighty-nine, the rest were ninety-threes or some such. I actually don't mind it. A little thin, but with some earth, country earth, a hint of duck footprint, you know, an echo of a sort of honking, braying –'

'Before what?' said De Courcy.

'Ouf,' said James, shrugging like a Frenchman. 'This piece for *Glitter* really took it out of me. I'm not going to do this shit any more, this what's new what's going on shit, I'm not cut out for it. It's not me. And I'm not going to sleep with any more Nicolas. *Or* Alisons, for that matter.'

'Man delights you not,' said De Courcy.

'Exactly.'

'Nor woman neither?' De Courcy leaned towards him and held out his hand. James didn't know what the gesture meant. De Courcy kept his hand outstretched across the sofa, and James took it, awkwardly. The fingers were warm and soft. De Courcy was looking him in the eyes and his cheeks were burning. He must be a little drunk. James wouldn't look him in the eye. 'What's this? Congratulations?'

De Courcy dropped his hand and looked away mysteriously. James stuffed it into his pocket. 'You see,' he said quickly, 'it's been an accident all along. This hip stuff.'

'Oh,' said De Courcy softly, 'I don't think so. I don't think so at all.'

'I *know* so,' said James.

'*Prepare for Satan*,' screamed Acton's equipment.

'But I'm getting out,' said James. 'That's why we're celebrating.' He reached for the bottle.

'All right. Congratulations. Now what about your love life?'

'*Prepare to die,*' boomed Acton's tape.

A crashing and singing from the kitchen told them Fiona had arrived. 'Jam bottle *Jesus,*' she yelled, her voice approaching De Courcy's open door. 'That boy is such a tard I'm surprised he's not getting the check.' She strode into De Courcy's room and slid a wine glass out of the rack over his desk, then sat on the Shiraz prayer mat. She was wearing, unusually, a dress, a madras cotton summer dress with a short skirt that rode up her thighs as she folded her legs under her.

James caught a glimpse of white underpants. He said, 'You're supposed to face the other way.'

'What?'

'Mec-ca,' said De Courcy, dragging it out. 'You'll see at one end the pattern tapers slightly, because it's pointing towards –'

'Sit any way I goddamn please,' said Fiona, holding out her glass. 'I'm not surprised you boys are going a little shack wacky, sitting in here drinking all the time. Like a frigging chapel in here.'

'What are you so upset about?'

'That boy, I swear, what a quiff, what a quiffina.'

'Buck? Not exactly, I would think.'

'Well, whatever. You know what I mean. The guy is so stupid he doesn't know if his arsehole was bored out or chewed out.'

De Courcy coughed on some wine. 'Sorry?'

'And *mean*, I im-*a*-gine. Lazy as a pelt, and selfish. That man wouldn't piss down your throat if your heart was on fire.'

'I take it,' said James, 'you and Buck have had a little fight.' He winced a little as he saw the pad of flesh roll a little on her waist where the dress gripped her; it was troublingly stirring. Her shoulders were bare too: freckled. Her red hair bounced. He felt the wine swell in him.

'Got something out of it, though.' She poked a finger into her bra and pulled out a little plastic baggie. She threw it at James, who caught it. It was warm from her skin.

'Since when did you smoke this stuff?'

She shrugged. 'I guess I used to in Meat Cove, in high school, we all did. I haven't for a while. But I ran into Donny MacDonald at the Load and he gave me some, because we were all going to smoke it together, because Bucky was supposed to be celebrating his first B plus and his first semi-finals with the team, but he had to go be an asshole and ruin it all.' She was fumbling with papers and matches; James hadn't seen whence she had procured these. '*Hup,*' she said, in an intake of breath. 'Had to be an asshole as usual. Gotta love it. Pass that back to me.'

'Oh now just a minute,' said De Courcy, 'just how old do you think we are? Are we high-school teachers or rock music critics or what? Do you really think we're going to sit around a bedroom and smoke – what do you call it now? I would have no idea. Look at me. Do you see any evidence of a ponytail? Do you see any base-ball cap marked with faux medieval logo of heavy metal band? Really. Imagine. I *ask* you.'

'I wouldn't mind,' said James. 'We're out of wine.'

'I wouldn't turn my nose up at it if I was you,' she said. 'It's forty bucks' worth, and Buck is going to be some pissed when he reaches into his jacket pocket for it.'

James snorted; De Courcy was outraged. 'Honestly, what is this? Do we have to demean ourselves like this? I mean do we just drink wine for some brain-damaging high, some brutally physio-logical –'

'Yes,' said James. 'You don't have to have any.'

Fiona had rolled the joint and lit it; the manury smell filled the little room. James kept glancing quickly at her legs, hoping for another glimpse of cotton between them. What with the two bottles of wine and no food, he was no longer worried about what it meant that he might be stirred by the sight of Fiona's legs. He was stirred.

'Oh no,' said De Courcy, standing up. 'Not in my room. I'll have to live with the smell, I'll be having ghastly Proustian experiences for days, memories of CBC producers' parties where they play jazz. Put that out or smoke it somewhere else.'

'Oh, come on, Dec, don't be –'

'Out.' De Courcy's cheeks were burning.

James was getting tired of him anyway. 'Come on Fiona. In the living room. We'll be right back.'

De Courcy sat on the sofa and grabbed a book from a pile; he opened it dramatically and frowned into it.

He sat with Fiona on the living-room sofa. Aside from a team of heavy boots stomping up and down the stairs through the wall like an army exercise, the neighbourhood was suddenly strangely quiet. Even Acton had switched off his machinery. They smoked in silence for a few minutes, passing the joint back and forth. James coughed a lot but felt no other effects. He looked at Fiona's knees, crossed. 'So,' he said. 'So you think this thing with you and Buck, is it serious? I mean is this a real problem?'

Fiona shrugged. 'I don't know, Jimmy. We always have these things.'

'I know you do.' He was staring frankly now, running his eyes over her round shoulders, the sturdy thighs. He decided he loved Fiona, her solidity, her funniness, her practical sex, he was going to marry her and go and live in Cape Breton with her.

She turned to look him in the eye, one eyebrow arched, and passed him the joint.

'This is done,' he said, and snuffed it on a magazine cover on the trunk that served as a coffee table. He smiled at her and shifted closer. The ancient sofa sank and rolled. She looked away. James could smell her, faintly sweaty and shampooey. His heart was hammering. Gently, he put his arm around her shoulders.

She stiffened, gave him her quizzical look again. 'James?'

'Yes.' He dropped one paw onto her knee. It was hot and soft.

'Uh, James.'

'Yes.' He slid his palm up her thigh.

'Are you serious?'

'What?'

'I said, are you *serious*?' She giggled and brushed his hand off her knee. She shifted away from him and said, 'I don't think so, you know.'

James retracted his arm around her as if it burned. 'No. No, of course not.'

'No. Of course not.'

He sighed.

She took his hand and said, 'I think you're a little bit wasted and you don't know what you're doing.'

'Of course I know what I'm doing.' He knew his face was red.

'Well, it's just not a good idea. What with me and Buck and all ...'

'And I'm just not your type. I know.'

'No,' she said gently, 'it's that I'm not your type.'

He smiled, relaxed a little, patted her hand. He said, 'Let's roll up another one.'

She smiled and picked up the papers and the baggie. 'All right. Let's just do that. Might relax us.'

She had the next one lit and handed to James when there was a banging on the front door. 'Pizza,' said James, rising. The floor was at a funny angle as he walked to the door. He walked carefully. He yelled, 'Decko, PIZZA'S HERE!'

With the smoking joint in his hand, he swung open the door.

There were two extremely large policemen.

They wore blue uniforms and blond moustaches and shiny black belts hung with chunky black objects, and they had thick torsos from their bulletproof vests and thick, hanging, flexing, forearms and peaked hats and in fact everything you could expect them to have.

'Goodness,' said James, 'what a cliché.' He had immediately dropped the joint and stood on it.

'Looking for James Willing.'

James gulped. 'That's me.' He couldn't back up to invite them in or he would expose the smoking joint. So they stood chest to chest, his foot pressuring the floor. 'Can I help you?'

They were looking over his shoulder, exchanging glances. 'Uh. Yeah,' said one. 'You make a noise complaint?'

'Oh. Oh! Yes! Yes I certainly did.'

'Well, we came to check on it. Should be no problem now.'

'Oh, thank you.' James paused. It was indeed eerily quiet. 'So, you mean you, you talked to people?' A light flashed on behind the policemen, silhouetting them: Elsie. James couldn't see her past them. They were unimaginably enormous; his neck hurt to look up at their faces.

'We talked to the guys in the alley; should be no problem with them tonight at least. We arrested one.'

'Oh. What for?'

A minimal hesitation. 'I'm not at liberty to say. Anyway, we talked to Mrs Pimentel about her radio, which was in your complaint?'

'Oh. The one I filed with city hall. Yes.'

'Well, anyway, we delivered a letter which explains to her that she's liable for a five-thousand-dollar fine for noise pollution if we have another complaint, it looks very official and everything, so that should help there. She took it pretty serious.'

'Goodness. Poor Mrs Pimentel.' James was doing his best to concentrate on listening and on keeping the joint covered and on not swaying too much at the same time.

'And we talked to the guy upstairs, guy with the recording equipment?'

'Acton! But I didn't complain about him.'

'Well,' one officer chuckled, 'when we got here we heard such a racket we went upstairs to check it out. I think we gave him a little scare.'

'Jes–dear me.'

'So we'll be dropping by next week to check on all these noise sources, give them another friendly reminder, even if they're quiet for a while. These things, you know, they tend to go quiet and then start up again, so we like to remind them that we're still here. Now you can call us at any time, too, I'm Sergeant McNab, and here's my card. Any recurrence of this problem, and we'll send a car around.'

'Wow,' said James, swallowing. His mouth felt very dry. 'Poor Acton.'

'Okay?' The taller one was still trying to look into the apartment. And he was sniffing noticeably.

'Oh. Okay. Thank you. Thank you very much for your ...' James trailed off.

Still they hesitated. 'Everything okay in here?' A smug smile.

'Oh yes, perfectly fine, thank you.'

'Nice smell in here,' said the wider one, folding his arms. Another smug smile.

James opened his mouth and closed it again.

'Incense,' said a voice behind him. 'Officers, I want to thank you for your prompt response. Would you like to come in for a second? A cup of coffee or small glass of whisky?' De Courcy had his hands on James's shoulders. He was trying to move him out of the way, but James wouldn't budge. 'James, step aside so the officers can come in.'

'No, thanks,' said the taller one, still smiling. 'As long as everything's okay here.' Both policemen took steps backwards.

'Thank you again, then.'

One turned, and past him James could see Elsie in her bathrobe in her doorway. The other still stood with his arms folded and that irritating smile and said, 'Don't light too much incense, now.'

De Courcy, now standing beside James, said warmly, 'No sir. We just light a little now and then, in the summer the garbage in the courtyard gets so –'

'Or at least don't light incense and then call the police over, you understand what I'm saying?' He was looking at James. 'Bright guy?'

James nodded. 'Yes sir. No sir.'

'Good night.'

They clattered down the metal staircase.

'*What is happen?*' shrieked Elsie.

'Nothing at all,' said De Courcy, stepping onto the deck. 'Everything is fine.'

James left him to work on her. He stepped off the crushed joint, kicked it under a radiator and went back into the living room. Fiona was sitting on the couch with her legs crossed, clearly exposing a rhomboid of white. She was on the phone, speaking softly. 'I know, baby,' she was saying. 'I know. It's okay. It was stupid.'

James looked once more, ruefully, at the glowing thighs, and walked past her into De Courcy's room. He opened a desk drawer and took out the cheapest bottle of wine he could find, which was still not cheap. He found a corkscrew on the desk.

De Courcy came in a minute later. James handed him a full glass. 'Thanks.'

'What was that nonsense about not moving out of the way?'

'There was a whole joint under my foot.'

De Courcy sat in his armchair and began laughing. James laughed too and soon they were both laughing so hard that they were whooping a bit and making a loud noise. There was a thump from above.

'Acton!' shouted James, and they laughed harder.

'Poor Acton!' wheezed De Courcy. He had tears on his cheeks. 'Cheers.'

After a while they quietened. De Courcy stood up and said, 'So. We were talking about the women business.'

James shook his head violently. 'No. No, I've settled it. I'm out of the women business.'

'Ah.' He paused, looming over James, and said, 'An excellent choice.' And then he did something he had never done before: he bent, put his hands on James's shoulders, and leaned forward as if to kiss him.

'Whoa,' said James, twisting out of the way. He stood up, stepped aside. 'What the fuck?'

De Courcy was suddenly red and stiff, swinging his arms in the centre of the room. He looked away.

More calmly, James said, 'You've never done that before, Dec.'

'No,' said De Courcy faintly, 'but I've always wanted to.'

There was a long silence. James sat again and said, 'Oh.' He chewed for a time on the inside of his mouth. They were both bright red. 'What a night. I didn't mean to be rude, Dec, I'm sorry. I just … you know I'm not into that. I'm not like you.'

De Courcy sat across the room in his armchair. He ran his hands through his hair. 'I never was really sure.'

'Really?'

De Courcy shrugged.

James considered for a while longer. 'This is a problem, isn't it?'

De Courcy tried to laugh but it wasn't convincing. 'No, no. Not necessarily. Not at all. We can forget all about it. Just because … just because I'm in love with you.'

James puffed out his cheeks. 'Really?'

'Yes. Very.'

James kept sighing and chewing. All he could say was, 'Boy.

That's a drag.'

'Yes.'

'Has this been ... has it been for a while?'

'Yes. A long while.' His voice cracked a little.

They weren't looking at each other. Finally James said, 'I'm sorry.'

'So am I.'

James looked up quickly and saw that De Courcy's chin was puckered and there might even be tears in his eyes. 'Yikes. Look, I didn't realize you'd be so upset. I mean, this is a big surprise for me, right?'

'Is it? I thought you knew. Of course you knew.'

'No.' He shook his head. 'Honestly, I didn't. It didn't occur to me.'

De Courcy nodded gravely. He took out a dark purple handkerchief and dabbed at his eyes. He drained his glass of wine and grabbed the bottle from the desk. When he stood up, he was wobbly too.

'I'm sorry,' said James.

'Nothing to be sorry for.'

James stood up, looked at his watch. 'Well,' he said guiltily, 'I'd better get back. First night in the new place. I took some stuff over this afternoon; I'll move the rest once I can borrow a van later in the week. But I'd like to spend a night there, you know. It's all messy and ...'

De Courcy left the room. James went into his own little room and packed a bag full of clothes. He dragged it into the living room. Fiona was gone. The kitchen door was open onto the quiet night. De Courcy was messing with discs and the stereo. He put on some old eighties electronic dance music and turned it up. He stood looking at the stereo as it clicked and thumped. Tick, tick, tickytickytickyticky tick, tick, tick, tick.

'Well,' said James. 'Thanks for the wine. And you know, don't worry about it, everything will be fine, we'll still be ...' He stopped himself.

'Yeah,' shouted De Courcy over the music. 'I feel like dancing.' He began to dance in the middle of the living room. The music was New Order. *How does it feel, to treat me like you do ...*

'Haven't heard this for a while,' shouted James. He knew he should stay and talk to De Courcy, make it less awkward. 'Nostalgic?'

'I guess. Those were the days.'

'Yeah.' He stood there for a moment. 'Oh, the pizza.'

'It may be lost in the night, I fear.'

'Yeah. I'm not hungry, anyway. That joint made me a little ...' He found his wallet and extracted bills. 'If it does come, I'll leave some money for it.'

'Don't bother.'

'I'll leave it here, on the kitchen table. Okay? I'm tired and I'd better go.'

'Uh-huh.'

'You're okay?'

'Sure.'

'Okay. See you.'

'See you.'

James hesitated again. He listened to the pounding music of his adolescence and felt dizzy and sick. De Courcy seemed to be lost in it. James shouldered his bag and left.

In the courtyard, he could still hear De Courcy's music booming. He looked up and saw him in the yellow light of the kitchen, dancing with concentration as if in a discotheque.

On the way down the alley, he passed the pizza delivery man and pointed out the fire escape to him. Then he scuttled out into the hot street.

The walls gleamed white. He hadn't put anything on them yet, but he had found a bed and stacked his framed things in the main room and put his clothes in the closet and set up the desk against one wall. There were windows in two walls. He moved the old desk chair that he loved fractionally closer to the desk, so that he was lined up perfectly in the centre of the wall, framed by the window on his left. It looked onto a small fenced garden with a tree and a tire swing and a sagging garage. He found this garden exorbitantly pretty, something out of a New England travel brochure. The tire swing had worried him at first, but he still hadn't seen a single child emerge from the neat brick house next door. He held himself still and listened: he could hear the odd car swishing past the front of the house. And, if he was very still, the humming of the small refrigerator. And *both* the windows were open.

He took an exultant breath and looked at his ordered desk. Today was the first day he was going to do something on it. The first task was to look – just look, he didn't have to actually read it – at the new issue of *Glitter*, which was symmetrically placed in the bare centre of the desk. It was a task he had been putting off but which had to be done eventually, if only to prove his manhood.

The cover showed Boben's weathered face. His eyes were closed, suggesting deep thought. One gnarled knuckle was at his chin. The redness in his skin suggested years of wind-burn, regular dogsledding perhaps, all the nobility of the natural life. He looked majestic. Words across the cover read, 'Who is this man? And why is he so cold?' And below that, 'JAMES WILLING warms up LUDWIG BOBEN, the man behind the Eskimo groove.'

James winced. He had hoped they had taken his byline off it at least. He chewed on his cheek as he flipped through the magazine, briefly distracted by a photograph of a woman slathered in ice cream who was apparently an actress, and by an article on how to

clean umbrellas. It had never occurred to him that umbrellas
might need cleaning.

But he knew he was putting off the inevitable.

The Boben spread looked magnificent. They had used all
Nicola's black-and-whites, and the effect was one of gravity. The
paintings in subtle shades of grey, Boben's tweedy clothes, the
trees through the window behind his head, it all looked archaic
amid all the glossy colour on the other pages: a world of timeless,
lapidary genius. The pores on his skin, the very hairs in his ears
looked wise.

With a bubble in his stomach, James read the first paragraph:
'Addicts of *Breaking the Ice* know by now exactly where to rewind
and slow down, just to relive in its frosty ecstasy the icy tongue-
lashing hard-headed Hardbird gets from snow siren Alicia
Montgomery – what some might call the defining moment of the
current Northern craze. Who might have predicted the onslaught
of boreal chic? Who indeed, but the educated fans of the North's
true leading man, the writer who has been quietly tracking the
windswept Alaskan paths of the dogsled and the igloo for some
twenty ...'

James put it down. He yelled, 'God damn stinky quiff o rama,'
and then quietened, remembering his new surroundings. He had
to get up and drink water before he could continue.

He read the article through quickly. Some of his original lines
stuck out here and there, lumpy and plain, wooden logs in a neon
façade. Most of Mrs Boben's quotations were intact. He noted that
Boben had been 'rocketed to the international stage' by the *Prairie
Afternoon* prize; its value was not mentioned. He noted that
Boben had 'the kind of smoldering sexuality that reminds you of
ancient and long-forgotten courtly rites, the incense of the long-
house, the suppressed tension of the sleeping animal.'

The last paragraph ended, 'And what's next for the mature
observer, as he sweeps his eagle eyes over the glacier? He is coy
about upcoming projects. But be sure that he won't be content to
watch the fire dwindle as the Northern Lights begin to glitter –
and be sure that film rights to any new project will be eagerly
snapped up. And when the next tome of the Mariner series washes

up in the cities, we'll be thinking *Oscar.* You heard it here first.'

Then a bullet, and then, in tiny italics, 'James Willing lives in Toronto.'

There was no mention anywhere else in the article of Canada. James stood, laughing, and looked out the window. The swing was still motionless. He turned to the desk and picked up the magazine and began tearing every page into strips. There were many pages, and he decided to shred each page both horizontally and vertically.

It was absorbing work, so when the phone rang he almost absently picked it up.

He stayed his hand just in time. It could be any number of dangers: Raymond Cottager from *Reams,* Julian from *Edge,* De Courcy being stoically polite, even Alison or Nicola. Although he doubted that. He waited until the ringing died.

If he was in fact as decided going to reject any work that Julian or anyone like Julian offered him, then now was the time to begin to think about what he might do for work.

He stood at the window and felt, for the first time in months, a slight breeze that was not hot. It might even have been cool. He stuck out his hand to feel it. Soon it would be the fall and everyone would be allowed to wear sweaters again, which made them far more comfortable anyway.

He focused. If he had absolutely nothing to do in his life, he would soon run into difficulties with such things as adequate food and shelter, he knew, he realized this, but it was an extraordinarily pleasant feeling, in this white room.

He shuffled over to the bed, whistling, and lifted up the frame to get at the violin case underneath. He pulled it out and dusted it off. He sat at his desk and tuned the instrument.

He put a rag under his chin and nestled the wood there. He hesitated before playing. He couldn't remember the last time he had played. His hand looked awkward; he wasn't even sure if it was at the right angle. He stretched his fingers, then played a scale, and it whined a bit. The attack wasn't crisp, but the scale was right.

But since he had nothing else to do, he repeated it a few times and it lost some of the harshness. He made a nice round hollow sound with some resonance and played a bit of Scarlatti, then a bit of 'Death and the Maiden', and then a Fauré lullaby. Then he got up and fumbled in boxes for a few more minutes until he found a sheaf of sheet music and sat down with that.

He played a bit of a Milhaud piano quartet which was awfully difficult and his finger strength wasn't up, and then found Richard Catherell's 'Northern Prelude', which he had always loved and could play easily.

It was quiet and simple and melancholic, and as he played it he thought about how good, how really good this guy was and why nobody had ever done a big thing on him, a profile or something, since he was still living in Montréal and probably wouldn't be for much longer, and especially since it was basically modernist stuff and you could make a big deal out of a high-modernist revival that was going on as a reaction to both the clangy post-modern stuff *and* to the mushy and monotonous neo-romantic and rhythmic minimalist stuff, especially since you could probably find examples of it in other art forms as well, like that painter with the shaved head in Berlin who had got all that attention doing that sort of fauvist or more like early Kandinsky stuff, whose name James was prevented from recalling by the phone, which commenced ringing. He answered it without thinking. 'Hello? Damn.'

'Damn what?'

'Oh. Hello Julian. *Damn.*'

'Are you okay?'

'Fine. I just, ah, dropped something. Listen, Julian, I can't do any work for you. I'm sorry. Whatever it is, the answer is no.'

'Well, well, well, mister big shot, mister don't-call-us-we'll-call-you, hey, mister star quality, don't get ahead of yourself. I haven't offered you anything.'

'Oh.'

'Yet.'

'Well, you see, that's just –'

'I'm calling, actually, mister swollen-head, to say congratulations. I just *wanted* to say how totally *impressed* I was by the article in *Glitter*.'

'You were?'

'Everybody is, your name is on everyone's lips. You're a big star.'

'Uh-huh.'

'It was very smoothly handled, James, very smoothly. In fact, MacRobert was asking about you.'

'Really?' MacRobert was the editor-in-chief.

'Oh yes, and in fact two television producers have called here, one from Global, one from Talk, wanting to know how to find you and I refused to give out your number.'

'You did?'

'Well I know how you don't want that sort of work right now.'

'Right.'

There was a cool silence from Julian. You had to admire it. James was no match for Julian. James said, 'You really liked it?'

'It was very smooth. I particularly liked how you didn't make a big deal out of Boben's Canadianness. Some writers would have gone overboard with that.'

James cleared his throat. 'Yes. Yeah. I thought it would be a little, a little cooler that way. Not to stress it.'

'Of course. How right you were.'

'Thank you.'

'Anyway, I want to make you an offer before *Glitter* snaps you up permanently.'

'Here we go. No.'

'James, just hear me out. This was MacRobert's idea, and it's a big deal. Your own column, James. Monthly.'

'No.'

'Really easy stuff. Profiles, personality pieces, like the Boben one. Whoever you want to do. It's all about you, though, your voice. We call it Willing People, right? It'll be super fun. Just, you know, whoever's hip this month, like this Fijian chef who's at –'

'Nope. No. Thank you. I'm out of it, Julian. For good. Thank you anyway, but I'm not interested.'

'James,' said Julian calmly, 'it would pay very well. It would pay very well indeed for what it is. Fifteen hundred bucks a month. You could live on that.'

James looked out the window and drew a deep breath. 'Nope.'

After a few seconds, Julian said, 'All right. No problem. If you ever reconsider, you just let me ...'

James let him talk for a minute. He looked at his violin, the sheet music on the table. As soon as he hung up, the apartment would be in silence again and he would wonder what he had done.

'James?'

'Sorry. Did you ask me something?'

'No, no. Just saying goodbye.'

'All right. Thanks anyway, Julian.'

'Not at all. Are you all right?'

James was silent. He picked up his violin, plucked a bit. His fingers were stiff already, the tips sore. He said, 'Listen. I have something for you.'

'All right.'

'There is one thing and one thing only that I will write for you. It's good and you should take it.'

'All right. I'll take it. What is it?'

'Classical music.'

'What?'

'Classical music. A column.'

'What do you mean? You mean like orchestras and – James, come on. A little *élitist*, isn't it? Nobody's interested in that.'

'That's all I'll do. No more restaurants, no more underground fashion, no more club beats. Take it or leave it.'

A long silence. 'Well,' said Julian finally. 'It's a little weird. I kind of like it. It would be kind of quirky, with your reputation.'

'We have a symphony orchestra here,' said James. 'We have musicians and composers in hiding all over the place, I know them. I know all about them. And I can make it interesting.'

'To younger readers?'

'Yes. I know all about what's going on in Prague and Vienna, too. And I can, I can make it relevant, I can write hip and sexy, you know I can.'

'Interesting,' said Julian. 'Hip classical music. It might make us look kind of cool.'

'Good,' said James, swinging his feet onto the desk. He leaned back. 'It's a deal. Here's how it's going to work: I write an essay every issue – not a service piece, not a news piece, not an article, but an *essay* – on some trend, some idea I've had about music, some new composer – but the music only. I could explain what makes it interesting and what you're supposed to listen for. I could compare, say, the rhythmic minimalist stuff to techno music, and show how they both happened at around the same time, one in high culture and the other in low. That's interesting, isn't it?'

'It is interesting. But –'

'I'm talking about popularizing this. Like that crazy nun who talks about paintings on TV.'

'Sister Wendy.'

'Exactly. I'm the Sister Wendy of music.'

'You could spin it into a TV show. We would get a percentage though.'

'Whatever,' said James. 'I'm just thinking about ideas right now. Or you could talk about how something happening in painting is like something happening in music. Like this guy, this painter in Berlin, I forget his name, guy with a shaved head, I was just thinking about this, his painting is basically neo-modernist, I mean it's like early Kandinsky, Blaue Reiter stuff, and don't worry, I could explain what that was and you could have pictures, and you could show how composers have a similar nostalgia and they're writing music that sounds as if it's from the same period, because it's a rejection of post-modernism. I mean people have only just started getting used to saying post-modern all the time and we go and tell them it's all over, it's tired.' James smiled. He knew what Julian wanted to hear. 'People would *love* to know about that. You know how impressive it would make your readers sound at a cocktail party to spout off about new trends in the high –'

'Okay, James,' said Julian, his voice edgy again, 'but as long as there's a *personality* involved, like if this painter is an interesting character, maybe we shoot him in his apartment, you know people have to have a *person* they can –'

'Nope.' James shook his head gleefully. 'That's exactly what it's not, Julian. Take it or leave it. No profiles, no celebrities, no daily routines and favourite colours and who designed their living room.

It's about lots of people at once, lots of little profiles, but mostly it's about their work, and their ideas, and my ideas. Maybe a review of a concert or several, but no news, no discussions of the musicians' union disputes, right? It's got to be serious. It's got to be totally serious.'

'Serious? I'm not sure I follow you.'

'I mean *ideas*. It's all about ideas. And it's fast-moving and funny and –'

'Ideas? James.' There was a sound of rushing air. 'James, hello, this is reality speaking. This is a *magazine*. Ma. Ga. Zine. Got it? Can you see me messing about with *ideas* –'

'Sorry to waste your time, Julian.'

A long silence. 'Ideas.' James could hear him thinking, rolling a pen on his desk. 'Ideas. No one has done that before.'

James waited.

'James.'

'Yes.'

'I think that's a brilliant idea.'

James said, 'Thank you. Two thousand dollars per column.'

'Two thousand dollars? Just how long do you think this is going to be, James?'

'About two thousand words, Julian,' he said, calmly. 'It's difficult stuff; I can't gloss over things. You know I can make it interesting.'

'But James, I can't give you two thousand bucks every issue, I –'

'Then goodbye, Julian. Maybe *Glitter* will be interested.'

'I'll talk to MacRobert about it. I know he'll object but ... I can usually have my way with him.'

'Good. Let me know as soon as you can, though.'

'Yes,' said Julian, his voice sounding more distant. 'Yeah. The hipster's guide to classical music.'

'Exactly. Picture the artwork.'

'I can see it now!'

'Yes. Two thousand dollars a month.'

'Well.'

James was silent.

'Well, that sounds reasonable,' said Julian weakly.

'Yes.'

Another long pause.

Finally, Julian said, more confidently, 'Frankly, James, I don't see how that would be a problem.'

'I'm getting started on my first one right now. Goodbye, Julian.'

'Goodbye James,' said Julian. There was reverence in his voice. 'Where would I be without you?'

James hung up and turned the computer on, then off again. He had an urge to write, in his new intellectual mode, by hand. He took a sheet of white paper from the printer. He found a working pen: luckily a good one, a black rolling-ball with a wide point. It was a good omen.

He wrote at the top of the page, 'Richard Catherell and the new modernism.' The ink flowed smoothly. The paper soothed his palm. The letters were black and thick.

He admired his handwriting for a moment, then began.

Last May in Berlin, a young painter with a shaved head named.

He got up abruptly. He paced for a moment and still couldn't remember the guy's name.

X began a series of canvases whose stylized.

In which human faces were.

In garish streaks of primary colour reminiscent of 1930s.

James pushed back his chair. It shouldn't be this difficult. He didn't need to go into too much detail; it was just a lead-up. Something was bothering him. Perhaps if he could remember the guy's name it would help the rest. But he could see the pictures clearly anyway.

Perhaps he was too excited after the phone call. His knee waggled and bounced on the ball of his foot. He listened for distracting noise. There was none. He tried to stop chewing his cheek and concentrate.

In which the harsh angles of subway cars and.

And what?

He stood up, exhausted. He knew he had a lot to say about this, he had to talk about Futurism and Suprematism and the modern neo-romantic stuff as both a reaction against high modernism and a nostalgia for it but for some reason he couldn't concentrate.

He stared agressively into the garden, in case there would be some children to shout at. He went still so he could hear the refrigerator's hum.

'It hums for thee,' he said aloud, and it stopped with a shudder.

Now the place was dead quiet. He chewed on his cheek.

With a sudden urgency, he strode to the boom box on the floor and spread out a pile of CDs. His hands shaking, he snapped open a plastic case – the blackest cover he could find: Hostilator X, the Vacuum Mixes – and jammed the disc into the machine. He slammed down the cover and hit play.

There was a shattering sound like glass, a siren, and a chest-hollowing blast from the box.

He lay on the floor, feeling his breathing slow as the beat began, vicious and regular as machine guns. When the snare and clap patterns were laid over the bass, his muscles relaxed, too.

Words came. *The chrome glare of the subway car. The romance of the fax machine.* He stood.

With the thumping all around him, he sat at the desk and began.

■ ACKNOWLEDGEMENTS

Excerpts from *Noise* have been published in *The New Quarterly*, *Kairos* and *Carousel*.

I am very grateful to the Canada Council, the Ontario Arts Council (Writers' Reserve Program), The Yukon Arts Council and the Writers' Development Trust (Woodcock Fund) for grants of actual cash money. I spent three months writing this book as Berton House Writer-in-Residence in Dawson City, Yukon; this program was funded by the Yukon Arts Council and by generous donations from Pierre Berton. Thanks to Pierre Berton, Max Fraser, Belinda Smith, John Steins, Paula Hassard and the people of Dawson who did so much to help me out. Architectural and musical knowledge was shamelessly and perhaps inaccurately stolen from architect and mathematician Matthew Lella, with many thanks. Thanks to Patrick Crean, Eugene Barone and the staff of the Bar Italia, Katherine Bruce for emotional and editorial support in the crucial early stages of the manuscript, and to Ceri Marsh for emotional and editorial support in the crucial later stages. Thanks to The Porcupine's Quill for their patience, to Doris Cowan for her Australian, and to my tirelessly supportive, meticulous yet always sympathetic editor – who put in at least as many hours as me on this book – John Metcalf.

Russell Smith was born in Johannesburg, South Africa, and grew up in Halifax, Canada. He studied French literature at Queen's, Poitiers and Paris (III). Since 1990 he has lived in Toronto, where he works as a freelance journalist. He has published articles in the *Globe and Mail, Details, Travel and Leisure, Toronto Life, Flare, NOW* and other journals, and short fiction and poetry in *Queen's Quarterly, Malahat Review, Quarry, The New Quarterly, Carousel, Kairos, Toronto Life* and other journals. In 1995 he won a Gold Medal at the American City and Regional Magazine Awards. His first novel, *How Insensitive*, was short-listed for the Smithbooks/*Books in Canada* First Novel Award, the Trillium Award and the Governor General's Award.